Picture
Perfect

Also by Fern Michaels

FERN MICHAELS

Picture Perfect

ZEBRA BOOKS
KENSINGTON PUBLISHING CORP.
http://www.kensingtonbooks.com

ZEBRA BOOKS are published by

Kensington Publishing Corp.
850 Third Avenue
New York, NY 10022

All Kensington titles, imprints and distributed lines are
available at special quantity discounts for bulk pur-
chases for sales promotion, premiums, fund-raising, ed-
ucational or institutional use.

Special book excerpts or customized printings can also
be created to fit specific needs. For details, write or phone
the office of the Kensington Special Sales Manager: Kensington Publishing Corp., 850 Third Avenue, New York,
NY 10022. Attn. Special Sales Department. Phone: 1-800-
221-2647.

Zebra and the Z logo Reg. U.S. Pat. & TM Off.

First Zebra Printing: February 2005
20 19 18 17 16 15 14 13

Printed in the United States of America

One

Davey Taylor didn't like the shine of the street lamp that cut through the darkness and played against the filmy curtains in his bedroom. The lamp created shadows that danced on the wall, menacing his toy chest and his favorite stuffed animals on the shelf above. Each night Davey would move his ragged, beloved Panda Bear from the shelf and place it where the shadows couldn't touch it.

Right now the lights in his room were all lit and the shadows were held at bay. If Davey moved back the curtain, he could even see his own reflection in the glass. But later, after Mom turned off the lights, those dark invaders would enter his room. His mother said he was too old for a night-light.

Straightening his room before he went to bed, as he had been taught, Davey pursed his mouth as he studied his dog calendar.

"Today is Sunday; yesterday was Saturday," he told the dog sitting quietly near his feet. "I'm supposed to change my pajamas on Saturdays, Tuesdays, and Fridays." His brow knit into worried lines. "I can't remember if I changed them last night or not, Duffy."

The Yorkshire terrier squirmed, as if uncertain of the tone of Davey's voice.

"See, I make an X on the days I change my PJs. There's no X for yesterday." Davey looked down at his dog, who tipped her head to one side. Shaking his head over his forgetfulness, he walked over to his chair and flopped down.

"Changing my pajamas," he said, with seven-and-a-half-year-old authority, "is one of those 'almost' things. You know, Duff, like I can almost reach the top cupboards. I can almost tell the time. I can almost walk to school by myself. Everything is 'almost.' I can't wait to grow up so I can be *most*."

The tan-and-black dog woofed in agreement.

Davey swiveled his bright blue eyes to the clothes tree. There were no colorful pajamas on the peg. A cherry-red windbreaker and a yellow slicker with matching hood were the only garments hanging there. Davey ran his stubby, little-boy fingers through his thick, flaxen hair, a sign that he was relieved. His breath exploded in a loud whoosh. He must have changed his PJs the night before after all, and put them under his pillow, otherwise they'd be hanging from the peg. As if sensing her master's relief, Duffy yipped happily.

"See these, Duff? They're my first pair of Reeboks!" Davey said proudly. "And I almost got them dirty today. I'm wearing them tomorrow with my new red jacket when we leave with Aunt Lorrie to go camping. Mom says you can't go camping with dirty shoes, Duff."

Duffy rolled over on the meadow of green carpet, taking Davey's excitement as a sign that it was time to play. Instead, Davey leaned over to pull up his pants leg. Duffy watched as first one strap and then another was loosened. She growled deep in her throat when the brace fell against the side of the desk. Crawling on her belly, she stretched herself to her entire two feet in length to show her disapproval.

Davey stood erect. He could walk without the brace; he just wasn't supposed to be ram . . . rambunctious. He liked that word even though he wasn't exactly certain what it meant.

Finding the PJs under his pillow, he stripped down and pulled the top over his head, then completed the job with the long-legged bottoms. Jumping onto the bed, he settled himself down with his new book, *Elliott the Lovesick Swan*. The long hand on his 101 Dalmatians watch told him it was almost time for his parents to come in and say good night. The new watch, a gift from Aunt Lorrie, was special. The only time he took it off was when he had a shower.

"Oh, man, I forgot to brush my teeth!" With only a few minutes until bedtime, he didn't want to waste them brushing his teeth. Davey threw back the covers and marched to the bathroom. He turned on the water, put his toothbrush under the flow and wet it. His eyes danced merrily as he purposely splashed a little water onto the marble vanity top. A giggle erupted as he gave the toothpaste tube a quick squeeze in the middle, then set it down. He scurried back to bed where Duffy watched him with droopy eyes.

"I made it look like I brushed my teeth, Duff, but I really didn't."

Picking up his picture book, he flipped through the pages. He wasn't interested in Elliott tonight. If only he could talk to his friend Digger on the CB radio. But "if only" was like "almost."

"Time for lights out, buddy," his father said, opening Davey's door all the way.

Davey looked up to see his mom and dad standing in the doorway. "I know, Dad. See, the big hand is almost on the six. Do I call it six eight or eight six?"

There was a trace of annoyance in Sara Taylor's voice when she answered for her husband. "No, Davey. You call it eight thirty or half past eight. The little hand tells you the hour and the big hand tells you the minutes." She refused to call the hands on his Dalmatian watch "paws," as her sister Lorrie had suggested. The boy would learn to tell time properly. "We went over all this on Saturday afternoon. I can see where we'll have to practice extensively when you get back from your camping trip."

Davey was undaunted by her displeasure. "I don't think I can fall asleep tonight. I can't wait for tomorrow. Gee, this is almost better than Christmas," he said, his voice bubbling with excitement. Almost. It *was* going to be better than Christmas, he just knew it.

Andrew Taylor walked over to the bed and grinned as he bent to kiss his son good night. "I think you're absolutely right. Do you have all your gear ready?"

Davey nodded. "I've had it ready for a whole week. Are you going to miss me, Dad?"

"Of course we're going to miss you," Sara replied instead. "By the time you get back from your trip, we'll be back from ours. We'll all be together again in just a few days. Did you brush your teeth, Davey?"

Davey squirmed. "Go see the toothbrush," he answered, avoiding the lie. He looked at his parents, noticing how close they were to each other. They were always like that, he thought. And Mom always knew what Dad was thinking or was going to say. He had heard the phrase "matched pair" and that was how he thought of his parents. A pair. Like a pair of socks or shoes. They matched. Wanting to be part of a pair, Davey drew Duffy close.

Wordlessly, Sara Taylor pushed the terrier off the bed. "I think I will check that toothbrush," she said, then leaned over to kiss him good night. "Did you find your PJs under the pillow?"

"Yep. See?" He lifted the pillow for her inspection.

"Davey, we do not say 'yep.' It's a slang term and I don't want you to use it."

Her voice was firm and Davey made a note to try and remember. Mom's voice was *always* firm. He liked Dad's voice better because there was usually a smile in it. But he liked Aunt Lorrie's voice best of all because there was usually a secret waiting to be told. Hers was a tickly, fun kind of voice. You couldn't fool Aunt Lorrie. She would have known about the toothbrush right away.

Davey felt guilty for liking Aunt Lorrie's voice more than his mom's. Impulsively, he reached out, hugging her around the neck. The stretching pulled back his pajama sleeves from his arms.

Sara Taylor's cinnamon-brown eyes fell on the needle marks dotting her son's arms. But her movements, when she extricated herself, were icily controlled. There was no hugging pressure on her part, no smile in her eyes, when she firmly pushed him back onto his nest of pillows. "Good night, Davey. Sleep well."

"G'night, Mom. G'night, Dad," the boy said quietly. He felt funny inside, as if he'd done something wrong. He lay very still until the door closed behind them.

Seconds later, he scooted to the bottom of the bed. Duffy lay stretched out on a small carpet bearing her name.

"C'mon, Duff. You can get up here now." The little dog was on the bed in one leap, her tail wagging furiously. "I've got that funny feeling again, Duff. As if we did something wrong."

Chubby hands cupped the terrier's face in a firm grip. Bright blue eyes stared unblinkingly into Duffy's melting brown ones. "We didn't do anything wrong today, did we?" Duffy wriggled, trying to get free to snuggle in the warmth of the blankets.

Davey stared into the dim corners of the room, trying not to look at the light that filtered through his curtains. Why did his stomach feel so funny after Mom and Dad said good night? All those times in the hospital, his stomach had felt bad, too. The tubes going into his veins, his sore puffy knees making him want to cry. But he hadn't cried. Instead he'd gripped the pillows and clenched his teeth so hard he'd been afraid they'd crack into pieces. "Don't cry, Davey. Only babies cry," his mother had cautioned. "You must be brave and not do anything to upset your father." He had felt sick whenever Mom said that to him, her eyes willing him not to cry.

He remembered the day the tall doctor told him he was going to get a different kind of treatment— a blood transfusion through the jugular vein. Davey had steeled himself not to cry in front of his dad. Instead, he'd grinned and waved to his dad as they wheeled him to the special room for blood transfusions.

Pills and shots, shots and pills for days afterward, and Davey had taken it all, like the brave little man his mother had told him he must be for his father's sake. He'd been carefully instructed from infancy that Daddy's wants and needs came first. Even when the pain in his joints was so bad he couldn't walk, still he hadn't cried. Davey's eyes had searched his father's each time he visited. There was always acceptance in his father's eyes, an acceptance that was totally ignorant of the price Davey was paying just so that his dad could laugh and smile when he came to visit.

Davey had hoped his mom would be proud of him, but if she was she hadn't said so. He didn't understand. He'd done as he'd been told. He'd been brave. Behaved like a grown-up. With a child's sure instinct, he'd recognized that he was a trial to his parents, less than perfect, a disappointment.

Once when his aunt had visited him, she'd commented on the shadows under his eyes and asked if he was in pain. He'd been hesitant to say yes, but Aunt Lorrie had persisted until he admitted it.

"Why didn't you say something to your mom when she was in here?"

"I . . . I wanted to but—"

Before Davey could finish his answer, his mother and father had entered the room and stopped him from continuing. That night, after visiting hours, Lorrie came back. Wordlessly, she lowered the bars of the youth bed and sat on the edge. There, in the dark, she took him in her arms and held him.

"It's okay to feel tired and sore, Davey," she told him, her voice as soft and sweet as the darkness. "It's all right. You can cry if you want to. No one will hear. I know it hurts," she crooned, reaching out to share the weight of his misery, acknowledging Davey's pain, accepting it.

Silently Davey clung to her, taking from her the courage to continue with his charade and face the ordeal. At last he slept, his body weak with exhaustion. But he hadn't cried. Not then, nor the last time either. But knowing that it would be okay to cry lightened his burden.

Now the worst was behind him; he was home, and there were just the daily shots of antigen. He had done what his mother wanted; he had been brave. He hadn't cried. He hadn't upset his dad.

Now, sitting with Duffy in the darkness of his room, trying to avoid the light coming through the curtains, Davey felt that tightness in his middle, again the alarm that said he'd done something wrong. That his mother didn't approve.

In a flash he was off the bed and across the room, dodging the light. He created a windmill of motion as he pulled his toys from the toy chest and sent them sailing across the bedroom. "See, Duff. Here it is," he whispered triumphantly, grabbing onto his stuffed giraffe.

Back on the bed, with Duffy crouched between his legs, Davey held the stuffed giraffe up for inspection. "You see, Duff, how shiny Jethroe's eyes are?" The giraffe's bright, shoe-button eyes stared back at him. "Look, Duff," the little boy commanded, "Jethroe's eyes never change, no matter how I move him. I don't like this giraffe!" he cried suddenly, and his lower lip trembled as he stared at the toy.

"You know why I don't like that old thing, Duff? I'll tell you. It's . . . it's 'cause I feel like Jethroe sometimes. All wobbly and tired. Aunt Lorrie says it's okay to feel that way sometimes. But Mom doesn't." Seven-and-a-half-year-old wisdom rose to the fore. "If I cry and act like Jethroe, Dad will get upset. Mom doesn't want to see Dad upset."

Duffy snuggled deeper into the covers. "Aunt Lorrie knows I hurt sometimes. She knows I feel like Jethroe. She says it's okay to feel like that because those trips to the hospital for blood tests take all the . . . energy out of me. Energy, Duff. Like what's in the batteries that make my RC car go. The blood tests take all my energy."

Davey pitched the giraffe across the room. The backward motion of his hand nearly toppled the picture of his parents that rested on his nightstand. "Whew, that was close," he sighed as he grappled with the slippery frame. Even in the near darkness it seemed he could see the photograph of his smiling parents. Holding the frame carefully by the edges, he turned the picture to the light that came through the curtains. His gaze intent, he brought the faces closer, then held them at arm's length again. Gingerly, he replaced the picture on the nightstand.

His whisper was fierce, almost savage, as he pulled up the covers. "I like Aunt Lorrie best! Mom and Dad really only like each other."

A soft whine and much wiggling and the little dog was safely tucked against the pillow next to Davey. "You know, Duff, when I get all my energy back, I'm going to . . ."

He was asleep before he could complete his thought.

* * *

In the corridor leading to their bedroom, Sara linked her arm through her husband's and squeezed. "I want to talk to you about something, Andrew."

Andrew smiled around the pipe clenched in his teeth. "I'm all yours, as soon as the door closes." He turned and leered suggestively at his wife.

Sara laughed, tossing her blonde head. "That, too."

"Why don't we go down into the den and have a nightcap? It's early and we're all packed and ready to go."

"Mr. Sanders is downstairs. I hardly think an FBI agent, even one as nice as Stuart Sanders, is conducive to a relaxed drink and lovemaking. Why don't you," she said, dropping her voice to a whisper, "turn on the gas log, shower, and wait for me? I'll go down and lock up and bring our wine up here. We haven't made love in front of the fire for ages. It's time," she purred.

Sara always had a better idea, or so it seemed to Andrew, as he returned her grin. "Hurry," was all he could say. God, how he loved and desired her. He would never cease to be amazed that she returned his feelings. A man could search his life through for the right woman and never find her, but he'd found Sara and she was perfect. She fulfilled his every need. There seemed no amount of energy and caring that Sara would not put forth for his happiness. She had even interrupted her career as an English literature professor to bear him a son. At the time, she had been thirty-nine years old. He knew it had been no small conces-

sion on her part to make their union even more
perfect.

Desire, hot and potent, coursed through him as
he turned the key to light the fire. Sara would return in exactly the amount of time it would take
him to shower, dry off and put on the bathrobe
she'd bought him for his birthday.

Sara descended the long, circular staircase. Halfway down she called softly, "It's all right, Mr. Sanders.
I'm just coming down to lock up and get a drink
for my husband and myself."

Stuart Sanders waited at the bottom of the steps.
His appraising, businesslike gaze took in the
woman's cool blonde beauty and her regal bearing. He could appreciate her neutral tone of voice.
He wasn't a servant, or even a family friend; he was
an acquaintance and Mrs. Taylor addressed him as
such. It was acceptable.

"I'll stay with you, Mrs. Taylor, until you go back
upstairs."

Sara recognized the order behind the words.
"Of course, Mr. Sanders."

Stuart followed her from one end of the house
to the other as she checked the locks and turned
off the lights. Even though he had locked up himself, she'd explained that the nightly ritual helped
her to sleep better. He waited in the doorway of
the den while she retrieved a couple of glasses and
a bottle of wine from the built-in bar fridge. They
weren't just glasses, he told himself, they were antique wine goblets and the wine was one of those
fifty-dollar-a-bottle varieties.

He felt no envy as he surveyed the expensively appointed room. The whole house reflected Sara Taylor's conservative style and exacting taste. It was totally unlike his own place, where the furnishings—bought one at a time—never seemed to match. The clink of the crystal echoed through the room as Sara prepared to go back upstairs. There was nothing personal in Stuart's gaze at her. She looked like a sophisticated movie actress in her ivory satin robe and slippers. Too thin for his tastes. He liked a little more flesh on his women. Besides that, he'd never cared much for blondes; Sara's smooth delicate complexion lacked the vibrant flush he preferred.

Sara's sister, on the other hand, Lorrie—now there was a woman. She was just the opposite of Sara in coloring and temperament. On top of that she was unattached. He'd liked her the moment he'd met her.

"Would you get the lights for me, Mr. Sanders?"

"Sure. Can I help you carry any of that?" Stuart offered.

"It's quite all right, I can manage. I like doing things for my husband. It's all part of being a good wife." She smiled at him, her widening lips and soft tone belied by her expressionless eyes.

Stuart Sanders returned to his position in front of the television screen. He didn't like Sara Taylor. She was cold. Icy. At first he'd thought she was only that way with him, but then he'd realized she acted like that with everybody, and worse with her sister.

Sibling rivalry, he thought. Maybe there was something in their past that had come between them. Whatever the reason, it was none of his business. His business was to protect the Taylors, not get involved in their lives.

Maybe after the trial, when he wasn't on assignment, he could ask Lorrie out.

"You're something, honey," Andrew said, taking the wine bottle from her. "Right on schedule. I just this minute stepped from the shower."

Sara laughed, a warm rich sound that sent tingles up Andrew's spine. He loved to watch her when she laughed. The mirth began around her mouth and ended in her eyes, and he knew it was for him alone. Wanting to savor the moment, he poured the wine slowly while Sara settled herself against a mound of cushions in front of the fire. He handed her a glass and sat down beside her. "A toast. How about to—"

"Our happiness," Sara said, extending her glass. Her eyes were glowing, full of desire as she met Andrew's gaze.

It was Andrew who looked away first. "Tell me, what did you want to talk about?"

Sara placed her goblet on the raised hearth. "I've been thinking that Lorrie is spending too much time with Davey. What do you think?"

Andrew's mind raced back in time. He frowned. "You may be right. We can't allow her to intrude into our lives and Davey's affections. I wish you'd mentioned it sooner, Sara. How long has this been troubling you?"

"A while. I wasn't certain I should say anything. Not until I saw the way Davey looked at that ridiculous Dalmatian watch, and noticed the way he's beginning to use slang words. Lorrie's responsible for that, I think. After this camping trip, we should have a talk with her. And," she held up a warning hand, "we have to be prepared for some hysterics."

Sara brushed the hair back from Andrew's forehead. Her touch was cool, confident and soothing. Beneath her fingers, his brow wrinkled in a frown at the thought of the inevitable confrontation with his sister-in-law. He knew that she loved Davey almost to a fault. That was the problem: Sara found fault with that love. How like Sara to put Davey's welfare above her love for her sister—her only living relative. Andrew was glad Sara would deal with the unpleasantness herself. She would handle it just the way she handled every situation he found disturbing or distasteful. He trusted her judgment— she always did the right thing at the right time. Still, Andrew really liked Lorrie and he knew Davey loved her. An unsettling sensation grew in the pit of his stomach. "We must think of Davey first . . ." he began, half-developed contradictions forming in his mind. He had never been any good at personal relationships. He was really only comfortable with the undeniable truths of the laws of physics and higher calculus that he taught at Montclair College. And, of course, with Sara.

"Yes," Sara smiled warmly, "Davey must come first."

"The little guy is really excited about the camping trip. I think it will be a good experience for him. Since Lorrie is a doctor, we can leave for Florida without worrying about him. I meant to go up to his room this afternoon and set up his train tracks for him, but I got involved with something else and never got around to it. I'll have some free time when all this trial business is over, I'll be able to do it then." Reaching for Sara's hand, he asked, "Want to sit in with the grand old master of locomotives when he does his thing?"

"I'd love to," Sara assured him, pleased that Andrew always included her in his plans. "I was thinking of taking some time off myself, a day or so at least, and taking Davey to the apple orchard. We could watch them bake pies and buy some to bring home. Davey does love apple pie."

Andrew frowned. "I thought you were going to take him a couple of weeks ago. Didn't you?"

Sara laughed ruefully. "Unfortunately, no. Something came up and I couldn't make it."

"Was he disappointed?"

"No, not that I could see." Sara sipped at her drink, eyeing her husband over the rim of the glass.

"Okay. Next thing we have to talk about is our trip tomorrow. Nervous?"

"No," she answered flatly.

"I wish we didn't have to go through with this. I hate the whole thing. And I never liked the FBI's decision to place Sanders and his partner in this house. You know, Sara, I've been thinking. You don't really have to go with me. I'm the one who has to testify, and I don't want you to be upset."

"I'm going and that's final. I wouldn't dream of letting you go off without me. We belong together. That's the way it's always been. Where you go, I go. Final."

Andrew ran his fingers through his thatch of dark hair salted with gray. Sara smiled, knowing the gesture signified relief. "I don't like the fact that our names are being splashed all over the papers. And calling me a hostile witness . . ."

"Andrew, I don't pay any attention to nonsense like that. The media is the media. Period. You know how they like to latch on to what they think is a story. Everything is going to work out, so I don't want you losing any sleep over this. Promise me. After tomorrow, or the next day at most, this whole ordeal will be over."

Andrew drank his wine. "I never thought they'd link me with this business, Sara. Not after we took the precaution of moving out of Miami and coming here to New Jersey."

"I know all that, darling. I thought we'd escape this dreadful mess too, but it hasn't worked out that way. Don't blame yourself, Andrew."

"Jason Forbes was a good student, Sara. Bright. Lots of potential. And now he's dead. Maybe if I'd come between them there in the university library . . ."

"It wouldn't have made any difference," she assured him. "Kids make drug deals every day—in libraries, in classrooms, even in churches. You just happened to witness a buy. You couldn't have known it would end up in murder."

"But that doesn't excuse the fact that I didn't go to the police the minute I heard about the murder. Now, because I didn't, and because Jason told his roommate that I'd witnessed his buy, it looks as though I was trying to cover up something."

"Well, we both know you weren't doing anything of the kind. Mr. Sanders says that the only reason you're called a hostile witness is because you didn't come forward voluntarily but had to be subpoenaed. Once you testify, the State will have its case wrapped up, and we can go back to our normal lives. And Mr. Sanders and his partner can go home and leave us alone."

"I should have stepped forward voluntarily, Sara. I should have reported the threats I'd overheard as soon as the body was discovered."

"Hush, darling, you'll only upset yourself." Sara cradled Andrew's head against her soft bosom. "You were only trying to protect Davey and me, and we love you for it. Even the FBI recognizes that our lives are endangered, otherwise they wouldn't have put us under twenty-four-hour guard. I love you, Andrew Taylor, with all my heart for all my life."

Andrew's pulses pounded as Sara's face swam before his eyes. It never failed to happen when Sara prompted their lovemaking with those words. God, how he loved her. He knew his life would be meaningless without her. They shared their lives, careers, and interests; theirs was a coming-together, a blending, a loving. His hand slipped beneath the soft velour of her robe, touching her breast. Through the years he had learned the special phrases and words that heightened her response and brought her to life beneath his touch. He told her how he loved her, how they fitted one another like hand and glove. How perfect she made his life, how perfect she was, her beauty, her womanliness. How complete they were, one with the other, inseparable. And Sara responded, listening, prompting his words with touches, kisses, and murmurs.

Her eyes became liquid, her mouth ripe and open for him, accepting his kiss, his tongue. He loved her like this, soft and yielding. His pulses quickened, his senses sharpened as he waited, knowing she would slip out from under him and turn, leaning over him, assuming her usual dominant position.

Her thighs were lean and hard-muscled as they closed around his body, the heated, warm center of her pressed against his belly, rubbing, pleasuring. He submitted himself to her mastery without any inclination to assert a masculine role, trusting her implicitly, always trusting himself to her.

Wineglass in hand, Sara watched his reaction as she tipped the rim, allowing the sweet liquid to trickle down his chest, pooling on his belly. The chilled wine, her hot tongue. She felt his hands stroking and pressing her head, heard him groan with pleasure. "Your mouth, Sara, your beautiful mouth . . ."

Contact between their bodies was wet, slick, so warm. Artfully, she lowered herself onto him and felt him fill her body. She felt she was dissolving, melting. He seemed to become a part of herself. The muscles in her pelvis became rigid; she could feel her womb contract. It was as though she were birthing him.

At the moment of climax she brought her hard-tipped breast to his lips, encouraging him to suckle. And while she held his head, feeling the life spurt into her, she crooned, "Sara's baby, Sara's sweet, perfect baby."

Blue light glaring from the television washed the faded colors of the sparsely furnished room. Hands gripping the arms of the chair, he sat with his booted feet planted solidly on the floor, his bulky torso leaning slightly forward, poised as though he were about to spring up. The images on the screen flickered. He stared at them, unblinking, but didn't see any of the action, didn't hear the blaring sound. Chill, wet patches on his back betrayed his anxiety. Perspiration broke out above his sullen mouth and on his scalp beneath his dark, military-short hair. Cudge Balog was waiting, listening for the dull thud of hooves deep inside his head. Cutting hooves which dug into his brain matter, tearing and gouging at it. It would start slowly, with only a hint of the weight and power to come.

He had been watching TV, his thoughts on Lenny Lombardi, who, Cudge knew, would soon be pounding on the door, demanding repayment of the borrowed fifty dollars. There was a crap game in the neighborhood tonight and Lenny would want to sit in well heeled. Little bastard. He didn't need the fifty. Lombardi got more than he could spend from his drug-dealing racket. It was only pot, none of the big stuff, because he didn't want trouble with the syndicate. Still, Lombardi made more in a week than Balog would see in a month of breaking his ass on construction jobs.

Cudge's short, thick fingers dug into the threadbare fabric covering the chair. Pressure crowded the back of his brain, driving his squarish head into his neck as his powerful shoulders hunched to bear the weight. Soon, he knew, the hooves would pound through his skull—an unleashed power, irrevocable and ruthless. A dark, hulking shape would break loose from that area of his mind where he kept it penned, under control. Thinking about Lombardi had opened the gate.

As far back as Cudge could remember, the hoofed beast had lived inside his head. As a kid, he'd thought of it as a huge prehistoric monster with a long, arching neck and rows of jagged, fierce teeth. But then, at a summer camp for underprivileged city children, he'd seen a bull. He'd known then, he'd recognized the thick hulking body, the menacing drift of weight. Black, with dagger-sharp horns and fiery snorts of breath. He feared it but, in doing so, he feared a part of himself. When he was provoked and lost control of the gate, it was there—lurking, skulking, ready to burst forth from the recesses of his brain. A pounding, all-powerful force, hooves striking, horns slashing, searching for escape. Finding none, it would stampede wildly, smashing his reserve, pulverizing his restraint, compelling and dominating him until he *became* it.

Some said it was temper. Cudge knew better. It was the bull.

Brenda Kopec—or Elva St. John as she preferred to be called—sat on the lumpy daybed, her back against the wall. Her attention was riveted on the man in front of the television. She watched his profile with feral alertness, knowing he was a firecracker about to go off.

The instant Cudge had turned on the TV, she'd immediately lowered the volume of her small cassette player and jammed the earphones onto her head. Elva knew the words to Elvis Presley's "Blue Suede Shoes" by heart, but she wanted to hear the song from beginning to end. As her foot tapped to the rhythm, the scowl on Balog's face deepened. Elva knew he wasn't really watching the TV. She'd known that from the minute he had turned it on. He was thinking about that little rat-faced Lenny Lombardi. Cudge was mad and getting madder by the minute.

As though feeling her eyes on him, Balog turned

and glared at her. His square, snub-nosed face registered contempt. Veins swelled in his short, thick neck. With a speed that belied his bulk, he tore the earphones from her head; when she grappled for them, he struck her. Hard.

Elva brought up her arms defensively. "Why'd you do that?" she whined. If she cried, Cudge would hit her again.

" 'Cause you're breathin'. Shut that damn thing off and sit still. I'm trying to watch TV."

"No, you're not. Anyway, you've seen that one before. It's the one where—" Instantly, she was sorry she'd opened her mouth. Cudge sent her another look which made her cower and slip off the end of the daybed.

He stood and loomed over her. "How many times you heard that dumb song, Brenda? Oh, 'scuse me," he sneered at her, "you wanna be called Elva now. In honor of Elvis Presley. Well, he's dead and you're nothin' but a dummy. Say it, Elva—you ain't nothin' but a dummy."

Elva swallowed hard. The side of her head smarted from the blow. She knew better than to argue with Cudge. "So, okay, I'm a dummy."

"You always get hit because you never know when to shut up." His words were accusing, placing the blame for his actions on her. "Now, shut up, if you know what's good for you. Already I missed the first part of the show."

Righting herself, cautious to stay out of his reach, Elva put the cassette player in the paper shopping bag on the floor beside her, where she kept all her meager possessions. If Cudge decided they were moving on, he wouldn't give her five minutes to get her gear together. Wishing she were in-

visible, she settled herself again on the worn daybed.
She wanted to cry. She wanted to run. But she
never would. Cudge scared her sometimes, but the
outside world scared her more. At least Cudge
took care of her. Sometimes he wasn't so bad, she
told herself. Once he'd bought her a purple scarf,
and he often took her to the movies. Every Elvis
cassette she owned had come from Cudge. So why
did she take such pleasure in goading him the way
she did? Even when he was raging at her, even
when he hit her, there was a small part of her that
took abject pleasure in it. Not that she was a pervert, or an S&M freak, or anything like that. No, it
was more that she was little and helpless, so it felt
good to be able to get a rise out of a hulk like
Cudge. It gave her a kind of power, knowing she
could set him off any time she wanted. It made her
stronger than him, in some strange way. But Cudge
was right—she *was* a dummy. Someone smarter
would know how to get a rise out of Cudge and
aim it at somebody else. Whenever she set him off,
she was bound to get the brunt of it.

Suddenly she felt contrite with tenderness for
Cudge. He had his own problems to deal with. And
he wasn't so bad, not really. So what if this dumpy
room wasn't the Ritz? People like her and Cudge
would never make the Ritz. They'd be lucky if they
ever saw the inside of a Holiday Inn. She risked a
quick, sidelong glance at Cudge to see if he really
was watching TV. If he was, she could lean back
and relax. She stared at the screen, fearful that any
movement would alert Cudge that she was restless
or scared. Her toothache was coming back and she
wanted to massage her cheek but she was afraid to
move.

"Some day I'm gonna get one of those portable satellite dishes so's I can see some really sexy shows," Cudge said during a commercial.

Elva shrugged.

"Why ain't you sayin' anything?" he demanded irritably.

"You told me to shut up, that's why. I'm a dummy, remember?"

"That's your trouble, you never know when to shut your mouth. Here," he said, fishing in his pocket for money, "go get us a pizza, and I want the change. And listen—"

"I know, I know—I should tell that guy to put on extra cheese and not charge me for it."

Cudge laughed. "You really think that old man has the hots for you, don't you? Well, he don't. And if he did, he knows better than to mess with you. Thirty minutes, Elva, and you better be back here handing me my first slice. Don't lose the change!" He laughed again, his flat blue eyes narrowing.

Feeling like a trapped rat, Elva scuttled away. If she ran, she might make it there and back again in thirty minutes. Tony might be nice and give her somebody else's pizza when she told him it was for Cudge. Tony would do that for her, maybe.

Her skinny body bent into the wind, she hurried along the deserted streets of Newark's Ironbound section. The tap of her high heels echoed hollowly off the sleeping, brick-fronted tenements. She was wary, jumping at imagined shadows, at the prowlings of a conspiracy of cats lurking in an alley. Her worn navy parka was warm but it hung loosely on her slight frame. She pulled it higher, burrowing her chin into it against the late October cold.

Just ahead, less than a block away, she saw the dim red halo outlining the storefront of Tony's Pizzeria. She broke into a run, eager to be near the warmth of Tony's ovens and out of the menacing darkness. For an instant she panicked. Pushing her hand deep into the pocket of her parka, she searched for the ten-dollar bill Cudge had given her to pay for the pizza. Torn tissues and gum wrappers tumbled out, were caught in the wind and fell onto the sidewalk. Biting her lower lip, she prayed silently that the ten would magically appear. The last time Cudge had sent her out to buy something, she'd stupidly lost the money and had to go back to face his rage. She gave an audible sigh of relief when her skinny, twitching fingers found the bill. Holding tightly to the money, as though fearful some unseen force might pluck it away, she made a dash for the pizzeria.

The glass-paned door was steamed up, dripping moisture from the heat of the ovens meeting the cold outside. Throwing her weight against it, she entered into the light and warmth of the restaurant. The jukebox was playing a popular song and Tony, behind the counter, was singing along in his broken English.

"Hey, Elva! Whatcha doin' out so late? Don't y'know li'l girls should be in bed by now? I'm just closin' up. Business, she's bad tonight. Every Monday, it's the same." His white apron was stained with tomato sauce and the bright overhead lights accentuated the stubble on his jowly face.

"I ain't so little," she protested shyly. "I told you, I was eighteen last month."

"Elva, you always gonna be a li'l girl. It make no

difference how old you gonna get." He smiled at her, showing a space between his front teeth.

Elva liked Tony. He was always friendly and he seemed to know instinctively how scared she was of everything and everyone. "Cudge wants a pizza."

"So? He wants a pizza. I'm just closing up." Tony saw the dread in her dark eyes. "Why you wait so long? It's late. I've got a family waitin' for me," he complained, leaning over the counter. "Hey, how's your eye? It's not so nice what he does to you, that guy. Why you wanna stay with him?" His finger touched her cheek just below her left eye where, only last week, she had been black and blue from another of Cudge's beatings. "Poor little thing," Tony commiserated. "You oughta leave that son of a bitch." He stared at her, pity in his eyes. "Sure, Elva, for you, anything. What kinda pizza you want?"

Cudge heard the door slam as Elva ran out. He really had to hand it to her—when she wanted she could really get that skinny ass of hers moving.

He wished he had a beer. The dull thudding in his head was getting louder; a beer might help. It was a piss-poor world when a man couldn't have a beer. Elva always had her Kool-Aid in the fridge. His sullen mouth turned down. He was starting to hate Elva almost as much as he hated that sticky-sweet, artificial drink. It was getting to be time to rip the rug out from under old Elva. Time to move on and he liked to travel light.

Cudge let his eyes drift back to the blurry picture on the TV. It was an old rerun. Hutch was say-

ing something to Starsky. Now that Starsky was a
real man. *Starsky, if you hoot with the owls all night,
you won't be able to soar with the eagles in the morning.*
Cudge rolled Hutch's words around in his head
then said them aloud. He liked the sound and the
meaning. He repeated the sentence four times, till
he was sure he'd remember it. It was just the kind
of thing a guy would say to his best buddy.

A knock sounded and the door opened. "Cudge,
you in here?"

Lenny! The thudding in his brain matched the
beating of his pulses. He knew it! It'd been a sure
bet that as soon as Lenny'd heard about the float-
ing crap game, he'd come looking for that fifty. Some
best buddy Lenny was. Lenny Lombardi would
pick the gold from a dead man's teeth; he didn't
deserve the words Cudge had just heard on the TV.
He was a jerk. The whole world was full of jerks.

The muscles in Cudge's neck went into a spasm.
He feigned a smile, showing his teeth. "C'mon in,
Len. Wanna drink? Elva's got some Kool-Aid in the
fridge." He liked the stupid look on Lenny's face.

"Nah. I didn't come for Kool-Aid. I saw that Olive
Oyl old lady of yours runnin' down the street. What
did you do? Threaten to beat her again?" Lenny
loved to torment Cudge about his uncontrollable
temper.

"What's it to you?" Cudge drawled menacingly.

"Nothin'. I come for the bread you owe me.
There's a hot crap game and I want to sit in." Lenny
sauntered around the room, hands jammed into
his pockets. "Cough it up, I'm in a hurry."

Cudge's fist tightened. The lone ten-dollar bill
in his pants pocket seemed to be burning his leg.

He didn't need this cocky little dude with his pointed shoes giving him grief. "I ain't got it."

Lenny's pinched face flattened. He worked his tongue between the space in his front teeth, making a hissing noise that set Cudge's nerves on edge. "You told me that three weeks ago. Your time ran out, now pay up."

Cudge laughed, an obscene sound. "I told you I ain't got it. Gimme another week. Christ, Lenny, we been friends for a long time. You gonna blow it all for a lousy fifty bucks?" He watched Lenny keenly.

Lenny looked nervously over his shoulder before turning back to Cudge. It was a habit Cudge found irritating. Always looking away and then back again, diverting his attention, making him look over Lenny's shoulder himself, making him half expect to see someone there.

"Looks like I'm gonna have to take it in trade, old buddy."

Cudge's mouth tightened. Both hands balled into fists. "Yeah? How?"

"By taking that camper sittin' down at the curb, that's how. And your truck goes with it. Give me the keys. When you come up with the bread, you get it all back. Simple."

"You ain't taking my rig so get that idea right out of your head. You want collateral, take Elva's cassette player and tapes."

"Hey, man, I don't want your junk. Just give me the keys to your wheels. I gotta get going if I wanna sit in on the game."

Cudge's mind raced. The hooves pounded in his brain. Without his truck he'd be sunk, unable to get to the construction sites where he could pick up some money, even though he had to work his balls off just to keep body and soul together. He had to think of something. Think fast. Before the thundering hooves blotted out all reason. Lenny was a sneak, a real bastard, when it came to money. He had to get rid of him somehow.

"Don't even think about pulling a fast one, Balog. I know you got money. You think I'm stupid or somethin'? Your old lady was going into Tony's, probably for a pizza and some beer. If you can eat, you can pay your debts."

Cudge got to his feet, Elva's tape player in hand. He had no plan as he stared at Lenny Lombardi. He could almost hear the creak of the gate that kept his rage penned in the back of his head. His shoulders hunched from the weight pressing against the top of his spinal column. "I ain't got it. If you can't take my word for it, you ain't my friend."

"Friends don't welch on loans," Lenny told him. At the look in Balog's eyes, he edged back.

Cudge laughed, an unpleasant sound. Lenny backed up another step, lurching into the kitchen table. His eyes seemed to measure the distance to the door. "Okay, okay. Forget the wheels. I'll give you another week to come up with the scratch. Look, I gotta go now," he bleated as he put the table between himself and Cudge.

Suddenly the beast was loose. It took off at a gallop, snorting fire. Pressure moved from the back of Cudge's head to a point at the center of his skull. Instinct told him that if he frightened Lenny enough the fifty bucks would be called even, and he could forget about ever paying it back. He took a deliberate step in Lenny's direction, hefting the cassette player in his beefy hand.

It was the sheer terror on Lenny's face more than his words that provoked Balog. "You're crazy, man! Crazy!"

Havoc broke loose in Cudge's brain. He became the beast, sensing his prey, moving in for the kill. Blood surged into his face; his skull throbbed and pounded. Fiery breaths scorched his thoughts; dagger horns gouged and ripped.

Lenny stood speechless, his eyes round with fear. Urine pooled around his shoes. A sound erupted from his throat—a sick, choking sound. He made a run for the door but Balog was there ahead of him, blocking the way.

Cudge snorted; saliva glistened on his chin. Lenny froze. Only his eyes moved as the cassette player lifted and crashed down on top of his skull.

"Take my wheels, will you?" Cudge raged, slamming the cassette player again and again into Lenny's head. "You ain't my friend. Now get your ass out of here before I throw you down four flights of stairs."

Lenny lay with his face pressed against the floor. Cudge stood over him, seeing only the back of his friend's head. "Get up! Move, you little turd!"

He prodded the still form with his boot, was surprised when there was no movement. He squeezed his eyes shut against the sudden stab of pain in his temples. When he reopened them he noticed the widening pool of blood on the floor.

Cautiously Cudge crouched to the ground, the cassette player still clutched in his hand. He turned Lenny faceup, thinking how light he felt, how his still form offered little resistance. The wide, staring eyes panicked him and the cassette player fell from his hand.

Jesus. He didn't need anyone to tell him that

Lenny was dead. The jerk was dead! Jesus. Oh, Jesus. He had killed his best friend!

As Tony punched down the yeasty dough and stretched it over the shiny pan, he watched her. As always, his heart went out to her. She was still a kid. Other girls, by the time they were eighteen, were more woman than child. But not Elva. She would always remain a child, a frightened, winsome, confused child. Too bad she had to meet up with that animal, Balog. A nice guy could be the salvation of a timid kid like Elva, but in the hands of the hulk she was damned. Pity. She wasn't a bad-looking girl. Too skinny, of course, and a little pinched-looking, and her eyes were always on the edge of panic, but she was pretty in a shy sort of way. With a little fixing she could be really pretty. A haircut and a little meat on her bones would make a world of difference. And something, Tony thought, or someone, to take that haunted look from her eyes.

As he scattered mozzarella cheese on the pizza, Tony found a chunk and handed it to Elva, noticing her severely bitten fingernails. She took the cheese from him with a shy smile and nibbled at it. He pushed the prepared pizza into the oven and went back to cleaning the counter. "Elva—what kind of name is that? Ol' Tony never hear it before you come here."

"It's a name I just like," she answered between nibbles.

"So, it's not your name?"

"It is now. My name used to be Brenda Kopec," she said, putting the last morsel into her mouth.

"Brenda! That's a nice name. Soft, like you. So,

how come you change it? My own two daughters, they want names like Brandy and Tiffany. What's wrong with Maria and Theresa anyhow? I'm never gonna understand them. So, tell Tony, how come you changed your name?"

"I call myself Elva after Elvis Presley. I heard somewhere that Elva was the girl's name for Elvis."

"Elvis, huh? He dead long time now, you know."

"Gone but not forgotten. As far as I'm concerned, he's still the king and I love him!" she said with rare emotion.

Tony glanced up, struck by the sadness in her voice. It held the same note he had heard in his wife's voice whenever she mentioned their own dead son.

"I've read all the books written about him, seen all his old movies, and I've got all his songs on tape. He was a gentleman, Tony. A real gentleman. And generous." She pulled at her dull brown hair, her fingers working in agitation.

"You like your fellas generous? So what are you doing with that cheap son of a bitch, Balog?"

"He ain't so bad. Sometimes I think he's scared inside, just like me. Only he don't show it like I do."

Tony shrugged. There was no accounting for these American girls. He only prayed that his own daughters wouldn't end up with anybody like Cudge Balog. If Elva was right about Balog being scared of something, Tony couldn't imagine what it might be. He'd seen guys that Balog had worked over and he knew what the man's fists could do to a face. It was only a matter of time before he killed someone, and Tony hoped that it wouldn't be Elva. She was a good kid, even if she was a little stupid. Maybe if she weren't so scared all the time she wouldn't be so dumb.

Elva hurried back to the apartment, balancing the hot pizza carefully so the gooey cheese wouldn't run to one side. She wondered how long she'd been gone. It seemed like a long time, and Cudge would get mad if she kept him waiting. Suddenly, she couldn't remember if she'd picked up the change from Tony's counter. Cudge was a real stickler when it came to money. She stopped in front of a tenement and propped her leg on the stoop, balancing the pizza on her knee. The heat penetrated the cardboard box and stung her leg as she frantically dug through her pockets, looking for the change. Her panic began to turn to hysteria when she couldn't find it. She thought of going back to Tony's to see if she'd left it on the counter and glanced back along the street. The red light over Tony's door had gone out. What should she do? Maybe she could catch up with him at his car . . . Just then her fingers touched cold metal and relief flooded through her. She'd found it; she hadn't been stupid after all. For safekeeping, Elva dumped the coins into her bra, then gripped the pizza box again and hurried back to Cudge.

She smiled in the darkness. Everything had gone right for a change. Cudge wouldn't have anything to yell about.

When Elva turned down Courtland Street, she recognized the familiar outline of Cudge's Chevy pickup truck and the flat square shape of the pop-up camper hitched to its rear. They rarely went camping, but just a few days ago Cudge had talked about taking a weekend in the country. Like so many things Cudge talked about, Elva never expected to see it come to anything.

She loped up the front stoop of their building and into the dimly lit hallway. Urine and stale cooking odors came to her nostrils. Just as her foot was on the first step leading upstairs, the door to the landlady's apartment swung open.

"Oh, it's you. I thought maybe it was you he was knocking around up there." Mrs. Fortunati's thin gray hair fell over her eyes and she brushed it away with an impatient gesture of her work-worn hands. "You'd better get your ass up there and see what's going on. I was thinking about calling the cops."

Elva gulped at the sinking feeling in the pit of her stomach. The night was ruined; Cudge had done it again. Now it wouldn't matter that she had bought the pizza and brought home the right change and had done everything just exactly right. Cudge was going to be nasty and find something, anything, to be mad about anyway.

"Well, what are you waiting for? Get up there! From the sound of it he was tearing the place apart." She moved to the banister and watched Elva go up the stairs as she issued her last warnings. "I'm telling you now, there better not be any trouble or out you go! The both of you! Him in particular!"

Elva waited outside the door, dreading going in. For all Mrs. Fortunati's ravings, it was quiet now. Only the cries of the baby from up in 4B broke the silence.

She fumbled with the doorknob, balancing the pizza box on her knee. The door opened a mere three inches. Cudge had latched the chain hook. Puzzled, Elva opened her mouth to call him, then winced. The temperamental tooth with its rice grain of decay was going to ache all night.

"Cudge," she whimpered, "open the door, will you?"

"Elva?" It was a hoarse whisper from the other side of the door.

Something was wrong. Cudge never whispered. He yelled and put his fists through walls, but he never whispered. "Yeah, it's me," she responded. "What's the matter? Why are you whispering?"

The door was forced shut, jamming against a corner of the pizza box, and she heard him fumbling with the chain latch. Then it swung open again and he grabbed hold of her arm and pulled her into the apartment. The bare lightbulb over the kitchen table swung back and forth, creating wild shadows and rhythmic patterns of light.

"Get in here, dummy. Where the hell were you?" He was angry but he was still whispering, and the annoyance on his face was mingled with something else. Something dreadful she had never seen there before. Now it wouldn't matter that she had done everything exactly right. Nothing would matter except that Cudge was mad and, one way or another, she would pay for it.

"I . . . I went for the pizza like you told me. I even got the change."

"Shut up. I gotta think!"

Elva shrank back, still clutching the pizza box. Something was wrong, awfully wrong. What? She'd never seen Cudge like this, so quiet and scared. He moved away from her and sank down on the edge of the daybed, his head in his hands. The TV was still on but the sound had been turned off. She watched him, not daring to turn her eyes away.

Then suddenly, like an uncoiled spring, he jumped to his feet and punched the wall, his lips drawn back over his teeth in a frightening grimace.

"Stupid little shit! He never should've tried to bust my hump. He should've known I didn't have fifty bucks to pay him back." His fist pounded the wall again, punctuating his words. "Thought he'd take my truck and rig. Thought I was stupid or something. He should've known!"

Elva pressed against the wall, eyes wide with terror. In all the time she had lived with Cudge she'd never seen him like this. Cudge was scared. Scared shitless.

"Don't look at me that way!" He turned on her, slamming his fist into the cardboard pizza box, knocking it to the floor.

"You ruined it." Automatically she bent down to pick up the box but Cudge hoisted her to her feet.

"What the hell are you messing with that for?"

"I . . . I just wanted to clean it up."

He shook her, almost making her teeth chatter. "Oh, yeah? Well, see what you can do about cleaning *that* up!" He turned her around so she came face-to-face with Lenny Lombardi. Lenny was lying on the floor, his face barely recognizable. If it hadn't been for his familiar trench coat and slick dark hair, she wouldn't have known him.

Elva knelt down beside him, her hands extended in a gesture of helplessness. Lenny wasn't breathing!

Her mouth opened but before the sound could rip from her throat, Cudge had his beefy hand clasped over her lips, covering her nose, cutting off her air. Waiting for her to be quiet, he hissed a warning not to scream.

She stared up at him over his hand, her eyes wild and panicky, then shook her head violently, fighting for breath.

"Will you shut up?" Cudge growled. " 'Cause if you don't, you'll get some of the same."

The cords in Elva's neck threatened to burst; she was feeling dizzy and sparks were shooting off inside her head. Frantically, she nodded.

Cudge waited a long moment before removing his hand. For an instant, she believed he never would, that he would hold her there forever and ever. Her feet kicked out, touching the soft, unyielding body wedged against the wall. Sickened, she ceased her struggles.

"Now, shut up. One sound out of you and you'll look just like him!" Cudge warned in that creepy whisper, a scared look narrowing his eyes.

Full of revulsion, Elva made her way to the daybed, away from Lenny—from what used to be Lenny. She clamped her hands over her mouth to stay the questions. Unable to control herself any longer, she began to tremble as the words tumbled out.

"Why? Why'd you kill him? He was your friend! My God! You killed him!"

Cudge raised his hand, threatening her. "I told you to shut up! I don't wanna hear your mouth! Shut up!"

Elva was beyond the point of hysteria, she was verging on dementia. "God! You killed him! You killed Lenny! Your best friend! God!"

"If you don't shut up so I can think, you're gonna get what he got!" Cudge knocked the lamp beside her onto the floor. "One more word, Elva, one more word and you're gonna get it! You stupid broad! I gotta think!"

"But the police! What are you gonna do? They'll find out!"

"Quit your babbling, I gotta think!"

She shuddered with horror. Cudge had killed Lenny Lombardi and he would do the same to her if she didn't keep quiet. Everyone always said Cudge would kill somebody someday and Elva had silently agreed with them, never realizing how his potential for violence fascinated her. But Lenny was his friend.

Cudge paced the floor, his hands constantly kneading his skull in exasperation. While he paced, he kept up a constant monologue, muttering curses at Lenny, whining complaints and praying to God for a solution.

Bit by bit the quarrel between Lenny and Cudge became clear to Elva as she stole quick looks at the body that lay stuffed between the table and the wall.

"We have to get out of here," Cudge said, intensity sharpening his blunt features. "And we have to get him out of here, too, before anybody starts wondering where he got to."

Elva looked up, puzzled.

"You're an accessory, you know," he informed her. "If I hang, you're gonna hang, too!"

"Me? I didn't do anything! I just came in here and found . . . him."

"It don't matter, baby," Cudge told her, his voice showing concern. He knew how easy Elva was to handle—stupid, dumb broad. All he had to do was make her think he cared for her and she came crawling, willing to do anything he demanded. "Look, baby. According to the law, you should have run out of here and gone straight to the cops. You didn't, so that means you're aiding and abetting. That makes you an accessory and what I get, you get too! Understand?"

Elva really didn't understand, but she knew that Cudge was smart when it came to the law and he sounded as though he knew what he was talking about. If he said she was an accessory, then she must be one. He'd been busted by the cops enough times to know what he was saying. "But what can we do? Where can we go?"

Cudge smiled to himself. Poor, stupid Elva. "Look, baby, we've got to get out of here and we have to take him with us. I figure we can stuff him into the camper and take off somewhere and bury him."

A tear trickled down her cheek. "Poor Lenny."

"What about 'poor Cudge'? What about me? That stupid jerk tried to rip me off—he got what was coming to him! And now I ain't got no best friend." He knew that would bring Elva around. There was nothing that could swing Elva around like cheering for the underdog. Just make her feel sorry for you and you could lead her around by the nose.

"Cudge, I didn't mean anything like that." She went over to put her arms around him. "Sure I know how hard this must be on you and all. Lenny was your friend and I know you didn't mean to . . . to hurt him."

"That's right, honey. I never mean to hurt nobody. I just don't know what comes over me sometimes. Hey, I'm sorry I hit you before. Real sorry. Sometimes I don't know my own strength. But don't back out on me, baby. I need you. More now than ever."

Elva's heart went out to him. Poor Cudge, he just couldn't help himself. Any more than her father had been able to control his temper. Hadn't Mama always forgiven him? Hadn't Mama known that she was Daddy's very own salvation here on earth? Daddy had known it too. He always called Mama his own angel. Deciding she couldn't do any less for Cudge, Elva squeezed him hard. "Just tell me what you want me to do. I'll do anything to help you, Cudge, you know that."

"Good girl." He answered her hug with a kiss on the cheek. "Only don't go getting the idea you're doing it for me. It's for you too, baby. Christ, what would I do if they ever took you away from me because you're an accessory?"

"Don't worry, Cudge," she said soothingly. "Nobody will ever take me away from you."

Cudge Balog smiled and began formulating his plans for moving the remains of Lenny Lombardi into the camper.

Two

Listening to Sara's slow, regular breathing, Andrew knew she had fallen asleep. She had climbed into bed beside him after their lovemaking in front of the fire, placed her head on his shoulder and settled down. Now, as he lay beside her, he thought about their trip to Florida the next morning.

No need to worry about packing; Sara had seen to it, and much better than he could have done himself. They would be escorted by federal agents to the airport; and there was no concern about tickets or reservations; the government had seen to everything. They would simply board the plane and, once in Miami, go right to the courthouse. Their hotel accommodation was being kept secret even from them, so there was no possibility of a leak.

No matter how often Sara tried to reassure him, Andrew still felt uneasy for not coming forward to testify of his own volition. Nothing should have kept him from going to the authorities as soon as he'd learned that Jason Forbes's body had been discovered behind an all-night supermarket. Forbes had been only twenty, a promising student in Andrew's second-year physics class. While Andrew hadn't known the young man outside class, he had found him to be affable and to have an above average aptitude for higher mathematics.

Tomorrow Andrew would be asked to review his acquaintance with Forbes on the witness stand. There was little he could say beyond an impersonal recital of Forbes's class attendance and scholastic record. The prosecuting attorney wouldn't be looking for a personal history, Andrew reminded himself. He would want to know the details of the last time Andrew had seen Forbes alive.

It had been in May. The university library had been dim and cool, especially in the stacks where he was doing research in preparation for the coming week's classes. It had been quiet, so quiet one could almost hear the proverbial pin drop. With a scholar's contentment in the musty, hushed atmosphere, Andrew had gathered up the heavy physics texts. This was a little-used area and he had expected to spend the entire time alone at a table in the far alcove. He had been so immersed in his work that he hadn't even been aware of any noise until he heard angry voices. Curious, he had stopped to listen.

There were two voices: one with the unmistakable tenor of youth; the other harsher, older, more authoritative. They were arguing in hushed tones but their words were clear and distinct. The older voice was accusing the other of "holding out . . . starting your own business . . ."

"No!" the younger man had protested. "That was

all I picked up. Honest!" He continued to protest the accusation, his tone becoming more nervous, fearful and wheedling. Impelled by curiosity, and a vague recognition of the younger voice, Andrew had quietly closed his book and moved to the archway of the alcove.

He'd recognized Forbes immediately. His accuser was a man in his late forties, of heavy build, wearing a Hawaiian-print shirt. Andrew had never seen the man before but there was something menacing about him and the way he was leaning toward Forbes. He was a dangerous man, Andrew thought, one he wouldn't want to deal with himself. He wondered if he would have Forbes's courage in standing up to him.

"We know you're lying, kid. I've been told to tell you that you'd better get the rest of the stuff to us by ten o'clock tonight . . . or else." The man had jabbed his index finger into Forbes's shoulder for emphasis. "We don't like kids who hold out on us. We know you picked up ten kilos, so how come you only delivered eight? At street prices that would make you a nice little bundle, wouldn't it, kid? Think about it, you've been playing around with the big boys and you'd better come across."

Forbes's complexion had turned pasty white beneath his Florida tan, and he'd choked out his words with difficulty. "I don't have it, I tell you. You've got this all wrong."

"You've got it all right, kid. We know you do. Word got back to us about that little sale you made yesterday. Ten o'clock, kid, the usual place. Be there with the stuff. Oh, and don't try running home to mama. We've got our connections in St. Louis, too." With the speed of lightning, the man had punched Forbes in the stomach, the blow sending the young man gasping to his knees. Then he'd turned and strolled away, his heels clicking along the aisles of books.

Andrew had hurried over to Forbes to see if he was hurt. As he stepped forward, Forbes staggered to his feet, rubbing his abdomen. A low whistle escaped him, and Andrew thought he heard him mutter a curse.

"Are you all right?"

The young man stood frozen, staring at Andrew.

Andrew had taken a step toward the student, but the forbidding expression on Forbes's face stopped him. Jamming his hands in his jeans pockets, Forbes walked out.

For the rest of the day, the scene he had witnessed replayed in Andrew's mind. That Forbes was involved with drugs was obvious. Florida was the U.S. entry point used by many drug smugglers; from there the drugs were distributed to major cities. There was also no doubt that Forbes had gotten hold of two kilos of whatever—cocaine, heroin or marijuana—and had kept it. The only uncertainty was whether or not he would return it. If he had made a sale the day before, did that mean he no longer had the drugs? What would happen to him if that were the case? The question had occupied Andrew throughout dinner, until Sara had complained. Finally, he had confided in her.

The following day, Forbes's body had been found behind the supermarket. Was that the "usual place" the older man had spoken of? The campus was thrown into turmoil by the murder, and an investigation was launched. Detectives and policemen scoured the campus for information. No one approached Andrew to question him; yet he was becoming increasingly uneasy. Two weeks passed and still he wrestled with the question of whether or not to come forward with his information. Then more information had come to light. Forbes had been found to be involved in drug trafficking, along with his roommate, Franklin Pell. Still, nothing in the newspaper reports indicated that the police were any closer to finding Forbes's killer. Andrew knew that the police rarely revealed all information to the press, yet every day he scanned the papers, finding out more about Forbes after his death than he had ever known about him in life. It became an obsession.

In the midst of it all, Andrew and Sara had had to respond to job offers made to both of them earlier that year by Montclair College in New Jersey. They had talked it over and agreed they would be fools to leave the "Sunshine State" for the long, cold Jersey winters. But now the opportunity to leave Florida and escape even the remotest involvement in the Forbes case appealed to them. They would leave as soon as classes ended in order to set up housekeeping and prepare for the fall semester.

By the middle of July, the Taylors had moved into an old Victorian house on the outskirts of Montclair. Andrew seemed to be his normal self again, and Sara was occupied with setting up housekeeping and redecorating. Even Davey seemed to adjust to the move with little difficulty; in fact, he thrived on the additional attention provided by Sara's sister, Lorrie, who lived nearby. September came, and with it a structured schedule, marshaled by Sara, of classes, study, chores, and school for Davey. Then the murder in Florida had caught up with them—Andrew and Sara were picked up during their classes by federal agents. Franklin Pell had informed the police about the circumstances leading to his roommate's death, revealing that Forbes had told him that Professor Taylor had witnessed the confrontation in the library. Pell's testimony had leaked to the newspapers, but before the news could be picked up by the wire services, the government hastily arranged for the Taylors to be picked up and questioned.

The drug ring Forbes had been involved with was one of the biggest in the country. Andrew's testimony was vital in linking the syndicate to Forbes's death, and hence to other crimes. The government had been waiting for such a link—it would be instrumental in breaking up a wide circle of corruption which it was determined to destroy. Without Andrew's testimony, the connection between Forbes and the syndicate would be weak, and if the government knew this, so did the killers. Even Franklin Pell had no direct contact with the syndicate. His only contact had been Forbes himself.

With awesome speed and thoroughness, the government put the Taylor family under twenty-four-hour guard. The syndicate's main objective would be to prevent Andrew from appearing in court—an end most likely to be achieved the same way they had dealt with Forbes.

Sara had been wonderful throughout, dealing with the government interlopers with the same efficiency with which she ran the house and her career. Davey liked the men who followed him to school and stood outside his classroom even though he didn't understand exactly why they were there. Sara had deemed it unnecessary to tell him too much. It was more important, she said, that Davey saw his parents coping with the unusual happenings in their household and going about their lives as normally as possible.

Andrew hated the news media most of all. They referred to his caution in coming forward with the information that could "crack the most infamous drug ring operating in the United States" as though he had deliberately held back. While he didn't have any illusions about being a hero, Andrew despised their use of the word "caution." He knew it was a non-libelous euphemism for "coward."

Sara turned over onto her side, sleeping deeply now, her blonde hair fanned over the pillow. The sweet, round shape of her haunches pressed against Andrew and he smoothed his hand over her hip, following the line to the slim valley of her waist. He envied Sara her peace, wanted it for himself, wished he could find sleep instead of lying there thinking.

A soft cough from Davey's room drew his attention. He smiled as he thought of his son. Andrew didn't share Sara's reservations about Davey's growing dependence on Lorrie, but he didn't disagree either. Sara, as his mother, was much closer to Davey and his needs than he was; he would rely on her instincts.

Andrew and Sara had been married nearly fifteen years before Davey was born. They had been resigned to never having a child when the miracle was announced. Methodical thinkers both, they spent the time prior to Davey's birth discussing and rediscussing their ideas of child rearing. Happily, they'd found they agreed on almost every point. At the time, they had been teaching in a small college in upstate New York, their professional lives neatly blending with their home life. It had been an idyllic time, filled with scholastic achievements and music and love. And even though both were just past forty, they were certain that their long-awaited child could only enhance their lives.

Shortly after Davey's birth they had learned he was a hemophiliac. When he was nine months old, Sara had discovered a swelling near the base of his spine. When the doctor entered the examination room, the first thing he'd asked was, "How long has he been this color?" Andrew remembered how upset Sara had been, feeling she had been remiss, but neither one of them had noticed a change in the baby's complexion. Thinking about what had happened next still caused Andrew to break out in a sweat. After a preliminary blood test the doctor had informed them: "This baby is dying. Get him to the hospital, fast! Your son is a hemophiliac and his condition is critical."

That immediate crisis had passed, but it had launched a whole new lifestyle for the Taylors, one predicated on preventing Davey suffering even the slightest injury. Simple things would send them rushing to the hospital emergency room—bumps, bruises, cutting baby teeth, Davey biting his tongue when he fell taking his first steps.

Those had been bitter days and Sara, in particular, had agonized over the situation. Hemophilia was a blood disorder passed from mother to son. Having no brothers or uncles on her maternal side, Sara had been completely ignorant of the fact that she carried the gene. She was burdened with a guilt that could never be overcome. It was *her* fault that Davey was imperfect. She had immediately planned a campaign to protect her son in every way possible. The baby's crib and play areas were padded. Expensive special shoes with rubber soles were purchased so Davey wouldn't slip. Occasionally braces were necessary to assure that his limbs grew straight. Each little episode bordered on catastrophe. In addition to dealing with the harrowing medical problems of hemophilia, the Taylors had to live with anxiety and uncertainty every day. And still accidents would occur. Because of Davey's young age, his tiny veins sometimes could not accommodate transfusion equipment, and he would have to be strapped to a hospital bed for hours.

Sara's strength of will kept the family on as even a keel as was possible. She could ease Andrew's mind and offer hope when there was none, holding out for the day when Davey could be put on an antigen program. Before researchers had succeeded in isolating the two anti-hemophilic factors—Factor VIII and Factor IX—patients with bleeding had to lie in bed while bottles of plasma containing clotting factors were dripped into their veins. Then pharmaceutical companies had developed a way to freeze and concentrate the factors, making it possible for patients to self-administer the drug with daily shots. Unfortunately, Davey had developed antibodies against Factor VIII. It took more and more of the concentrate to block his bleeding, and Sara and Andrew feared that he would die from his next injury or spontaneous bleed. So when he was accepted into the antigen program researching suppression of antibodies, his parents were relieved. As long as Davey received an uninterrupted daily dosage of antigen, he would be able to live a normal life.

That word "uninterrupted" still made Andrew uneasy. In this life of uncertainties, was that really possible? It had to be. At this point, Davey's hemophilia was controlled. But, by the very nature of the antigen, it was possible that Davey's own body defenses could reject the drug. Then it would be useless, and the only treatment that would be effective would entail hours strapped to transfusion devices. Sara and Andrew had been instructed how vitally important it was that Davey received the antigen at the same time every single day. Even one day without the injection could set up a chemical reaction in his body, whereby the drug would be rejected and rendered useless forever. There would be no turning back. Once a week, Davey's antigen level had to be checked; it was imperative that it be kept at a level which coincided with his growth.

Sara's sister, Lorrie, was a doctor; she realized the problem. So well, in fact, that she had made a decision not to have children, knowing the odds were against her since she, too, carried the hemophiliac gene. Lorrie had happily anticipated getting married and having a family until Davey's condition was discovered. After that she'd devoted herself to her pediatric practice.

Sara threw her arm over her husband's chest and Andrew nuzzled against her, aware of the fresh scent of her shampoo which lingered in her hair. Trying to set his worries aside, he settled into an uneasy sleep.

* * *

Cudge sat beside Elva on the daybed. He was certain he had used the right words to settle her down and make her help him. She'd come up with an idea for disposing of Lenny's body; though he'd never admit it, it was more than he could have done.

"Question is, how do we get him downstairs to the camper?" Cudge touched Elva's cheek, brushing back a strand of hair. "We can't just drag him down the stairs and pretend he's drunk. Not with his face all . . ."

Elva's eyes scanned the room and came to rest on the three paper bags that held the laundry. A small bottle of fabric softener and a box of detergent were beside the bags. Frowning, she saw the rusty ironing board with its scorched, dirty gray cover leaning against the wall. She forced her eyes to go to Lenny's body and then back to the ironing board. "I got an idea, Cudge."

"Yeah? What?" He knew it was going to be something stupid but he'd better hear her out and make her feel important. This wasn't the time to fight with her and get her screaming loud enough to wake the dead.

"Like you said, we can't just take him down the stairs and pretend he's drunk or sick or something. That nosy old Mrs. Fortunati is awake and she already told me she was thinking of calling the cops because of the noise coming from our apartment. That must have been when you were hitting Lenny and—"

Cudge's hair almost stood on end; the black look in his eyes stopped Elva's flow of words. He clenched his hands to keep them from shaking.

"What did that old snoop say she heard, Elva?" It was a monumental effort to keep his voice steady.

"Nothing. She just said it sounded like you were tearing the place apart." Elva saw him relax. That wasn't anything new with the landlady. She was always saying she was going to call the cops, and she even did once because the baby in 4B was sick and cried all night long. "Anyway, I was thinking we could put Lenny on the ironing board, pile the dirty clothes on top of him and pretend we're going to the laundromat. Then you can put him in the camper and drive him away somewhere."

Cudge's eyes widened. "Sometimes you ain't so stupid after all. It just might work. Hey, you look like you're gonna be sick. If you gotta puke, do it in the toilet."

"I ain't gonna puke. I just don't like seeing dead people. It reminds me of . . . They look like chalk, and they don't move no more. Not ever."

The regret in her voice was lost on Cudge who was busy putting the ironing board next to the body to measure it. "He'll fit. Come on, don't just sit there, give me a hand."

"Cudge, I . . . I can't touch him," Elva cried.

"Move it, Elva!"

Elva shuffled over to the body and bent down to grasp the legs while Cudge took hold of it under the armpits. Lenny landed with a thump on the rickety board. Elva backed away, her hands going to her mouth to stifle a retch.

"We'll tie him on it. I don't want him rolling off in front of Mrs. Fortunati's apartment door."

"I don't like that Mrs. Fortunati. She's got little beady eyes that see everything."

Cudge ignored Elva and began to heap dirty clothes over Lenny's body. Beads of perspiration dotted his upper lip as he leaned back against the table. "Okay, that was the first step. Now we gotta clean out this place and make tracks. Get your junk together."

"I got it all in a paper bag. The rest is on top of your friend. Now what?" Elva asked, moving as far away as possible from the ironing board.

"Get everything together. We ain't coming back here ever again. Take all the food and then clean up this mess." He gestured to the pool of blood under the table. "Make damn sure you do a good job. First thing I'll take down to the camper is the TV."

"Cudge, I hate blood. It makes me sick. I can't do it!"

"You're going to do it and you'll do it now, before I punch a hole in that thing you call a head. Move it!"

"I always get the shitty jobs," Elva protested as she kicked at a filthy dish towel. With the toe of her shoe she picked up the rag and dropped it into a supermarket grocery bag. The towel was so threadbare it barely soaked up any of the blood. Not wanting to be alone with Lenny in the kitchen, she raced to the bathroom and waited till Cudge came back into the apartment. A roll of toilet paper in her hand, she walked back to the dingy kitchen. She unrolled the sheets and wiped the mess up with her foot. Satisfied that the blood had been wiped up, she poured a glass of water on the floor and repeated her actions. It was kinda sad, she thought, one roll of toilet paper was all it took to wipe up a man's life.

"You got everything?" Cudge asked belligerently.

Elva was tossing food from the refrigerator into a paper bag. "Should I take the eggs?"

He rolled his eyes. "Yes, you should take the eggs," he mimicked. "Take everything. Come on, we ain't got all night. We'll take him down first, but I want to make sure the coast is clear. I left the back of the camper open—all we have to do is stuff him in."

Elva gritted her teeth before picking up her end of the ironing board. "Wait! We have to put the detergent and softener on top to make it look real."

"Christ, Elva, we ain't really going to the laundry. Leave the damn stuff."

Elva was not to be deterred. The detergent and fabric softener were plopped on top of Lenny's stomach. Halting abruptly in mid stride, Elva's voice was a high-pitched stuttering squeak. "You can't, you just can't . . . We have to spray him with something."

Cudge's fists were white-knuckled tight. "Why?"

Elva gulped. "Be-because he'll smell. Dead bodies smell. They start to . . . to rot or something. I'm telling you what to do—I didn't say I knew what to use," she blurted. Her toothache was pounding away like a trip hammer.

Cudge stared at Elva. His voice was almost patient. "I ain't exactly planning on carrying Lenny around for very long. I don't think he'll have a chance to smell."

"Soon as he gets stiff, he'll smell."

Cudge hated the certainty in Elva's voice. "We don't have anything around to spray him with. Come on, grab your end."

"What about . . . what about the mothballs in the bottom of the sink? That's enough to kill any kind of smell. You could stick some in Lenny's coat pockets."

It was evident to Elva that Cudge was going to go along with her idea by the way his gaze shifted to the bottom of the sink. She darted between the table and the body. Her skinny arm was trembling so badly that Cudge jerked the container of mothballs from her hand. "This better work, you dizball."

Elva backed away till she was standing in the dingy living room. Cudge sneezed four times in rapid succession as he stuffed the white pellets into Lenny's pockets. "Okay, he's preserved now. You got any more crazy ideas, now is the time to spit 'em out. I ain't planning on touching him again. Let's go. Get back over here—you think I can do this myself?"

Elva advanced one step then backed up two. "I can't, Cudge, I just can't do it," she whined.

"Listen, you're the one who came up with this whole idea. Now grab hold of the damn thing and let's get him down to the camper."

She stared at Cudge. As usual he was right. The ironing board and the mothballs had been her idea. It never occurred to her that if Cudge hadn't lost his temper and killed Lenny, she wouldn't be standing here now, ready to cart a dead body down to the street.

"Grab hold, and God help you if you let him slip," Cudge snarled.

Elva shivered as she picked up the narrow end of the board. Her hold secure, she stopped again, the wide end of the board jamming Cudge in the small of his back.

"What now?"

"The detergent and bottle of softener," she explained. With a mighty effort, she reached to the top of the sink.

All the way out of the apartment and up to the top of the stairs, Lenny's body jounced with each step they took. Elva tried to look anywhere but at the ironing board. Halfway down the stairs she spotted the feathery trail of soap powder spilling onto the steps. Maybe if she didn't say anything, Cudge wouldn't notice. She repeated the thought over and over again, thinking about the trailing powder, remembering the fairy tale about the children who left a trail of bread crumbs in the forest so they could find their way back home. Elva St. John had had a home once, but something told her she never would again.

A sound like rain pelting on a roof made Cudge stop at the fourth step from the bottom. Elva's eyes popped open as she toppled over the ironing board. Cudge lost his hold and the load slid down the remaining steps. Bile rose in Elva's throat and soured her mouth. "Oh, my God, quick, pick him up! Somebody might hear! Pick him up!"

Cudge moved swiftly to right the board and rearrange the laundry on top of its burden. "I guess you know that funny noise was those damn mothballs falling out of his pockets. Run around here and get that front door open."

Elva obeyed, never letting her eyes rest on the bundled board. Cudge grimaced with effort as he dragged the board forward, holding the door open with his shoulder. "Get around and grab the other end. You and your bright ideas."

Huffing at her end of the board, Elva whispered, "I ain't even sure they'll work in his pockets anyway. Maybe you should've stuffed them in his ears." She could almost see the stubble stand on end on the back of Cudge's neck.

"Either you shut up, Elva, or you're gonna be in the back with Lenny, and it's *you* who's gonna get mothballs in the ears. Dumb shit!"

His voice was tight and choked. Elva smiled to herself. She could risk being smug. With her own eyes she'd seen Cudge gag while he was stuffing the pellets into Lenny's pockets. It was nice to know that Cudge was afraid. "I'm just trying to help," she whined. "I keep tellin' you, I ain't smart. I just know things."

"Right the first time," Balog grunted, bearing almost the full weight of the board and Lenny down the front steps and out to the curb. "Okay, now when I say 'shove' you push your end in. You got that?"

Elva let her breath out in a sob the minute the camper was closed and the top half lowered. She could imagine poor Lenny squashed in there, in the darkness. "Cudge?" she said hesitantly.

"Jeez, what do I have to do to make you shut up? What?" His tone was hushed, little more than a whisper instead of his usual yelling. Elva liked that; it was the one good thing that had happened all night.

"Should we go back and pick up the mothballs?"

"I'm going back in to get the food and make sure you didn't leave anything. You wait right here and don't go getting any ideas about taking off. You go when I say you go. Got that? And quit your worrying about the mothballs."

It was spooky sometimes the way Cudge could

read her mind. No matter what he said, she wasn't getting into the cab of the pickup until he was right there beside her. She didn't know what hurt her more—her shoulders from carrying Lenny down two flights of stairs, or her tooth.

The streetlight seemed friendly as Elva leaned against the pole. Her thoughts, however, were gray. She'd been this close to death before, only this time it was easier. She didn't really care about Lenny Lombardi, not the way she had about little BJ. She couldn't cry for Lenny—she had spent all her tears on her little brother. And she didn't feel guilty either. She hadn't even been there when Cudge killed Lenny. Not like with BJ when, if she hadn't been so scared for herself, she might have been able to do something to save him.

The worst behind him, Cudge looked around the apartment and felt nothing except relief. There were no visible signs that anything had happened in the kitchen. He walked through the apartment, taking his time to see that nothing had been left behind. If—and it was a big if—they had to come back for any reason, they could just walk in the door. The rent had been paid for the next month; there was no reason why anyone should come nosing around.

Cudge made his way down the dim stairway. The mothballs littered the filthy stair treads and, unconsciously, he counted them. When he reached the fourth step from the bottom, he stopped and inched his way closer to the greasy wall. It hit him then. He was a murderer. He felt like a land mine ready to explode. A grin spread across his face, easing the tension between his shoulders. He was the only one who knew he was a murderer—he and

Elva. Nine mothballs. Wiseass Elva would have to go. It would be his secret then; no one would ever know. One balled fist smacked into the other.

He was still grinning when he loped down the steps to the sidewalk. The camper looked just fine, and Elva was leaning against the telephone pole. "Get in, Elva, and don't you so much as blubber. Not even once, hear me?"

Elva's toothache was getting worse. If only she could fall asleep and wake up when the pain was gone. If there was someone who could promise her that, she might give up one of her Elvis tapes.

"I'm gonna drive around for a while till I decide what to do with Lenny. You keep your eye peeled for cops, or anything that might get us into trouble."

"Like what?" Elva whispered. "I want to know so I don't get us into trouble."

"Like some goddamn jerk trying to mug us as we drive around. I have to think, so watch with both your eyes. I know that trick you use sometimes, when you close one eye and stare with the other. Maybe you think it's sexy, but you look like a ghoul. Now, start looking."

Cudge drove carefully, his eyes alert. While he was searching the apartment, he'd toyed with the idea of burying Lenny in the Watchung Mountains. It was as good a place as any. There wouldn't be too many people on the steep mountain roads. The trees were thick and dark around Bernardsville, and he had more than enough gas to get him there and back. Back to what? He couldn't think that far ahead.

As he drove along, his thoughts were confused. It seemed like he was always in trouble of some kind. When he was a kid, he had been in one scrape after another, but he'd always managed to save his hide at the last moment. So far, the cops had nothing on him except a few drunk driving charges. He had been deprived. He was being deprived now. Pity was drowning out all reason. Pity for himself, pity for the circumstances that controlled his life. When he was a kid, he'd never had anything, except the clothes on his back and what he could steal. Now he was a man, but still he had nothing.

Three

Lorrie Ryan maneuvered the small motor home around a bend. She enjoyed driving the RV, found it relaxing.

She had been looking forward to spending time with Davey for weeks now. She'd gotten Dr. Petti to cover for her. He was a good pediatrician and his small patients liked him, to say nothing of their mothers. Tall, dark, and handsome Douglas Petti. Too bad he was already spoken for. Lorrie was at an age where most of the men she met were already spoken for, or divorced, or losers.

Her thoughts turned back to the camping trip ahead of her. She'd made a dozen cupcakes for her and Davey to share. Not the best diet in the world, but Davey did so love them and this trip was special. If he wanted, she would serve them for breakfast, lunch, and dinner. Davey had a sweet tooth, just like her. She knew she'd better not let Sara know that cupcakes were on the menu for all of Davey's meals. Sara followed a strict regimen in the kitchen, even down to how many times Davey chewed his food.

Sara was okay, Lorrie told herself, she was just a little overorganized. Even as a child, Lorrie could remember her older sister saying "A place for everything; everything in its place." Today, that included Andrew and Davey, she thought.

Sara was Davey's mother and of course she wanted what was best for her son. Lucky Sara, she'd got the best material to work with. Davey was the most remarkable, resilient child Lorrie had ever known. Lorrie looked ahead, anticipating a left-hand turn several blocks on. Andrew was the one who surprised her, she admitted to herself. She'd always thought of him as the absentminded professor, oblivious to everything except mathematical theories—a little sloppy, disorganized, terribly forgetful. The fact that he didn't balk at Sara's "organization" surprised her. Andrew was a good guy, a dear really, even if he was just a little *too* comfortable and secure. That was Sara's fault. Lorrie didn't think it would even occur to Andrew to rock the boat, to make a fuss. He seemed to think that if he was happy, everyone else must be too.

Unfortunately, that didn't hold for his son. Davey had been over-protected, over-organized and raised strictly by the book. Lorrie remembered how Sara hadn't been able to keep a nursemaid while she was teaching at the college. No one was able to adhere to her stringent schedules. Time to get the baby up, time to feed him, time for a bath—Christ! The woman was a living automaton. Lorrie wanted to blame it on the fact that they came from a big family and that every time their poor mother even tried to set a time for dinner, she had a mutiny on her hands, but the fact was, Sara was different. Lorrie knew that Sara didn't approve of her sister's influence over her son. Andrew was a great guy, but he wouldn't stand in Sara's way if she suddenly decided to put an end to Lorrie's relationship with Davey.

Lorrie didn't understand Sara. Never had, and probably never would. The fifteen-year gap in their ages had caused a gulf of understanding that couldn't be bridged—until Davey, that was. Davey had brought them together. His medical condition had forced Sara to turn to Lorrie for help and answers.

Carefully executing the left-hand turn, Lorrie glanced in her side mirror. All this business with the drug racket in Florida had put a crimp in Sara's style. Especially since it was plastered all over the news. It was difficult to picture Andrew as the lead witness. A hostile witness, since he had to be subpoenaed to come forward. It was going to be a rough few days for him, she was sure. He wouldn't like being cross-examined on the witness stand. Lester Weinberg was representing the syndicate, and he wasn't exactly a pussycat lawyer. When he had Andrew on the stand, he would do whatever he could to rip apart Andrew's testimony. There was a lot at stake—more than just some thug threatening a kid entangled in the rackets. That thug was a known connection with the syndicate, and if the government could pin the murder on him, it would lead to other important convictions.

"Poor Andrew," Lorrie whispered aloud. "And poor Sara. She must be fit to be tied." She wondered how Sara was coping with all those FBI agents underfoot; Sara who didn't even like live-in help. During a recent phone conversation, Andrew had told her that Sara had had one of those agents removed from the case. The man had removed his jacket in front of Davey, exposing his shoulder holster and gun. Lorrie couldn't say she blamed Sara for getting angry, but she could have cut the man some slack and just asked him to keep his jacket on. But that was Sara—unbending, unyielding, unforgiving.

Lorrie would have liked to make excuses for her sister—after all, Sara only wanted what was best for Davey. But she went too far. She demanded perfection from people. And, if they didn't live up to her standards, she cut them down ruthlessly, without conscience, all in the name of what was best for her son. And for Andrew, too, now that Lorrie thought about it.

Lorrie had a good idea of where she stood in Sara's eyes and had learned to accept it. One of her friends, a staff psychologist, had suggested that Sara might be jealous of anyone besides herself having a place in Davey's or Andrew's life. He'd warned her to be careful, not to let herself get hurt, no matter how much Davey meant to her.

Tears welled in Lorrie's blue eyes as she thought about the love she felt for Davey. She didn't want to steal Davey away from Sara; she only wanted to have a part in his life, to be his favorite aunt, even if she was his only aunt. For all that Lorrie felt sorry for Andrew and Sara and all they were going through, she was glad for the chance to spend some time alone with Davey. She would love him and pamper him as he had never been loved and pampered before. And maybe, just maybe, after all this was over and done, Sara would consent to letting her take him some place again.

Davey kept vigil at the front windows, waiting for the first sight of his aunt's motor home coming down the street. It turned the corner, a white and green RV with a wide expanse of tinted windows, and gold decals that proclaimed it was "King of the Road." "She's here! She's here!" he shouted excitedly, hurrying into the dining room with Duffy chasing at his heels.

Andrew and Sara Taylor sat at the table with their morning coffee. "Well, get over to the door and help Mr. Sanders let her in, Davey," Andrew said, smiling as he put down his mug. "Mr. Sanders knows she's coming."

Davey raced to the front door, almost running headlong into Stuart Sanders who was at his usual post in the foyer.

"Hey, little buddy, what's your hurry?" Sanders asked, well aware of Davey's excitement about his first camping trip.

"Aunt Lorrie is here to take me camping and to the zoo! I'm going to sleep in the RV and cook outside and everything!" Davey's bright blue eyes shone, and a heightening flush colored his little-boy cheeks.

"So I hear," Sanders said jovially, keeping a professionally watchful eye on the RV as it pulled into the Taylors' wide driveway.

"Let her in, Mr. Sanders, she's taking me camping!" Davey pleaded.

Sanders had his keys ready to insert into the

double locks as soon as Dr. Ryan reached the door. As a matter of routine, he had already unsnapped the flap on his shoulder holster although, as per his instructions, it was done in such a way that Davey didn't notice.

Lorrie knew her every movement was being watched as she climbed the steps to her sister's front door. What a way to live! Constantly monitored and watched, unable even to open the front door without a security check. Hearing Davey's voice on the other side of the door, she didn't bother to knock.

"Hurry up, Mr. Sanders," Davey was urging.

The moment the barrier was gone, the little boy threw himself into his aunt's arms, hugging her tightly. "Can we go now? Huh? Can we?"

Lorrie laughed as she knelt to hug her nephew. "Yep, in just a few minutes. Are you all packed and ready to go?"

"I've been ready since before it got light." Davey sniffed the air. "What's that smell?"

"Smell? What smell?" Lorrie asked, sniffing the air as Davey had done. "I don't smell anything."

"I do," Stuart Sanders said. "I believe it's your perfume, Dr. Ryan. Chanel Number Five, isn't it?"

Lorrie released Davey and stood. "Why yes, as a matter of fact it is, Mr. Sanders," she said. "Does your wife wear it?" she asked, fishing.

"I'm not married."

"Oh, I see . . ."

"I worked a case once that involved a perfume manufacturer," Sanders said, as if to explain.

Lorrie nodded. In spite of his stern expression, Stuart Sanders was a very good-looking man. She'd noticed him the last time she'd come to see her sister and, though he hadn't spoken more than a few polite words, she'd found herself discreetly watching him, wondering about him.

"Where are your mom and dad, Davey?" Lorrie asked, looking around.

"In the dining room. Here comes Mom now," Davey said quietly, moving back. Duffy scampered between his legs, knocking him slightly off balance.

"Whoa there, young man." Mr. Sanders grabbed his shoulder and held firm until Davey was steady on his feet.

Sara Taylor's eyes held a guarded look as she walked toward her sister and the FBI agent.

"You're right on schedule," she said, offering her cheek for Lorrie's kiss. "Come and sit down for a few minutes."

"But Mom . . ." Davey whined with impatience.

Sara rested her hand on top of his head. "Your aunt and I have a few things to discuss before you go, Davey. You go on up to your room and get your bag."

"Okay, but hurry!"

Lorrie followed her sister back to the dining room.

"Lorrie! You look like a real camper, decked out in Wranglers and all." Andrew stood up and gave his sister-in-law a quick kiss.

"I am a real camper, Andrew. I've even got my American Trails card." Lorrie sat down and looked toward the stairs. "Davey's really excited, isn't he?"

"That he is!" Sara answered. "I only hope he's this happy at bedtime. He's never spent the night away from us before, except for hospital stays."

Lorrie reached across the table and patted her

sister's hand. "Now, don't go worrying. I'll take good care of him, and if he has any problem tonight he can just crawl in the bunk with me."

Sara pulled her hand away. "I don't want you taking Davey into bed with you, Lorrie," she said flatly. "Andrew and I have never done that and, frankly, we find it unacceptable."

"Hey, okay," Lorrie agreed, trying to make it sound like it was no big deal. "If that's the way you want it, I don't have a problem."

Andrew leaned toward his wife. "It might be rough on him, Sara, being away from home for the first time. What harm—"

"No, Andrew," Sara interrupted. "I won't hear of it. Once you start something like that . . ." She shook her head.

Lorrie smiled. "I understand, sis. If you say no, then it's no. I really don't anticipate any problem anyway. He'll probably be so worn out, he'll go to sleep right after supper." Lorrie hated to ingratiate herself with her sister this way, but she would do anything to prevent Sara from coming between her and Davey. A familiar sadness crept up on her as she thought of the children she would never have because of the gene she carried.

As if reading her thoughts, Sara moved away from the table, returning with a small box which she set before her sister. "Here's Davey's medication. Keep it refrigerated. His usual time is at noon. That makes it easy to remember." A hint of a frown drew her brows together.

"Noon," Lorrie repeated. "I won't forget."

"I know I shouldn't worry, but I do," Sara said. "Davey's been doing so well, and his doctors say it's mainly due to the strict regimen we adhere to. Last month he had another test for antibodies and he's still very low. As far as we're concerned, that's great. He could possibly go on using the AHG for a long time to come."

Lorrie had made a point of keeping up on the latest research. Approximately eight percent of all hemophiliacs would develop an antibody with specificity against Factor VIII, making it less effective in stopping the bleeding. AHG was more or less a replacement for the factor that Davey's own body didn't manufacture. By adhering to a strict daily time schedule, it was more likely that the antibody buildup could be avoided. In Davey's case, it seemed to be working and, with any luck, he would be able to live an almost normal life, free of the spontaneous bleeding beneath the skin and into the joints that resulted from what was, for most kids, minor trauma—a spill from his bicycle or a skinned knee. Without AHG, the antibody levels would shoot up, especially if there was a disproportionate amount of stress present. That's when all systems were go, as far as the body was concerned—the adrenaline flow increased and the heart pumped faster. AHG was touted as a miracle treatment, as long as the antibodies didn't develop to cancel out the new, refined Factor VIII.

"Well, you don't have to worry about Davey this weekend. I'll take good care of him." Wanting to change the subject, Lorrie pulled a brochure out of her pocket. "I've got some really great plans for the next two days," she said, sliding the brochures toward her sister. "I thought we'd spend most of today at the Philadelphia zoo, then come back into Jersey and spend the night at my favorite campground. It has all the modern conveniences,"

she added. "Then tomorrow morning, I'll take
him to New York City. I've got tickets to the laser
show at the planetarium. Then back to the campground for tomorrow night, and home Wednesday
afternoon. What do you think?"

"Sounds great!" Andrew interjected before Sara
could find fault with the plans. He knew she would
worry about Davey becoming over-tired and over-
excited.

"Yes, I . . . I suppose that will be all right."

"Of course it is, honey," Andrew said. "Davey will
love it. Only one word of warning, though," he
added, looking at Lorrie. "Don't tell Davey about
the planetarium until tomorrow or he won't sleep
through the night. Ever since he saw the advertise-
ment for the laser show on TV, he's been begging
me to take him and, well, with everything that's
been going on around here lately, I haven't been
able to take him anywhere." Andrew smiled and
shook his head. "All your plans sound like so much
fun I feel like playing hooky and coming with you."

"Oh, no you don't," Lorrie scolded her brother-
in-law playfully. "This is my chance to have Davey
all to myself and you're not invited. I intend to
treat that kid as if he was my own. Better."

Sara straightened her spine. "I suggest you remember that Davey's our child, not yours, Lorrie,"
Sara said, avoiding Andrew's warning glance. She
knew he didn't think this was the right time to tell
Lorrie they intended to reduce her time with Davey.

Lorrie paled, her sister's cruel words cutting
her to the quick.

At a sound from the doorway everyone turned.
Davey was standing there, Duffy clutched in his
arms. The little boy's face looked crestfallen.

"What's the matter, son? Not having second thoughts, are you?" Andrew teased.

Davey sniffed. "It's Duffy. She doesn't want me to go. Look at her eyes, she's been crying."

"Duffy will be fine in the kennel," Sara told her son.

"I don't want her to stay all alone in a kennel. I want her to go with me!" He glanced shyly at his aunt, feeling like a crybaby yet unable to help himself.

Lorrie smiled warmly. "Come here, Davey." Slowly Davey walked over to her, Duffy still held tightly in his arms.

"That's one sorry-looking dog you've got there. I think you're right. She doesn't look to me as though she'd last a day without you. We'd better take her with us."

Immediately Davey brightened. "Really? Did you hear that, Duff? Aunt Lorrie said you can come with us!" He set her down. "I'll go get her dog food," he said, turning to leave. "C'mon, Duff. We need your leash and your dish, too." Davey scampered off to the kitchen, leaving his aunt to bear the weight of his parents' remonstrances.

"Lorrie, are you sure you want to do that?" Andrew asked, looking doubtful.

"Where will Duffy stay while you're at the planetarium and the zoo?" Sara questioned, not liking a last-minute change to the plans she had carefully made.

"In the motor home. She'll be fine. I should have thought of it before."

Davey ran through the dining room carrying Duffy's red plastic dish, a metal-link leash and a bag of dry dog food. He headed for the front door with Duffy scrambling after him, yipping at the sight of her leash. "I'm going to tell Mr. Sanders that Duffy's going with us!"

Davey dropped the bag of dog food and the rest of Duffy's possessions next to the front door. "Duffy's coming too!" he told Stuart Sanders.

"Is that right? Good for Duffy! Hey, Davey, come over here. I've got something for you." Sanders withdrew something from his pocket. "It's a penlight, just like the Boy Scouts use." He flipped the switch and displayed the light against the palm of his hand.

"Gee! Thanks, Mr. Sanders."

"And see, it has a chain attached to it so you can hook it through your belt loop, like this." Sanders attached the penlight to Davey's narrow belt loop and dropped it into the boy's pocket. "For your very first camping trip."

Davey's smile was the agent's reward. Shyly the youngster reached out to shake hands, just the way his mother had taught him.

Lorrie called Davey back to the dining room and held him on her lap, the brochure spread out on the table in front of them. She pointed to the pictures of the campground where they would be spending the night.

Davey pored over the pictures, then looked up. "Mom, you said I could call Digger on the CB to say goodbye. Can I tell him about my camping trip, Mom, can I? I want to tell him that we're staying at a campground right near Wild Adventure Park, and that at night you can hear the lions roar."

"Yes, Davey, you can call him but don't be long."

After Davey had left the room, Andrew turned to Lorrie. "That CB was a godsend. Best thing you could have given him. He loves it."

Lorrie smiled, pleased that Andrew was pleased. "Well, I knew Davey would be cooped up in the house for a while because of the trial and all. I'd remembered one of my patients, a little boy with severe physical limitations, talking about a Junior CB Club and how much fun he had talking to other kids."

"Davey would be on it all the time if we let him," Andrew said. "But Sara and I explained that operating a citizen's band radio is a responsibility, and I'm proud to say that Davey doesn't abuse it. One half hour each afternoon, that's all. After all this is over, we promised Davey he could meet this 'Digger' in person."

"Digger? That's a funny handle. I've heard some of them are outrageous. What's Davey's?" Lorrie asked.

"Panda Bear," Sara answered, long white tapered fingers shredding the paper napkin near her cup. "It's the only one he came up with that Andrew and I would agree to. You should have heard some of the others."

"I'm so glad you approve of Davey belonging to the Junior CB Club, Sara. I wasn't sure you would."

Sara faced her sister. "I don't approve of some of the 'lingo' that the CBers use. It goes against my grain. Whatever happened to the Queen's English?"

Elva and Cudge sat stiffly on the front seat of the Chevy pickup truck, fully aware of Lenny

Lombardi's body behind them on the floor of the pop-up camper.

Cudge kept a careful eye out for traffic signals and speed limits. This was definitely not the time to attract the attention of some cop who might demand an inspection of the camper. Cudge damned himself for painting the truck with wild colors and applying decals that just barely came within the limits of the law. Cops were always stopping vans and pickups, looking for drugs, and the wild decorations on the old Chevy just begged for police to get nosy, if only on principle.

The CB on the dashboard emitted its usual static, picking up a trucker here and there. He intended to keep the CB going all the while they were on the road, regardless of Elva's whining protests that she wanted to listen to her Elvis cassettes. If there were speed traps or any cops in the vicinity, he wanted to know while he could still do something about it.

They headed west out of Newark, traveling city streets. Elva had never seen Cudge drive so carefully. She knew better than to complain about the static coming from the CB that was giving her a roaring headache. This was no time for Cudge to lose his cool.

About nine o'clock they were going through the town of Montclair. As they entered the town, the transmission on the CB became clearer.

". . . that sounds great, Panda Bear. When will you get back? Over." A click.

"We'll be back Wednesday, Digger. How long will you stay in the hospital to get your legs fixed? Over." A click.

"Don't know, Panda Bear. Where are you camping? Over." A click. The second young voice sounded louder, clearer, coming through the speaker.

"Down at a campground near the Wild Adventure Amusement Park. Aunt Lorrie says you can hear the lions roar at night. Over."

"Too bad the park isn't open yet," Digger said. "I know you'd like the Ferris wheel they have there. Over." Click.

"That's what Aunt Lorrie says is so great. When the park is open, it's so crowded you can never get in; this time of year there won't be hardly anybody there. It'll be like being out all alone in the woods. Over."

"Have a great time, Panda Bear. Wish I could go with you rather than to the hospital. Over."

"Digger? I hope they fix your legs this time. Over."

"Yeah, me too. Gotta go now, Panda Bear. Have a great time for me. Out."

"I will, Digger. I know I will! Out."

The transmission ended and the static sounded again.

"Get that map out of the glove compartment, Elva," Cudge instructed, keeping his eye on the road. "Find out where that Wild Adventure place is."

Federal Bureau of Investigation Special Agent Stuart Sanders stood outside Davey's door. He could hear the excited voices on Davey's CB. He still had some time. He would wait till the conversation was over before he said goodbye.

The agent looked into Davey's immaculate

room, so different from his nephews' bedrooms. Where were the personal touches? Everything was expensive, from the porcelain clowns on the shelf to the leather-bound editions of Dickens. An interior decorator might find it in perfect taste, but to Sanders it seemed like a model room in a department store. Where were the bits and pieces of games that were standard in a kid's room? Where were the stubby crayons in coffee cans? Or the slipper without a mate? Where were the comics and storybooks that took a kid on trips to fantasy land? He knew if he looked under the bed he would find nothing but a clean, vacuumed carpet. There would be no forgotten toys, no dirty pajamas, no pennies. Just a clean floor. As he watched the Yorkshire terrier nip at Davey's pant leg he thought, at least Duffy was real. Davey was real.

It was impossible, but the bed was already made. It annoyed him. His sister's kids never made their beds till five minutes before their mother came in from the office, and then all they did was throw the comforter up over the pillow. There was no life in this room. Sanders had a sudden urge to scoop up the dog and the kid and take them to his sister's house with the noise and disorder that four boys made. Nancy would take one look at Davey and cradle him in her arms and croon some indistinguishable words that only kids understood. Nancy called it "mother magic." Disgust washed through him. This room, this kid, could use a double dose of Nancy.

The minute Davey broke his connection Duffy barked to let Stuart know it was all right to enter the room. Walking in, he held out his hand. "I came to say goodbye, Davey."

Manfully, Davey extended his hand. "It was nice of you to come up to see me and Duffy, sir."

Stuart Sanders squatted down till he was at eye level with the little boy. "Listen, tiger, I hope you have a whale of a good time on your camping trip. Take good care of this bundle of dynamite," he said, motioning to the dog.

"I will, sir. And, sir, thanks again for the flashlight. I have it in my jacket pocket so I can use it whenever I want."

Stuart stared into Davey's bright eyes. Despite the room, the kid would be all right. Stuart felt it in his gut. His eyes dropped to the needle marks on Davey's arms.

Davey grinned when he noticed Stuart staring. Playfully, he punched the agent on the arm. "I almost don't need them anymore."

Suddenly, Stuart didn't want to leave. He had never in his life believed in premonitions or anything supernatural, but he was experiencing something now. And the dog, the dog was staring up at him with what Stuart would later describe as questioning eyes. "Davey, I'm going to give you a card that has my cell phone number on it. If you ever want to talk to me, or if you think I might be able to help you sometime—you know, if you ever join the Scouts or something like that—you call me. It doesn't make any difference what time it is, day or night. If I don't answer, you just leave a message and I'll get right back to you."

"Sure, Mr. Sanders," Davey said, taking the business card and sticking it in his hip pocket. "Maybe you should give me two, one to take with me and one to leave here in my desk."

Stuart got to his feet. He didn't know why but it

was important for him to make the kid promise. "Okay, but first I want you to promise me that you'll call me if you need me." Deliberately, he made his tone light.

Duffy barked sharply and Davey's tone was solemn. "I promise, Mr. Sanders."

"Listen, tiger, you got any money on you?"

Davey shook his head. "Mom and Dad said I don't need any money."

Sanders winced slightly. "I'm sure they're right, but when I was a kid, my dad always gave me some pocket change to carry around in case I needed to make a phone call and all I could find was a pay phone. I think you should have some. Here, take these three quarters."

Dutifully, Davey accepted the three quarters and stuffed them down into his pocket with the business card. The jangle sounded nice.

"As long as you have money in your pocket, you're always just a phone call away from having someone to talk to. I have to go, tiger. You and Duffy take good care of each other, okay?" He choked a little as he tousled Davey's hair.

"Got everything, sport? Ready to go? Your mom and dad have a plane to catch to Florida and we can't hold them up." Although Davey was aware that his parents were flying to Florida, Lorrie knew he wasn't aware of the reason. He had been told it was on school business.

"Everything's ready. Right, Mom?"

"You'd better be on your way, son," Andrew said, then turned to his sister-in-law. "His gear is on the front porch. Sanders took it out a while ago."

Sara, issuing last-minute instructions, was still talking when she pecked Davey on the cheek. Her hand lingered a moment on his shoulder before she stepped back.

Andrew Taylor clapped Davey gently on the back and patted his head. "I want you to be a good boy for your aunt, and don't give her any trouble."

"And keep Duffy out of trouble," Sara instructed. "We'll see you in a few days," she added quietly.

Lorrie knew she had been dismissed. It was Sara's inimitable style. She didn't just say hello or good-bye like other people. Not Sara. She welcomed you for the moment and then, when some invisible clock in her head reached the appropriate time, she dismissed you. As she ushered Davey out the door, Lorrie wondered if Sara ever dismissed Andrew that way, and what he thought of it if she did. Or if he was even aware of it. Sara was her sister and she loved her dearly, but she had to acknowledge she *was* different.

"Doctor Ryan," Stuart Sanders said, following Lorrie out the door and down the steps. "If I could have a word with you, please."

Lorrie turned around. "Sure, just let me open the door to the motor home so Davey can get in."

"Of course. I'll just wait right here," he said, standing back.

While Lorrie unlocked the motor home door, Davey turned to see if his parents were watching him from the long panes beside the front door. Not seeing them, he scanned the living room windows. There was no shadow behind the lace curtains.

"C'mon, Duff," he said, turning toward the motor home. Aunt Lorrie stood beside the open door, waiting to give him a hand up the steps. "I can do it myself," he said, wanting to show her that he was self-sufficient.

"Okay then, but how about if I give Duffy a boost?" Lorrie's eyes met Stuart Sanders's amused gaze. At Davey's nod of agreement, Lorrie lifted Duffy and put her inside. "You two look around while I talk to Mr. Sanders, all right?"

"All right, but hurry!" Davey replied, then disappeared into the motor home behind Duffy.

Stuart Sanders rolled his shoulders and straightened his tie in preparation for his talk with Lorrie Ryan. It was funny, where criminals were concerned, he had always been aggressive and sure of himself, but with women—especially unattached, attractive women—he was a different man entirely, awkward and never quite knowing the right thing to say or do. "I only need a minute," he said, reaching into his coat pocket as Lorrie came toward him. "I wanted to give you my card. It has my cell phone number on it. If you need me . . . for anything, I want you to call."

Lorrie stared at him, worry etching lines into her forehead. "You don't think—"

Sanders put his hand on her arm, stopping her from completing her sentence. "Let's not borrow trouble by speculating on things that may never happen. I just want you to know that I'm only a phone call away, and that means help is only a phone call away. Understand?"

She nodded. "That's very considerate of you, Mr. Sanders."

"Stuart. Call me Stuart."

"Stuart, then." She took the card from his hand,

looked it over, then slid it down into her right front pocket.

"You do have a cell phone, don't you?"

"Yes, it's in the motor home. Do you want the number?"

He took a pen and a little spiral notebook out of his inside pocket and jotted down the number. "I gave Davey a card, too," he told her. "He does know how to use a telephone, doesn't he?"

"Of course, he does. Along with a CB and a computer," she said proudly.

He smiled. "Davey's a lucky boy to have an aunt who loves him so much."

Lorrie's eyes started to tear up. "No, Stuart," she said, shaking her head, "I'm the lucky one to have a nephew like Davey. He's one in a million."

"I know. So are you."

"Aunt Lorrie!"

Lorrie turned toward the sound of Davey's voice. "Coming, Davey."

"You'd better hurry," Sanders said.

"Yes, I . . ." Something—Lorrie wasn't exactly sure what—had just passed between them, something that left her feeling a little lightheaded. "Will you be here when Davey and I come back from our big adventure?"

"I'm not sure. It depends on what happens with your brother-in-law."

"Aunt Lorrie!"

"Goodbye, Stuart. And thank you for your concern."

"You're welcome, and have a good trip."

Lorrie climbed up into the motor home and closed the door behind her. "So, what do you think, Davey? This is going to be your home for the next couple of days. Like it?"

Davey looked around, his eyes wide with excitement. "It's a house! A real house! On wheels!"

Lorrie smiled. She was proud of the recreation vehicle and had selected each accessory with great deliberation. The thick, forest-green carpeting added softness to the hard-surfaced, utilitarian appliances. The first thing Davey asked her to show him was his bed. Laughing, Lorrie pointed to a bunk over the driver and passenger seats.

"Where are you going to sleep?" Davey questioned, looking around for a big king-sized bed like his parents used.

"In the back," Lorrie said, sliding back the bedroom door. "You see, just like home."

"Wow. It is. It really is."

"Okay, now. Sit down and I'll buckle you in." As Lorrie secured the safety belt across Davey's chest and lap, she said, "I want you to know this expedition is in no way a Mickey Mouse production. This is a first-class, grade-A, super-colossal expedition to the Philadelphia zoo and other points of interest. Any comments?"

"Nope," Davey responded with mock solemnity.

"First things first. Let's go through our check list. Your medicine. What time do you get your shot?"

"You know. Every day at noon."

"Right. I'll set the alarm on my watch for twelve noon just in case we're having so much fun we forget what time it is. Dog food! Did you remember to bring dog food?"

"Yep. It's under the table. Duffy eats twice day."

"Okay, then. I guess that's it."

Davey chattered excitedly as the RV ate up the miles on the crowded highway. He was having a good time just sitting in his seat, talking to Aunt Lorrie about his CB buddies and the movies he'd seen. He thought about his mom and dad when he saw an airplane and wondered if it was their plane. He waved, just in case it was and they were looking out the window. Were they thinking about him the way he was thinking about them? He listened with half an ear to Lorrie talking about the Philadelphia zoo. He had never been to a zoo before. His CB buddy, Digger, had told him it was humungous, whatever that meant. It must be good, he reasoned, because his buddy got all excited just telling him about it. He'd said it was almost as good as being there just telling Davey so he would know what to expect. A giggle erupted in his throat. Panda Bear was going to the zoo!

A large white dome with red lettering caught his eye as the RV slowed to merge with the traffic. "What's that, Aunt Lorrie?"

"The dome? It says 'Cherry Hill.' That's the name of a town near Philadelphia. It's a kind of welcome for travelers, it lets them know that Cherry Hill is the next turnoff."

Davey shrugged. His attention was diverted when a battered pickup truck painted with bright designs pulled up beside the motor home. He stared at it and saw it was pulling a big square box on wheels. The glare on the window made it impossible to see who was sitting in the front. It didn't really matter who it was. He would never see them again once Aunt Lorrie turned off the road for the zoo. On closer inspection he saw that the pickup truck was pulling a pop-up trailer. Davey watched the truck as it moved still closer to the RV. A man and a woman were sitting in the front. He stared at the woman; she looked scared. His eyes widened when he saw the man reach out and slap her across the face. He swallowed hard as he clutched Duffy.

"Another five minutes and we'll be getting off the turnpike. Are you excited, Davey?" Lorrie asked heartily.

"Uh-huh," Davey mumbled as he slid a piece of gum into his mouth. The woman in the pickup wasn't like Aunt Lorrie or his mother. She was more like Millicent, the babysitter who used to watch him when his parents went out. Only she wasn't pretty like Millicent. And Millicent would never look scared like that, or cry like the woman in the truck. Millicent said only babies cried, and that you had to be tough to survive. When he'd repeated what Millicent had said, his mother had got him a new babysitter, Mrs. Goodeve.

Davey's golden eyebrows drew together as he stared pointedly at the girl in the truck. She gazed back at him through the glass before wiping at her eyes with the back of her hand.

"Get ready, Davey, here we go, exit four. Time to get off and make tracks for the zoo. I vote to see the monkey cage first. What about you, Davey, what do you want to see first?"

Davey turned, trying to get a last look at the pickup and the girl with the white face.

"The elephants," he said, distracted. Why had the man hit the girl? What could she have done? She had just been looking out the window.

*   *   *

Cudge Balog caught a look at the RV beside him. Sitting in the passenger seat there was a blond kid holding a dumb-looking pooch. Wet nose prints slopped up the side window.

Cudge was driving as carefully as he could. No way did he want a trooper pulling him over. Damn, he wasn't even going to sneeze for fear his foot would jam down on the accelerator. Slow and easy was the way to do it. No wise-ass trooper with polished sunglasses was going to chew him out for anything, real or imagined.

Cudge's hands tightened on the steering wheel. A bead of sweat dotted his upper lip. "Why ain't you saying anything, Elva? It ain't like you to sit so quiet. You up to something or what? If you got any ideas at all about jumping out or taking off, forget it." His voice was mean and low.

"You told me to sit here and keep my mouth shut. Make up your mind. Either you want me to talk or you want me to keep quiet." God, now why had she said that? She was so in tune with Cudge's voice that she knew exactly what his next move and statement would be. You did what Cudge said when Cudge said it, and you didn't ask questions. You didn't volunteer anything with Cudge either. What was wrong with her? Why was she acting this way? Her stomach churned and she felt bile rise in her throat. She was afraid to stay with him and afraid to leave him. Fear of walking the streets, with no place to go at the end of the day, was worse than living with Cudge. Everyone needed someone, something—a place that was their own at the end of the day when darkness fell. She remembered only too well the darkness of the pantry where her father had locked her to punish her.

She hated the dark and the creatures that came out in the dark. In a way, Cudge was like one of the rats back in the apartment; his eyes were just as beady, his lips as thin, his ears as pointed.

Cudge ignored her; this was no time to let Elva get under his skin. He had to concentrate. "I want you to keep your eyes peeled for anything suspicious, like a trooper in an unmarked car, that kind of thing. Keep what wits you have sharp. If I get pulled over for any reason, you just sit there, deaf, dumb and blind. Don't open that mouth of yours. You got that, Elva?"

"Yeah, I'm watching. How am I supposed to spot a trooper in an unmarked car? They don't wear their trooper hats in plain cars. I might pick the wrong person and then you'll get mad," she whined.

"You can always tell a trooper because they wear those fancy polished sunglasses. I'm obeying all the traffic rules, so I think we're safe, but that's usually when something goes wrong. There's no way I could make a run for it in this old buggy. If we get caught, it's jail for both of us. You're an accessory and don't you ever forget it."

"I won't," Elva said. She had to think about what she was going to do when they got to the Wild Adventure campground. She knew she couldn't stay with Cudge after this. Enough was enough. Even her fear of the dark and the creatures that prowled in the night weren't as bad as winding up as dead as Lenny, and that's what would happen if she stayed with Cudge. She couldn't let him know what she was planning. The thought of leaving him was so daring, so alien to her, that she broke into a cold sweat. Fear—it always came down to fear. If Cudge made her help dig the grave for Lenny, she would bawl. And if he made the grave wider than it needed to be for Lenny, she would die on the spot—he wouldn't have to kill her.

"Damn you, Elva, didn't you see that trooper? What the hell is wrong with you? Look, in the next lane, that's a trooper or my name ain't Cudge Balog. Pay attention. I ain't gonna tell you again."

"He don't look like a trooper to me," Elva said defensively. "There's two kids in the backseat. Troopers don't ride with kids. I'm watching the best I can."

"Okay, okay. He could still be a trooper. Just because he had kids doesn't mean a thing. Always go by the sunglasses. They try and trick honest drivers. I'm gonna move up now and get in the right lane. Keep your eyes peeled on the road and don't screw up, Elva."

"If you're moving to the right lane, what should I be looking for? There ain't no traffic to the right of the right lane." Her gaze shifted from Cudge's profile to her window. BJ! The kid in the RV looked just like her little brother BJ. Another bummer. There was really something wrong with her. BJ was dead. She stared at him for a moment before she turned back to Cudge.

Cudge clenched his teeth. One long arm reached out and yanked at Elva's shoulder. Before she knew what was happening, she felt the hard sting of his hand against her face. She blinked as scalding tears burned her eyes. She turned away before Cudge could see the result of his handiwork. The little boy in the RV, his dog clutched to him, was staring at her as she wiped the tears with the back of her hand. He looked scared, the way BJ used to look scared.

"You bawl one more time and you've bought it, Elva. We'll get off this pike and get something to eat. We have to kill time. I don't want to show up at that campground too early."

Elva said nothing, wishing she knew who the little boy with the dog was. He looked just like BJ—same color hair, same bright blue eyes, same scared look. Only this kid had a dog to love. Poor little BJ had only had her, and what good had that done him? When it counted, she hadn't helped him at all. The little kid in the RV was alive and BJ was dead. And here she was with Cudge. How soon would it be before she joined BJ, wherever he was? Fear of the unknown or fear of Cudge—it was six of one and half dozen of the other.

It was mid afternoon when Lorrie and Davey left the reptile house. Lorrie took long gulps of fresh air to get over the creepy feeling the snakes had given her. Duffy frolicked at their feet, evidently glad to be outdoors even if she was confined to a leash.

Lorrie glanced at her watch. "I think we've had enough zoo for one day. What do you say we head for the campground and set up camp?"

"I didn't like the smell in that snake house, did you, Aunt Lorrie?"

"No. It was awful," she said with a shiver. "Are you tired, Davey?" she asked, noticing how slowly he was walking.

"A little. But that sure was fun." His voice was full of awe. "I think Duffy is more tired than I am. What are you cooking for dinner, Aunt Lorrie?"

"Hamburgers, baked beans, and cupcakes for dessert. How does that sound?" Lorrie asked, looking down at the little boy.

"Great. I love hamburgers with lots and lots of ketchup."

"Climb up then, and let's head for camp," Lorrie said as she unlocked the RV. "Next stop, Wild Adventure!"

"Duffy and me, we'll sit here at the table, okay?"

Lorrie belted him in then headed for the driver's seat. She followed the yellow exit arrows through the parking lot and, just before pulling out onto the highway, turned to check on Davey. He was sitting up, sound asleep, Duffy lying across his lap. She hoped she hadn't overdone it. That brace was pretty heavy to lug around. Poor little guy. He was exhausted. She wondered if maybe she shouldn't have left sooner.

Lorrie shook away the bad thoughts and concentrated on the fun they'd had. She was acting like a mother hen, over-protective of her chick. It was just that she was so crazy about him she wanted to do everything right. She would hate to see Sara's wrath if something went wrong.

She turned off the highway into the campground and followed the signs to the office. The place looked pretty deserted and she wondered if maybe she shouldn't find another campground, somewhere more of a year-round variety. On the other hand, the lack of people meant that she and Davey would have more of an opportunity to spend time together, without distractions.

"We're here," she called behind her as she turned the key in the ignition. In an instant, Davey went from being sound asleep to wide awake. Before

Lorrie could get out of the driver's seat, he had his seat belt unbuckled. "You wait here while I get us signed in and find out where our campsite is. Did you ever see such glorious colors?" she asked as she craned her neck to look at the giant trees with their spirals of autumn leaves.

A few minutes later, Lorrie climbed back into the RV with a map and a card to hang from the rearview mirror. "I took a site at the far side of the pond." The manager had told her she would be near an elderly couple from Massachusetts with an Air Stream trailer, and a New Jersey couple with a pop-up trailer.

The RV slid into a deep rut and bounced out. Davey struggled to hang onto Duffy. "Aunt Lorrie, I have to go to the bathroom."

Lorrie grinned. "Hang on till we're parked, Davey. I don't want you walking around in the motor home while I'm driving."

"I can't wait to get out and see everything. Right, Duffy?" Exactly on cue, the terrier woofed.

Lorrie passed a garishly decorated pickup truck with a pop-up trailer parked in a grove of trees and knew she was heading in the right direction. "Our site must be just around the bend and to the right," she said, more for her own benefit than Davey's.

Davey turned to look out the long side window. He rubbed at his eyes and stared at the pickup. It looked like the one he'd seen on the turnpike. His thoughts were diverted when Lorrie deftly maneuvered the RV into the assigned slot. As soon as they stopped, he unbuckled his seat belt and headed for the bathroom.

Stepping down out of the RV, Lorrie stretched luxuriously. Davey joined her seconds later, zipping his jeans. "Is it okay if Duffy and I take a walk?"

Tousling his blond head, Lorrie was once again taken with her nephew's grammar. Sara's influence, no doubt. Most of the kids who came into Lorrie's office would have said, "Duffy and me." "Sure," she said, "but first let's set down the rules. Look at your watch. The big hand should be on the nine and the little hand almost on the five. What time is that?"

"It's fifteen minutes before five o'clock," Davey said proudly.

"Right. Now, when the big hand is on the three, I want you back here. And you must stay within earshot. Do you know what that means?"

"That means you have to hear me if I call, or I have to hear you. Right?"

"Right again. Now, Davey, what time do you have to be back here?" she questioned, just to make sure he understood.

"Fifteen minutes after five," he said.

"Don't let Duffy wander off, and if she does, call her, don't chase after her or you could end up getting lost."

"Aw, you shouldn't worry, Aunt Lorrie, Mr. Sanders gave me a real Boy Scout flashlight and money for a phone call. See!" He rummaged in his jeans pocket for his two gifts.

"And I'm impressed." Not for the world would she tell Davey there were no phones attached to the trees. And as far as the little penlight went, he'd be lucky if he could see his hand in the dark with it. "I think you can make it. Remember, big hand on the three."

He started to leave then winced.

"What's the matter?" Lorrie asked, concern drawing her brows together as she noticed the pained expression on the little boy's face.

"It's . . . my leg brace—I must have it strapped too tight or something. Dad knows how to fix it." A shadow slipped over Davey's face, and Lorrie knew he was suddenly anxious about being separated from his parents for the first time.

"Let's have a look. Maybe I can help."

Davey lifted his pant leg. Hunkering down to inspect the brace, Lorrie grimaced when she saw how the leather straps were cutting into the fragile flesh of his calf. "No wonder. Your sock slipped down. How long has this been irritating you, Davey?" From the abrasion on his leg and the look on his face, Lorrie knew it must have been bothering him for some time. "Oh honey, this was hurting you at the zoo, wasn't it? And you didn't say anything. Why?"

"Mom and Dad told me not to cause any trouble."

"Davey, you're the best kind of trouble I could ever have. I love you, don't you know that? There's no way you could be any trouble to me. Now, sit up here on the step so I can fix that brace. I'll pull up your sock and loosen the strap a notch." As she worked, Lorrie noticed the new shoes that had never had an opportunity to get dirty. It wasn't fair, she told herself. Davey was too overprotected, too housebound. Instinct told her it wasn't the hemophilia that made Andrew and Sara restrict Davey to the house. A child who played in his room all day was a lot less trouble than one who was in and out, bringing in dirt onto Sara's spotlessly clean carpet.

"How's that?"

Davey tested the brace and smiled. "Way better.

Do you like my new shoes? Mom says I can't wear them all the time. Is that because Reeboks are special?"

Lorrie thought a moment. "Well yes, Davey, in a way they are. They're for playing and running. You should consider yourself very lucky. Some children who wear a leg brace must wear heavy, high-top shoes. But your brace is only to give strength to your leg. See how it's made? This strap slips under your foot so you can wear it with any shoe."

Davey nodded. "I saw a boy in the doctor's office and his braces went over his knees. He had to push these clamps so he could sit down. But I don't know why he had to wear those braces. And I don't know why I have to wear mine."

"Didn't the doctor tell you that it's only for a short time? When you were a very little boy, before you started your shots, you injured your knee and it bled. You don't have to worry about that any more—the bleeding, I mean. The brace keeps your shin bone in line with your knee joint." She ran her fingers down the length of Davey's leg to show him what she meant.

"Oh," the boy murmured, pondering her explanation. "But I can walk real good, and I can run." Suddenly he wrapped his arms around Lorrie's neck, giving her a tight hug. "I love you, Aunt Lorrie. You're a foxy lady."

"And just where did you hear that term, young man?"

"In the Junior CB Club. But don't tell Mom what I said. She doesn't like it when I learn new words."

"I promise. It's our secret. I'm your secret foxy lady."

"Hey, Aunt Lorrie, that could be your handle on the CB. I'm Panda Bear and you're Foxy Lady!" Delighted with himself, Davey trotted off, Duffy at his heels.

Lorrie watched them go. There was a slight unevenness to Davey's step because of the brace, and his red nylon windbreaker blended with the autumn colors in the woods. Her eyes focused on the blond head and she wanted to reach out and touch him again. Duffy's short legs stirred the thick layer of leaves on the ground as she followed her master. With the same sense of loss that she always felt whenever she parted from the little boy, Lorrie turned to go into the motor home and begin dinner.

She was stirring some brown sugar into the beans when a mental picture of Stuart Sanders came to mind. It had been a long time since she'd felt an attraction toward a man, and never a man like Stuart Sanders—big, tall, a rugged sort of guy. She supposed he had to be rugged to be an FBI agent, chasing after all those criminals.

"Too much TV," she said aloud, then laughed at herself. Too much TV was right. After a long day at work, all she wanted to do was sit down in front of the TV and be entertained. The hospital shows were always good for a few laughs. The truth of it was, the long hours were of her own doing. A workaholic, her peers called her. The last time she'd had a date was . . . She was horrified to realize she couldn't remember her last date.

Prior to Davey's birth she'd dated a lot, and had thoughts of marriage and a family. But once Davey had been diagnosed as a hemophiliac, things had changed. She had changed. A family was no longer an option, at least not until medical science gave prospective parents the option of choosing the sex of their children. Until then, she would remain childless. But she needn't have given up men, she realized. It had just happened. She wasn't sure exactly why.

Now Stuart Sanders had reignited a fire within her, a fire she'd thought was dead. And if she wasn't missing her guess, he was equally attracted to her. She hoped she wasn't missing her guess. It would be nice to get to know him better.

"Stuart." She tested his name on her tongue. It had a nice sound. "Stuart Sanders."

Davey and Duffy kicked their way through the fallen leaves until they reached the pond. The water was still and a deep, mossy green, and the red and orange of the sunset broke through the surrounding trees to create a golden path on the pond's surface.

"I saw this on TV, Duff," Davey said. "Now watch. You pick up a stone and skip it across the water." Duffy sat patiently on her haunches, watching pebble after pebble hit the water with a splash, then sink.

"Guess it's another 'almost,' Duff. I can *almost* do it, can't I?" Losing interest, Davey picked up a twig and poked at the dry pine needles and soft leaves. He was surprised to see the snowy shoelaces on his new shoes were now a dirty brown. He laughed delightedly; now they looked used, like Aunt Lorrie's.

Pushing back the sleeve of his windbreaker, Davey took note of his watch. The big hand was on the one. He had two more numbers to go. "C'mon, Duff, let's see what's over on the other side of the pond."

John and Sophie Koval stood outside their silver trailer, watching the newcomers' motor home bump down the road. Sophie wiped her hands on her apron, relieved that there were going to be other campers besides themselves and those . . . those hippies! Camping certainly wasn't turning out to be the lark that John and the brochures had promised. "Meet new friends, see the country, get back to nature." The "new friends" had turned out to be large families who couldn't afford to get away from home any other way, and instead of the nice, sociable bridge games to liven the evenings that Sophie had envisioned, she'd had to endure the sounds of children squabbling, their parents yelling at them, and the sight of endless lines of laundry hanging between the trees. The smell of that disinfectant they used got everywhere, even into the dirt. In every campsite it was the same, and now even the shiny new inside of their trailer smelled of it. At night it filled her nose and seemed to parch her throat. Whoever it was who said there was no place like home must have gone camping.

Now that summer was over and the northeastern states were well into fall, John and Sophie felt lonely and apart from everyone and everything. Most of the campgrounds were desolate, like this one, stopping places only. They would rest overnight then, in the dew-heavy mornings, they would break camp and ride on, sometimes for hours at a time, pushing the speedometer and the clock to arrive at their next destination before dark. As the days grew shorter, camping was becoming more of an ordeal, just like the very thing John had promised they would leave behind.

Sophie longed for the ease and comfort of her home back in Massachusetts, where she could spend the afternoons watching her soap operas on TV instead of growing stiff from long hours in the car, watching for obscure turnoffs to their next destination. John's retirement was becoming a trial and a punishment.

"Why couldn't we have gotten one of those nice buses, John? Then I could stay right in the back and prepare lunch or dinner and still be able to talk to you."

"Watch your soap operas, you mean. I've already told you, Sophie, those things guzzle gas. We've got to watch our pennies now. Social Security doesn't bring much and you know it." He watched her from behind his wire-rimmed glasses. The annoyance that he felt whenever she complained about their new lifestyle made him chomp down on his pipe. For over thirty years he'd made a nice home for her, given her an easy life, while he went to work every day at the mill and dreamed of the day he could retire. He'd given up most of his dreams and all of his energies for Sophie's comfort, and he wasn't going to let her make him feel guilty now.

"They looked like nice people, didn't you think?" she asked, changing the subject, almost able to read his mind after all those years. "Maybe we could go over and meet them later."

John's eyes narrowed. "No, don't think so. Be getting dark soon and you've got supper to fix.

Imagine they do too, what with setting up camp and all."

Sophie frowned. She didn't like this new John, and she certainly didn't like their new lifestyle. She didn't know who or what she could trust anymore. Gone were all the comfortable, familiar things from over the years. Instead, in their place, everything was stiff and new. She comforted herself with the knowledge that she had at least refused to allow John to sell their home. She'd just wait for him to tire of this vagabond existence, and then she could go back to her nice electric range and a refrigerator that could hold a week's supply of food. She couldn't get used to shopping every other day at strange supermarkets where she couldn't seem to find the simplest item.

Worst of all were the doubts she had about John. It had been fine back in Massachusetts when he drove her to the neighborhood supermarket and even to the shopping mall. But out here, on the open road, John had become a man she didn't know, a stranger. A . . . a Seattle cowboy! His driving had become aggressive instead of defensive. He was constantly cursing under his breath about this one cutting him off, or that one driving with his brights on. She was worried he would do something stupid, like flip someone off. Nowadays, instead of flipping you back, they just shot you! Road rage—that was another part of this new life that frightened her.

Looking at her husband, she saw him staring off in the direction of the camp where those hippies were parked. She knew they were hippies because of the way their pickup truck was painted. "You're just as glad as I am that we're not alone here with those hippies, aren't you?" More than a question, her words were a challenge.

"Sophie, they don't call them hippies anymore. And I don't see what the problem is. We're bound to meet people from different walks of life. You've got to learn to live and let live." He'd never admit it, but he was glad there were other campers besides themselves. Elderly people were easy prey for some types. "Go on in and get dinner, Sophie. We've got a long drive ahead of us in the morning, and I want to get started early." He refolded a road map and traced the lines with his fingers. "The manager of this camp told me about a real nice place down near Virginia Beach."

Cudge watched Elva set up the barbecue grill. "Why are you using that? Why don't you use the stove?"

Elva continued to pour briquettes into the grill. " 'Cause we don't have any more propane, that's why." She lifted her head and glared at him.

Ignoring her unspoken accusation, Cudge leaned against the camper. "What's for supper?"

"Eggs, corned beef hash, and Kool-Aid."

"Shit."

"Well, if you'd stopped at the store the way I wanted we could be having hamburgers or something. Eggs is all we got. And beans. You want beans?"

"Shit. That's what it is. Shit. I could go for a steak, rare and juicy, and maybe a baked potato."

"Yeah, well, couldn't we all," she snipped.

"Don't we have anything besides Kool-Aid? A beer maybe?"

"If we did, you'd have drunk it before now. All we have is Kool-Aid."

"Hey, I don't like your tone. Don't get smart with me." His voice was suddenly menacing. Elva hung her head a little lower and went on trying to start the fire.

"Be careful with that charcoal lighter. I don't need you setting fire to yourself and having to go to the hospital. We still got some work to do." He gestured to the closed pop-up with his head.

After cranking up the top section that served as the roof, Cudge opened the front and back canvas wings that expanded into bunks. "We have to do this right or else somebody might ask questions. Just keep the door closed so nobody can see inside," he warned.

"I need the eggs and stuff," Elva said. "And I don't want to go in there, so you'll have to get them."

"What's the matter? Little Elva afraid that Lenny'll jump up and bite her ass?" Cudge mocked.

"So what if I'm afraid? I don't like dead people. You killed him, so you go in there and get the food."

"Don't get fresh, Elva. I'm warning you. I've had more than a man can take today, and I've been real patient with you."

"It's not my fault that we were stopped by the state trooper. You're the one who had the truck painted that way."

"Shut up, Elva."

Elva looked at Cudge, saw the way his lips were curled in a snarl, saw his eyes boring into her and the way his neck seemed to disappear into his shoulders. Prickles of apprehension rose on her arms;

she could feel them through the scratchy woolen poncho she had crocheted for herself. "You gonna get me the stuff?" she squeaked.

"Yeah, I'll get it. But you better not turn chicken on me tonight when we haul his ass out of here. I took a walk around before and I found the ideal spot. It's down in that shallow gully." He pointed to a spot near the pond on the far side of the campground.

"How are we going to get him there? I can't carry him that far."

"Well, you're going to. Just make up your mind. What do you think I feed you for? Just remember, you're an accessory, Elva, and I don't want to hear any of your shit. You just do what I tell you, understand?" His fingers closed over her arm like a vise and Elva wriggled away.

"Lemme go! I understand. Just lemme go!"

"I don't want you screwin' up the way you did with that trooper."

"That wasn't my fault! He was on your side and you should've seen him in the side-view mirror. It wasn't like he was in an unmarked car or anything like that."

"So you say. And I say you should've been watching! That was a close call, too close."

They had been on the turnpike after riding the back roads around Brick Township. It was too early in the day to appear at the campgrounds without provoking questions. Elva had her nose buried in the map, looking for the exit, and Cudge was tuned to the CB, listening to the truckers' conversations over the airwaves. Usually he could count on truckers to report a "Smokey" in the area, but not this time. The next thing Cudge knew, the bright blue light of a trooper's car was flashing and he was being instructed to pull over.

"Not a word, Elva," he said before getting out of the pickup.

"I'll need to see your driver's license and your registration, please," the trooper said, the afternoon sun reflecting off his mirrored sunglasses. Like most troopers he was tall, taller than Cudge, but he didn't have Cudge's bulk. Sizing him up, Cudge decided he wouldn't have the least bit of trouble in pounding the man to the ground. Then he saw the trooper's side holster and the blue-black grip of his pistol.

"Where are you heading?"

Cudge was so preoccupied with half-formed plans of escape he hardly heard the question. "Huh? Oh, we're camping. Heading north."

"Sir, your license says you're from Newark. That is north."

"Uh, we have been camping, in Maryland. We're heading home."

The trooper leaned forward to peer through the dirty window. The passenger was a young woman, at least ten years younger than her companion. "Would you open the door, sir," he asked Cudge.

"What for? There ain't nothing in there that shouldn't be," Cudge bristled. He didn't want the trooper talking to Elva, and he didn't like his condescending attitude. The trooper called him "sir" but it could have been "shit" from the way he said it.

"Open the door, sir."

"Okay, okay." Cudge pulled the door open. The trooper looked in at Elva, who was sitting with her legs up underneath her on the seat. His trained eye observed the girl's long, dull brown hair, her painfully thin body, and the worn clothes. He also noticed the panic in her eyes. "Everything all right, miss?" He spoke from over Cudge's shoulder, some instinct telling him he didn't want this man behind him where he couldn't see him.

Elva nodded.

"Are you Mrs. . . ." he glanced at Cudge's license, "Balog?"

Elva shook her head.

"How long have you known Mr. Balog?" He deliberately asked a question that would require a verbal answer. Something was wrong here—he could almost smell it. His mind clicked back to his last radio transmission, calculating how long it would take for assistance to arrive.

Elva remained silent, her eyes searching Cudge's.

"Miss, how long have you known Mr. Balog?" the uniformed trooper persisted.

A long pause ensued. Elva's eyes were locked with Cudge's. The scent of trouble grew stronger in the trooper's nostrils.

"Jesus Christ! Will you tell him, Elva? What's wrong with you anyway?" He was shouting, knowing that he was alarming the trooper, yet unable to control himself. The beast in his brain pawed, the hooves biting into tissue, alerting him. Struggling for control, Cudge lowered his voice. "Elva, for crissakes!" He thought of Lenny hidden in the pop-up, saw the blue flash of the dome light on the trooper's car, and felt the threat of the trooper's pistol.

"Miss, would you like to get out of the truck, please?"

Elva shook her head, her face whitening.

"Elva, for crissakes, do what he tells you."

"Would you please assist the lady from the cab, Mr. Balog?" Something was amiss here. The girl's silence, the panic in her eyes, the man's agitation. Even the pickup truck looked like trouble—electric colors, slogans, and decals that were just short of obscene. Only the pop-up trailer was still a light beige, devoid of decorations except for a few four-letter words fingered in the grime. In fact, the pop-up was in pretty good condition compared to the old Chevy pickup pulling it. "I'd like to see your registration for the trailer."

Cudge's eyes widened, his hand shook as he pulled Elva from the truck. What in the hell did the cop want to see the registration to the trailer for? His glance darted from the trooper to the trailer and back again. "Damn you, Elva, this is all your fault. Why wouldn't you answer him like he wanted?"

"You told me to shut my mouth and not to say a word," she whined.

"Shut up," he hissed. "If he wants a look inside, you better be in this truck when I take off or else I'll leave you on the side of the road."

"Cudge, I didn't—"

"Shut up!"

"Any problem over there?" the trooper inquired.

"No, no, nothing's wrong. Right, Elva?"

Elva nodded.

"Crissakes! Tell him, willya?" Cudge saw the trooper's mouth tighten and he could sense his eyes narrowing behind those glasses.

"Your trailer registration, please."

Digging in his wallet again, Cudge presented his registration.

"What have you got in the back?" the face behind the glasses asked, checking the information
on the card Cudge had handed him.

"Whatever goes into a camper—a toilet, sink,
beds." The trooper was starting to piss him off.
He'd like to punch his fist right into those glasses
and push them through the back of his head. The
silent pawing in his head became the restless shift-
ing of weight, leaning against the gate, wanting to
be let out.

"Let's take a look."

"Christ, you know how much trouble it is to open
one of those things? To say nothing of putting it
together again. I've been thinking of getting a regular trailer, one of those Air Streams or something.
This kind is a real pain in the ass."

"Let's take a look, buddy. Now!"

Gone was the "Mr. Balog." No more "sir." Now it
was "buddy." Cudge's spine stiffened and a light
spray of sweat broke out on his brow. He moved to
the rear of the trailer; his mind raced but no solution came to him. This was all Elva's fault. Damn
Elva.

"Mind telling me what I did wrong? I wasn't speed-
ing or nothing. I was just cruising along. This is ha-
rassment."

"Police brutality!" Elva prompted. "Tell him,
Cudge, you want to talk to your lawyer!"

Balog's eyes rolled back in his head. If she said
one more word, he was going to let her have it.

"Finally found your tongue, miss? What's this
about police brutality?"

"You have no right to bother us. We weren't
doing anything. You can't just sneak up on people

like that. Cudge told me to watch out for cops, and I was, but you came up on the wrong side."

"Shut up, Elva, for crissakes, shut up!"

"While you're cranking open your camper, I'll call in your license," the trooper told him in a somber tone that made Cudge wonder whether or not he'd heard what Elva had said about watching out for the law. "Get going!" There it was, the authority, the suspicion that made Cudge's skin prickle.

The trooper moved toward his patrol car, senses alert for danger. It wasn't unheard of for a trooper to be shot down just asking a guy for his registration. Damn those politicians for cutting back on two-man teams. If he ever needed a partner, it was now. There was something fishy going on here, and he didn't like this Balog. And when that mouse he was traveling with decided finally to open her mouth, it was to tell him that she'd been on the look out for the law. Was she trying to tell him she was being kidnapped? What was in the camper? Drugs, contraband cigarettes? What? Not only was he going to call in Balog's license, he was going to ask for assistance.

Turning his back on the couple, he took the few steps to the patrol car. He could feel Balog's eyes on him, piercing and angry. For a second back there, when he'd asked what was in the camper, Balog's anger had become almost tangible, thick and viscous. For that one second he had felt as though all his air had been cut off and he was trying to breathe through a vacuum.

Christ! He was getting paranoid, jumping at shadows. Still, that feeling had been real—a warning. Fleetingly, he thought of how many times his wife had begged him to change jobs. His brother-in-law had even offered him a job managing one of his used-car lots. Maybe it was time to consider it. Scared troopers didn't do their jobs properly; and the ones who did often ended up with half their head blown away.

He wondered again how far away the nearest assistance was.

The patrol car was still flashing its blue lights when a loud squawk sounded through the open window. "Car 169, Car 169, proceed to mile 43 southbound. Emergency vehicle needed. Car 169, collision at mile 43, New Jersey Turnpike. Assistance en route, do you read?"

The trooper looked at Cudge and Elva and then back at the patrol car. He hadn't realized how damp his shirt had become or how eager he was to get away before he found out what Balog was hiding in the camper. Thrusting the registration and license back into Cudge's hand, he hurried to his car and took off, lights flashing, siren blaring.

"Get in the truck, Elva. Move!"

"Cudge," she whined. "Cudge . . ."

Cudge blinked and Elva's whining brought him back to the present. "Are you going to get me the eggs? This fire's ready. And don't forget the black iron frypan."

For a long moment Cudge looked at her, the menace and power in his gaze so tangible that she backed away. "Cudge, what's the matter? Cudge, don't look at me that way, I don't like it."

Wordlessly, Balog stepped inside. If he had to look at her for one minute longer, he would kill her.

* * *

Duffy scampered ahead of Davey, intent on chasing a gray squirrel. Davey shook his head with exasperation. The squirrel would run up a tree, and Duffy would have led him on a merry chase for nothing. Nearby a cook fire was burning; he could identify the smell from when Dad barbecued steaks in the backyard. As expected, the squirrel escaped up a tree, leaving Duffy barking near the base.

"C'mon, Duffy, you can't climb trees and that squirrel won't come down until we're gone. C'mon!"

Reluctantly, Duffy obeyed, coming to heel near her master. Davey looked at his watch. The big hand was on the two. That gave him one more number to get back to Aunt Lorrie. He frowned. Running through the woods with Duffy was so much fun, maybe Aunt Lorrie wouldn't be too upset if he got back when the finger was almost off the three. That would make it almost one more number. No, he'd promised to be back on time and he would be.

The trail led away from the pond to the road. If he turned to the right and followed it around, he would come back to their campsite. Breaking through the growth at the side of the gravel road, Davey took another glance at his watch. He wasn't certain how far it was back to the site, and he thought he would have to hurry. Anyway, his legs were tired, and even though Aunt Lorrie had fixed his sock and adjusted the strap, his calf was still sore.

"C'mon, Duffy! I'll race you back to the RV!"

Duffy woofed, stubby tail wagging and ears lifted, watching Davey for his next move. When she saw that Davey wanted to run, she obliged happily, scooting ahead to lead the way.

Just around the road's bend, Elva and Cudge were eating when their attention was caught by Duffy's yips and Davey calling to her. They watched the little dog and the boy run headlong into their campsite. Elva recognized Davey immediately. He was the little boy who looked so much like BJ, the one that she had seen in the RV on the turnpike.

"That's a cute little dog you've got there," Elva called to Davey, bringing him up short. Davey's pride in Duffy was evident in his shy smile. He liked hearing that Duffy was smart and cute.

"Her name's Duffy," he told Elva, realizing that she was the woman from the pickup who looked like Millicent, his old babysitter. Remembering the man who had hit her, Davey turned to see Cudge sitting on a camping stool, his elbows on his knees, and an empty dish in his hands. Davey didn't like this man who had such a mean face and eyes that could eat you up.

"Where's your campsite, kid?" Cudge asked. It was a piece of information worth having. If their campsite was too close to where he intended to bury Lenny's body, then he'd have to make other plans while it was still light out.

"Over there, on the other side of the pond," Davey told him, fidgeting beneath Balog's appraising stare. Duffy's exploring nose was put to the ground and she followed it to the tip of the man's boots. For an instant Davey thought the man was reaching down to pet Duffy; for some reason he couldn't explain, he didn't want the man to touch his dog. "Duffy, come here," he ordered.

He wrinkled his nose; something smelled strange

over here near the man's camper, a bit like the way his snow jacket smelled before his mother hung it on the line to air. It was the little white balls in the pocket that made it smell that way—mothballs, Mom called them. Curious, he dropped his eyes to the ground, expecting to see some sign of the candy-like balls. He decided he liked the smell on the other side of the pond better.

"Hey, kid, how many brothers and sisters you got camping with you? Not too many, I hope. I don't like all kinds of noise at night when I'm trying to sleep."

"I'm the only . . . I don't have any brothers or sisters. I'm camping with my Aunt Lorrie."

"I don't want to scare you or anything, but you shouldn't go walking through the woods after dark. I hear there's bears and wild cats that'll eat that dog of yours for supper." A satisfied smirk lifted the side of Balog's mouth as he saw Davey gulp.

"Aw, why d'ya have to scare the kid that way? There ain't no bears in these woods!" Elva raised her voice and moved forward, her half-eaten eggs sliding around on her dish.

"Shut up, will you? That's right, kid—there's no bears, only tigers, and there's nothing they like better for supper than a nice juicy little dog like that one." Balog looked around for Duffy. His eyes darted to the open door of the pop-up—in the shadows he could just make out the small dog nosing around the blanket-wrapped corpse. In two long steps he was at the camper and a second later Duffy came flying out.

Duffy grappled for her footing, barking in pain. To Davey's wide-eyed horror, Cudge leapt down and grabbed the dog by the scruff of the neck, shaking her helpless body. "Damn little bitch! I'll teach you to go snoopin' around where you don't belong!"

"Cudge! Stop it! Cudge!" Elva screamed. "For crissakes, leave the dog alone! Put her down, Cudge! Cudge!" She grabbed hold of Cudge's arm.

With a mutter of disgust, Cudge threw the dog to the ground, ready to plant a boot in her side if she came after him.

"Get your dog, little boy, and get away from here!" Elva shouted.

Sparked to action by Elva's commands, Davey moved forward and scooped Duffy into his arms.

"Get out of here!" Cudge thundered. "Don't come snooping around here no more, you hear? And if I see that dog again, I'll kill her! Understand?"

Davey didn't move. His mouth dropped open, his wide eyes stared at the man. He couldn't think, couldn't breathe.

"You brazen little son of a bitch!" Cudge made a motion toward the boy, who was clutching his panting dog.

"No, Cudge, don't. You can't!" Elva knew Davey wasn't being stubborn and brazen, he was just scared stiff. Just like BJ. Just like herself. "Don't hurt the kid, okay?" she pleaded with Cudge. "He's scared, that's all. Just scared."

Cudge shook Elva's hand from his arm, the movement tossing her backward to the ground. The behemoth in his brain was charging the gate now; he had to get control and force it back. His heart pounded with the effort; his knees became rubbery, incapable of holding his weight. Warning signals were going off inside his head, telling him that if he wasn't careful, he'd have trouble with the kid's family.

Jaw jutting forward, fists clenched, Balog leaned over, placing himself at eye level with Davey. "Get out of here," he growled, "and if you want that dog to stay alive, keep her away from me!"

Suddenly, charged with a rush of energy that enabled him to move his feet, Davey turned and ran. Though the brace on his leg hampered free movement, and Duffy's weight was heavy in his arms, he still found the strength to run. His Reeboks pounded the dirt road, sending up spirals of dust. His laces snapped and twisted together in agitation, his socks slipped downward, wrinkling at the ankles. The nylon windbreaker whispered, louder and louder, urging him to run. Faster! Faster!

Down the road, through the trees, Aunt Lorrie's RV stood sentinel, waiting for Davey's return. He could see it now, all lit from within, a welcome refuge. He put Duffy down and watched her carefully, checking her for injuries. He walked on and Duffy followed—her movements seemed normal. She was all right.

Davey bent down and gathered Duffy close to him. Her cold wet nose brushed against his flushed cheek. One thought only raced through Davey's head— he must *never* let Duffy go near that bad man again.

Four

Lorrie was concerned about Davey's behavior. He hadn't said more than a few words since he'd returned. She sat watching him as he ate his hamburger. She could hear his shoes rubbing against each other restlessly beneath the picnic table—when kids did that, something was wrong. She restrained herself from lifting the colorful picnic cloth and peeking to see if she was right. She sipped her coffee, never taking her eyes from Davey.

Davey reached for his glass of chocolate milk and swigged it down. "I'm finished, Aunt Lorrie. That was good. I even liked the hard stuff on the hamburgers."

Lorrie threw back her head and laughed. "Tell it like it is, Davey. Your aunt flubbed up. That hard stuff is called burnt crust. I promise you the cupcakes will be much better."

Davey grimaced slightly. "Can I save mine till later?" He wanted to go inside the camper and lie down and think about the woman who looked like

Millicent. He waited dutifully to be excused from the table. The moment his aunt nodded, he went inside the RV and sat down at the table. If he thought about the woman, he would have to think about the bad man.

"He was mean, Duff," he whispered to the little dog. "And bad. We have a lot of things to think about, Duff, so you be quiet or Aunt Lorrie will come in and take my temperature." Duffy settled herself on Davey's lap.

All manner of jumbled thoughts raced through the little boy's mind as he absently reached for his new *Goosebumps* book. His voice, when he spoke next, was controlled yet squeaky. "You weren't around, Duff, when Puffy got put in the ground. She was killed by a bad person who was going too fast in his car. Then they gave me you. You were supposed to be a boy dog, but Aunt Lorrie got all mixed up and gave you a name before she figured out that you were a girl dog. I don't want that bad man to get you, Duff. I don't want you to get killed. That's why we aren't going back there again. Now, you have to listen to me when we wake up in the morning. You have to stay with me." He wagged a finger under Duffy's nose. "We're going to stay on this side of the pond so we don't see him!" For answer, Duffy snuggled closer to the little boy. "I was scared and so were you. I could tell."

Idly, Davey flipped a page of the book then played with the sharp corner until it was limp. When he saw how he'd curled the edge of the paper, he spat on his finger and tried to smooth it out. He pursed his lips then quickly turned three pages before he risked a look at the door. Aunt Lorrie wouldn't really care if he curled the pages. Books were supposed to be fun—she had even given him some of her own from when she was a little girl that had crayon marks and spilled jam on the pages.

"Now I've forgotten what I was thinking about." Then Davey swallowed hard as the specter of Cudge's face appeared before him again. He didn't want to think about him, or the woman who looked like Millicent anymore. "C'mon, Duff, let's go get our cupcakes, and maybe Aunt Lorrie will let me talk on the CB."

He opened the door and looked out. "Aunt Lorrie, can I have the cupcake now, and can Duffy have one, too?"

"You bet." Lorrie smiled happily as she untied her red checkered apron. What a relief. Davey was fine. He'd just been tired from his long tramp through the woods. Maybe it wouldn't hurt to take his temperature, just to be on the safe side. Immediately she quashed the idea; she wasn't going to be a mother hen. "So tell me, big guy, where did you and Duffy go and what did you see?" Lorrie asked, peeling back the cupcake wrapper.

Davey settled himself on the picnic bench. He couldn't lie, especially to Aunt Lorrie. "We walked around the pond and we visited the people in the camper. You can't see their truck from here, but it's there. I guess that's all we did. Duffy doesn't like it over there."

"I see," Lorrie said as she watched Duffy devour her treat.

Davey wiped his hands on his blue jeans. "Aunt Lorrie, will you let me talk on the CB before I go to bed?"

"Sure I will, Davey. Tell you what, why don't you

get ready for bed, and when you're clean, you can talk for a while."

Lorrie's gaze followed the little boy inside the RV. Something was wrong, she just knew it. He'd been distracted throughout dinner. Was he homesick? It was perfectly reasonable that he should miss Sara and Andrew. After all, this was his first time away from them. He was doing remarkably well, all things considered.

Cudge's voice was hardly more than a whisper. "It's almost ten o'clock, Elva. Time to take Lenny out. I've been watching that RV on the other side of the pond and their lights have been out for more than an hour. Get that shovel out from under the bunk. I can't wait to get rid of old Lenny and split."

Elva was snuggled down in a blanket near the campfire. She sat up. "Are we leaving here tonight?"

"Nah! I told you before, we can't make any false moves. Everything has to look natural. C'mon, give me a hand."

This was the moment she had been dreading—the moment when she would have to go near Lenny. "How are you gonna get him to that place you picked out this afternoon?" Her dun-colored eyes drifted away from Cudge towards the fire, the light. She didn't want to hear Cudge say she had to help carry him. If he told her she had to touch Lenny, she'd be sick right here and now.

"Same way we got him out of the apartment—on the ironing board. He's still tied on it, ain't he?"

"Cudge, I don't want to do it! It's dark and I don't like dead people." Her whining grated on Cudge's already tightly strung nerves.

"You'll do what I tell you. Now, get your ass over here and grab your end of the ironing board." He cursed viciously as he dragged the narrow end of the board over the aluminum step so Elva could grasp it. "Now, pull it out and I'll grab the other end." He checked his pocket for the flashlight.

Balog led the way through the light underbrush near the road and into the darkness under the trees. "Just keep up and make sure you hold up your end."

"It's too heavy."

"You made it down the stairs at the apartment all right. You've got the light end, so shut up and quit your whining."

"Maybe people get heavier when they're dead. Maybe that's what they mean when they say a 'dead weight.' I don't think—"

"That's right, you don't think! I've had enough of your bright ideas. Christ! The smell of those mothballs is making me sick."

The harvest moon shone through the trees and, once their eyes had adjusted to the night, they were able to see surprisingly well. "See, it ain't so dark. What's to be scared of? We'll be through before you know it."

Elva trudged along behind Cudge, struggling with her end of the ironing board, wishing she could put it down even for a minute. The aluminum frame was biting into her fingers. If only she could stop and change her grip.

"Okay, here it is," Cudge whispered, huffing with the exertion. "Drop your end and I'll slide him the rest of the way down. Take this flashlight and turn it on so I can see what I'm doing. And for crissakes, keep it pointed at the ground."

Elva took the flashlight and turned it on, pointing it at the ground in front of Cudge. She trembled violently, making the light skitter in all directions.

After sliding down the embankment to the shallow gully, Cudge asked for the shovel that had traveled along on Lenny's stomach. Careful not to touch the blanket, or to think about the body beneath it, Elva gingerly lifted the shovel and handed it to Cudge.

Cudge felt better now that he was at Lenny's last resting place. It wasn't bad, he told himself. Lots of trees, quiet, shade in the summer—Lenny could have done worse.

"Are we gonna bury him with my ironing board?" Elva's voice squeaked.

"Dumb broad. No! How'd you like to spend the rest of eternity strapped to an ironing board? Point that light over this way." Clearing away the underbrush, Cudge put the spade into the loamy earth and forced it deep with his foot. Shovelful by shovelful, the rich, black dirt piled up beside him as he dug deeper, calculating the size of the hole into which Lenny would fit.

"Your turn, Elva, and I don't want to hear any complaints. Just dig while I take a breather."

Cudge's venomous growl left no room for argument. It wasn't long before the perspiration was dripping down Elva's face and between her shoulders. She didn't want to be a grave digger. How deep was deep enough? Her arms ached from the unfamiliar exertion. Now she had to stand in the hole to excavate the heavy earth. The woods surrounding them seemed unnaturally quiet. "Quiet as a grave," her mother used to say, and now Elva understood it.

"Move over, Elva. I want this done and over with. You operate somewhere between slow and stop, and we ain't got all night." The grave was almost four feet deep—Cudge decided that was deep enough. "Get over there and untie him from that board. Then you can help me roll him into the hole."

"I . . . I can't," she gulped. "Don't make me, I can't touch him!"

"When I tell you to do something, I mean for you to do it. He'll roll easy; don't think about it."

His no-nonsense tone propelled Elva toward the body. Shakily, she untied the knot that held Lenny to the board, trying not to touch the body or feel the yield of flesh beneath the blanket. One good thing, she thought. Cudge was right about Lenny rolling easy. The incline of the gully aided her efforts as she prodded and pushed toward the grave. She nearly gagged from each dull thud the body made as it rolled over. "Watch out, Cudge, here he comes," she said in a quivering voice. The loud thwack of Lenny's body falling into the grave made Elva squeal with fright. An awful sound. The last sound poor Lenny would ever make.

"Right. He's down. Now we shovel the dirt back on top of him."

"No! Wait! He's . . . he's lying on his face." The flashlight beam revealed Elva to be right.

"So what, he'll be facing the way he's going."

"No, we can't, you have to turn him over. He was your best friend, you can't leave him like that."

Revulsion filled Balog at the thought of touching Lenny. What if the blanket slipped and Lenny was looking up at him? Christ! No man should be expected to see his best friend before he threw the dirt over him. Yet Elva was right. Besides, if he left Lenny face down, Elva would never stop whining or let him forget it. He was tempted to tell Elva to turn Lenny over, but the grave was shallow and narrow; it would take a fair amount of strength to position the body within its confines. He shuddered. "Here, hold the light and get ready with the shovel. And whatever you do, don't shine it on his face. I don't want to look at him."

Taking the flashlight, Elva trained it into the grave. Cudge slid in near Lenny's feet and grasped the body near the shoulders to turn it. Some demon of perversity made Elva flash the light on Lenny's face just as Cudge turned him over.

"God!" Scrambling as though his life depended on it, Balog climbed out of the hole, his stomach heaving, his lower intestines loosening. The underbrush holding his legs seemed to be Lenny's hands pulling him back into the grave. He propelled himself forward into the darkness, where he retched and felt himself almost foul his pants.

"Cudge, Cudge, you all right? I didn't mean for the light . . ."

"So help me, Elva, what the hell's wrong with you anyway?" Cudge spat, clearing his mouth, knowing the sour taste of his own bile. "Get that shovel and start covering him over, and if you stop, even for a minute, you're going in there with him. You got me?"

Elva grabbed the shovel, pushing the dirt into

the hole to cover Lenny as fast as she could. She'd seen Lenny's face, and it was something she never wanted to see again. It was worse than what had happened to BJ.

Twenty minutes later, they were finished. Cudge played the flashlight around the area, scanning the gully till he was satisfied everything looked normal. At the last minute he added a fallen branch, heavy with red-gold leaves, to the new grave.

"Can we go now, Cudge? I hate this place, I really hate it." In the chill night air, Elva shivered all the way back to the campsite.

"There's no point in hanging around here," Cudge told her in the light of their campfire. He brushed the dirt from his jeans. "I'm going to take a ride and find a bar. I need a few beers. You're staying here so nothing looks suspicious."

"You want me to stay in that pop-up after . . . Cudge, a dead body was in there and it stinks."

"The stink is your own fault. Just where else do you think you're gonna sleep tonight? It's cold out here and we've only got thin blankets. What's the matter, Elva—afraid of spooks coming back to haunt you?" he taunted.

"I'm not as scared as you," she shot back. "I ain't the one who almost shit his pants."

Without another word, Cudge jumped into the pickup and drove down the road. The taillights became fainter and fainter until they were just tiny red eyes staring at her through the darkness. Now she was all alone in the darkness, with Lenny's body only yards away in the gully. It was like being left in a graveyard. Death was all around—she could feel it and smell it. It was cold, so cold. If only she wasn't afraid to go into the camper, but Lenny's body had been there for all those hours.

A gust of wind swayed the trees, knocking a dead branch to the ground near her feet. Elva screamed and covered her face with her bony hands. Then she crawled up the steps into the pop-up.

Five

Morning arrived fresh and clear. The sunlight streaming through the hardwood trees sent a kaleidoscope of color through the motor home windows. Davey climbed down out of bed, yawned and looked around for Duffy.

"I let her out to go to the bathroom," Lorrie said, hugging him. Davey yawned again. "You are a sleepyhead this morning, aren't you?" Lorrie kissed his forehead, discreetly checking for fever. It was cool. He was fine. And she was a worrier. "After you get dressed, I thought we'd go fishing for an hour or so, then we'll break camp and head for our next destination."

"Where are we going?"

"It's a surprise." She hunkered down to his level. "But you're gonna love it." She brushed his light, silky hair back from his forehead. It would need cutting soon.

"I am?"

"Yep. Now get a move on. Time's a'wastin'," she

said, patting him on the backside. As soon as she stood up, she heard Duffy barking outside the door. "C'mon, girl. Time for you to eat, too," she said, opening the door. The little dog bounded up the steps into the motor home and greeted Davey as if she hadn't seen him in a week.

Breakfast consisted of cereal, a banana, chocolate milk and a cupcake. Afterwards, Davey and Lorrie got their fishing gear and headed toward the pond.

"They don't seem to be biting," Lorrie said morosely after only fifteen minutes.

"How do you know there are any fish in the pond?"

"I don't, but it looks like a good place for fish, doesn't it? Besides, Davey my boy, there's more to fishing than meets the eye. It's not always important to bring home the dinner, if you know what I mean."

Davey looked up at his aunt, his head tilted to one side, trying to understand.

"Look, it's this way. Fishing is about getting out into the fresh air and sunshine. You sit around, watch the water, listen to the birds, and commune with nature. Understand?"

"I guess. If you say so."

"Davey, you have the instincts of a true sportsman!"

It was nice when Aunt Lorrie smiled at him the way she was now. Her eyes got crinkly and it made Davey feel warm inside.

"Tell you what. We've got a little time to kill before we take off, so why don't you take Duffy for a short walk and I'll stay here and fish. I'll prop your pole up and whistle if there's a tug on your line.

Then you can come back and reel in your fish. How's that?"

"Aunt Lorrie, maybe if you didn't whistle, the fish would bite."

"Davey! I have to whistle to let the fish know where to find the bait." She watched with amusement as Davey pondered her answer. When the boy shook his head from side to side, Lorrie burst into laughter. It was clear Davey had his own views on fishing.

Elva watched Cudge sleep. Even though she had pretended to be asleep when he'd returned to the camper in the early morning hours, she hadn't been able to relax. He had come back drunk; within seconds he'd fallen across the bunk, his loud snores bouncing off the canvas walls of the pop-up. She had been even more afraid with him there than she had been alone. She'd seen him like this before, many times. When Cudge got drunk, he got even meaner.

Inside the pop-up everything smelled of mold and mildew, sour liquor, and mothballs. Bright sunlight shone through the nylon mesh windows, which were backed by clear plastic to keep out the wind. The plastic warped the sun's rays, making lacy patterns on the filthy floor. Elva scraped at the floor with the toe of her shoe. The grime was embedded so deeply that her rubber sole left no mark. That annoyed her still more.

Elva needed to use the bathroom. There was a pot stashed in the camper, but she didn't want to use that. There were showers and bathrooms at the end of the road, but she didn't want to have to walk that far. She decided to wait.

Cudge mumbled in his sleep and thrashed about on the narrow bunk. Elva held her breath. Was he going to wake up or would he sleep some more? His long arm hung disjointedly; from where she sat she could read the numerals on his watch. Ten minutes past eight.

Most people were up by eight o'clock. The woman and boy in the RV across the pond were probably up and eating their breakfast. Maybe they were finished with breakfast by now—they were probably arranging their day, the kitchen all tidied up, both of them dressed in neat, clean clothes. They must have money, Elva decided. You had to have money to drive an RV that only got six or eight miles to the gallon, and dress your kid in new clothes to go camping!

Slowly Elva stretched one cramped leg from beneath her. She rubbed her aching calf before bringing her other leg out straight in front of her, careful not to make a sound. She took turns massaging each leg and, when she was certain she could stand, she slowly inched to her knees, holding onto the handle of the small refrigerator door for support.

A hand gripped her from behind and she heard Cudge's voice. "Wherever you thought you were going, Elva, forget it. We have something we have to do this morning, and then we'll get out of here."

"I wasn't going nowhere. And what do we have to do this morning?" She was surprised to see him so lucid and alert. Something told her that he had been awake all this time, thinking. And when

Cudge Balog started thinking, it didn't bode well for her.

Balog swung his legs over the side of the bunk. His watchful eyes never left Elva's face. "We have to dig Lenny up."

Elva gasped, the wind knocked from her. The thought of going down into that gully, even in bright daylight, started her shaking. "Why?"

" 'Cause we don't have any money, that's why. Lenny was on his way to a crap game, wasn't he? Well, he wouldn't go unless he was well heeled. I blew what money I had last night in the tavern, or else I was rolled in the can. Don't open your yap, Elva; I'm in no mood for you."

Oh, God! She couldn't look into that hole again and see Lenny's eyes staring up at her. It was a sin to open a grave, wasn't it? She couldn't do it; but one look at Cudge's face told her she would.

Standing, he loomed over her. "You're the one with the bright ideas, so how come you never thought about taking the money out of Lenny's pockets? Why do I have to think of everything? Every cent we've got is buried in that hole with what's left of Lenny Lombardi."

Cudge was looking at her strangely. And his voice, while hardly pleasant, was different somehow. He wasn't yelling. Normally, he'd be yelling at her. Something about him was making Elva's flesh crawl.

"Go outside and take a look around. Where's that Kool-Aid you made last night? Christ, I feel as though my mouth's lined with cotton."

Elva handed him the plastic pitcher of grape Kool-Aid. "We can't go down there in the daytime. Somebody might see."

"So what if they see? All they'll see is us taking a little walk. What's wrong with that? One of us will stand guard while the other digs Lenny up. We need that money."

All Elva heard was the word "we." "We" meant both of them, which made them a couple. She liked it that Cudge was thinking of them in those terms. It made her feel special, like she meant something to him.

"Go outside and see if anybody's moving around out there. We don't want anybody to come up on us when we have Lenny laid bare to the daylight." He laughed, a horrible sound that made the bile rise in Elva's throat. She nodded and closed the door behind her.

Shading her eyes as she peered off into the distance, she couldn't see anyone or anything. The campground was thick with trees and undergrowth, making it impossible to see very far in any direction. The campsites were all set away from the road, with a modicum of privacy. Off in the direction of the pond and the gully there was nothing to be seen. With only two other camping parties besides themselves, Elva really hadn't expected to see anyone.

Stepping out beyond the perimeter of their campsite into the bushes, she dropped her jeans to her ankles. She'd better go now, otherwise she'd probably pee in her pants when Cudge opened Lenny's grave. Cudge's bellow made her hurry, pulling her jeans up quickly.

"Took you long enough," he grumbled as she stepped back into the clearing. "Get over here and give me a hand with the camper. I'm going to close up the sides so's all we have to do when we're fin-

ished is throw the shovels in and crank the top
down."

Obediently, Elva helped him fold in the canvas
eaves and put away the barbecue grill and utensils
they had used the day before. She knew they should
have been put in before the canvas eaves were folded,
but she was afraid to argue with Cudge this morning. In went the ice chest, the nearly empty bag of
briquettes, and the dirty frying pan. Used paper
plates and plastic cups littered the campsite and
she began to clear the area.

"Leave it! We paid enough to stay here; let them
clean it up. I ain't no garbage picker. Grab the
shovel and let's go."

Following him through the woods, Elva dragged
her feet. The thought of what they were about to
do revolted her. It was a sin, she knew it.

At the edge of the pond Cudge stopped, coming
up short, waving her back with his hand. Across
the pond, a woman sat fishing. "Dumb broad, she's
not going to catch anything there," Balog whispered. "I don't like it."

"Me neither. Cudge, let's forget it. Huh? It's a
sin to dig up a body. I know it is."

"Shut up. It don't look like she's going to walk
this way, and even if she did, it'd take her a while
to go around the pond to the gully. By that time,
we'll have old Lenny dug up and planted again.
This time, permanently."

Elva swallowed hard as she followed Cudge.

Davey tossed a stick high in the air, watching to
see where it would land. "Go get it, Duff. Bring it

back." The little dog scampered off to do his bidding. Davey followed her into the grove of trees that circled the pond.

Again and again he threw the stick and followed Duffy. Once or twice he turned around and looked back; his Aunt Lorrie was growing smaller and smaller as he walked away. Now he couldn't see her at all. Looking at his watch, he realized he'd walked for three numbers, and his eyes widened as he looked around him. He was on the other side of the pond now, the side where the mean man was camping.

His first thought was of Duffy. He could see her, carrying the stick back. There was a funny smell in the air. The smell like his snow jacket. "Good girl, Duffy. Here, give me the stick. Time to go back and see if we've caught any fish. I don't like it over here; I don't like the way it smells."

Duffy cocked her head to one side, growling deep in her throat. Someone was there. Davey looked around, trying to detect the direction the sound came from. He thought he heard a voice. He held his arms out to Duffy who needed no second urging. "Shhh," Davey whispered close to the dog's ear. "It's that mean man. Be real quiet, Duff."

The little boy moved away from where he thought the sounds were coming; crouching low. Afraid for his dog, he went deeper into the woods, hiding in the low growth of scrubby pines.

He heard the sounds again, and he knew he had chosen the wrong direction. They were there, right in front of him. He could look between the green branches and see them. "Quiet, Duff. Quiet. That man said he'd kill you if he saw you again. We have to be still, and hide and wait till they go away." Davey wished he and Duffy hadn't walked so far, hadn't gone out of earshot of Aunt Lorrie.

The girl who looked like his babysitter kept wiping at her eyes. She looked scared. The man was digging with a short-handled shovel, and it crossed Davey's mind that he was digging for buried treasure. Davey wanted to know what was in the ditch; he wanted to see what buried treasure looked like. He dropped to his knees to get a better look and accidentally let go of Duffy.

"I hit something," Cudge said. "God, he's buried deeper than I thought."

Elva forced herself to look down into the open grave. She couldn't speak; her tongue was stuck to the roof of her mouth.

Davey looked at the open hole. A man's shoe. A man's leg. A blanket. What was the man doing in the hole, and why did the mean man have to dig out the dirt?

The truth dawned on Davey. After his cat had been run over by a car, his dad had dug a hole in the backyard and buried him. His dad wrapped the cat in a clean towel, not like the dirty blanket the man was wrapped in. When you were dead and didn't breathe anymore, they put you in a hole and planted flowers. But there weren't any flowers here. He felt a vague disappointment that he wasn't going to see a buried treasure of gold coins and jewels. Just a dead man.

"Get in there and go through Lenny's pockets, Elva." Cudge's voice was cool and controlled. He had purposely kept a thick layer of soil over Lenny's face, knowing he didn't have the stomach to see it in broad daylight. Besides, something was eating at him. Elva kept saying it was a sin to open a grave. What the hell? It was a sin to kill!

"What? I can't . . . no, Cudge, I won't do that. I'll puke." Elva's face was a sickly green.

"Do what I tell you and quit your yapping. We need that money, Elva. I did all the digging."

His last remark stopped her. Illogically, she saw the practicality in what he wanted her to do. And he *had* done all the digging. Hesitantly, she jumped down and braced her legs on either side of Lenny's, trying hard not to retch.

Cudge saw her hesitate. "C'mon, Elva, we ain't got all day. Just get the wallet. Try the back right-hand pocket first."

Elva's hand made contact with the blanket, but it might have been the slime of a giant slug, the way it made her recoil.

"Do it, damn it! Get it and hand it up!"

Lenny was heavy and cold. She could feel how cold he was, right through the blanket, even through his clothes. She managed to lift him slightly and get her hand underneath him, feeling for the rectangular bulge that would be his wallet. Closing her eyes, she found it and pulled it free. Cudge reached down and grabbed it away from her.

"Good girl, now try the other pockets. He must have had a good-sized roll." While Elva struggled with her revulsion and Lenny's stiff body, Cudge opened the wallet and pulled out two twenties and a single. "Find it, Elva. This can't be all he had. Lenny liked to go into a game well heeled." Putting the bills into his own pockets, he dropped the wallet onto Lenny's chest.

"I think I got it, Cudge," Elva told him, her spirits lifting because he had called her a good girl. "It's a wad, all right."

"Hand it over." Must be a couple of hundred dollars, he told himself, satisfied. Ol' Lenny was worth a lot more dead than alive. "Try those other pockets."

"I already did and there was nothing. Cudge, I don't want to touch him anymore. And jeez, this blanket stinks. I think we used too many mothballs."

"Search him, Elva, do like I tell you." His hands closed over the shovel handle, eyes intent, watching. He wouldn't like hitting Elva and rolling her into Lenny's grave, but he had to do it. She was stupid, and stupid was dangerous.

Elva looked up to plead with him, to tell him that it made her sick to touch Lenny. She had to convince him that there was nothing else in the earth-damp pockets. Her mouth opened but no sound came out. Cudge was staring down at her, shovel held high over his head. Doom crowded her and she knew she would soon be lying next to Lenny. "Cudge! No, don't!"

A sharp yipping followed by an angry bark broke the stillness.

"What the hell?" Cudge shouted, leaping back from the open grave. The shovel flew from his hands and clattered to the ground. "I thought I told you to have a look around, Elva! Now you've blown it!" He grabbed her hand and yanked her out of the grave. "It was that kid's mutt. Where the hell did it go?"

"I don't know! I don't know!" she wailed.

"Get him! Find him! I'll fill in the hole!" Cudge's words were cut off by a streak of black fur charging from the bushes.

Davey was stunned. He stood transfixed by the sight of Duffy running toward the mean man and the crying girl. Growls and snarls burst from Duffy as she tried unsuccessfully to chew at the man's leg. Davey wanted to run to get his dog, but the girl was running toward him. For one instant he looked directly into her eyes.

"Run, kid! Run as fast as you can," she ordered in a loud whisper. "If he gets his hands on you, he'll kill you and you'll end up like Lenny. Run, damn you! Run!" That's what she had said to BJ, but BJ couldn't run. BJ had just stared at her, willing her with his great saucer eyes to help him. But she hadn't. Couldn't. This kid wasn't moving either. Panicking, she reached for him, pushing, shoving. "Now, damn it! Run! Get away from here!"

Davey eyes went from the girl to the man. He had to get Duffy before the man did. Davey charged past the girl, calling Duffy's name. Quicker than mercury, the boy caught up with his dog, grabbed her and ran as fast as he could. Duffy was still growling, erupting into agitated barks as Davey climbed the ridge of the gully, heading for safety, for Aunt Lorrie.

Encumbered by his leg brace, Davey slowed. Duffy fell from his arms, tumbling into the leaves. Half dragging his leg behind him, Davey scooted beneath low overhanging branches, in and out of the brush, Duffy loping behind him. Behind him, he could hear something tearing through the woods, breaking branches, snapping twigs, pounding the soft earth.

Davey had to hide; he had to keep Duffy safe. The dog ran ahead of him, ears erect, tail held high. Davey followed her through the brush into the bright sunshine, toward a winding road. They had to hide. *He'll kill you,* the girl had said.

On and on Davey ran, shoe laces snapping.

The truck and pop-up sprang into Davey's line of vision. The camper was half-closed; the sides were folded in, but the door stood open.

Duffy picked up speed, heading away from the pop-up, toward Aunt Lorrie's RV. Davey was breathless, nearly exhausted. He knew the man was close and could probably see him now that he was out in the open. The decision was made. He ran up the aluminum step into the camper and slammed the door shut behind him. He had to hide where the man couldn't see him. Duffy was smart; she would find her way back to Aunt Lorrie.

Covering his mouth with his hand to quiet his ragged breathing, he crawled to the back of the camper, down between some empty boxes and the bunk. He waited, listening. There was no sound, no scratching from outside to tell him that Duffy was out there. Just silence.

A loud bellow ripped close to Davey, making him jump. "That goddamn kid got away and it's your fault, Elva. You dumb broad! Once that kid tells his folks what he's seen, it's curtains. The manager has our license number and knows who we are. That means jail, Elva. We'll be locked up for the rest of our lives."

Davey held his breath, expecting the man to

walk into the camper any minute. Instead, a rusty creaking sound filled the pop-up, making it vibrate. The scraping of metal against metal pierced Davey's ears, making his teeth hurt. Daring a glance upward, he saw the camper's roof lowering, coming down to squash him like a bug.

Six

Elva climbed into the truck, her face white with terror. She had every reason to be terrified of Cudge, but being left behind was somehow more frightening than what he might do to her. "You were going to kill me back there!" she hissed as she lifted herself onto the seat beside him.

His face was set in lines of panic and it gave her some small satisfaction to see him this way. Big, bad Cudge Balog, scared of what a little kid could do to him! "Don't try and lie to me, I seen it in your face." She wanted to hear him say she was wrong, that she was crazy and imagined things. She needed to believe that she was safe with Cudge Balog.

He turned the ignition key, foot pressing on the gas pedal. The engine cranked and almost caught before winding down. Again, he pressed the gas, twisting the ignition key viciously as he pumped the pedal, willing the engine to turn over, dreading the thought that he might have flooded it. He

was sweating. Elva looked at him, desperately wanting him to defend his actions back at Lenny's
grave. "I ain't going with you!"

Before she could think twice she was out of the
truck and running across the dusty road, heading
for the cover of the trees. Bullet-swift, Cudge was
out of the cab and racing after her.

Resolution died in Elva even before she felt his
hands on her shoulders. "This is all your fault,
Elva! You're not running out on me now. Get it
through your head. Get in the truck and don't
open your mouth unless I tell you. In a couple of
hours we're gonna be wanted for murder because
of that kid and his mutt. Murder, Elva! And it's all
your fault."

Cudge wasn't sure which way to go—north or
south? Maybe he'd stand a better chance if he
ditched the camper. No, he'd worked too hard to
get it, and he wasn't going to part with it. Why did
that mangy mutt have to show up? Of all the bad
luck! And that kid—what had happened to him? If
only he could have gotten his hands on him. "By
now that kid is spilling his guts to his aunt. Hear
me, Elva? That kid is blabbing and his aunt is
going to the cops. We got another hour of freedom and then . . . *pow*!" His arm shot out toward
Elva but she ducked and managed to miss it.

Elva huddled against the door, unable to move,
fearing that if she did, Cudge would try to hit her
again. If the cops got her, she would be locked up.
If she made a move, Cudge would kill her. Why
couldn't she win, just once? At least the kid had
gotten away. If it hadn't been for her, he would be
dead and his parents would be crying over his
body, trying to figure out what had happened. She

was a heroine of sorts. She had saved the kid and got the good-looking guy. Only Cudge wasn't a good-looking guy and she didn't want him. Still, the kid had got away, thanks to her, and she felt good about it. She wished she could bless herself and maybe go to confession. She could do it in her mind. Cudge wouldn't have to know she was praying and confessing. In the name of the Father and the Son and the Holy Ghost, amen. Bless me, Father, for I have sinned. It has been many years since my last confession, since . . . since BJ. Father help me, somebody help me, she cried inwardly.

There was no priest behind a screen in a small confessional. She was in a dirty pickup with a murderer. What good was pretending to go to confession? She needed a real priest to give her penance. The kid was safe; that's what was important. If there was a God up there somewhere, then He would know she had saved the little boy.

"Get the map out, Elva, and make it snappy. You know where we are; find some back roads and give me directions. We'll head south and maybe our chances will be better once we hit Delaware and Maryland. We'll ditch the pop-up as soon as we can. I'll smear the license plates with mud and maybe we can hole up in some other campground. For now, it's the only thing I can think of. Don't even say you're sorry, because I don't want to hear your sniveling. I'm dumping you, Elva, first chance I get. You ain't nothin' but trouble."

Elva clenched her teeth and then bit her tongue. Dump me, my ass, she thought bitterly. Kill me is more like it. Still, she was glad she'd helped the kid. She would do it again in a heartbeat. She felt suddenly defiant as she flipped the map over. Maybe she was stupid like Cudge said and, then again, maybe she wasn't. "If you take Route 535 south for a while, you can either pick up 33, or at that point look for some other back roads. There ain't too much on this map, or if there is, I can't see it, the print is too small. This map must be twenty years old. The amusement park ain't even on it."

"Do you see any campgrounds listed?" Cudge asked.

"No."

"Then get out the camp guide and find one. Do I have to think for you, too?"

Elva dug under the seat and pulled out a tattered loose-leaf book. With nimble fingers she found the page she wanted. "There's two KOA camps open and the others are closed for the year. This is October."

"Shit!"

Davey was wedged in between the bunks on either side of the pop-up. It hurt when he took a deep breath and something was pounding inside his chest. If only Duffy were here to hug. He sniffled, wishing he had a tissue to blow his nose. The dark didn't scare him, only the smell of mothballs was making him sick.

Motion, rocking—the camper was moving! The tires were bouncing over the road; the bad man was taking him away. Davey realized that the man didn't know he was trapped inside the camper. If he just stayed very quiet and waited, he would have his chance to get away. Wait, instinct told him. Wait.

The rocking wasn't so bad now. It didn't seem as

though the wheels of the camper were bounding over holes and ruts. No, it seemed almost smooth, like when he rode his bicycle off the back lawn and onto the paved drive. It was a road—a highway, Davey thought, making the connection.

His legs hurt. The leather strap from the brace was cutting into his good knee, making it throb like a drum. He wanted to cry, but instead he bit his lip and tried to work the strap free of his good leg. If he could just catch the metal brace against the side of the refrigerator, he might be able to push with both hands and roll free. Time and again he tried and failed. A sob caught in his throat. If only Duffy were here. Again he tried hooking the side of the brace that curved around his shoe against the greasy refrigerator, and this time he was successful. The metal brace clanked against the refrigerator with a loud bang. Would the man and woman hear? What would they do to him? Would she help him get away again? Somehow he knew the man wouldn't let that happen.

It was cold in the pop-up; a draft was coming up from the crack where the sides and floor of the camper met.

How long was he going to have to hide in here? He had to go to the bathroom. He wished he could see what time it was. When he didn't get back at the time Aunt Lorrie had said, she would start looking for him.

He *had* to get out of here and back to Aunt Lorrie. He sighed deeply. How nice it would be if she suddenly appeared from out of nowhere and took him in her arms and held him close. He would sniff and sniff until he couldn't sniff anymore. Then he would hug her as tight as she hugged him.

Maneuvering a little, he tried to relieve the pressure in his abdomen, but it wouldn't go away. A look of horror crossed his face when he felt a warm trickle. He'd tried, but hadn't been able to hold it. Tears stung his eyes as the wetness seeped into his clothes. Only babies wet their pants.

Lorrie clapped her hands in delight when Davey's fishing pole bobbed up and down in the water. She looked around, calling his name, wanting him to be the one to reel in the fish.

A quick glance at her watch told her it was just after ten. Davey should have been back by now. "Davey! Davey!" she called. When he didn't immediately appear, she reeled the fish in herself, then removed the hook and set it free. "Oh, well. Maybe next time," she said to herself as she gathered up their fishing gear. Lorrie shielded her eyes against the bright sun. "Just where is that boy?"

As if in answer to her question, Duffy came scampering toward her. "Hey, there, Duff, where's your master? He was supposed to be back here five minutes ago." Duffy stood at Lorrie's feet, wagging her tail. Fully expecting to see Davey at any moment, Lorrie laughed and headed back toward the motor home. Maybe Davey was waiting for her there.

He wasn't. She set her gear down, put her hand over her eyes and scanned the campground for a sign of her nephew. "Davey! Davey, it's time to leave," she yelled, her voice rising.

She looked down at Duffy. Davey never left Duffy alone, and Duffy never left Davey alone. Something was wrong. She could feel it. Oh, God, she had to find him. What if something happened to him?

She felt herself begin to panic, but couldn't help it. She raced around the campground, shouting Davey's name over and over. Eventually she noticed that the little dog was right on her heels. "Some watchdog you are. Where is he, Duffy? Find Davey," she pleaded. "Go on, girl, find Davey."

Duffy raced ahead, her short legs whirling the dry leaves in her wake like spindrift. Faster and faster the little dog raced, Lorrie right behind her. Gasping for breath, Lorrie skidded to a stop when Duffy pulled up short, wildly barking.

Lorrie walked around, peering into the brush and beneath the low-spreading evergreens. Nothing. Over and over she called Davey's name, her voice becoming hoarser with each agitated call. Davey was nowhere that she could see. She looked down at Duffy. She was staring at something but Lorrie couldn't see what it was. "What is it, girl? Is it Davey?"

Duffy woofed with excitement and ran around in circles. Lorrie knew that dogs had sharper eyes than people, but for the life of her she couldn't see anything. She scratched her nose. It must be the smell of mothballs that was making Duffy act strangely. "I don't see him, Duff," she said, scooping the dog up into her arms. Her heart raced as she headed back to the motor home, wondering what to do. Practically every day the news carried a report of a child being abducted, sexually assaulted and killed. Every day! This was the nineties for God's sake. Things were different from when she'd grown up. If only she'd thought about that before she'd let Davey go off exploring.

Oh, God, she groaned. What was she going to tell Sara? "I lost your son." Where *was* Davey?

Stop it! she told herself. You're jumping to conclusions. In all likelihood, Davey had just forgotten the time. After all, it was his first camping trip and there were lots of things to see and do, things he'd never seen or done before. She would wait a little longer. Eventually, he would look at his watch and come running. If he wasn't back in a half hour, she would take action.

Lorrie let her thoughts jump ahead, creating scenarios she prayed wouldn't happen. First, she supposed she should visit the other campsites and ask if anyone had seen Davey, then she should alert the campground managers and enlist their help in a search. If they didn't turn anything up, then she should call the police. Once it got dark, she would call Sara and Andrew. Or should she wait till morning? No, they had a right to know as soon as possible. After all, Davey was their son. Their son, not hers. Never hers again after this. Christ, she'd be lucky if Sara ever let her set eyes on the kid again. Maybe on his eighteenth birthday, Sara would take pity on Lorrie and let her see her nephew come of age. Her thoughts were getting more ridiculous by the second. Goddamn it, where could the kid be? Why had Duffy come back by herself? Did Davey send her back for help or had the little dog just tired of the walk and wandered back on her own?

She waited.

After precisely thirty minutes, she headed out to visit the other campers. They'd gone. Both couples. The smell of mothballs made her realize this was the same spot she and Duffy had stood at ear-

lier. She hadn't noticed before, but the site was littered with trash. She remembered the pickup
truck, the way it was painted, and wasn't at all surprised.

Lorrie took off at a run for the manager's office
and told them her problem. They grabbed their
jackets, locked the door and headed out to search
for Davey.

"Don't worry, ma'am. We'll find him. Kids wander off all the time but they always turn up," the
manager assured her.

Lorrie nodded, thankful for his assurance, but
not altogether convinced it would turn out that
way this time.

"Now, tell us what he looks like and what he's
wearing."

Davey sneezed then immediately clapped his
hands over his mouth. He sneezed again as dry,
gritty dust blew up at him through the crack between the floor and sides of the pop-up. Angrily,
he pounded small fists against the side of the refrigerator and tried to kick out at the cardboard
boxes near the toes of his shoes. It was so dark inside the pop-up, he couldn't even see his shoes.
He'd be willing to bet they were dirty. Maybe even
ruined. As soon as he found Aunt Lorrie he would
throw them away. Would three quarters buy new
Reeboks? Three quarters for two shoes sounded
right to him. He sneezed again, then again. He
was hungry and he wanted a drink. He wanted out
of this dark, smelly place. He lashed out with his
foot at the carton filled with Cudge Balog's bar-
bells. His foot shot back as quick as a rattler. Gently,

he nursed his aching foot by holding it in both hands. "I want out of here!" he shouted. "Let me out of here!" The only response was a jolting thump as the pop-up hit a bump; another spiral of dust came in through the crack.

Suddenly, his head jerked up and he strained to hear. Was the camper slowing down? His tongue worked frantically in his mouth as he tried to wet his lips. He needed more spit if he was going to shout so someone could hear him. The woman would let him out when she heard him call. But how was he going to know where the bad man was? What would he do if it was the man who raised the top? The woman would try to help him, he was sure of it. The camper *was* slowing down. He would be quiet and wait.

Cudge eased up on the throttle. "Keep your eyes peeled for a gas station, Elva. This ain't the time to run out of gas. You listening to me?"

"Yeah, I hear you. I don't see anything but grass and trees. I'm hungry," she whined.

"Ain't we all. My advice to you is to suck in your gut because it might be a long time before we eat."

"Can't we stop and get something from the pop-up? How long would it take?" Elva persisted. "I can't remember the last time I had something to eat. I'm really hungry, Cudge. If I don't eat, I'm gonna be sick. I can feel it in my stomach."

"Jesus Christ! You don't hear too good, do you? After that dumb stunt you pulled this morning, you don't deserve to eat. You had the kid, Elva. You actually had him in your hands, and what do you do? You let him get away. That kid is spilling his goddamn guts to the police right now, and all you can think of is your stomach."

Elva slouched back against the seat. Cudge was probably right. Scared as he was, he was right. Maybe, when they stopped for gas, she could crank open the top and get something. How long could it take? A minute, two or three at the most. It took that long for the tank to be filled. She decided she would risk it. She needed her strength to run if she found the opportunity. Her stomach seemed to settle down with her decision.

She wondered where the little boy was right now. Was he talking to the police like Cudge had said? She had tried to help. Cudge would never understand; he was too concerned with not being blamed for Lenny's murder. Her stomach heaved as she remembered the body in the open grave. Poor Lenny, he didn't even have a coffin. The worms and bugs would eat through the blanket real quick. Her stomach heaved, then eased as she swallowed hard.

Elva risked a quick glance at Cudge. She really wasn't hungry. She might not be the smartest person in the world, but right now, this minute, if somebody offered her a Big Mac, she wouldn't be able to swallow past the fear in her throat. Cudge had tried to kill her back there and he would try again. She must never forget that, never pretend to herself she hadn't seen that look on his face when he wanted to put her in that hole with Lenny. It was okay to pretend sometimes, when reality hurt too much, but this time pretending could get her killed.

"Dammit, Elva!" Cudge spat. "I can't depend on you to do anything. See that gas station? That's where you get gas. I thought I told you to keep your eyes open." Elva shrugged. When you were going to die, what did it matter if you saw a gas station or not? Cudge's foot moved from the gas pedal; he swung it to the right and brought it down with all his force on Elva's ankle bone. She yelped in pain as she jerked her foot away. "Next time you do what I tell you." Cudge laughed at the expression on Elva's face. "Now, try and act normal."

The pickup truck bounced over and through deep ruts as Cudge maneuvered around the entrance ramp to the gas station. A home-made sign with big red letters said shocks were a specialty of the station. "Rip-offs," Cudge muttered, "they probably dug the damn holes themselves."

The truck pulled alongside the pump. It was so old it looked like something out of a Presley movie, none of the fancy digital stuff that was on the gas pumps in the cities. No, this one was a real antique. For that matter, so was the station itself.

"You sit tight, I gotta take a leak first. Jesus, this place don't even look like a gas station." Elva looked around for some sign of life. The place looked empty. Disobeying Cudge's orders, she opened the door and got out. Limping, Elva walked to the opposite side of the pumps. Maybe she should pump the gas herself to save time. She was just about to lift the nozzle from the rack when she heard music and saw a needle-thin youth coming out of the garage, carrying a boombox. "What'll it be?"

Elva almost laughed. She couldn't remember when the last time was that she'd seen a gas station attendant. Usually, there was just some guy sitting in a glass box taking money.

"Fill it up with unleaded, please," she said in a loud voice. She moved away from the pump toward the pop-up.

"Let me out of here," she heard someone say. She looked around. The voice came again, louder. It was coming from inside the pop-up. It was the kid. Oh, God. Elva's brain felt like cold, wet spaghetti as her eyes went to the door marked MEN.

"Hey!" the muffled voice called again. "Let me out!"

Elva slouched against the side of the pop-up. "Is that you, little boy?" She waited, hardly daring to breathe as the attendant danced around on one foot, watching the nozzle with unseeing eyes.

Davey's eyes closed in relief. She'd heard him. Where was the man? They must have stopped at a gas station. He could smell the fumes and "fill it up with unleaded" was what his dad always said when he stopped to get gas. "Please let me out," he yelled excitedly.

"You say something to me?" the boy asked, turning down the volume on the boombox. "You want the water and oil checked? Hey, are you all right? You look kinda sick."

Elva's eyes remained glued to the restroom door. "Sick? No, I'm not sick. The water and oil are okay." As if he cared whether or not she was sick. He was just being polite. She felt sorry for him; he kept scratching at his acne. For want of anything better to say, she blurted, "You got a problem or what? How come you bounce around like that on one foot and then the other?"

The boy held up his boombox. "I got music in my soul. My boss, he don't understand. He likes rock'n'roll. You sure you're okay?"

"Yeah, I'm okay. I like rock'n'roll too. Especially Elvis Presley. I have every single one of his tapes but I usually listen to them with earphones," Elva confided.

"Whatcha doin' way out here?" the boy asked.

Elva clamped her mouth shut. What business was it of his what she was doing out here—wherever here was. She'd better play it cool. It would be just like Cudge to get jealous.

"Let me out, please let me out!" came the muffled plea to Elva's left.

"Shhh," she whispered into the crack. "Be quiet. I have to think. If Cudge hears . . ."

"What did you say?" the pimply faced youth asked as he slammed the gas pump back onto the rack.

"Nothing," Elva replied. Her eyes flew to the old-fashioned numbers on the gas pump. Twenty-four dollars ninety. Cudge would have a fit. Let him. Right now she had enough problems. Where was he anyway?

"I heard you say something and I saw your lips move. My ma used to talk to herself before they took her away. You better watch it. *She* said she didn't talk to herself either."

Elva's heart fluttered. What if this kid said something when Cudge got back? What if he said she was talking to herself? Cudge wasn't dumb. "Yeah, you're right, I wasn't actually talking, I was kind of singing. I miss playing my tapes. I was just saying the words to a song to myself. That's what you saw me doing. I ain't like your mother, believe me, I ain't."

The boy looked skeptical as he held out his hand for the money.

"You have to wait a few minutes till my . . . till Cudge . . . Here he comes." She didn't know if she was sorry or relieved. "Hey, why don't you turn your set up a little so I can hear that song? I haven't heard anything but the CB for two days." Anything to drown out the feeble, muffled pleas of the little boy.

"You got it!" Never taking his eyes from Elva, the attendant turned up the volume. "And now for all you Metallica fans, here's their latest . . ." The disc jockey bellowed so loud Elva clamped her hands over her ears.

"Shut that goddamned thing off," Cudge shouted.

The gas station attendant's eyes widened. Then his eyes locked with Elva's. Defiantly, he turned the volume up even louder. Blaring music ricocheted around the pumps.

"I thought I told you to shut that thing off!" Cudge bellowed.

"That's what you told me all right, but this is my turf, buddy, and I don't give a damn what you say. Pay up and get that junker of yours out of here."

Cudge balled his hands into hard fists. Who the hell did the kid think he was with all those ugly pimples on his face? He was just about to raise his fist when he saw the boy looking at the license plate. "Okay, okay, play your damn radio. I got a headache and that's why I asked you to turn it off, but never mind. Here, keep the change."

"Big spender, a whole quarter," the kid smirked.

"It's twenty-three cents more than what your service was worth!" Cudge shot back.

Elva stared at the boy. As defiant as he was, she

knew he would have helped her if she'd asked. Why hadn't she asked? Why had she just stood there and done nothing? Now it was too late. Her window of opportunity had closed with Cudge's return. The kid stared back at her, pity in his eyes as she climbed into the cab of the pickup truck.

"You're a loser, Elva. I saw the way you was sucking up to that kid. Well, let me tell you something. I saw that bastard look at our license plates. He's going to remember us. You in particular."

"No, he isn't," Elva said defensively. God, what was she going to do about the little boy? She had to get him out before he suffocated. Reason, crystal clear, seemed to come back to her. He couldn't suffocate with the cracks in the outer shell of the pop-up. She knew there had to be hundreds because of the way road dust filtered inside and stuck to everything. The boy might be stiff and sore but he wouldn't die, not like BJ. Not if she could help it anyway. She saw herself letting the little boy out of the pop-up, spiriting him away and taking him back to his family. They would call her a hero and give her a reward and everyone would live happily ever after. Everyone but Cudge.

She was cold, almost as cold as she imagined Lenny must be. Cudge was perspiring. Served him right, she thought viciously, as she rolled up her window.

The pickup came to life beneath Cudge's hands. Slowly, it moved past the attendant, who made a show of turning down the volume of his boombox.

"Let me out of here," Davey yelled. "Open the door and let me out!"

The attendant's eyes widened in question. He

followed the trailer for a few feet, his head cocked, then stood watching as it pulled out onto the highway.

The station owner walked out to where the kid was standing. "Anything wrong?" he asked.

"I thought I heard . . ."

"What?" the owner prompted.

The boy shrugged. "Ah, it must have been my imagination. It sounded like there was someone in that pop-up. A kid, but . . . Nah! That ain't possible."

"Why not?" the man asked, staring after the pickup.

"'Cause there ain't no room in there once those things get folded up. If there was somebody in there, they'd be smashed. Must have been my imagination."

"It was probably one of those new radio commercials," the owner said, pointing to the kid's boombox. "Back to work," he said, then headed toward the grease pit.

"I think I'll write down their license plate anyway. You never know."

Davey knew they were on the move again. "Let me out of here!" he screamed. "Open the door! Let me out!" Why hadn't the girl opened the door? She'd heard him. He knew she'd heard him because she'd answered him. So why?

Davey thought for a moment. Maybe she was scared the man would see her letting him out. Maybe she was afraid he would punish her if he saw her. Davey scrunched himself even tighter into the space between the refrigerator and the hard, wooden bunk. It was dark and smelly, but it was better than having the man catch him. The girl would let him out as soon as she could. She might even take him back to Aunt Lorrie. His eyes drooped wearily—he was so tired, and he didn't feel well.

Seven

Stuart Sanders watched the people in the anteroom with clinical detachment. It was a hell of a job, all things considered. When you came all the way from New Jersey to Florida you expected to get a little sun and fun, not to sit inside a courthouse waiting for the prize witness to be recalled to the stand.

The waiting was hard on the Taylors, too. Annoyance was clearly written on both their faces, yet Sanders would have staked a week's salary that he was the only one aware of it. There they sat, chatting in companionable comfort, occasionally puffing on a cigarette.

As he watched them, he realized it was difficult to imagine Sara Taylor without her husband, just as it was difficult to picture Andrew without Sara at his side. He tried, unsuccessfully, to complete the family picture by imagining Davey between them. His eyes narrowed as he watched a stocking-clad leg move just a fraction closer to the trouser leg. No, there was no place for a little boy. Sanders saw an intimate smile play around Andrew's mouth as he looked up from his magazine, acknowledging the pressure of Sara's leg. There was no trace of a smile on her face as she lowered her gaze to her own magazine.

Sanders had seen their silent communication when Andrew Taylor had been questioned on the stand by the prosecutor, Roman DeLuca. The preliminary questions had focused on Andrew's university position, and were designed to show the jury that he was a solid, upstanding citizen, testifying at personal cost and possible jeopardy to himself and his family.

Then the prosecuting attorney's questions shifted to Andrew's relationship with Jason Forbes. It had become clear to Sanders that, whenever a question was put to Taylor, he sought out his wife, who was sitting in the first row, just behind the table where Roman DeLuca's assistants were taking notes.

Andrew Taylor's poise and confidence were unshakable, even under the hostile stare of the accused killer, and his confidence was reinforced by small, almost imperceptible nods of Sara's head. Her eyes never left her husband and, from the proud set of her shoulders and the slight smile around her lips, Sanders realized that she was giving Andrew her approval.

Sanders turned his attention to DeLuca, saw him look back and forth between Andrew and Sara, much as he had done himself. DeLuca was sharp, almost as sharp as him. Sanders studied DeLuca's expression and knew that he, too, had seen the silent signals between husband and wife. Sanders wondered how unshakable Andrew would be in his testimony if Sara weren't in the courtroom.

He hoped the trial wouldn't continue much longer. He'd always considered himself a patient man, but he decided now that he liked his company a little more jovial. He disliked the hushed whispers and dusty rooms, the smell of furniture polish and dry, cracked leather. Most of all he disliked the stale air and the austerity of the countless courthouses in which he had spent half of his life. And, to be honest, he disliked the Taylors. The thought surprised him—he'd never thought himself capable of such intense dislike. It bordered on hate. Everyone had faults, he supposed, and God knew, he was far from perfect himself. That was it! The Taylors were just too perfect to suit his tastes.

At that moment he would have given his soul to be with Lorrie Ryan and Davey, visiting the zoo, laughing at the animals' antics, eating popcorn and drinking sodas. Or had the trip to the zoo been planned for yesterday? He couldn't remember.

Now, where had all that come from? he asked himself. He glanced at the clock above the judge's head. In the weeks he'd stayed with the Taylors, he'd grown especially fond of Davey. Maybe because he felt sorry for the little kid. In the Taylor family, Davey was the odd man out, so to speak. Wanted, yet a bother. A flawed intruder. A wrinkle in the fabric.

Sanders had never had any kids of his own; his one marriage, ten years ago to a career-minded book editor, hadn't produced any children. His wife hadn't wanted them, and at the time, neither had he, though now he couldn't remember the reason why.

Spending time in Davey's company had brought out feelings in him that he hadn't known existed—feelings about home and family.

Lorrie was also an intruder. Where her feelings went, she wore her heart on her sleeve, loving Davey as if he were her own. Men weren't supposed to see or understand the subtleties that went on between women, but any fool could see that Sara disliked her sister and especially disliked Lorrie's love for Davey.

It wasn't right, he thought. Any kid who had gone through what Davey had gone through deserved a lot more love and nurturing than Sara offered. Davey should have been Lorrie's kid, not Sara's. Sara only loved Andrew and Andrew . . . Sanders wasn't sure what was up with Andrew; he seemed deaf and dumb to what Sara was doing. Why they'd had a child at all was beyond him, yet he was sure Davey hadn't been a mistake. The Taylors didn't make mistakes.

Sanders wished he had a cigarette, but he'd emptied his pack of Marlboros a half hour ago. He'd have to go out into the hall to see if he could bum one off one of the court clerks.

"Mrs. Taylor, I'm going outside for a smoke. If you need me, I'll be right outside the door." That was another thing that angered him—why did he always defer to her?

Sara nodded, not bothering to glance up from her magazine.

Outside the courtroom, Sanders spotted a clerk standing next to a potted palm, smoking a cigarette.

The man nodded at Sanders's request but was slow to get his pack out of his pocket. As Sanders waited, he imagined he could taste the acrid, hot smoke on his tongue.

"Thanks," he told the clerk as he put the filter tip between his lips. A lighter flashed and he drew deeply, the spiraling smoke making his eyes narrow. A vibration against his waist told him he was being beeped. He pulled the cell phone out of its belt case, opened it up and pushed the button to retrieve his voice message.

"This is Lorrie Ryan. I need to speak with you. It's an emergency," the voice said.

Sanders recalled the premonition that had prompted him to give Davey and Lorrie his business card.

He pushed a second button to see the phone number, then pushed it again to dial it automatically. "Lorrie, this is Stuart Sanders. What's wrong?"

"Oh, Stuart. It's Davey. He's gone. I've looked everywhere and can't find him."

"What happened, Lorrie?"

"I—Oh, God." Her voice was an anguished cry.

"You have to calm yourself, otherwise I can't help you," he said in his FBI voice.

She sniffled. He could tell that she was trying to regroup. "Right after breakfast, we went fishing," she began. "There's this cute little pond . . . We weren't catching anything and Davey got bored so I suggested he go for a short walk with Duffy. He knew we would be leaving soon . . ."

"Lorrie?"

"Duffy came back without Davey."

"Christ," Sanders swore beneath his breath. "How long has he been gone?"

"Duffy never leaves Davey's side," Lorrie said, not answering his question. "This is all my fault. I should have been more careful. I shouldn't have let him out of my sight, not even for a minute. If anything's happened to him, I'll never forgive myself."

"Let's not borrow trouble, Lorrie. You don't know that anything *has* happened to him. How long has he been gone?" he asked again.

"Since about nine thirty this morning."

"For God's sake, Lorrie. It's almost four. What took you so long to call me?"

"What? I . . . we . . . the managers and I—we've been searching the campground and—"

"Who else knows he's missing?"

"The police. I called them when we couldn't find him."

"I wish you'd called me first, Lorrie." Sanders glanced at his watch. Three fifty. Another five minutes and the court would adjourn for the day.

"Called *you* first? But I thought it was more important to call the police and get them started looking for him. I called you because . . . because I need you to tell Sara and Andrew."

Sanders's sharp gray eyes traveled the length of the corridor, coming to rest on the nattily dressed young lawyer who was assistant to the defense. In the old days, he would have been called a mouthpiece. Not for the first time Sanders wondered why a promising young attorney would align himself with known syndicate bosses. It occurred to him that Davey might have been kidnapped by a branch of the syndicate and was being used as a pawn to discourage Andrew Taylor from testifying.

"I'll tell them." He pulled a notepad out of his pocket. "Tell me exactly where you are, Lorrie."

Lorrie quietly gave Sanders the name and location of the campground. "Stuart . . . this couldn't have anything to do with . . . What I mean is—you don't think Davey's disappearance has anything to do with Andrew's testifying in this case, do you?"

Sanders hesitated before answering. "Anything's possible, and the thought has occurred to me." He was instantly sorry he'd admitted his suspicions. "I want you to sit tight. Leave your cell phone on so I can get back to you." He swallowed the lump in his throat. "Lorrie?" He wished he could reach out and touch her, comfort her.

"What?"

"Everything's going to turn out all right. I promise. You'll get Davey back unharmed."

"I pray to God you're right, Stuart. I can't tell you how much I love that little boy."

"You don't have to. I already know." He paused. "I'll be back in touch with you in a couple of hours." He pushed the "end" button and stood there, staring into space.

Davey had been kidnapped. It was exactly what the FBI had been guarding against; the reason he'd been moved into the Taylors' house. What kind of scum would snatch a kid? The kind of scum Andrew Taylor was testifying against, he answered himself. They were everywhere. And kidnapping was only the tip of the iceberg.

His steps were heavy as he made his way down the hall. In a husky whisper he repeated the phone conversation to his associate, Jake Matthews, giving him orders to report to headquarters. "I'll be waiting here, so make it snappy. I don't want to tell the Taylors until I get an okay from upstairs. There's a good possibility the boy is just lost."

Matthews nodded and took off at a run. He was back ten minutes later. "Something is brewing around here, Sanders," the younger man told him. "I get the feeling that everybody is watching and waiting. What's your hunch? Do you think that friends of the syndicate have snatched the Taylor kid?"

Before he replied, Stuart Sanders took a last drag on his cigarette, watching the conversation outside the courtroom door between Lester Weinberg, counsel for the defense, and his young assistant. "Matthews, it's enough to know that the bad guys probably already know the kid is gone. Our aim, right now, is to keep the Taylors from knowing until we get the go-ahead. You'd better get word to Roman DeLuca. As state prosecutor, he's got to know that his case might fly out the window if Taylor refuses to jeopardize his son by testifying."

Lorrie's white-knuckled fingers dug into the flesh of her upper arms. In spite of Stuart's words, she couldn't find the comfort she so desperately needed. All she could do was wait. She kept going over her phone conversation with Stuart. Was it possible that Davey had been kidnapped by someone affiliated with the syndicate? If Davey had been kidnapped, then it was reasonable to assume that he was safe somewhere. But if he'd just wandered off—what had happened to him? Where was he? More often than not, kidnapped children were found dead. It was easier to think that Davey was lost and that, before too long, he'd come wandering out of the woods, safe and sound.

Lorrie watched the police prowl the woods, their dogs sniffing and straining at their leashes. The local police had called in the state troopers for extra manpower. It was late in the day, and Lorrie had been told that if the boy wasn't found by morning, the police would alert the media and widen the search. The blood had rushed to Lorrie's head at the thought of Sara seeing her son's picture on national news.

Where was Davey? What could have happened to him?

Davey Taylor was as close to a flesh-and-blood son as she was ever going to get. He was part of her, no matter what Sara or Andrew said to the contrary. She loved him as much as Sara did—maybe more. A sob rose in her throat and tears spilled down her cheeks.

Leaning against the doorframe, looking out, Lorrie thought about Stuart Sanders. She wondered what difference it would have made to call him first. He was in Florida. How could he help find Davey from there?

It was nearing dusk when Lorrie saw a tall, lanky police officer come into the clearing. Suddenly uniformed figures were everywhere. "What? What is it?" Lorrie yelled.

The lanky officer backed off a step when he saw Dr. Ryan running toward him. "Stay here, ma'am. This isn't for you to see. No," he answered her unasked question, "we didn't find the boy. This is something else. Stay here," he repeated firmly.

"No," Lorrie said just as firmly. "I want to see

what it is. Whatever it is, will it help you find Davey?"

"I don't know," the officer replied.

In spite of his orders, Lorrie followed him through a stand of trees to what looked like a hole . . . or a grave.

"Put some muscle into it, Delaney. If there was a six-pack in that hole you'd have it out by now!" a local policeman with a noticeable beer paunch bellowed.

"Whatever's down here isn't going to come up any faster with you yelling, Jackowsky. And who the hell appointed you my superior? You want speed, grab a shovel and do it yourself. If not, shut up and let me do it my way." Delaney hefted his shovel and gently prodded into the soft dirt.

Standing at the edge of the hole, Lorrie saw the outline of a body. An adult's body, not a child's. She breathed a huge sigh of relief.

"Simpson, get in there with Delaney and help him," Jackowsky ordered. "We don't want any marks on the body made by our department."

Simpson sneezed. "Jesus! What's that smell?"

"It's mothballs!" Delaney lifted up a shovelful of dirt containing several of the white balls. "Suppose this is somebody's idea of how to preserve a body."

Jackowsky didn't laugh.

"Okay, so it's not funny. What we got here is a white male, twenty-five to twenty-eight years old. Hey, his eyes are open!"

"Cover his face," Jackowsky said, offering a used handkerchief. "This ain't no funeral parlor, you know," he grumbled. "Lift him out while I call this in."

Minutes later, Jackowsky returned. "The chief is

on the way with the coroner, and if you're one of those guys that's gonna puke, do it somewhere else. What's that you got, Simpson?"

"Looks like the guy's wallet. Hell, I picked it up and now my prints are on it."

"Then throw it back in." Jackowsky sighed as if to say how tired he was of dealing with rookies like Simpson and Delaney.

Lorrie whispered a prayer of thanks. It wasn't Davey. Thank God, it wasn't Davey.

"Now, ma'am," Jackowsky said. "You'd best be getting back to your RV and taking a pill or something. Or you won't be able to sleep tonight."

"Officer, I appreciate your concern, but I'm a doctor. I've seen dead bodies before. Who is he?"

"I don't know, but we intend to find out. Ma'am, why don't you go back to the camp and we'll get back to you as soon as we clear this up."

Lorrie looked around and counted a total of seven policemen and troopers. "I know this is going to sound ungrateful, but there are seven of you here. Why do you need seven people to dig up one body? Why aren't at least four or five of these men out looking for my nephew? I'm sorry that the man is dead, but nothing can be done for him. Davey is just a little boy, and he needs all the help he can get, and you aren't doing anything."

Lorrie felt herself bordering on hysteria. She decided to leave the gravesite before she said something she was sure to regret. Behind her, the seven men were silent.

Lorrie shivered. As soon as she got back to camp, she would make herself a cup of coffee— no, a pot of coffee—and build a campfire. A big campfire, one that could be seen from a long distance. It would warm the searchers as they came back with their reports, and it would serve as a beacon for Davey, a way for him to find his way back through the dark of night.

Today had been the kind of day you prayed would never happen, the kind of day that always seemed to happen to other people. Tomorrow had to be better. But, unless Davey was found, tomorrow would be worse, and every day after that would be worse than the one before. And then there was Sara. Oh, God, Sara. Sara would arrive and . . . She didn't want to think about it.

Lorrie imagined her sister receiving the news. Of course, she would take the next plane out of Miami. Lorrie shivered again, not with cold but with fear of Sara and how she would react—or rather, retaliate. Because that's what Sara would do. Lorrie felt guilty thinking that of her sister, but she knew her well enough after all these years. It would be Sara against Lorrie and the police; Sara would stay on the sidelines, yet somehow she would manage to control everything and everyone. There would be no closeness, no weeping together, no hoping together. Sara never shared her emotions with anyone but Andrew. She would be the judge and the jury, and Lorrie would never get an acquittal. Sara would find her guilty and judge her accordingly.

Lorrie turned her thoughts to building the fire. She piled up the kindling and set more rocks around the firepit. When everything was ready, she set a match to the construction and watched the flames spread through it.

She wished Stuart Sanders would call again and reassure her, like he had earlier. This was one of those times when she really needed a good man to lean on. Someone she could share her fears with. Someone who would hold her while she cried her eyes out. When this was all over, and Davey was safe and sound, she was going to think seriously about pursuing a relationship with the man.

Lorrie looked up to see three patrol cars coming her way. Their lights were flashing but their sirens were silent. Must be the coroner and his entourage, she thought. A short while later, Officer Delaney came over to speak to her. "We still have men combing the woods."

Lorrie nodded.

"The coroner says that the man we found in the grave died of massive head injuries. Either he hit something or something hit him. We're pretty certain it was the latter. As you know, there was a wallet in the grave. The description on his driver's license seems to indicate that the deceased is Leonard Lombardi of Newark, New Jersey. Do you know him?"

"No, I don't. It was murder, wasn't it?"

"It's looking that way. Right now, there's an allpoints bulletin out for the two other campers who were here last night. According to the manager here, one was an older, retired couple. The other couple, they were a lot younger, real lowlifes from what the manager's wife says. Seems they were camped in the vicinity of the grave. Both couples left early this morning. We're checking it all out."

"What about Davey?" Lorrie asked anxiously. It seemed to her that the excitement of finding the body was taking precedence over the search for her nephew.

Delaney became defensive. "We're working on

that, Dr. Ryan. There's always the possibility that your nephew's disappearance is linked with the dead man. I'm not saying that's the case, ma'am, only that it's a possibility."

Lorrie's voice was low and controlled when she questioned the young officer. "Did the manager say if he knew where the other couples were heading? Campers, as a rule, usually make inquiries about where their next stop is going to be."

"The older couple, the Kovals, said they were going to Virginia Beach. They should be setting up camp there around about now. We have a call in to the local police and we're waiting for them to get back to us. The young couple is another story. They paid in advance and didn't stop on their way out. The guy didn't even have a hookup, so we don't know when he left or where he was heading." Delaney looked up as someone boomed his name. "Hold it, looks like something just came in. Stay here and I'll be right back, ma'am."

"I'll wait, officer," Lorrie said quietly. "I won't get in your way."

She dug a trail in the powdery dirt at her feet, fighting to keep her emotions in check. Delaney returned shortly.

"What did you find out?" Lorrie asked, hoping, praying.

"The young couple I was telling you about— well, the pickup is registered to an Edmund Balog of Newark. Yesterday he was stopped on the turnpike by a state police officer. Seems there was some uneasiness on the part of the trooper. He was checking Balog's license when an emergency call came in. There was an accident further down on the pike and he had to cover it. We have a call in to the officer now. He'll be going off duty soon and will call in. I'm afraid that's all I have to report for now. Why don't you go back to your RV? I give you my word that as soon as I hear something, I'll report to you. The other teams will be checking in, and the new crew will be coming on duty. We may need you later. What do you say?" he asked hopefully.

"Did you get an address for the couple in Newark?" Lorrie asked.

Officer Delaney looked pained. "Yes, ma'am, and right now there's a team of officers on the way. I don't know if you know anything about Newark, but the address is in the Ironbound section. Tough neighborhood, if you know what I mean."

"I know the area. I worked a free clinic there for six months." Lorrie assumed the officer suspected Edmund Balog of kidnapping Davey or he wouldn't have brought him up. "Officer, if this goes out to the media, you need to let them know about Davey's medical condition."

"When was he supposed to have his shot?"

"Noon."

Delaney looked at his watch. "It's five-thirty now."

"I guess all I can do is pray that nothing happens to Davey to cause him to bleed. I don't have to tell you that, without the proper medical care, he could bleed to death in a very short time."

"We're doing everything we can, ma'am. I wish we could do more, but we can't. Things like this take time."

"Thank you, Officer Delaney. I appreciate you keeping me posted." Lorrie began to go back inside the motor home, then turned to the officer. "I just made a fresh pot of coffee. Would you like a cup?"

Delaney nodded. "Make it hot and strong. The manager's wife thinks coffee is colored water." He gave Lorrie a conspiratorial wink, then excused himself a moment and hurried back to the police car where Jackowsky was gesturing to him.

"She okay?" Jackowsky nodded toward the motor home.

"As good as can be expected," Delaney replied. "Shouldn't we have something on the kid by now? Too many hours have gone by for him to have simply wandered off."

Lorrie fixed herself and Officer Delaney a cup of coffee. She stood in the doorway of the van, waiting for him to return with whatever news he had just been given. Over and over she pleated the hem of her cotton shirt, her long, tapered fingers creasing the material, smoothing it out, and pleating it again.

"I used to love this time of year," she said when Delaney returned. "Now I hate it. It's starting to get chilly. It was downright cold last night. Davey had only that windbreaker on; it just has a thin flannel lining. I wonder if he's hungry."

"Nothing much new to report," Delaney said as he took the cup of coffee from her hands.

"Whatever it is, please tell me."

"That older couple that was going to Virginia Beach—they turned out to be duds. Zero. They didn't see your nephew. They had some thoughts about the young couple, but that's all they were. Mrs. Koval says she heard a lot of yelling and screaming, sounded like they were having a verbal altercation. Mr. Koval said he was sleeping, and his wife always hears yelling and screaming. He blames it on all the soap operas she used to watch and something about a fish tank. Sometimes this happens. People don't want to get involved and they mind their own business. The Kovals are a mind-your-own-business couple—and those are the words of Detective First-Grade Harry Thatcher. They checked out fine. Sorry."

"Thanks for coming back to tell me, Officer Delaney. You'll let me know about any further developments, right?"

"I'm going off duty shortly. One of the other men will check in with you. We've set up temporary offices next to the manager's quarters. If you need us, or if the boy comes back on his own, you'll know where to find us. Try not to worry."

Sanders's ulcer was beginning to act up, and he had the two-and-a-half-hour plane ride back to New Jersey to look forward to. And an airline dinner. He popped two Rolaids into his mouth, hoping to ward off what he knew would be an acute case of indigestion. The thought of sitting beside Sara Taylor for the entire trip played hell with his whole body chemistry. Perhaps she would sleep, or he would. Although the latter was out of the question—he'd have to remain awake to play bodyguard. Ridiculous. It was like playing nursemaid to a barracuda in open water.

He wanted this case to be over and done with. He wanted Davey back home, safe and sound. He yearned to take Lorrie Ryan into his arms and tell her everything was going to be all right, but he didn't know if it would be. It had to be, dammit. It just had to be. Davey Taylor was one hell of a special little boy and Sanders couldn't bear the thought of anything bad happening to him.

His footsteps were silent in the thickly carpeted hallway which led to the Taylors' hotel suite. Could it have been only half an hour ago that he'd presented them with the facts about Davey, carefully omitting any mention of the possibility of foul play? He'd intentionally reinforced their suppositions that Davey was lost or had wandered off. Whatever it was that he'd expected, it hadn't happened. Sanders knew that he had wanted to be the one to tell them because he'd wanted to see Sara Taylor go to pieces. He should have known better, he told himself, and wondered when he'd become so vicious in his thinking. If it had been any other woman, he would have dreaded telling her that her son was missing. But not Sara Taylor. For once he wanted to see her rattled, confused, and desperate. Out of control.

Andrew Taylor was the one Sanders pitied. The man kept running a frantic hand through his hair, his features drawn and pained. Sara had been the strong one, comforting her husband, telling him that she agreed with Sanders and was certain Davey had wandered off.

For a long moment, Sara's eyes had commanded Sanders's attention. Was he wrong, or had he seen an accusation in their depths, even while her hand tenderly stroked Andrew's arm? A thought came to him. Andrew Taylor's witnessing of that scene in the university library had upset the order of Sara's household. Things were beyond her control and she blamed Andrew.

Matthews stood outside the Taylor suite, arms crossed over his chest. "They wanted to be alone," he explained.

Sanders nodded and rapped on the door. Andrew opened it, the anguished lines of half an hour ago gone from his face. Sara had worked her magic with him once again. But how, Sanders wondered, did you get a man to forget that his son might be in grave danger?

"Mrs. Taylor, our plane leaves at six-ten. A car will pick us up. The airport is only a few minutes from here. Can you be ready?"

Sara's eyebrows shot up. "Mr. Sanders, I won't be leaving with you after all. My husband and I talked it over, and I'm going to remain here with him."

Sanders was incredulous. Wild horses wouldn't have kept his sister away if one of her kids had been in trouble.

"And Mr. Sanders," Sara continued in her cool voice, "tell my sister I'll be calling her shortly." The words held a threat; Sanders pitied Lorrie Ryan, and Davey too. Every child needed a loving, tender mother figure in his life. Somehow he just knew that if Sara had anything to say about it, and she would, Lorrie Ryan might as well forget she'd ever known and loved little Davey Taylor.

"Now, Mr. Sanders, I don't want you to waste your time trying to persuade me to go back with you. My mind is made up. I must be here with Andrew. We started this together, and we'll finish it together. What kind of wife would I be if I deserted my husband now when he needs me? You'd better hurry; you don't have much time and there's bound to be traffic at this hour. We wouldn't want to be responsible for you missing your plane. After all, it is your job."

Sanders turned to Andrew. "Mr. Taylor, do you agree with your wife's decision to remain here?" *Make her go, dammit! Make her be a mother to that kid for once in her life.* But Sanders did not give voice to his thoughts. He'd been warned that the Taylors weren't to be unnecessarily alarmed—at least Andrew Taylor wasn't. He was the key witness in the trial, and his testimony was all important in the case against the multimillion-dollar drug ring. The State needed to prove a connection between the murdered man and the syndicate, and Andrew would provide the connection.

"Both you and my wife have assured me that Davey has just wandered off from the campsite. What would Sara's presence accomplish? Lorrie will do all she can; we know that. Right now, as I see it, the imminent danger to Davey is his missing his shot. Unfortunately, nothing can be done about that until he returns."

Sanders couldn't believe his ears. Taylor was talking as though Davey were a naughty child who had wandered away, and would return when he was good and ready! Sanders wanted to take Andrew and shake him and hear his stiff neck crack. Still, he couldn't go against departmental orders. Even a hint that Davey might be held by friends of the Miami syndicate could discourage Andrew's testimony.

As time went on, Sanders was becoming more and more skeptical of that possibility. Surely, if Davey had been kidnapped, the Taylors would have been apprised of that fact; word would have been gotten to them, either directly or through the Bureau it-self.

"As my husband has told you, Mr. Sanders, we'll be staying here until Andrew takes the stand. To-morrow afternoon, at the latest, and then we'll be back in New Jersey. By that time, Davey will have returned."

Sanders stiffened. What kind of mother was Sara Taylor? That poor little kid. Christ, he felt like smashing something. Smashing her! Something was on fire in his stomach—his damn ulcer was acting up. At least he could sleep on the plane and hope for the best. Just because she gave birth to Davey didn't make her a mother. Schooling his face to impassivity, he said goodbye and walked away. He hoped he would never have to see either one of them again. Back in New Jersey he would be in the field, his responsibility to the Taylors over. From this moment on, his only contact with them would be through Lorrie Ryan.

Leaving their hotel room, he sent up a silent prayer. *Hang in there, little buddy. I'll find you some-how.* He dismissed the lump in his throat. Must have something to do with the ulcer, he told him-self.

Andrew Taylor watched his wife through nar-rowed lids. Another day and they would be back home, safe in New Jersey. Now why had he used the word "safe"? Here they were, locked in a hotel room with an armed guard outside the door. How much safer could he be than he was at this mo-ment? He still wasn't certain of Sara's decision to stay with him. Was it a mistake for Sanders to go back alone? Sara had made the decision to stay at his side; he'd known she would. Her argument that two heads were better than one convinced him. Sara was always right. Everything that could possibly be done for Davey was being done. Sanders would take charge. Davey was alone, lost in the woods, but Sanders would find him and take him home safely. Sanders was a man to depend on.

Andrew's shoulders slumped as he recalled the look on the agent's face when Sara had told him she wasn't flying back with him. Her duty, she had said, was to stay with her husband. Sanders should have understood that, but Andrew knew he hadn't. At first the look had been one of disbelief, but that had given way to sour acceptance. His goodbye had been barely audible. Sara was right; she was always right. Davey had just lost his bearings and would turn up before dark.

Sara walked around the edge of the bed and lightly touched Andrew's shoulder. "Would you like roast beef or chicken for dinner?"

"What do you suggest?"

"I think a broiled spring chicken sounds fine. With a garden salad and some fresh peas—it's much too hot for a heavy dinner. Andrew, you aren't upset with me because I decided to stay on with you, are you?"

"Of course not, Sara. Why would you even think such a thing? I know everything is being done to find Davey. The truth of the matter is, we would probably be in the way. Besides, he'll turn up before dark. I know I always did." He laughed. "I used to get lost at least once a week and always managed to find my way back."

"And Davey is his father's son," Sara said briskly.

"After dinner I'm going to call Lorrie. I want to know how this happened. She always was a feather-brain. I'm so disappointed in her that I hardly know what to do. It just bears out, Andrew, what I told you before we left home. We must curtail her involvement with Davey."

Any doubts Andrew might have had concerning Lorrie's attentions toward his son were wiped away with Sara's words. It was uncanny how she was always right. "I quite agree, Sara."

"Police!" Sara made the term sound obscene. "It isn't bad enough that we're surrounded with guards and police twenty-four hours a day, but now we have to be subjected to more of them. What would you like to drink, Andrew? Why don't we order wine and we can have it for the rest of the evening. It will help us to unwind and relax."

All Andrew heard was the word "relax." He had been looking forward to a double scotch, straight up. A couple of liters of wine while he went over his testimony would certainly help. Sara was one step ahead of him all the time. Scotch wasn't really a drink to sip in a hotel room. He hoped the wine-glasses had long stems.

"I think I have it all now. You don't want dessert, do you?" Sara said, putting the hotel pen back in the desk drawer.

If he ordered dessert, he would still be eating after Sara was finished.

"No."

"I didn't think so." Sara's eyes twinkled down at him. Fondly, she stroked his hair. "I'll give this to the guard and you can watch the news while we wait."

Just as Sara was about to open the door a sharp

knock sounded. She glanced at Andrew—he was already engrossed in the early evening news. It was probably just the guard wondering why she was taking so long with the dinner menu. She smiled as she opened the door, the menu extended ready to hand over, then backed off a step, her eyes flashing between the bellboy and then to the guard.

"A message came in for you a few minutes ago, ma'am," the bellboy offered.

Sara looked at Jake Matthews. "It's all right," he assured her. "We've checked it out. It just came in. Is that your menu? Good, the boy can take it down when he leaves. I'll tip him, Mrs. Taylor. You go back inside now and lock the door."

Sara made a face the minute the door was shut—as if she needed to be told to lock it. The message was probably from Lorrie and full of all kinds of apologies, or else to say Davey had returned to the campsite. She sat down next to Andrew and withdrew a slip of paper from the envelope. She read it once, then read it again. The message was brief: *It's urgent that you call 943-0773 as soon as possible.* There was no signature, just the time the message had been logged in.

Sara read it again. Was it a local number? It was certainly a Florida number or the operator would have included an area code. What could it mean? Should she show it to Andrew? He would worry. Roman DeLuca. Of course. It didn't matter that she detested the suave district attorney. She would wait till a commercial came on before telling Andrew.

The anchorman's voice droned on as he reported on the plight of the Albanian refugees. A sleek Mercedes flashed on the screen as a pitch came on for a local car dealer. "Darling, look at me," Sara began. "It seems we have a message. A bellboy gave it to me when I opened the door to give our dinner menu to the guard. Read it and tell me what you think."

Andrew read the curt message. He shrugged. "Did you show it to the guard?"

"Of course not, Andrew. After all, we are entitled to some privacy. Perhaps it's something personal, although I can't think what it could be. It appears to be a local number, or at least a Florida number. At first I thought it might be a message from Lorrie, or even Mr. Sanders, but I don't think that's the case."

"Well, there's only one way to find out—call the number and see what it is," Andrew suggested.

"I don't know if that's such a good idea, Andrew. Perhaps we should wait for Roman DeLuca to get here and show it to him. I really don't want to get involved in anything else right now. It could be some pervert, or a weird person who watches the news and does things like this. You know how some people get a thrill out of tormenting others. It could even be a threat against us."

"I don't want anyone threatening you, ever," Andrew said adamantly. "We'll wait for Roman to get here and let him handle it."

Sara smiled. "How gallant of you, Andrew. I think it's wise to wait, too."

Andrew let out a long sigh. She agreed with him. He smiled at her in an intimate way and she responded in kind. Gently, she blew him a kiss. He smiled again as the caravan of Mercedes cars left the screen to be replaced again with the silver-haired, somber-faced news commentator.

Sanders settled himself in his aisle seat aboard the 747. He hoped the flight would take off on time and that they wouldn't have to wait in line on the runway. He hated waiting. It seemed all he ever did was wait. Wait for this. Wait for that. Waiting was something most people thought he did well because he never complained. But he didn't do it well. Not at all. His insides always felt as though they were on fire. He detested inactivity almost as much as he hated certain people. Once he hated someone, God Almighty couldn't get him to revise his opinion. And by the same token, when someone got close to his heart, that person stayed close forever. His sister said he loved with a vengeance. Maybe he did, he thought sheepishly.

Out of habit, he reached for his pack of cigarettes, took one out, then remembered: no smoking. What the hell! The half dozen he would have smoked during the flight would be that many fewer nails in his coffin. He'd always thought that when he went down for the count it would be with the big C. He was already coughing and hacking in the morning. The thought of his own death didn't bother him. It was the death of other people that made him want to lash out.

Davey Taylor. Was the kid suffering, wherever he was? Sanders leaned back and grasped the cross he always wore around his neck. He didn't like takeoffs any more than he liked landings. It used to be that as long as he could smoke and sleep in between, he didn't care. But things were different now. The silver bird climbed and climbed then leveled off. The "No Smoking" sign, a laughable relic of the last decade, went off. Maybe if he had a bourbon and water, he would be all right for the next two and a half hours. He opened his briefcase and pulled out the Polaroid he'd taken of Davey Taylor wearing his red windbreaker. A deep, paternal feeling for the little boy swelled in him. There was something about this kid, something that bothered him. Something he just couldn't put his finger on. He would have to chalk it up to a gut feeling, and twenty-three years with the Bureau.

Back in Miami he'd felt that someone, or some force, was at work against the kid. Over the years he'd learned to trust his feelings, even if others didn't. When he'd told the chief about it, he'd listened, nodded and asked for some concrete evidence or substantiated facts. Sanders didn't have anything concrete—just a feeling, a gut feeling. Both agreed it was possible that the little boy was being used as a pawn, but Sanders thought it more improbable than probable. So what was it then—this feeling of his?

All of a sudden Sara Taylor's face appeared before him. She had a cool, patrician kind of beauty, he had to give her that. But that was all he would give her. She'd said her place was with her husband. How could she ignore her son like that? Was it possible she knew something Sanders didn't? Had she really bought into his bogus theory that the kid had just wandered off? Who knew what she was thinking behind that frozen mask she wore. Sanders might not know what made Sara Taylor tick, but there was one man who thought he did know—Roman DeLuca. Sanders had watched the suave district attorney during his first meeting with the Taylors. DeLuca sized Sara up in five minutes flat, and immediately discounted her—much to Sara's chagrin.

Sanders stared at the snapshot of Davey for a while longer. He couldn't shake his feelings. He kept thinking that he'd see something in the photo that would make it all clear. Some answer, some clue. But there was nothing. He laid the picture back on top of a yellow legal pad, groped for a paper clip and attached it to a wad of sheets. He didn't want to lose it. Satisfied that the picture was secure, he fished and fumbled inside the briefcase, looking for his favorite treat—salted peanuts. He found two bags and laid them on the seat next to him.

Eight

Cudge Balog wished he had three eyes—one for watching the road, one for watching his back, and the third for watching Elva. He didn't like the way she was acting, nor did he care for the creepy way she kept looking at him. And, he thought grimly, she hadn't bawled at all when he'd kicked her ankle. That wasn't like Elva. Crying and whining were the things she did best, besides making Kool-Aid. Time to give her another jolt.

He took his eyes from the road for an instant and sneaked a look at her. She was nervous, of that he was certain, but it was annoying him that she was in control of it. "I was thinkin', Elva. You know, in prison they give you anything you want to eat for your last meal. What would you order, Elva? This is as good a time as any to decide because you been belly-aching how hungry you are. What would you order?"

Elva knew exactly what Cudge was trying to do.

Unnerve her. Make her fall apart, and then, when she was hysterical, he would kill her. She couldn't let that happen. She had to help the little boy get out of the camper and get away. She couldn't let Cudge do anything to her until the boy was safe.

Cautiously, she turned in her seat and stared at Cudge for a long time. It was Cudge who was becoming unnerved now as he kept glancing at her then quickly looking back at the road. Her voice was light, almost airy, and seemed to come from far away. "I think I'd order veal cutlets, because of what they cost. And shrimp. Big juicy ones with a real spicy sauce to start with. Baked potatoes, with lots of sour cream. And rolls. Hot ones with butter. And that dessert I always hear about, Cherries Jubilee; whatever it is, it sounds good. And beer. A really icy cold beer. Coffee, with rich cream, none of that fake stuff, to top it off. Maybe a peppermint Lifesaver to settle my stomach as I walk down death row. What are you gonna order, Cudge?"

Cudge glared at Elva. She'd turned the tables on him. She made her question sound as though it was certain he'd have to order his last meal because he was definitely going to be convicted. "You're dumb, Elva. You'd be so piss-ass scared you wouldn't be able to eat a thing. And if you did, you'd puke your guts out."

"Maybe you'd be too scared to eat, but I wouldn't." That should settle him down for the time being, she thought. She had to think about the little boy and how to get him out of the pop-up. She wouldn't mess up this time, not again. Poor little thing, he must be miserable, cooped up in there. I won't let anything happen to you *this* time, BJ, she crooned to herself. *This* time I'll make sure you're safe. Don't worry, BJ, I'm gonna take care of you. Somehow, I'll make him let you go.

Cudge didn't like Elva's wiseass answers. By now, she should have been a glob of putty, jabbering away at him to stop tormenting her. Stupid broad. Instead, she was sitting there in a dream world, smiling to herself. It was her smile that started to awaken his anger. Maybe she was thinking about Elvis Presley again. No, that wasn't the usual dumb smile she had when she was dreaming about Elvis. This was more ominous. Maybe she was plotting his death, just the way he was planning hers—this very minute. Old Elva might be skinny as a pencil, but she was wiry and strong, like a bull terrier.

He hated Elva and everyone else. But mostly, he hated that little bastard who was finking on him to the cops. If he'd had a gun, he would have killed the two of them on the spot. People like Elva and that brat kid could ruin a person's life. He'd get out of this mess yet, and without Elva.

Hours passed as Cudge concentrated on his driving. For Elva, it was impossible to think clearly with Cudge being so controlled at the wheel. The road map in her lap was nothing more than a blur. Her neck and shoulders were stiff with the effort she was making to sit straight in the jouncing truck seat. Her ankle throbbed painfully and her tooth was aching. She was sure of just one thing: she had to find a way to open the pop-up and set BJ free. Even if she died doing it. Once in a while God and the fates allowed you a second chance, and this was hers. She couldn't flub up, not now. Maybe she should pray for a miracle. Or just pray. Did she re-

member how? Maybe there wasn't a God after all.
If there was a God, what was He thinking of, to
allow BJ to be penned in the camper and her to be
stuck with Cudge Balog? God was as make-believe
as Ali Baba and the Forty Thieves.

Right now Cudge would have bet the remainder
of Lenny's bankroll that Elva was up to something.
He didn't like the ramrod stiffness of her back,
nor the way she stared straight ahead. This silence
was different from the times when she had her
damned earphones on. "There's a rest stop ahead
at the next exit. I think we can get some eats. Elva,
are you listening to me?"

"I ain't hungry."

"What do you mean, you ain't hungry? You been
busting me to stop and eat, and now you ain't hungry. Why ain't you hungry, Elva?" he asked suspi-
ciously.

"Because I ain't."

"Well, I am, and we're going to stop. We can get
a carryout order. You go in and get it, and I'll wait
for you. We need to fill up the water bottles anyway. Make up your mind, we're stopping."

Elva hoped her relief wasn't evident. If she had
learned anything at Cudge Balog's knee, it was
that to disagree would make him more determined.
Just a little more playacting and maybe she could
free BJ. "I can't do it, Cudge. My foot hurts too
bad, and I'll be limping. Someone will remember
that I limped. You have to be careful and use your
head now."

"I got a bad feeling about you, Elva, like you're
planning something."

"Yeah, like what I'm gonna buy you for Christmas.

What I said is the truth. If you want to be stupid, go ahead, but don't say I didn't warn you. I didn't ask you to kick me."

Cudge eased up on the gas pedal as he turned off at the exit sign. It was a Denny's.

"Where you gonna park this thing?" Elva asked quietly. "Maybe it would be best if you park right in front. That way no one will think it's at all suspicious. It's just a suggestion." Now, if she was half as smart as she thought she was, Cudge would park at the end of the parking lot, away from all the families with their little kids. The last slot would be perfect. She could open the pop-up, scoop up BJ and run like hell.

"Maybe that's what you would do, but it ain't what I'm gonna do. I'm parking at the end of the lot. There ain't enough cars around to lose ourselves in the crowd. We don't need to be noticed. You keep your yap shut, and do *what* I tell you *when* I tell you. You got that?"

"Does that mean you're going in for the food? I told you I can't walk. Look at how swollen my ankle is. I think you broke a bone or something."

"You're walking, Elva, and I'm gonna be right behind you. And I don't want to hear any more of your crap about someone noticing you either. Ain't nobody gonna pay any attention to you."

"Oh, yeah, what about those two guys?" Elva said, pointing toward the entrance.

Cudge's eyes followed her finger. Two troopers in tight gray pants and the inevitable polished sunglasses were just getting out of an unmarked car. His features tightened. One hand curled into a fist. The two men walked slowly through the entrance. There were booths alongside the long row

of windows. Would the troopers sit at the counter
or take a booth? Either way, he had to make some
kind of move. If they sat down in one of the window booths, they had a clear view of the entire parking lot. Should he go in alone, as Elva had suggested,
and take out the food, or should he drag Elva with
him? Christ, what should he do? It was the smirk
on Elva's face that forced his decision. She wouldn't
dare try anything. "You're coming with me. We'll
eat inside. Act like we didn't do nothin' and everything will be all right."

Elva squared her shoulders. "*We* didn't do anything; *you* did it." She felt more powerful at that
moment than she had ever felt in her life. "Ain't
you afraid I'll spill my guts to those cops? I could,
you know. Just remember that, Cudge. You should
have killed me back at the campground when you
had the chance."

Cudge's pent-up rage swelled and his eyes rolled
back. Elva watched him, neither afraid nor relieved.
Nothing mattered to her anymore, except freeing
the little boy who looked like BJ.

"Okay, okay. You stay here and watch the rig.
Make sure no one comes nosing around." Each
word was slow and distinct, spoken with great effort. He had to close the gate *now*, before it was too
late. A loud sigh escaped Cudge's lips. What he
had to do was convince Elva he was going to take
care of her.

"I been thinking, Elva, about what you just said,
that I was gonna kill you. You're wrong. I wasn't
gonna kill you. You ain't never done anything bad
to me like Lenny did. Jesus, Elva, you're all I live
for. Look what you've done for me so far. Without
you, my ass would be in jail. I ain't never gonna

forget that. I mean it, and as soon as we get out of this mess, I'm gonna bankroll this wad and take you to the Poconos, to that lodge where they have heart-shaped bathtubs. I was even thinking of marrying you. I don't expect you to believe me, but it's what I want and I think it'll work. What do you say, honey?"

"I ain't as dumb as you think I am, Cudge. I know wives can't testify against their husbands. I ain't ready to get married, and if I never see a heart-shaped bathtub, I'll live. You can't snow me anymore, Cudge, so forget it. If you're gonna get the eats, get 'em. Them troopers must be wondering what you're doing just sitting here. Most people either go to the bathroom or the restaurant when they stop at a place like this. You're gonna look suspicious if you don't get moving."

Cudge knew she was right. If she was telling the truth and she couldn't walk, then he was safe. "Okay, I'm going in. You get out and stretch your legs like everyone else. Hop around on one foot and stay put. Don't you have to go to the bathroom?" he asked as he suddenly remembered that she hadn't gone when they'd stopped for gas.

"I don't have to go. I didn't drink any Kool-Aid today."

"You better be here when I get back, Elva."

Elva nodded. She would be here, but the kid wouldn't. There was no point in fooling herself—there was no way she could walk, much less run, with her swollen ankle.

"While you're getting the food, I'll open the pop-up and get out the water bottles to save time."

"Like hell you will. I can just see you cranking it the wrong way and bam!—one pop-up shot to hell.

You know you can't do nothin' right. I'll do it when I get back. If you even think of trying to open my rig, your neck is gonna look like your foot. Now, you get out and we'll talk a minute and then I'll walk real slow into the restaurant, and you damn well better act like you know what the hell you're doing."

Cudge stretched luxuriously, as if he had all the time in the world. He worked first one leg and then the other. He hitched up his jeans and threw back his shoulders like a man who was bone tired from traveling all day. Walking to the back of the rig, he thumped on the pop-up. It was his, all his. The one thing in his whole stinking life that was his alone. No one was going to take it away from him, and no skinny bag of bones was going to crank it open and screw it up. "You stay right here, Elva. I'm gonna be watching from the restaurant."

Davey woke with a start. The trailer wasn't moving anymore. He squirmed around, trying to get comfortable. Why had they stopped? Was it nighttime? Where was the woman? Would she let him out? He was about to shout when he heard the man's voice. He had to be quiet and not make a sound. He had to act the way he did in the hospital and be brave. Be quiet and still. No matter how scared he was. One, two, three strikes and you're out! His dad often said that. This was his third time. If the woman didn't get him free, he was out. His dad had never said what happened when you were out. But Davey thought he knew. He was tired, almost too tired to care. He frowned in the darkness. It was a different kind of "almost."

As soon as Cudge entered the restaurant, Elva made her way to the back of the rig. "Little boy, can you hear me?"

"I hear you. Let me out of here! I can't move. Please let me out."

"I'm gonna let you out soon as I can. Can you be quiet for just a little longer? I know you must be hungry, but I can't do anything about it right now. Cudge just went inside to get some food. I think he's going to open the pop-up, and you gotta be ready to run. Do you think you can run? Little boy, can you run?"

Davey's thoughts were jumbled. He knew he couldn't run. He was too tired and too weak. But he had to say yes or she wouldn't help him. "Yes," he said loudly.

"Good. There's two cops here, and if you run inside the restaurant, they'll take you back home. But you have to be quick. Real quick. Are you okay? You ain't sick or anything are you, little boy?"

Davey thought a minute. "I'm almost sick. I didn't get my shot today."

"What shot?" Elva asked fearfully.

"I'm a hemophiliac."

"You mean you bleed?" Elva asked in horror.

"I used to, but now I get shots. Please, can't you let me out before *he* comes back?"

"You have to trust me, little boy. I'm gonna help you." If the kid didn't get his shots, he might die. She would be just as guilty as Cudge this time around. He was just a kid, a little boy like BJ. She had to do something. The hell with what Cudge said. What did she care if the cranks fell apart? Her hand was on the crank ready to turn when Cudge walked through the doorway. Behind him were the two troopers. Elva froze. "Little boy, something's wrong. Be real quiet."

"Here we go, honey. Food at last," Cudge shouted with false gaiety. Elva stared at him. Didn't he see the troopers behind him?

Suddenly a voice shouted. "Sir, sir, the cashier wants to see you." Cudge ignored the voice. Elva gagged and her face drained of all color. As if in slow motion, she watched one of the troopers put a hand on Cudge's shoulder. "Hey, mister, you deaf or somethin'? The cashier wants you back inside."

Cudge turned slowly and stared at the two troopers. His brain was swelling, every instinct prepared him to fight, to defend himself. The very sight of a uniform could do this to him, but to have the trooper speak to him—*touch* him! A hoof cut into the soft tissue of his brain. A hulking, dark shape shouldered the restraining gate. Only a superhuman effort quelled the restlessness of the beast and held him behind the gate. "Me?" he asked stupidly.

"Yes, you. The cashier wants you back inside."

The trooper's partner smirked as Cudge turned and walked back into the restaurant. "They're all alike, those campers. A couple of days on the road and they're in another world. Kind of airless around here, isn't it?" His fingers worked at his collar.

"I thought it was me," the first trooper said quietly. "You ever hear about the Santa Ana winds? They say they make people do crazy things, kinda like a full moon." He laughed sheepishly. "Come on, let's get it in gear and hit the road. I got a date tonight that would set your hair on end. She's got the biggest knockers on the East Coast."

"Seeing is believing," the second trooper grinned.

"I don't take a cop's word for anything. Everyone knows you can't trust a cop."

"Yeah, right," the first trooper said with a grin as he climbed behind the wheel. The car came to life just as Cudge hit the parking lot. "Would you believe they shortchanged me?" he said, holding out his palm with thirty-seven cents in it for proof.

The trooper stared at the change for a full second. His eyes behind the polished glasses were cold. He nodded curtly and switched from park to reverse. Cudge stood back respectfully and watched till the yellow Plymouth left the parking lot.

"Close your mouth, Elva, and get in the truck."

"What about the water bottles? We ain't even got a drop. We need the water. You crank open the top and I'll get the bottles. You'll have to fill them though."

"Christ, you're stupid. Two cops just left here. We were eyeball to eyeball, and you want to hang around here to get water? We ain't opening that pop-up till we make camp. When the shit hits the fan, those guys are gonna remember me. Now, get your ass in that truck and let's move!"

As Elva started to hobble back to the truck, a noisy family got out of a maroon station wagon close by. Seven children squealed and shouted as they romped about the parking lot, trying to catch a frisky, fuzzy-looking dog. Cudge and Elva were suddenly surrounded by yelling kids and a barking dog. "C'mere, Bizzy. Good girl. C'mon, we got some popcorn for you."

"Jesus Christ!" Cudge shouted to be heard above the noise. "Get that damn dog out of here and get him out now! All of you get out of here. I want to start this rig up and I'm running late."

"Bizzy is just sniffing your pop-up, mister. You got something in there she likes. She's not hurting anything. See, she's just trying to get in to see what you got," a boy in tattered overalls grinned.

"Well, I ain't got nothin' in here for your dog, so get her out of here."

"We can't catch her," a little girl with pigtails complained. "She's fast, mister. Her mother's name was Flash; that's why we picked her from the litter."

"I don't give a damn what her mother's name was. Get her out of here!"

"Kids, kids, what's going on here? Where's the dog?" The kids' mother approached, gathering her children into a close group like baby chicks. Her eyes flicked over them as if taking a habitual head count. Her work-worn hands pushed back frizzy hair from her forehead. "Hey, Max, you better get your butt out here and settle this. These people want to get on their way and your kids are holding up the works. Max, you hear me?"

"Yeah, yeah, I hear you. I been listening to you all the way from Milwaukee. What's wrong this time?" a bear of a man demanded as he climbed from the dust-streaked station wagon.

"There isn't any problem," Cudge said patiently. "We just want you to get your dog, Flash, out of here so we can be on our way."

"Name's Bizzy. Flash was her mother," the girl with the pigtails chirped.

"What you carrying in that pop-up, mister, that attracts our dog? She usually ain't interested in other people and their belongings. Kind of a mind-your-own-business mutt, if you know what I mean," the man said.

"Just get that dog out of here. We're running behind schedule now."

Max LeRoy stared at Cudge in a way that said he didn't like what he saw. "Bizzy, up," he commanded in a sharp, clear voice. The little dog leaped in midair to land in his arms. He nodded curtly to Cudge and, without so much as a word, the kids backed off, allowing Cudge and Elva to enter the pickup. It was Mrs. LeRoy who memorized the license plate, without realizing what she was doing.

Elva sighed heavily. She felt like an old newspaper that had been cut up to paper-train a new pup. How much more could she take? And the kid—how much more could he take? What if he started to bleed back there, all alone, and then died on her? *Please, God, don't let anything happen to the little boy. I don't care about me, just don't let anything happen to him. I know that I was thinking before that there wasn't a God, but you must be real or Cudge would have found him by now. I don't need a miracle, just a diversion of some kind. You can't let him die, he's just a little boy, hardly more than a baby?* Elva choked back a tear. She knew God did let little boys die; he'd let BJ die.

"What are you doing, Elva? Tell me you ain't talking to yourself. Please tell me you ain't."

"Okay, I ain't talking to myself. I was praying."

Cudge's eyes widened. His head bobbed up and down. "It figures," was all he said.

"Where we going and how much longer are we going to stay on the road?" Elva demanded.

"Soon as I see a spot that looks like it's off the beaten track, I'll stop. You feeling frisky, Elva?" he baited her. "That why you wanna stop so quick?"

She ignored him, her mind racing ahead. The

kid had said he could run, so he must be all right.
Little kids were always hungry. Whatever it was
Cudge had bought, she would save her portion for
the little boy to take with him.

Cudge was so full of it. First he tried to kill her,
then he thought he could make it all better by calling her honey and telling her he'd take her to a
lodge in the Poconos with a heart-shaped bathtub.
As if that would make everything all right. The
thought was too ludicrous even to warrant a smile.
She was just beginning to realize how stupid Cudge
really was. Now, when it was too late.

"Elva, get that map out and take a look-see. I just
seen something that makes me nervous. Take a
look over there and tell me what you see. Ain't that
the same diner and ain't that the same gas station
we seen when we started out? It is!" he bellowed.
"There's that mom-and-pop camp store. Of all the
friggin' luck!" For the first time in his life Cudge
felt raw gut fear. They were right back at the scene
of the burial. The kid would have told his folks.
There'd be cops everywhere. Fear swooped up
into his throat and he gagged. What should he do?
Head back to Newark? Turn around and drive all
night? Camp? Where?

Elva felt herself go limp. This was her miracle.
Think, she had to think. "That's good, ain't it, Cudge?
Who would ever think we'd come back here? We
can even stop at the store and get the water and
stuff." She hardly dared breathe. "We don't have
to camp in the Wild Adventure campground. We
don't need no hookups. You could pull deep into
the woods. A flashlight is all we need. What do you
think, Cudge?" she asked anxiously. "But we better
get off the road now, before it gets dark." The little

boy will be able to find his way to the highway before the black night descends, she thought. "Take a look at the sky, looks like rain to me. If we're going to stop, we better do it now." Childishly she crossed her fingers, waiting for his answer. Make it the right answer, she pleaded silently. You're almost free, little boy, she said over and over in her mind.

Cudge risked a glance at Elva, then made up his mind. She was probably right, but he wouldn't give her the satisfaction of telling her so. Without thinking, he signaled a right turn and was off the road.

He had done what she wanted; now she would let the little boy out. Elva's teeth clamped together in relief.

"You're right, it's gonna rain pretty soon." Cudge frowned. "Elva, you notice anything, feel anything?"

Now what? "What's wrong?"

"Feels like we're limping, like maybe we're getting a flat. I'll have to check it out when we stop."

This couldn't be happening. All the tools were in the pop-up in a tool kit under the bunk. Cudge would crank it open and then it would be all over for her and the little boy. She tried for a light tone. "You're just uptight, Cudge. I don't think there's anything wrong."

"We'll know soon enough." He drove a little way beyond the campground to a general store. "I'll pull up around the back and take a look. Here's some money—you hobble in and get a few things. No gabbin', Elva."

The moment Cudge braked the pickup, Elva had the door open and was outside in the damp air, pretending to check the tires on her side. She moved toward the pop-up. "Little boy," she whispered, "whatever you do, don't make a sound."

Cudge bent down to inspect the tires on his side. "The rear tire's really low. Must have a slow leak. I'm gonna have to change it, but I think we can hold out till we make camp. Go get our stuff and make it snappy."

"Cudge, I gotta go to the bathroom real bad. You go in and get the stuff," she said, holding out the money.

"All right, but I ain't buying no Kool-Aid; goes against my grain to buy that crap." He watched her limp to the restroom.

When Elva was done, she opened the door and looked around the tiny parking area. Thank God he hadn't cranked open the camper. "Little boy, can you hear me? Say something. Are you all right? You ain't bleeding, are you? I been real worried."

"I'm okay. Let me out. When are you going to let me out?" Davey pleaded.

"I was going to do it now, but Cudge is watching me. We're going to stop real soon because it looks like it might rain. You gotta be ready to run real fast. I'm sorry I couldn't let you out before, but he was watching all the time. I couldn't take the chance. You just have to hang tight for a little longer. I'll get you out, I promise."

A promise. That was real, Davey thought. Something true that happened even when you thought it wouldn't. Like when Aunt Lorrie made a promise. "Okay, I can wait."

"I ain't gonna be able to run with you, but you'll be able to make it by yourself. I got a flashlight you can use. It's the best I can do. Shhh, he's coming now."

"Who the hell you talking to, Elva? I seen your mouth going a mile a minute from inside."

If it had worked once, it would work again. "I was singing to myself, like this," she said miming the words to an Elvis favorite. "I miss not hearing my music."

"Get in. I got eggs, bacon, instant coffee, bottled water, beer and some cupcakes. They had a special on Coke so I got two six-packs. Here's a can for you," he said generously. "I got us a little information. A quarter of a mile down the road there's a deserted quarry. What do you think?"

Deserted. Would the kid get lost, or hurt, trying to get away with only a flashlight to guide him? "Yeah, sounds good to me," she said. She hoped it wasn't too far off the road or the kid wouldn't be able to make it to the campground. "You don't want to be driving on dirt roads with that tire like that," she cautioned.

"I won't. Just till we're out of sight. Beats the shit out of me how we ended up back where we started. See those trees over there? That's the back of the Wild Adventure Park, and to the right of that is where old Lenny's planted. It's your fault, Elva. Somehow you screwed this all up. Everybody said that 1998 was a big year for assholes, but you carried over to '99."

There was no point in arguing with Cudge. The more he talked, the less time he had to think. She could listen to his harangue with one ear and still use her brain to figure something out for the little boy. God, where was it all going to end? Imagine returning to the same place they'd started out from. She knew in her gut that God was punishing her and Cudge. But the little boy shouldn't be punished. He hadn't done anything. Cudge wasn't going to hurt him, except over her dead body.

"Here we go—hold on now." Deftly, Cudge maneuvered the truck around potholes as big as craters. "Son-of-a-bitch!" he exploded as he swerved to avoid one yawning hole only to hit another. His head hit the roof of the truck and Elva bounced almost as high. "Goddammit! I think the tire blew." He shifted into neutral, opened the door and banged it shut. "Shit!"

"Did it blow?" Elva asked fearfully.

"Damn right it did. I don't even know if I can get this rig out of here. Slide over, Elva, and gun it. I'll push from here."

Elva did as she was told. The rig jockeyed back and forth and then was free.

"Okay, we're stopping right over there. There's room to back the pop-up under the trees. If it rains, we'll have some protection. I gotta put the spare on now before it gets too dark."

Elva was out of the pickup like a whirlwind. "Let me help you. Where's the spare, Cudge? And the toolbox? Just crank open the top and I'll get it for you."

"How come you're so helpful all of a sudden? You want to help, get me a beer and then shut up."

In her haste to pop open the beer can, Elva shook it and bubbles of foam shot up, soaking the front of her blouse. With shaking hands she held it out to Cudge, who grabbed it from her and consumed it in one swallow. "Gimme another and don't shake it this time."

He upended the second can, gulped down its contents in several noisy swallows, then tossed it into the brush. Before Elva knew what was happening, he had the spare tire off its rack on the rear of the pop-up. "If this ain't one hell of a mess," he said disgustedly. "I didn't get the spare fixed the last time."

Elva felt overwhelming relief. Now he wouldn't open the pop-up.

"I'm gonna have to unhitch the rig and try to make it into the nearest town to get the tire fixed. What time is it, Elva?"

She shrugged and looked at the sky. "Must be after five, at least."

"I suppose they roll up the sidewalks early, so I better get moving. I want some supper when I get back. That greasy hamburger wasn't fit to eat. Help me unhook the camper." Elva's hands were shaking so badly, she was next to useless. "Get out of here! You ain't no help at all. Okay, it's off. Now look, me and you, we gotta have a talk. I don't like the idea of leaving you here while I go into town, but I ain't got no other choice. This is my rig, see, and I gotta take care of it. It's all I got in the whole world—except for you, Elva. I want you to promise that you'll be here cooking supper when I get back. I shouldn't be gone more than an hour, two at the most."

She'd promise anything as long as he left. "Okay, Cudge. I'll be cooking supper when you get back. Where else can I go anyway? Don't worry, just get the tire fixed and get back here. You know I don't like the dark."

"First, I have to get my tool kit out the camper."

A drowning fear engulfed Elva. She couldn't let him open the pop-up, not now. "Cudge, if the garage man sees you with your own tool kit, he ain't gonna do nothin' for you. You know how those guys are.

He's gonna think you couldn't do it yourself, and you're only going to him as a last resort because you botched up the job. You don't like people making a fool out of you. You don't need it."

An ominous roll of thunder helped Cudge with his decision. He threw the spare tire into the back of the pickup and climbed behind the wheel.

Elva's tongue was so thick she could only nod in farewell. Miracles—they did really happen, and at the oddest times. Somehow she just knew that roll of thunder had come from God.

She limped down the road, watching till the pickup hit the highway, then hobbled back to the pop-up, grasping at low branches for support along the way.

"Little boy, I'm going to let you out now. Can you hear me?" she gasped. Not waiting for a reply, she yanked viciously at the crank and lifted the top. The worn, khaki canvas unfolded like a flower. "Where are you? It's so dark I can barely see you. Come on, little boy, I'll help you."

Davey wriggled out from his makeshift nest and slid down to the cardboard cartons. Elva quickly shoved them aside and reached for the boy. How wonderful he felt in her arms. He was okay. "You ain't bleeding, are you, little boy?" she demanded as she gathered him to her.

Davey let himself be hugged and petted. He liked it. He liked this girl who talked to him and told him not to be afraid. She was as scared as he was; he could tell by the way her arms were shaking, even if she was holding him tight. "No, I'm not bleeding. I told you, I get shots so I don't bleed. Can you call my aunt now and tell her to come and get me?" he asked hopefully.

"I ain't got no cell phone. All I can do is give you a flashlight and something to eat. We're real close to where your motor home was parked. You see those trees over there? That's where you were camped. And just over there is where Len—I mean, that's where we were parked. I think that if you go through the trees, you stand a better chance of finding the motor home than going to the highway. But you gotta get going. Cudge will be coming back pretty soon and I don't want him to find you here. I know it's scary in the dark. I hate the dark and don't like to be by myself, but you're gonna have to be brave. Do you think you can make it?"

She was hugging him so hard, Davey could barely breathe. With all his might, he pushed against her arms and gasped, "I think I can." When she put him down he asked, "What's your name? I have to know so I can tell my aunt how you helped me."

"Brenda. Brenda Kopec. C'mon now, we have to get you ready and on your way. Cudge will be back soon. Are you hungry?"

"Starved," Davey responded, with a weariness in his voice that made Elva clasp him to her again, squeezing and crooning softly. BJ's little face floated before her eyes. An acrid smell wafted into her nostrils. Dried urine. Poor kid. She thought about all the times BJ had wet his pants because he was scared. And the beatings, the constant beatings. As if a thrashing could make a little kid stop wetting his pants. Poor little BJ.

A quick glance at the sky told her the rain would arrive shortly. And then what? Could the kid find his way in the rain? It would be cold, and he'd get soaked in minutes. God, what if he started to bleed

in the rain? "Rain, rain, go away, come again some
other day," she crooned.

"Here we go, you sit down and eat. You gotta be
quick, BJ, and get away from here before Cudge
comes back." Elva's eyes were glazed and watery as
she watched the little boy wolf down the cupcakes
Cudge had just bought. Starved. BJ was always
starved. He could stuff himself one minute and be
looking for something else five minutes later. A
bottomless pit was what BJ was. A bottomless pit
who wet his pants when he was scared.

"Can I have something to drink?" Davey asked
as he licked at his fingers.

"I saved my Coke for you. Drink it all, I'm not
thirsty. It's kind of watery now because all the ice
melted." Davey gulped and gulped until the watery Coke was all gone. Carefully, Elva pulled at
the hem of her blouse and wiped at the cupcake
crumbs around his mouth. "There now, your
mouth is clean and no one will know you were
snacking."

Davey sat quietly on the step of the pop-up,
trusting the woman to help him. So what if she
called him BJ? Grown-ups made mistakes sometimes. Not all grown-ups; he corrected the thought
and sucked in his cheeks. His mother never made
mistakes. Thunder roared overhead and he flinched.
If you think a thing through to the end, you won't
make a mistake. That's what his mother always said.
Lightning danced across the sky, bathing Elva's
face in eerie yellow light. Davey flinched again.
Her eyes looked like Duffy's in the dark, all bright
and shiny.

He inched his way to the end of the step and
waited, his eyes on the trees. The woods were dark

and gloomy, like on the cartoons at Halloween. He wondered what time it was. When the lightning flashed he saw on his watch that it was close to six o'clock. Davey frowned.

Elva saw the little boy check the time. Jesus. She didn't remember him being so smart, and where did he get a watch? A stolen watch would only get him another beating. BJ wouldn't steal, though. Or would he? She looked around. It was darker now; she didn't have time to worry about where he'd got the watch.

Davey held out his hand. "It's raining, Brenda, what should we do?"

"Come on, get inside, and I'll light the lantern. I have to get you ready to go even if it is raining. I don't have an umbrella," she said fretfully. "I don't have a single thing that will keep you dry. I don't want you to get sick, BJ. You know there's no money for doctors."

"Aunt Lorrie is a doctor," Davey said helpfully. "If I can get to her, she'll take care of me."

"Sometimes you talk crazy, BJ. We don't have an Aunt Lorrie, just an Aunt Stella and an Aunt Helen. Don't you remember? There, the lantern is on. Isn't this cozy, BJ? Just me and you. I hate the dark as much as you hate the beatings. I think I'd rather have a beating than be locked in a dark closet with the rats and roaches."

Davey wondered if Brenda was making up a story so he wouldn't think about Aunt Lorrie. But he didn't want to be entertained. He just wanted to be out of here. He had to leave Brenda and the security of the pop-up, but first he had to get the flashlight she'd promised him. The one Mr. Sanders had given him was in his pocket, but he didn't think the light would be big enough to find a way through the trees.

Rain pounded the canvas roof. "It's raining hard, BJ. I don't think you should go out. Stay here with me. I hate the dark," Elva said, hugging her thin arms against her chest.

Davey felt confused. He didn't understand. "If I stay here with you, the man will catch me. I thought you wanted to help me get away."

It was Elva's turn to be confused. "BJ," she said patiently, "I'm supposed to take care of you, and I will. But you have to stay with me. I won't let anything happen to you. Not again. The last time it was all a mistake. I won't let that happen again."

"I want to go back to Aunt Lorrie. She's worried about me, I know she is. I want to go home." He had an idea. "You can come with me, Brenda."

"What time is it?" she demanded fearfully.

"The big hand is on the three and the little hand is on the six."

Elva screwed her pinched features into a frown. "Quarter after six. God, Cudge will be back here any minute now. You have to get out of here fast."

Davey didn't like the way Brenda's hands were shaking. He sighed. "I know. You said to go through the trees, right?"

"It's raining so hard. Let me think. The rain will slow Cudge down and he won't be able to see the holes in the road. Yes, through the trees. That way you won't pass him on the road. Will you be afraid to go through the woods?"

Davey thought about her question. The road and the bad man, or the woods and the rain and the dark. "No, but I need that flashlight you promised me."

A sob caught in Elva's throat. She couldn't let him go out alone in the dark and rain. God, she was tired, almost too tired to think. Where was Cudge? Probably in some bar. For a moment, the thought pleased her. If he was in a bar, he wouldn't be coming through the door any second now. The kid was safe, for the moment. If he were in a bar, he would start off with beer and switch to boilermakers, and from there anything that came in a bottle. He would be good for a couple of hours. She and BJ were safe, for now.

A deep bellow of thunder sounded above them. Elva shivered and drew Davey into her arms for comfort. Streak after streak of lightning skittered overhead, lighting the inside of the camper. Elva swallowed hard. She feared thunder and lightning almost as much as she feared the dark.

"We're going to sit quietly for a little while so I can think. I have to think about what's best for you. Do you understand that, BJ?"

Davey nodded and relaxed into the crook of her bony arm. He felt almost safe. Almost.

Nine

The sky was darkening, more from the threatening storm than from the oncoming night. The roads were almost deserted, even the main road that led back to the garage. The occasional car that passed was going in the opposite direction; the drivers intent on getting home for supper after a long day on the job.

Cudge stopped the pickup in the bay area of the garage. He was relieved to see a dim light shining through the door. Quickly he climbed out of the cab in search of the mechanic on duty.

"Hey, fellah," he said, trying for his most pleasant tone, "I've got a couple of tires what needs fixin'—could be I bent up the rim driving on a flat. I'm camped down the road and I left my wife there, havin' a fit because she's afraid of storms. I'll throw in a few extra bucks for you if you can fix it now."

"Ah, sure, why not? I was about to close up for the night, but a fellah can always use a few extra bucks. Keeps the wolves away from the door, if you know what I mean. It's gonna take me at least an hour." The tall, slim man wiped his grease-stained hands on the seat of his coveralls. "Why don't you go next door and have a beer? They got nude dancers in there for the afterwork crowd."

Cudge relaxed; the mechanic seemed more interested in the tire than in him. "Sounds good to me, I could use a cold beer." Sensing that the man expected him to make some remark about the dancers, he added, "I haven't seen a good set of tits in a long time."

"Ain't it the truth," the mechanic said, grinning. "I thought my wife had a good pair when I married her. You should see them now—two lemons and all nipple. Hell, it don't hurt to look, so I go in every so often and get my fill. Ain't nothin' wrong in lookin', I always say."

Cudge followed the man out to the pickup, where he retrieved the tire. Lowering his voice and looking over his shoulder, the man continued, "There's one little gal in there that's a piece of work. I ain't never been with her, but I heard about her. Calls herself Candy Striper and she's got knockers on her that'll knock your eyes out. You can watch her dance and dream a little."

"Sounds like a waste of good beer to me," Cudge grunted. Everywhere you looked there were perverts. "You said an hour, right?"

"More or less. When I'm done, I'll throw the spare back in your truck. But you'll have to pay up now, 'cause I'll be leaving soon as I'm done with your job."

Cudge handed over the money, with some extra as promised. He walked across the gravel-topped parking area surrounding the bar. A weather-worn sign beneath the orange neon proclaimed BEER— SNOOKIE'S. The thrum of music blared as some-one opened the door to leave. Cudge had been in bars like this before; the place smelled of beer and cigarettes, and sawdust littered the floor. There was a crowd at the curving bar but he spotted an empty stool.

Resting his elbows on the bar, he ordered a draft. He glanced around at the people; the place was packed. He grinned, thinking of what the me-chanic had said about his wife's breasts. Hell, any-thing was better than Elva's—her hard little breasts reminded him of overgrown walnuts, and you had to look to find the nipple.

Tinny music pounded as two scantily costumed girls mounted a step-stool to get up to the beer-splattered bar. Cudge stared at their jiggling bod-ies but his thoughts were a million miles away. Well, a few, anyway. On Lenny. On Elva. On the blabber-mouthed kid. On how he was going to get out of this mess he'd gotten himself into. He knew he had to think of a plan. Naked bosoms and gy-rating pelvises would have to wait for another day. It was getting late. Time for another beer and then he had to hit the road.

The music ended just as the bartender slid Cudge's beer down the length of the bar. Cudge took a long swallow and looked around. He hated dumps like this. Someday he was going to get all duded up and strut into a first-class cocktail lounge and drink champagne. He'd have a pearl-gray Lincoln Town Car, like undertakers drove, and a cigar clamped in his mouth. Cigars always added a touch of class, especially if they were

Havana cigars. He'd go to Canada to get them if he had to. He shook his head at his fantasy. This bar was his speed, and he'd never move on. The lousy cops would be on his tail anytime now. No point in fooling anyone, least of all himself. He had to get rid of Elva before dawn and travel light. Even if it meant ditching the pop-up and coming back for it later. He was shaken from his thoughts by a sweat-soaked man beside him calling out, "C'mon, Candy, show an old man how it's done."

"And after I turn you on, what am I going to do with you?" the second girl from the end shouted over the music.

"The same thing you did last week, baby. I got thirty bucks if you're interested."

The girl laughed and swayed her hips and cupped her breasts, making them stand erect. Cudge's interest peaked. He nudged the guy sitting next to him. "You got into her?" he demanded.

The man stared at Cudge. "She'll take on anything, mister, as long as you got thirty bucks. She locks in on thirty for some reason. Not a penny less. She likes two tens, a five, and five ones. Anything else is a problem for her." His round brown eyes stared at Cudge. "She gives you your money's worth, too. You interested?"

"Not if I have to pay for it," Cudge snorted. The day he'd pay a hooker would be the day he tied his cock in a knot.

"You're in the wrong place then, buddy. Candy don't hand out no freebies. She's putting her baby brother through medical school."

My ass she is, Cudge thought to himself.

"She likes her money up front too. You can't get around old Candy—she's a businesswoman."

Cudge took a better look at the prancing woman on the bar. "Old Candy" was right, but for looks she wasn't half bad. Better than scrawny Elva, at any rate. He'd been to bed with a bag of bones for so long, he'd almost forgotten how nice it was to be cushioned between a pair of thighs that had some meat on them. Her belly was slightly rounded and fleshy; it jiggled as she danced. Nice to slap his own belly into, he thought, feeling a sensation of life in his loins.

Thirty bucks. That's what she wanted. A dollar for each year of her age. Still, she did have a nice smile. Friendly. There hadn't been too many friendly people in his life lately, God knew. And her legs were long. Real long. Long enough to wrap around a man when he was . . . Cudge laughed at himself then, a dry, humorless laugh that made the man beside him turn to stare. What did he care?

Candy's bright smile took in everyone at the bar. Her skin was white, pale white, almost translucent under the blue-tinted lights. Again Cudge felt that stirring below his belt as she gyrated, her breasts bouncing. A long time ago, he'd seen one of the old-fashioned burlesque shows. The stripper had worn tassels on her breasts and could make them twirl in different directions at the same time. He bet Candy could do that; he'd love to watch her try.

"You got thirty bucks?" he asked the sweating man next to him.

"Right here," the man said, slapping the bills on the bar.

"You a gambling man?"

"In a manner of speaking."

"I got thirty bucks that says I can get Candy to

leave here with me with no cash up front. A freebie. You want to cover the bet or not?"

"You're on, man. I've known Candy a long time,
and she don't give it away."

"Hey, Candy, come on over here," Cudge shouted.

Candy Striper stared down the length of the bar.
A new dude. Looked loaded. Been a while since
she'd lain with someone she didn't know. What
the hell. His thirty bucks was just as good as anybody's. She didn't like his eyes though. Pig eyes.
And he had tattoos. She didn't like tattoos either.
Candy weaved her way among the bar glasses till
she was standing in front of the man. She squatted
down so he could whisper in her ear.

She laughed delightedly. "You putting me on?"

Cudge shook his head. "Tell my sweaty friend
here that you're coming with me and you're givin'
me a freebie."

"You heard the man," Candy told Cudge's neigh-
bor, who was watching her with a shocked expression.

Cudge scooped up the money and put it in his
shirt pocket. When you were on the run, thirty
bucks could be the means to an end. "C'mon, let's
go."

"Not so fast. I got a job to do here."

"Yeah, well, forget it," he answered. "I can't wait
around all night."

"Listen, I got a break coming after the next set.
Twenty minutes at the most and then I'm all yours.
Have another beer and watch me dance while I
warm things up for you."

Cudge almost told her to forget it, but the
promise in her eyes stopped him. And what was
waiting for him back at the pop-up? Elva? Skinny,

scared Elva. She would be there when he got back, cowering inside the pop-up, cheeks streaked with tears, body shaking with every clap of the storm.

"Okay, do your thing, baby," he told her, assuming his most debonair manner. "You ain't got nothin' I can't wait for."

A half hour later they left the bar. Outside, in the wind and rain, he looked at Candy. "How far do you live from here?"

"Behind the bar. This dump used to be a motel and those little one-room cottages are still out back. Were you serious about Las Vegas? I never been outside this town, much less to Las Vegas. Do you really know show people there who can get me a job on the stage? When are we leaving?"

"Right after you give me your freebie."

"Man, you can have all the freebies you want if you take me to Las Vegas. On the hour if you want. I gotta be honest with you though. I got this little problem. I don't mind giving if you don't mind getting."

"What the hell?" Then it dawned on him what she'd said. He had a condom in his wallet that he'd been carrying around for just such an emergency. He wasn't "getting" anything he didn't bargain for. "No problem."

"Where's your motor home? I like those things—all the comforts of home. You don't look like a rich promoter."

"Now, did you ever see a rich promoter?" Cudge demanded as he hustled her around the side of the bar. "I parked it behind the garage. This looks like the kind of neighborhood that means trouble."

"You scared me there for a minute. I thought

that pile of junk over there was yours. I wouldn't be caught dead riding in something like that." She motioned to his Chevy pickup, which was parked in front of the garage bay.

Cudge's eyes narrowed. "Wouldn't you now? Probably belongs to some hard-working slob who's sitting in that bar watching you gals toss your tits around."

Concentrating on keeping her balance on the gravel in her incredibly high heels, Candy led him toward the cottage nearest the road. A slat-ribbed dog near the door growled to show he resented their intrusion. Cudge watched the dog while Candy dug in her purse for the keys, clutching the edges of the sweater she had thrown over her shoulders to hide her nakedness.

"Don't let the dog bother you, honey. Just like the rest of us, he's only looking for a good meal." The door swung open and she reached inside for the light switch. "'Course, things are different out in Las Vegas. Nobody, but nobody, goes hungry out there. Say, how long did you say it would take to get there?"

"I didn't," Cudge answered, his voice harsh. He didn't like answering questions, especially ones that challenged his lies. Besides, if she was dumb enough to think she was good enough for Las Vegas, she deserved anything she got.

"Here it is, home sweet home. Should I pack first or do you want to ball? Don't make no difference to me."

"You got any alcohol around here?"

"Wine. A whole gallon. You want some?"

"Get it out, I feel like getting drunk. The guy sit-

ting next to me at the bar said you'd take on anything for thirty bucks. Is that right?"

"Thirty bucks is thirty bucks. I just close my
eyes."

"How come you sell yourself so cheap?"

"I really need the money. I'm putting my kid
brother through medical school," Candy said, un-
corking the jug of wine.

"You need a better story than that one."

"I'm not putting you on. My kid brother, Jackie,
is going to be an orthopedic surgeon someday. If
you get me a job on the line in Las Vegas, I can
send him more money. He's having a real tough
time. Do you know, just one medical book costs
seventy-five dollars, sometimes more! Here," she
handed Cudge a full glass of wine. "I think I'll have
some myself to get in the mood." She poured herself a glass, then took a sip. "So, how do you like it,
anyway?"

"The wine? It's vinegary."

"No, not the wine. Sex. How do you like your
sex? I don't want you to be afraid to tell me what
you want."

"What—are you kiddin'? Afraid? Me?" Cudge
laughed until his eyes started to water. When he'd
settled down, he glanced around the room. This
dump was no better than that furnished apartment he'd left in Newark. The iron bed in the corner looked like George Washington could have
slept in it, and the sheets probably hadn't been
changed since.

There was a Panasonic radio-CD player on the
table. Candy's brightly polished fingernail pressed
the "on" button and Kenny Rogers started to sing

"Lady." Candy casually shrugged her sweater off her shoulders. She always enjoyed watching the really cool-acting guys get excited when they got her alone. But something about the way this one was looking at her with those pig eyes of his worried her. Suddenly she realized that she'd been a gullible fool, and that he was nothing but a drifter with a silver tongue. He was no more a big promoter than she was Miss America. Still, a girl had to have hope, and working in a dump like Snookie's turned those hopes to needs.

"You were fibbing to me about Las Vegas, weren't you?" she asked, hearing the quake in her voice. The guy's eyes widened, then narrowed, and his expression turned evil. Candy decided she definitely should have stuck with the men who frequented Snookie's. There wasn't one who would go out of his way to do anything for her, but none of them scared her. She had to get out of here, away from this man.

"What's the matter with you?" Cudge asked. "You always get jumpy when it's time to hit the sack?" His voice was almost genial and Candy thought it must be a trick of the light making his pig eyes glitter and emphasizing the grim lines around his mouth.

Forcing herself to relax, she leaned over to undo the tiny straps on her shoes.

"No, leave them on. They make your legs look nice and long."

Now this was the kind of talk she was used to hearing from her customers. So what if he was a little kinky? She had a steady who liked to cross-dress. And even if he didn't take her to Vegas, there was still the thirty bucks.

* * *

Stuart Sanders lost no time once the plane touched down. He ran the length of the seemingly endless concourse; having no patience for the escalator, he bounded down the steps two at a time and elbowed his way through the milling travelers in search of the car that would be waiting for him.

Mac Feeley was waiting behind the wheel, cigar clamped in his mouth. He reached over to open the door for Sanders. "How goes it, big guy?"

"You don't want to know," Sanders replied in way of greeting. "Let's move it. Take the turnpike. Is this one of those souped-up jobs the motor pool hands out to speed demons like you?"

Feeley grinned. "This little number is slick—it starts out at ninety and works up to one eighty. You think you're flying. Five bucks says I get you there in thirty minutes."

"Is that with or without the siren?" Sanders asked irritably.

"Either or, you name it."

"I'd hate like hell to get pulled over and lose time."

"No way. This car has official government plates with the right code numbers, and I guess you didn't see the State seal on the door. You look done in. You hear anything? How did things go?"

"Nothing on my end. Mrs. Taylor elected to stay behind with her husband. She said she trusts me and the others to find her son."

Feeley switched the cigar from one side of his mouth to the other. "There's a lot to be said for motherly love." His voice was sour.

"What's new here? Any leads? How's the aunt

handling things? What's the latest on the guy with the painted truck? How did the old couple check out?"

"Dr. Ryan is worried but she's holding on. We tracked the older couple down in Virginia and asked a few questions, but it was a dead end. The local police think they have a few leads, but they aren't ones for sharing—they think this is their baby all the way down. Our guys had to pull badges to remind them who's in charge—what can I tell you? From here on out it's going to be legwork."

"What's your hunch, Feeley?"

"I'd like to know more about the body they found. Coroner's making his report in the morning, but it's pretty certain the stiff was beaten to death. Nasty head wounds. Leonard Lombardi, twenty-eight or so, lived in Newark. Putting the pieces together, we believe he was already dead when he was brought to the campground. Best lead we've got is a guy named Edmund Balog, aka Cudge Balog. Everything is pointing in his direction, right down to a report from a trooper who stopped him on the road. Said he was real nervous about opening the pop-up rig he was dragging. Emergency called the trooper away so he never got a look inside."

"Any connection with the syndicate, you think?"

"Haven't found any so far. And there's been no ransom demand. My thought is that the kid saw something he wasn't supposed to. Other than that . . ." Feeley shrugged ". . . your guess is as good as mine."

Sanders nodded. "I let this one get under my skin as far back as house duty in Montclair. I feel responsible, somehow. Did Dr. Ryan tell you Davey is a hemophiliac? He has to have a shot every day, regular as clockwork, to keep it under control."

"Yes. I know that if he misses his shots there's no telling if the drug will work for him anymore."

"Right. It's sort of an internal sabotage, his own body rejecting the drug that would keep him from bleeding to death. How many has he missed so far?"

"According to Dr. Ryan, only one—at twelve noon today. It's been over thirty hours since his last injection. Dr. Ryan has been on the phone with a specialist. No one knows how fast those antibodies in the kid's body will develop. Their best guess is that at forty-eight hours it starts getting critical. By the way, we have a code name for radio contact. Transmissions relating to this case are called in to Panda Bear."

Sanders laughed and shook his head. "That's the handle Davey uses in the CB club he belongs to."

"Yeah, we know. Dr. Ryan told us." Feeley bit down hard on his cigar. Everyone knew Sanders's feelings about kids, especially his sister's. Kids were okay, in their place, Feeley thought, but he didn't want any of his own. Not now, anyway. As if he had a choice, he laughed wryly to himself. His first and only marriage had come and gone before he'd realized what was happening. He hadn't been a bad husband, but he hadn't been a good one either.

"I thought you said you were going to get us there in thirty minutes."

Feeley looked at his watch. "You want to quibble about one minute and ten seconds, go right ahead."

As soon as the car stopped, Sanders grunted and climbed out. Why spoil Feeley's day, or night? "Who's in charge?"

"You are, now that you're here. You're senior officer. The local police will bow and kiss your hand, if you play your cards right. We've a temporary office set up behind the manager's office."

Sanders grunted again as he made his way to the camp store's grimy office. The fresh pungent scent of pine was everywhere. The smell reminded him of the air freshener the cleaning crew used in his own office. The autumn leaves heralded a new season that would soon give way to sharp, cold winds and, he hoped, snow. He liked snow, didn't even mind driving in it. Hell, he liked life and everything it had to offer. He felt a chill and stopped mid stride. "What do you think the chances are for a frost tonight?"

Feeley worked at the cigar in his mouth. He remembered Dr. Ryan saying that Davey was wearing a light windbreaker. A little kid could freeze, especially one in his condition. And the forecasts were predicting rain for tonight, possibly thunderstorms. "Jesus, I'm no goddamn weatherman. Fifty–fifty would be my guess."

Inside the storeroom, Feeley lounged against stacked cartons of cereal. He looked around at the boxes of merchandise that would eventually fill the camp-store shelves. Beans, Spam, instant coffee; he grimaced. His tastes ran to prime rib, baked potato, garden salad, fresh vegetables. Key lime or pecan pie for dessert. He looked around again to see what the storeroom held in the way of dessert. A meal wasn't a meal without dessert. He snorted as he removed the mangled cigar from his mouth. He should

have known—canned fruit cocktail. He trampled
the ruined cigar underfoot and put a fresh one in
his mouth. Sanders was shaking hands with the
local police. Feeley dexterously bit off the end of
the cigar. A butane lighter snapped to life, almost
singeing his thick eyebrows. He paid it no mind.
Black, evil-smelling smoke circled and spiraled
around his head. If nothing else, it would stop the
locals getting in his face and expounding their
theories, which, in his eyes, weren't theories at all,
but assumptions that any first-week rookie cop
could make.

"You've got a dead body with positive identification," Sanders said. "That's good. I have a missing
kid who's a hemophiliac. It seems to me you've
been doing a hell of a lot of work on a case that
should be cut and dried by now. It beats the hell
out of me how you haven't managed to pick up
that psychedelic truck and pop-up."

Eyebrows raised, jaws clenched and lips thinned
as Sanders drove home his point to the group of
policemen. "Good police instinct should have told
you that the boy is mixed up in this somehow. Your
all-points bulletin is worthless. And sitting around
waiting is pointless. We have to get moving. Now!"
He looked at each in turn and wondered if he'd
ever been so naive. "Okay, listen up. I'm the chief
and you're the Indians. You got it? If not, I have a
badge saying that's the way it goes."

Feeley blew another cloud of smoke in Sanders's
direction. He grinned to himself. Old war horses
could take charge quickly when they wanted to.

"Feeley," Sanders called over his shoulder, "see
that this picture is in every morning paper in the
area. Start with the *Asbury Park Press*. Don't let

them give you any crap about it being a color Polaroid shot either. If they even think about giving you trouble with the deadline, tell them you know the paper isn't put to bed till ten, and then there's a two-hour grace period. Call ahead if you want. Just get it done."

Sanders issued his remaining orders grimly. He believed that Davey was somewhere near the park. The moment the others cleared out, he spoke to Feeley across the makeshift table.

"If you're asking me what I think professionally, I have to say that I go along with the department. If you're asking me what I think off the record, I think the kid saw something and was picked up. He could be anywhere; he could be dead."

"What's he like—the kid, I mean?" Feeley asked curiously.

"He's got a lot of savvy, if you know what I mean. He's been through a rough time, and he's just now coming into his own. I know some adults who couldn't take the medical treatment this kid has been through. Do you think you could stand being transfused through your jugular vein? No? That kid has, many times. I'll tell you who he looks like. You ever see that airline commercial where the kid gets a pair of wings from the flight captain and then says, 'Oooh, thank you, Captain'? Well, he looks just like him. I'm sure there are thousands of kids who look like that, but Davey Taylor is special. Very special. I'm going over to the aunt's campsite now. Which way is it?" Talking about Davey made Sanders's stomach churn.

"Take the main road and follow it to the fork, then bear left. It's the only RV in sight."

Just as Sanders stepped outside, Lorrie Ryan

walked up. Sanders saw a woman who was stripped-down, naked with hurt. Nobody deserved to go through what she was going through.

"Stuart—I mean, Mr. Sanders—when did you get here? Where's Sara? Do you have word of Davey, is that why you're here?" Lorrie clasped her hands together and stared at him with wide, frightened eyes.

"Hey!" he said, taking her firmly by the shoulder. "Slow down." He tried to quiet her with his own calmness. "There's no word yet. And your sister—well, she elected to stay behind with Mr. Taylor." How bitter the words sounded.

"She what?" Lorrie looked incredulous.

Sanders tried to make his voice sound neutral, feeling that his own judgment would only serve to aggravate the situation. Christ, maybe he was getting too old for fieldwork. A desk job, that was what he needed. He repeated his carefully chosen words. "Mrs. Taylor elected to stay behind."

"Just what the hell does that mean?" Lorrie burst out.

Sanders kept control of his voice. "Mr. Taylor took the stand for thirty minutes today."

"What the hell does that have to do with Sara and Davey? She's the kid's mother! You did tell her what happened, didn't you?"

Sanders looked straight into her eyes. "Of course, I did, but . . ."

Lorrie clutched at Sanders's forearm and spoke softly. "I can't believe she would stay there. She has to be worried sick—how could she stay behind? Is there something you aren't telling me, something I should know?"

Sanders shook his head. He was truly at a loss

for words to explain Sara's behavior. "Your sister, Mrs. Taylor, she said she trusted me to handle the matter." He paused to let his words sink in. "Both Mr. and Mrs. Taylor believed that Davey . . . that he's simply wandered off and will find his way back." Should he volunteer the rest or be quiet? If he was going by the book, he'd keep his mouth shut, but he hadn't worked by the book in a long time. "Mr. Taylor was a very convincing witness today. It was unfortunate that the court adjourned at such an early hour or it could have been wrapped up and they both could have come."

Lorrie's eyes flashed with anger. "So, Sara's little Andrew made a good showing for himself under Mommy's watchful eye, did he?" She laughed with disgust. "Of course, you know she didn't come back to Jersey with you because she's afraid he'll screw up without her there to protect him. And if he screws up—well, let's just say she would feel that he had disgraced her. And God forbid that should happen. She's disgusting!"

Sanders sighed deeply.

"Poor Davey. He always comes last." Lorrie flung herself against the agent's chest and clung to him.

Sanders wrapped his arms around her and rested his chin on the top of her head. He'd wanted to hold her like this since the first time he'd seen her, but he would have preferred their first embrace to be under more pleasant circumstances. "Some people just have their priorities screwed up," he said, brushing her temple with his lips.

"Don't make up excuses for her. There is *no* excuse for her not coming here. None, and you know it, don't you?" She leaned back in his arms and looked up at him, waiting for him to answer.

If he hadn't known before, Sanders knew now that he was too close to this case. His emotions were involved. For an FBI agent, that was a cardinal sin.

"Lorrie," he began, not sure what he was going to say. "I . . ."

Lorrie glared at him, challenging him to answer, to be truthful with her. "Tell me I'm wrong, Stuart. Tell me there's a better reason for her to stay with Andrew than for her to come here."

"It's not for me to say, Lorrie."

With a pained expression, Lorrie glanced away. "You're right. It isn't. I'm sorry. I shouldn't have tried to involve you in our family's matters."

He smiled down at her. "I understand. You're upset."

Regretfully, Lorrie eased herself out of his arms. "Yes, I'm upset. But I'm sick and tired of Davey taking a backseat. He should be in the front seat all the time. Especially with his medical problems and—" She broke off, shaking her head.

"Why don't we walk back to your campsite? I could use a cup of coffee."

"Excuse me, sir." A young officer was heading towards Sanders.

"Yeah, what is it?"

"Phone call for Dr. Ryan." The cop held up Lorrie's cell phone. "You left it on the table outside your motor home. I thought you'd probably want someone to answer it," he said, handing it to her.

"Who is it?" she asked.

"Mrs. Taylor. From Miami."

Sanders watched as Lorrie seemed to shrink into herself. His voice was protective when he spoke. "Why don't you let me take the call? I can tell her you're trying to take a nap or . . ."

She smiled up at him. "Thanks, but that's the easy way. I'll talk to her."

Sanders watched her walk away. "I don't envy her that conversation," he said to Feeley, who had walked up behind him. "Sara Taylor is like a barracuda and Lorrie's a guppy in comparison."

"I don't know about Mrs. Taylor," Feeley said, "but I think you're wrong about Dr. Ryan. She'll handle the call."

Sanders nodded morosely.

Lorrie walked slowly in the direction of the motor home. "Is that you, Sara?" she asked calmly. She refused to permit Sara to rattle her.

"Yes, this is Sara, Lorrie. How could you have allowed my son to wander off? I trusted you. Andrew and I just can't believe you allowed this to happen. It's unforgivable. Well, has he returned yet?"

"No, Sara, he hasn't come back to camp yet. The police are still searching for him. Mr. Sanders arrived a short while ago. I don't think he's 'wandered off' as you put it. We all think it's more serious than a little boy lost in the woods. I'm not sure if you know it or not, but the police found a dead body near where Davey was playing. We're not sure if Davey saw or overheard something. We're doing everything we can. I'm sorry, Sara. I take full responsibility." Lorrie kept her voice firm and controlled.

"That's absurd. What could Davey possibly have to do with a dead body? You're grasping at straws, Lorrie, to cover your own ineffectiveness. There won't be a next time, I assure you. Andrew and I both feel Davey's wandered off. Andrew admitted that he used to do the same thing when he was a child. Like father, like son. I want you to call me the minute Davey gets back, no matter what time of the day or night it is." Her voice was frigid, bordering on open hostility. "I suppose if there's anything we can be grateful for in this . . . this outing you insisted on, it's that Davey's had his shot."

Lorrie swallowed hard. Evidently Sara didn't know Davey had been missing since early morning. "Davey missed his shot. He wandered off shortly after breakfast. I thought you knew," Lorrie said, gripping the phone tighter.

"Oh, for God's sake, Lorrie. What have you done?"

Lorrie's control snapped. "Why aren't you here, Sara? Why didn't you come with Mr. Sanders? Your place is here where Davey—"

"How dare you tell me where my place is! I'm here seeing to something very important and I trusted my son to *you*. The only reason you want me there is so I can make everything right for you, the way I did when we were children. You never did anything right, Lorrie. I was always the one who had to pull your chestnuts out of the fire and get you out of one scrape after another. Not this time. You, and you alone, are responsible for my son. I don't want to hear another word from you until you call me and tell me Davey is safe. Do you understand me, Lorrie?"

Lorrie felt goose bumps on her arms, not from the cold but from Sara's icy voice. *Hang up*, her mind shrieked. *Don't pay attention to what Sara's saying*. Sara was changing everything around, just like she always had. It was always Sara who began the arguments, not her. Yet she, Lorrie, had always ended up paying the piper. *Ignore her. She's upset. Don't say another word.*

"Lorrie, are you there? Answer me."

"I'm here, Sara. I was thinking about some-thing." It took every ounce of willpower she pos-sessed to square her shoulders. "I always tried to like you because you were my sister, but I don't like you, Sara. I didn't like you when we were children, and I don't like you now that we're adults. I love Davey—you know that. I won't bore you with what I've gone through today. There's no way you could possibly understand. Just because you're Davey's biological parent doesn't mean you love him more—or even as much—as I do. If you did, you'd be here. I don't have anything else to say, so I'm going to hang up. If I hear anything I'll let you know." Lorrie pressed the button to end the call. Damn Sara to hell.

"Are you all right?" Stuart Sanders moved around in front of Lorrie. He'd been right behind her while she was talking to her sister, not eaves-dropping, just waiting. He'd wanted to be there for her if Sara Taylor said something to send her over the edge.

When Lorrie turned around, he saw that her eyes were glistening with tears. "I'm okay," she said, her words belying her expression.

"Yeah, sure you are." He put his arm around her shoulders and led her toward the motor home.

Ten

The phone was still in Sara's hand when Andrew admitted Roman DeLuca into the hotel suite. Her conversation with Lorrie had not been satisfying, and it rankled that Lorrie had hung up on her. But Sara schooled her face to impassivity before facing the prosecuting attorney. Everything about him annoyed her. He was as bogus as a three-dollar bill, and he capitalized on his movie-star good looks, right from his meticulously clipped gray hair to the tips of his manicured fingers. A snakeskin briefcase matched his shoes and belt, and his dove-gray suit and sparkling white shirt were custom-tailored to his slim body in an expensive salute to his vanity.

Andrew had scoffed when she'd told him that she thought the impeccable attorney had his eye on the governor's seat. But Sara knew she was right, and Roman DeLuca seemed to read her thoughts. It didn't upset him, and somehow his reaction added to Sara's dislike.

"Mrs. Taylor," DeLuca said quietly. Sara nodded slightly in response. The phone receiver was still clutched in her hand. Was he wrong, or was there a glimmer of self-righteousness in her eyes? "Were you about to make a phone call, Mrs. Taylor?" he asked.

Sara glanced down at the phone. "Oh, no, as a matter of fact, I've just completed one. To my sister in New Jersey." Damn, now why had she needed to explain?

DeLuca noticed the stiffening of her shoulders; he had been right about the self-righteous glimmer. Sara Taylor must have just finished berating her sister, blaming her for the boy's disappearance. He wished he had arrived just a moment earlier to hear Sara's end of the conversation for himself. He would have liked to see her in action.

"Andrew, we must talk." DeLuca seated himself near the window, careful of the creases in his slacks. "Don't be alarmed. I want to congratulate you on your fine performance on the stand this afternoon. There's only one point that's annoying me." He looked up at Andrew from beneath his dark, bushy brows. "It's the way you look for approval from your wife before you answer a question." At Andrew's confused look, DeLuca continued. "Obviously you didn't realize that every time I asked you a question about what you'd witnessed, or your acquaintance with Jason Forbes, you looked to your wife before you answered. You almost never took your eyes off her. I even attempted to block your line of vision but, when I did, you started to get rattled and acted unsure of yourself and your statements. Rather than make you appear a fool, I allowed the visual contact between yourself and Mrs. Taylor."

Andrew was stunned. He knew he hadn't been a star witness, but he hadn't thought he'd done badly. And Sara had told him how wonderfully he'd performed on the witness stand.

"If the judge had let the defense attorney begin his cross-examination, you'd be on the scrap heap by now, my friend. The judge adjourned as a favor to me when he saw how perturbed I was by your attention to your wife."

"I'm sorry. I didn't realize . . ."

"Let's just hope the jury didn't notice. If they did, it may jeopardize our case."

"I don't know what to say."

"Say you won't do it tomorrow. Because if you do, I'll be forced to ask Mrs. Taylor to leave the courtroom. Do you understand what I'm saying?"

"Of course he understands, Mr. DeLuca. He's not a child," Sara snapped. "It was your own inept questioning technique that rattled Andrew."

Roman DeLuca's eyes narrowed to bits of chipped ice. "You should know, my dear, what makes your husband tick. I say he behaved like a sophomore, and so does the judge. Instead of giving me his undivided attention, he gave it to you. Why don't you ask him why?"

"I don't have to ask Andrew why. I was there. I saw what went on. You could have put Andrew on the stand earlier, but you didn't. Why? You deliberately waited till the end of the day before making your move. I want to know why, Mr. DeLuca," Sara said coldly. "I want to know now."

DeLuca smiled wryly. He didn't like Sara Taylor. Despite being sapling thin she had a ramrod strength. He possessed similar traits, but in Sara Taylor he detested them.

"Strategy, Mrs. Taylor. I don't exactly understand what you're accusing me of, and I don't believe you do either. I think you're just trying to turn the question I'm asking away from you." He gave a sly smile that he knew would irritate her. "For the sake of argument, let's just put it down to your desire to protect your husband. I'm merely making the point that a witness who continually directs the jury's attention away from his testimony is of little or no use. I know that Mr. Taylor's looking to you is merely a loving habit, but it's one that could lose this case for the State, and I won't have it." His tone was smooth, and he waited for the Taylors to digest what he had said before continuing. "Tomorrow is another day, Mr. Taylor . . . or didn't you say I should call you Andrew? Andrew, I'm here tonight to go over your testimony with you. I've studied your written deposition, and I think we'll work directly from that. If we can get it all together, you should be unwavering in the face of cross-examination." DeLuca smiled.

He's like a snake, Sara thought. She disliked DeLuca intensely, almost hated him. "You're very confident for a man who was so angry a moment ago," she remarked.

DeLuca's voice was urbane now, charming and suave. "Mrs. Taylor, what you mistook for anger was concern for Andrew, and yourself. As they would say back in New York, this is my turf and I know every blade of grass. I always win, Mrs. Taylor, remember that."

Sara's eyes narrowed. It sounded like a threat, or was it a warning? How dare the man? How dare he!

Andrew intervened. "Sara, before we go over my

testimony, why don't you show Mr. DeLuca the message that was delivered before dinner?"

Sara gathered her indignation close about her and walked stiffly over to the desk. She picked up the square of white paper and held it out, eyes cold and hard.

DeLuca scanned the message. "Well, who was it and what did they want?" he asked, listening closely for her answer.

"We didn't call the number. We waited to show it to you," Sara said. God, how she detested this phony movie-star lawyer.

"Let me understand something, Mrs. Taylor. You say this message was delivered *before* dinner, which, I assume, was between six and seven. Am I right?" At Andrew's nod he continued. "It's nine forty-five now," he said, teeth clenched. "Didn't it occur to either of you that this might be a message concerning your son who is missing, possibly kidnapped?" DeLuca glanced between the Taylors. Andrew looked horrified; Sara looked . . . Damn, nothing got to her. Nothing. He watched her carefully, almost admiring the way she took in his statement and managed to appear unruffled. Was it possible she didn't make the connection? He opened his mouth to drive it home. "Mrs. Taylor, I feel it my duty to tell you there's a possibility that someone associated with the drug syndicate we're prosecuting may have kidnapped your son." For one instant Sara appeared to be taken aback. But the heavy intake of breath belonged to Andrew, who sank down onto a chair. "You must believe I care about your son," DeLuca added in his most sober tone.

Sara was the first to rally. "Your concern is most

appreciated, Mr. DeLuca, but neither Andrew nor I owe you any explanations concerning our son or our private life. Experts, Mr. DeLuca, are handling matters back in New Jersey," she said stiffly, not liking the look in Andrew's eyes. "Andrew is here to do a job, and I'm here because I choose to be here. Do we understand each other? There's nothing in this case to suggest kidnapping. Davey has merely wandered off." Sara hadn't told Andrew about the corpse that had been discovered near where Davey had been playing. And she wasn't about to tell him now, not with DeLuca standing there ready to spring on her like a cat.

"But, of course, my dear. I understand everything you've done and said since our first meeting. I was merely thinking of you and your family. However, I must warn you—if the media gets hold of this . . . Why, I can't be responsible. They tend to start off with the term 'unfit mother' and from there it's usually a quick slide to a 'philandering, alcoholic husband.' I'm not saying any of it's true, or that I condone it—I'm just pointing out the possibilities to you. If my information is correct, Mrs. Taylor, Mr. Sanders urged you to take the next plane home. I would second that. Your husband, believe it or not, is perfectly capable of speaking for himself."

Sara was visibly shaken but she recovered quickly. She grabbed the message out of DeLuca's hand, picked up the phone and dialed for an outside line. Seconds later she replaced the phone and turned to face the two men. Her voice, when she spoke, was neutral. "It was a recording. Some insane person says he has our son and, if Andrew testifies, we'll never see Davey again. Obviously, this person is demented. Davey has just wandered off and is temporarily lost. If it was anything more serious, my sister would have told me. There *are* some people, Mr. DeLuca, who enjoy trying to make other people miserable. In spite of your seconding Mr. Sanders's suggestion, I'm standing by my decision to stay with Andrew. My son's escapade is in capable hands."

"Is that what you call it? An escapade?" Roman DeLuca questioned, his tone rising with disbelief. What a cold bitch she was.

"In my opinion, Mr. DeLuca, this matter is closed. Andrew, what's your feeling?"

Andrew looked from his wife to the attorney. "I quite agree, Sara. Why don't we get down to business, Mr. DeLuca? It's after ten now, and we have an early day in court tomorrow."

"Can I order something for either of you from room service?" Sara asked as if nothing had happened. Both men shook their heads. "Well, then, I think I'll leave you alone." Regally, she left the sitting room to go into the bedroom.

It was twelve forty-five when Andrew tapped on the door. "Mr. DeLuca is leaving now, darling."

"One moment, dear," Sara said, retying the sash of her peach-colored dressing gown. She opened the door and studied her husband's appearance. "Oh, Andrew, you look terrible. Take a shower, a nice hot one. It'll do you a world of good. Stand under the spray for at least ten minutes. I can see how tense you are. Relax, darling, this is almost over. By this time tomorrow it will be nothing more than a bad memory. You go along now and

I'll see Mr. DeLuca out. I've laid fresh pajamas out for you in the bathroom. I'll even pour us a nightcap."

Sara moved past Andrew, her scent circling above and around her. Andrew sniffed, liking it. Was it new, or were his senses exceptionally keen tonight?

"Mr. DeLuca, I'll see you out," Sara said formally.

The attorney dropped all pretense. Lowering his voice, he said curtly, "Mrs. Taylor, I want you on the morning plane back to New Jersey."

"I won't do that. My place is here with my husband," she answered tightly.

"Then let me put it to you another way. If you aren't on that morning plane, certain friends of mine will not be responsible for your son's safety. Now do we understand one another?"

Sara's world was turning upside down. She knew DeLuca would not repeat himself, nor would he ever admit to saying what he had just told her. "Certain friends" he called them; he obviously meant the syndicate against whom Andrew was testifying.

"Why?"

"It's not important for you to know why. Just be on that plane."

If he was saying what she thought he was, Roman DeLuca knew Davey's whereabouts, which did make it a kidnapping. Yet Stuart Sanders had led her to believe that Davey had wandered off and was having difficulty finding his way back. Or had she just accepted the first thing he'd said? She couldn't remember.

Poor Andrew. If anything happened to Davey,

Andrew would be devastated. She needed time to think.

"Can I have my office make your airline reservation, Mrs. Taylor?"

"No, you can't. I'm staying. You wouldn't dare have my son harmed. You're too respectable for that, Mr. DeLuca. And I understand you're thinking of running for governor of Florida."

"It's crossed my mind," DeLuca replied. "I meant what I said about your son. And remember something else—I always win."

A chill washed over Sara. Her tone, however, was just as menacing as his. "So do I, Mr. DeLuca."

"There's a first time for everything. You're out of your depth here. This is my turf, remember?" He smiled down at her. "I'll have a reservation made just in case you change your mind. I believe the flight leaves at ten after ten."

"Why are you doing this?" Sara hissed.

"Because I don't want you in the courtroom. Good night, Mrs. Taylor."

Sara Taylor stood for a full five minutes at the door after closing it on the attorney. She had caught a glimpse of Sanders's colleague in the hallway and, furious and frightened, had thought of calling him in to tell him about DeLuca's threat. But she knew he'd never believe her. Still, perhaps she should tell him about the phone message and the result of her call. Maybe he could trace it . . . But no, still no one would believe her. Who would seriously consider that the upstanding Roman DeLuca would subvert the very laws he had sworn to uphold? He hadn't achieved his current status by being careless. More compelling still was her own feeling that this was a personal confrontation between the attorney and herself. All she had to do to win was be smarter and faster than he was. As for going back to New Jersey, she would have to do that, too. She was going to have to buckle under to a hoodlum in a thousand-dollar suit!

"Sara? Where are you, darling?"

"Right here, dear. I was just turning off the lights. I'll be there in a moment."

Settled in the bed beside Andrew, Sara searched for the right words. She had to be very careful what she said.

"Andrew, there's something I want to talk to you about. I've been thinking that maybe I should go home after all. That I could be of more use there than here. There's a flight around ten tomorrow morning. What do you think?"

"I think that's a good idea. Mr. DeLuca assured me I would finish with my testimony by noon so I'll take the one-fifteen flight. I'm pleased you're going, Sara. I think it's important that, when Davey finds his way back, you're there for him."

Not for anything in the world would Sara let Andrew know that she was going back because of Roman DeLuca's implied threat. No, it hadn't been implied, it had been clearly stated and she had to deal with it. "I'll go with you to the court-house and see that you're settled in, then leave from there. I want to be sure that you're all right before I go."

"That's not necessary, Sara."

"Maybe it isn't, but it's what I want to do."

"Is there anything else on your mind, Sara? You haven't been yourself since DeLuca arrived. I know he upset you with all that eye-contact nonsense, but now that you're going home it's hardly important."

"You always see right through me, don't you, darling? Yes, something has been bothering me. It's about your testimony this afternoon. I can't be certain, but I think there's a small problem we've overlooked. Remember when we were in school and had to learn the answers to a long list of questions? I don't know about you, but I always had the answers down pat as long as the questions were asked in order. Once the questions were out of sequence, I failed miserably. I heard Mr. DeLuca going over your testimony with you. Everything was in sequence, and you had all the facts down perfectly. But what would happen if those questions were asked out of sequence?"

"By whom?" Andrew asked.

"Anyone. The attorney for the defense—anyone. It could rattle you, Andrew. It could rattle anyone!" she added, touching his shoulder lightly. "Darling, I have every confidence that you'll be wonderful. But perhaps it wouldn't hurt to have our own rehearsal. I'll go over the questions with you, just like Mr. DeLuca did, only I'll mix them up so you'll be prepared for any eventuality. Darling, in an hour or so, you'll be letter perfect. Remember that old saying, 'Anything worth doing is worth doing well'? Andrew, you've put too much time and effort and—yes, sacrifice to yourself and our family—not to be the best possible witness you can."

Sara waited, hardly daring to breathe, for his answer.

"Darling, I think you're right. You've hit the nail on the head. But why didn't Roman DeLuca warn me? Why didn't he think of it?"

Sara shrugged. *Because, dear Andrew, Roman DeLuca is part of the syndicate. He's a hoodlum and a crook, and with the help of "certain friends" he wants to buy himself the governorship. Roman DeLuca knows that without me in the courtroom he can make you appear a fool and your testimony worthless. If the state doesn't win a conviction for this murder, there will be no connection with the syndicate. And it will all seem as though it's your fault—the absentminded professor. That's why I have to go back to New Jersey and rescue our son. But I'll have both, Andrew darling—Davey and my pride in you. I'll have won!*

"Sara? You didn't answer me. Why didn't DeLuca think of asking me the questions out of sequence?"

Sara smiled warmly. "Who knows why lawyers do the things they do? Your job is to get on that stand tomorrow and be a credible witness. Now, let's get down to work. I want you to make me proud. I want to pick up the evening paper and see that you've proven yourself to the court. I want no sly innuendoes about my husband being an absentminded professor. Now, darling, here's the first question."

Sara mercilessly drilled her husband, making him word-perfect, unshakable, no matter what tack her questioning took. Hour after hour she pounded away, refusing to hear Andrew's complaints of weariness. At last, his responses were clear, confident and, above all, honest. None of her grilling had removed his spontaneity. Roman DeLuca was going to be in for a big surprise when Andrew took the stand; he would do an excellent job. Her husband wasn't going to be intimidated by some glib attorney, not if she had anything to

do with it. DeLuca's mistake had been to underes-
timate her. He hadn't realized how important
Andrew was to her, or to what lengths she would
go to be certain he appeared first-rate in the public eye. Sara smiled in the early morning light. It always paid to know one's adversary. A pity DeLuca
hadn't applied that rule to her.

"Enough, darling, you've got it down pat. There's
no possibility of becoming mixed up now. Truth is
on your side, and you've shown me a confidence I
hadn't realized you possessed. Each day, darling, I
love you more. I'm so proud of you."

Andrew returned Sara's smile as he basked in
her praise. He did feel confident now, able to handle anything. Sleepily, he reached out to his wife.

"Darling, you still have time for a short nap,"
Sara said. "I'm going to shower and pack for us. I'll
lay your suit out so you can sleep till the last
minute. I want you bright and relaxed when you
enter the courtroom."

"I'll be so relieved when you get back to Jersey,
Sara. If anyone can find Davey, it's you. You're so
capable. I have every faith you'll know exactly what to
do. All these hours I've been thinking about testifying, and I haven't given Davey much thought. I can't
understand why we haven't heard anything . . ."

"Hush, darling, everything will be fine. You'll
see. I don't want you worrying about Davey, or anyone. You have your civic duty to perform and
you'll make me proud. I know it. Now, close your
eyes and don't think about anything or anyone."

"Hmmm," he answered, closing his eyes obediently and nodding off.

Poor baby, he looked so tired, she thought. A
nap would refresh him then, within a few hours,

he'd rock DeLuca back on his heels and the attorney would be powerless to do a thing about it. She would have followed orders by returning to New Jersey, and Andrew would have testified in the service of justice, making himself a hero.

Roman DeLuca was a loser. He had counted on Andrew making a poor showing, something he must have depended upon from the first because Andrew had been a hostile witness. When Andrew had made his deposition with the State Attorney's office in New Jersey, it had been too late for DeLuca to do anything other than base his case on Andrew's testimony. And it certainly would have looked strange if Andrew refused to testify because she or Davey was threatened. No, DeLuca had to go along with appearing to be on the side of the law, while secretly undermining Andrew's testimony. But he hadn't counted on Sara, which was why he was forcing her to return to New Jersey.

But Sara could handle Roman DeLuca. He was nothing more than a scab on a sore, and scabs could be pulled off. In a few hours, that's exactly what would happen. She leaned back on the pillows, folding her hands primly on her rising bosom. She would sleep now and shower later.

Precisely twenty minutes later the alarm on her watch beeped softly and Sara woke instantly, ready for the day ahead. She climbed carefully out of bed and began to move about the hotel suite, putting everything in order. Noticing that Andrew was huddled beneath the covers, she adjusted the thermostat in the room. She looked around to see if she had missed anything. Satisfied that everything was in order, she stepped out of her nightgown, folded it neatly, and placed it on top of her

other clothes. She walked naked into the bathroom and stared at her reflection with clinical interest. For her age, she had a firm, supple body.
High, round breasts, narrow waist, flat belly. Long,
slender legs that, when flexed, were like steel
springs, or so Andrew said. She smiled.

Turning to adjust the showerhead and regulate
the water, she wondered briefly what kind of
women Roman DeLuca liked. Probably fleshy, big-
bosomed women who wore heavy makeup. He had
strong hands. Would those hands be gentle or savage on a woman's body? Her tense muscles relaxed as the steam spiraled upward in search of the
vent. What kind of words would he whisper into a
woman's ear? Her eyes narrowed. She could almost imagine. He would be a demanding lover,
uncontrollable when driven by lust. An animal,
savage in his intent, and even more savage as he
pounded against his prey.

Sara shook her thoughts away as she stepped beneath the spray. She didn't want to think about
that handsome, leonine head, the profile that
could have been minted into an ancient Roman
coin. The width of his shoulders, the slimness of
his waist, the length of his thighs, the power of the
man—the challenge.

The needle-sharp spray hit her breasts, erecting
her nipples. A sudden intake of breath brought
with it a mouthful of water. She doused her head,
struggling to control her traitorous thoughts.

He was there with her, watching her, his eyes
touching her with their glinting desire. He was
inches away from her, just outside the shower
spray. She could feel the heat from his naked body,
hotter than the shower, touching the most inti-

mate parts of her with the flaring licks of a blast furnace. He watched her, face impassive, eyes devouring, as she soaped her breasts, lifting them, displaying them for him, knowing that the drumbeat of his desire was quickening to wildness.

She was mad with her own sense of power over this man who had become her enemy. She was returning his gaze brazenly, impudence lifting the corners of her mouth. If she wanted, she could reach out and touch him, sending him beyond the parameters of sanity. She was preening beneath his gaze, perpetuating his madness for her.

A growing ache was voicing an appeal between her strong, supple thighs. Her skin felt pink, shining from an inner glow. Her breasts were heavy, hard, thrust high on her torso in a silent petition to be crushed beneath his hands.

As she was watching him, his hands dropped to his loins, holding himself. Taking her cue from her fantasy, her own fingers slipped between her legs; she was surprised by the heat that rivaled the steamy spray. She threw back her head, the water pelting the full length of her nakedness. As a low, throaty moan came from her throat, she recognized the need building in her. The misty steam was fast obliterating her fantasy image. Spasm after spasm racked her body. Her knees crumpled beneath her as she sank to the bottom of the tub, doubling over in a paroxysm of seemingly endless joy.

Eleven

It had been a long day. One of the longest Stuart Sanders could remember. How had he allowed himself to get so caught up in this case? A case should stay a case, and a kid a kid. But it wasn't like that this time.

His stomach rumbled ominously. He'd taken one look at the peppers and steak on the airline tray and pushed it away; he had no desire to tempt his ulcer. Lorrie led him to her motor home where, over a glass of milk and a turkey sandwich, Sanders had her tell him everything that had happened since breakfast.

"So Davey knew you'd be leaving soon to go to the laser show?" he asked.

"Yes. He knew, and he was very excited. He promised to stay close."

"Do you consider him responsible—I mean, as responsible as a kid his age can be?"

"Davey is very responsible," she answered. "He's had to be because of his medical condition."

"Right," Sanders said, nodding his head. He'd wanted to talk to Lorrie and get her take on the whole thing because she would have a different perspective from the cops.

"You think he was kidnapped, don't you?" she asked.

"I don't know what to think, Lorrie. There are too many pieces to this puzzle, if you know what I mean. They can't all fit." He got out from behind the table and took his plate and glass to the sink. "I'm going to go outside and walk around. Do I go left or right around the lake to find the grave?"

"There's a path that sort of veers to the right. It's a couple of hundred feet away. You can't miss it—there's a deep gully. You're not going to be able to see much and, from the sound of the wind out there, you might get blown away."

"Are you going to be up for a while longer?" he asked.

Lorrie gave him a watery smile. "You don't really think I'd go to bed while Davey's still missing, do you?"

"No, but . . ."

"I'm not Sara," Lorrie said, voicing his thoughts. "I know she would think it advisable to get some sleep so she'd be refreshed and ready for anything, but I'm not so logical or so . . ."

"Cold," Stuart inserted, without thinking. He shook his head. "I'm sorry. I have no right to criticize your sister."

"You don't have to apologize. I agree with you completely. There's no better word to describe Sara, except maybe for . . . heartless. I don't understand her and, even if I did, there's no excuse for the way she treats her own son."

Looking at Lorrie, knowing the guilt and pain she was suffering, made Stuart want to take her in his arms. As if reading his mind, she reached out and touched his cheek. "I know if there's anyone who can find him, it's you."

"I'll do my best." He put his arms around her and pulled her close.

"That's all anyone can do," she whispered.

Regretfully, Sanders left the motor home, the white beam of his flashlight guiding his way. He stopped as he neared the pond, sensing a presence. He turned and was about to reach for the gun under his armpit when he looked down into the pool of light and saw Duffy.

"How goes it, Duff? Kind of late for you, isn't it? You're supposed to bark when you see someone. Some watchdog," Sanders said as he dropped to his haunches to fondle the dog's ears. Duffy rolled over and let her paws go straight in the air, her signal that she wanted her belly scratched. Sanders obliged. "What happened, Duff? Where's the kid? Where's Davey? Jesus, if only you could talk."

At the sound of Davey's name Duffy woofed softly. She waited expectantly for Sanders to get on with his brisk massage. "You're one of those safe dogs that are meant to be good companions for little boys. I'm not blaming you, you understand. Hey, what's this?" Sanders's fingers encountered a swelling in the dog's groin. Duffy yelped and rolled over. "Let me see what that is." Obediently, the little dog came back to the crouching man. It was apparent that she trusted him as she started to nuzzle his ankle and whine. Sanders could feel the dog tremble as he gently ran his hands over her body. There weren't any other swollen areas but there was a small cut on her face. "Did somebody hurt you, Duff? It's okay, girl. No one is going to hurt you anymore." He picked up the fuzzy bundle. "We're going for a walk, Duffy. We're going to that grave and maybe you can tell me something in your own way."

Sanders unzipped his vest and held Duffy close to his chest, making sure the dog was comfortable. "I can't take any chances on you getting lost. You've been hurt and you deserve a ride." Duffy yipped, then buried her head in the man's warm shirt.

The wind whipped through the trees, whistling and shrieking. A three-quarter moon slid from behind a cloud, lighting the way for Sanders.

Duffy growled low in her throat. "Gotcha, girl. We're close, is that it?" Some familiar scent teased at Sanders's nostrils. It wasn't the leaves or the pine needles; it was something more commonplace, something he smelled only once in a while. He wrinkled his nose, trying to place the faint aroma. Christ, it was mothballs. Cautiously, Sanders approached the gully, the flashlight held straight in front of him. Duffy cowered against his chest, whimpering and whining. He hunkered down and peered into the gully.

Duffy jumped out of his arms. At first the little dog's bark was fretful. She approached the yawning gully then backed away, growling ferociously. Gaining her courage against some unseen or remembered terror, she used her front paws to dig into the soft earth. Sanders lowered the flashlight, illuminating the spot where Duffy was digging. Nosing and pawing, she made high-pitched whining noises, finally breaking into a howl, stopping only to stare up at him, waiting.

Sanders sifted through the dirt, looking for whatever the dog wanted him to find. The small, round pellet felt rock hard as he fingered it. It was a mothball! No bigger than the gumballs that kids got out of candy machines. "Good dog, good Duffy. I know this means something, but for the life of me I can't imagine what it is."

Sanders spent another half hour walking around, searching the area near the gully. He found nothing. Aside from the mothball in his pocket, it was a dry run, a bust. What had he hoped to find? Davey, of course. Always Davey.

Duffy backed off a step and barked. She planted her feet firmly on the soft earth. Her ears were straight up when she barked again.

"You got something in mind?"

Duffy backed off.

"Okay, show me." Duffy was swift as she turned to follow Sanders's order, and he was hard-pressed to keep up with the terrier in the dim light of the flashlight. Too much high-calorie food and too many cigarettes. He was breathless when he stopped next to Duffy. In all the time he had spent guarding the Taylors, he had never seen the dog so agitated. He lifted the flashlight higher into the leaves of the low-branched trees. A covered garbage can and a picnic table told him they were at a campsite. *The* campsite, if he was understanding Duffy correctly.

"Good girl," Sanders said, squatting down. "You've gotten me this far, now what? Where's Davey? What happened here?" He didn't feel foolish talking to the dog. Duffy whined then howled. Sanders swallowed. "I need more than that, Duff, if we're gonna find Davey." Duffy stared at Sanders, continuing to whimper and whine. The noise set the agent's nerves on edge. "Look, I get it—we're at a campsite. But what does it mean? Was Davey here? Were you here?" Duffy cocked her head as though she understood every word the man was saying.

Then she barked once, twice, a mean, chilling bark. Sanders watched as the dog dropped to her belly, shimmying toward him. When she was within five feet of him, she lay down then rolled over, belly up. Sanders reached out to touch Duffy, to touch the tender groin. Duffy let loose with a low growl and then leaped to her feet. Playfully, she pranced around Sanders, circling him Indian fashion.

"Son of a bitch!" Sanders exclaimed as he scooped up the little dog. "The bastard who was camped here is the one who hurt you. Kicked you, probably. Is he the one who has Davey? Show me, Duffy. Davey, where's Davey? What happened to Davey?"

Sanders lowered the beam of his flashlight to the ground. He squatted down and was able to make out tire tracks in the hardpacked ground. The truck with the pop-up had camped in this spot. It wasn't a startling discovery—any of the police officers could have told him if he'd asked. What was interesting was the way Duffy kept circling the back end of the campsite, where the pop-up had rested. To his mind, it suggested that Davey had been in the pop-up. He squinted in the yellowish light at the panting dog. "Davey was in the pop-up. You got hurt here and made it back to the motor home. But Davey wasn't that lucky, was he?"

Sanders kept walking around the back end of the campsite, trying to envisage what had happened to Davey Taylor. "You got hurt and probably ran off to lick your wounds. I'm not saying I blame you but the question is, did Davey hide in the pop-up or did the couple grab him and keep him in the truck with them? I think he hid. What do you think, Duffy old girl?"

The terrier whined in answer, nuzzling Sanders's leg. Satisfied that the agent was watching her, she lay down, her head on her paws. Sanders frowned. "Are you tired, Duffy?" The dog lay quietly, staring at him with wet brown eyes.

"I see, you're sticking with your story. That's good enough for me. C'mon, you deserve a ride back." He held out his arms to the little dog, allowing her into his shirt where she nestled her head on his chest.

He was walking back to Lorrie's RV when he saw a mothball laying on the ground. Thinking it was the mothball from the gravesite, that he'd somehow dropped it, he bent down and picked it up. "I'm getting careless in my old—" He broke off when his hand dipped into his pocket and discovered the first mothball still there. "Well, I'll be damned!"

Mac Feeley was waiting for him outside the motor home, an evil-smelling cigar clamped between his teeth. Sanders wondered what the agent looked like without the cigar. Jesus, probably naked.

"Everything's taken care of—the kid's picture will be in all the morning papers. Nothing's going on here. What say we get some shut-eye?" Feeley's tone was hopeful but he was resigned to what he knew Sanders's answer would be.

"I have to call headquarters. But first I want to talk to Officer Ordway."

Feeley grinned. "The guy's a piss, Sanders. He's combed his hair four times in the half hour I've been standing here."

Sanders chuckled as he approached the young, blond policeman. "Officer Ordway, isn't it?" he asked. "I'm Stuart Sanders, FBI. Were you around when they dug up Lombardi's body?"

"Yeah, and I'm still around. Pulling double duty is no way to spend your life, if you know what I mean," the young man told him.

"Did you see the body? Was there anything unusual about it?"

"Yeah, if you consider that bodies don't grow in the ground around these parts," came the flip reply.

Forcing himself to keep a cool head, Sanders persisted. "Were you at the scene?"

"I wasn't the one who dug him up, but it made the ones who did pretty sick. We don't have much crime down here. Drunks, petty thefts—this is a small town. Ever since Wild Adventure was built, things have picked up a little. Hired two new policemen last year, and there's room in the budget for another one this year. My brother's got a bid in for the job."

Sanders listened with pretended interest. "Sharp guy like you, you could go far. You look the type who keeps on his toes. Bet you've got it all over these locals. You should set your sights higher; maybe I can do something for you with the Bureau."

"No, thanks. If this is the kind of case you guys deal in every day of the week, I'll just sit back and collect a salary for traffic control. A few weekend family squabbles, a couple of buzzed-out teenagers, an occasional robbery—that's my speed. Don't get dirty that way." He picked an imaginary speck of lint off his uniform jacket.

"I heard digging up that body was real dirty work," Sanders tried again.

"The worst. The stench was awful. Don't think I'll ever be able to smell that stuff again without re-membering."

"What stuff?" Sanders asked, getting to the point.

Ordway stiffened as if realizing he'd spoken out of turn. "Ah, you know—the smell of death."

"Oh, sure," Sanders nodded. "But I thought Lombardi had been dead only twenty hours or so. Bodies don't usually start to stink that soon."

Ordway shrugged expansively. "Yeah, well, twenty hours or not, that son of a bitch stunk." He turned back to the magazine he was reading, apparently determined not to say any more on the subject.

Sanders grinned wryly. He'd figured the local police would hold back. It was always the same story—the search for glory. They wanted to be the ones to come up with the answers, and the only way to do that was to withhold information. It was a fact of life that Sanders understood, and he'd come up against it before. But what he had to do was make a definite connection between Balog and the dead man, and he could have what he needed right in his pocket. Lorrie had been there when they'd dug up the body. Maybe she could shed some light on things.

Lorrie was sitting at the table, staring out the window when Sanders opened the door to the RV.

"Did you find anything?" The look on her face was hopeful.

"I'm not sure. You tell me." He pulled the two mothballs out of his pocket and set them on the table. "I found one of these at the gravesite."

"There were dozens of them in the grave with the body," she confirmed, then glanced up at him. "You say you found one of the mothballs at the grave. Where did you find the other one?"

"At a campsite."

"Was there litter all around it?"

He nodded.

"That's where the couple with the pop-up were parked."

"I thought so." Sanders squeezed Lorrie's hand and went back outside. The cops had an all points on Balog and his companion for questioning but, as of now, they were prime suspects in a murder inquiry, and possibly a kidnapping.

Walking up to Feeley, Sanders said in a low tone, "Keep pretty boy over there occupied. I want to call in and I don't want him listening to my end of the conversation. Two can play this game."

"We got nothing in common," Feeley grumbled.

"Then asphyxiate him with your damn cigar. But keep him occupied."

The Bureau chief picked up the phone on the first ring. "Carmichael," he barked.

"Sanders here. Buzz, I want the okay to send Feeley into Newark. I've got a ninety-nine percent pure-gold lead I want him to check for me. We're just holding up the walls here, and the locals are withholding information. Feeley can be back by morning. I want him to check out the apartment that Balog was renting."

"You got it. No new leads on the kid, or is this part of it? You've only been there a few minutes and already you've come up with a snitch. How reliable is he?"

Sanders's face was pained. He could hardly tell the chief that his "snitch" was a dog. "Yeah, she's reliable," he answered without elaborating.

"Stu, I don't mind telling you this entire case is a pain in the ass. If I never see or hear from another local cop again, I'll die happy. Feeley tells me that Chief of Police Allen and his squad have been dubbed Allen's Assholes. True or false?"

Sanders strained to see Officer Ordway through the thick smoke coming from Feeley's cigar. He was combing his hair. "Sounds fairly accurate to me. I'll let you know my opinion tomorrow."

"You holding anything back on the kid, Stu?"

"Only theories and personal opinions. You know they count for zilch as far as the Bureau goes."

"Tell me about it."

"I'm pretty sure the kid wasn't snatched by any syndicate. It doesn't fit. What I've got is a possible connection between this Balog character and the dead man. I say, if I find Lombardi's killer, I'll find the Taylor boy. I think the kid saw something he shouldn't have, got scared and ended up in Balog's pop-up camper."

"Your snitch drop that in your lap?"

The pained look crossed Sanders's features again. "In a manner of speaking. You could say she pointed it out to me. I promised her the biggest steak dinner of her life if it pays off."

"Is that on or off the expense account? You sly dog, I always knew you had it in you. A word of caution from one who's been burned—that young stuff out there can be hard to handle. They don't mind givin' if you don't mind gettin'. You know what I'm talking about, don't you?"

Sanders grinned. "This little lady, I can handle. I'll check in midmorning. Have a good night, Buzz."

"You too, Stu."

A harsh violet-colored light was coming through the plastic drapes when Cudge opened his eyes. For the briefest instant he couldn't remember where he was, or why. Then he realized the glare was the security light in the parking lot behind Snookie's.

Candy Striper was in the bed next to him, turned on her side to face him. She wasn't pretty now with her makeup streaked and her mouth partially open. Why did he always end up with the dogs? Each time she exhaled, the odor of stale wine and cigarettes assaulted him. She was a pig, he decided. He'd known it last night, but he'd thought she may have something to offer. He only hoped what she was offering wasn't the AIDS virus. "Lie down with dogs, get up with fleas" as the old saying went.

His head felt heavy and he could hardly lift his arm to read his watch dial. Four-forty. In the morning? It had to be. It was yesterday evening when he'd brought the tire to the gas station next door to Snookie's. He sat up quickly, holding on to the wall for support. Shit! That mechanic had said he'd throw the tire into the back of the truck when he'd finished with it. What if someone had stolen

it? All those drunks coming out of Snookie's—
what if they stole his truck?

"Hey, what's the matter?" Candy groaned.
"What time is it?"

"I gotta get outta here," Cudge said, and rolled
over her to get out of bed. The mattress sank beneath his weight and the bedsprings screeched in
protest. Candy's body was lush and soft beneath
him and he remembered flashes of what it had
been like with her last night. Soft, warm, like he'd
been plowing into a featherbed.

"You got an old lady someplace looking for
you?" she asked sleepily.

Elva. How could he have forgotten about Elva?
What if she decided to skip out on him? Go to the
cops herself? Pin the whole rap about Lenny on
him. Then it wouldn't be just that little kid to worry
about, there would be Elva, too. Cursing under his
breath that he'd ever gone into Snookie's and got
entangled with Candy, Cudge searched for his
clothing. He never should have gotten sidetracked.
He should have stayed to watch the mechanic fix
the tire then gone right back to the camper, just
the way he'd planned.

"Hey, babe, any more wine left in that bottle?
My mouth's dry." Candy's voice was husky with
sleep and hangover.

"Get it yourself," he snapped. "I gotta get going.
Where the hell're my boots?"

"Find 'em yourself."

He bristled. "Watch your mouth. Where's my
boots?"

"How should I know? They're your boots. What
did you do with them?"

"I don't even remember taking them off."

"You didn't. I did," Candy smiled with satisfaction. "Hey, babe, why don't you crawl back in bed here? I got something to show you."

"Save it," he answered uncomfortably, not liking women to take the initiative. "Didn't you get enough last night?" He found his boots and something soft and rotten came off the bottom onto his hands. "Shit!"

"What's that?"

"Dog shit," he moaned, looking for something to wipe his hand on, finally deciding on the bedcovers.

"Hey! Don't do that!" Candy sat up suddenly to inspect the damage. "Christ, ain't you got no manners? Don't wipe that stuff on the covers. One thing at least," she said, turning on the lamp for a closer examination, "it's not dog do, it's apples. Even so, watch where you put it."

"Apples!" Sure, now he remembered those rotting apples on the road where he'd pulled over in the pop-up. He must have stepped on them and gotten bits of the pulp wedged between the ridges of his soles. Apples. Elva. He had to get back!

Candy settled back against the pillows in a languorous pose. "What's your hurry, babe? It's not even morning. Come on back to bed. This time it's for free."

"It's always free," Cudge growled, tying one of his laces. "Your kind always are."

"Like hell! That little parlor game we played is going to cost you exactly thirty bucks."

"Don't bug me, Candy, I ain't in the mood. Right now you're treading on thin ice. You think I'd pay to screw an old whore like you?"

"Old whore! Listen, you'd have to pay anybody to jump in the sack with you. And double if they'd been there once already. You ain't exactly Casanova," she mocked. "Tell me, you always have that much trouble gettin' it up or was it just the wine?"

Cudge loomed over her, standing close to the bed, hands curling into fists. "One more word and you're askin' for it. One more word. I don't want no more trouble, so just shut up!" He seemed to be fighting himself as he stood over her, forcing himself to back down, to quell his sudden rage. "Where's my shirt?" Not waiting for an answer, he looked around the shabby room.

When he moved away from her, Candy propped herself up on her elbow. "You don't really have any connections in Vegas, do you?"

"What do you think?"

"I think you were puttin' me on, so the deal's off. I told you, I've got expenses and that wine we drank together last night really knocked me on my ass. Far as I'm concerned, last night was a lost cause, and I ain't got nothing to show for it. So, how's about that thirty dollars I helped you win from that guy?"

"You gotta be kiddin'. That's my thirty bucks. I won it. You already got all you're gonna get."

Candy sat up in bed, the blankets falling away to reveal her full, round breasts. "The way I see it, you parked your ass in my bed and that'll cost you thirty dollars."

Balog faced her in the yellow lamplight, his eyes cold and hard. The air between them seemed to become dense and still. His square, cropped head burrowed into his powerfully wide shoulders; his barrel-staved chest expanded with each deep intake of air. Candy heard a high, frightened whine and realized with horror it was her own.

The corral gate in Cudge's brain swung open with nerve-cracking velocity. The beast lunged forward to freedom, sharp-edged hooves cutting into his brain tissue. Blackness obscured his vision. Rage ripped through him; he was almost senseless. Razor-tipped horns gored his sanity and attacked again and again.

Candy was helpless, defenseless as a rag doll in the jaws of a mad dog. She struggled against unconsciousness, fighting to stay alert, knowing it to be her only chance of survival. But when oblivion came, she surrendered gratefully.

The woman was still, no longer crawling across the floor to escape his onslaught. How long had she been like that? Still as death. Cudge backed away, stumbling over an overturned chair.

Incredulous, he looked down at his hands, just beginning to feel the tingle that preceded pain. He'd broken his little finger; it was sticking out at a crazy angle. Gritting his teeth, he straightened it and heard a sharp crack before it settled into place. Thinking he should wrap it to keep it in place, he searched the room, seeing one of the black stockings Candy had worn during her dance on Snookie's bar. It was thin and long, suitable. Winding the nylon around his knuckles, he looked around for anything he might have left behind. Now he had to pick up his truck and make tracks.

He didn't want to think about what he'd done to Candy. He didn't want to think about anything. He'd have to keep his head, keep his temper under control. From now on, he promised himself, every move he made would be planned. He wouldn't let the gate swing open again.

Davey woke slowly, trying to remember where he was. He opened his eyes to see Brenda still sleeping. Her arms were wrapped tightly around him. He had to go to the bathroom; it must be morning. He shouldn't have stayed, but Brenda had been so scared; he had felt her heart pounding when she held him. He didn't know what he had feared more: going off alone in the dark, or what the man would do if he found him.

He strained to see the hands on his watch. The big hand was on the seven and the little hand between the five and six. He felt confused, but knew he must leave the safety of the pop-up and try to find Aunt Lorrie. Through the mesh windows he could see daylight between the trees, streaking the sky a gunmetal gray. First, he had to go to the bathroom. He needed some food to take with him too, in case he got lost again. He had to be prepared. Should he wake Brenda and say goodbye? He should thank her for helping him.

Carefully and quietly, Davey inched from Elva's arms and stood up. He held his breath when his foot touched his discarded leg brace alongside the small refrigerator. Should he put it on? Maybe Aunt Lorrie would feel better if he wore it. He struggled with the familiar straps, trying to be quiet. Wincing in discomfort when the padded straps touched his chafed ankle, he remembered to pull his sock up the way his aunt had shown him.

Hurry, hurry, he told himself. He looked at

Brenda. He knew he should thank her but if he woke her up she might want to keep him with her the way she'd done the night before. Aunt Lorrie had told him once that sometimes the right thing to do was often the hardest. So it must be the right thing—to leave without thanking her, or saying goodbye.

The sound of a car coming close stopped him.

"Brenda, Brenda, wake up. He's here. Wake up, please wake up," Davey coaxed.

Elva sat up. "He's here, Brenda. I heard the truck."

"Oh, my God!" Holding Davey's hand, she scrambled out of the camper. "Run, BJ, run!"

Davey didn't hesitate. He was out of the camper and running as fast as his legs would carry him toward the trees. On and on he ran, the patch pockets of the red windbreaker ballooning. He fought for air as he staggered through the sodden leaves and twigs. It was good that they were wet and didn't make any noise.

He needed to take off the brace; it was slowing him down. Could he stop? Did he have time? He *had* to stop. He had to take the time or the man would catch him. He sat down on a matted pile of leaves. The straps were tight and still damp from yesterday when he'd wet himself. The brace was always easier to put on than take off. There, it was off. He couldn't take the time to appreciate how good it felt to have his leg free. He had to run. He had to run fast.

Cudge stood over Elva, his hands flexing as though working an invisible pair of grips. The long tendons in his forearms were hard and prominent under his skin. The meager light of early morning was behind him, throwing his silhouette into relief and hiding the brain-exploding rage on his blunt-featured face.

Elva backed away, shaking. She tried to tell herself that Cudge hadn't seen BJ escape, but she knew that was just wishful thinking. His posture was threatening, lethal. But BJ was safe.

"What were you doing here with that kid? How long have you been hiding him?" Her father's voice boomed in her ears, bouncing off her fear. She'd always been afraid of him, ever since she was a little girl. She'd never understood why Mama had married him or had children with him. There was no kindness in the man, only a love for the cheap hooch he bought in town.

"Papa, don't. I didn't do nothing wrong. Honest, I didn't."

She could smell the familiar liquor, sweet yet rancid, each time he exhaled. He'd been drinking again. There wasn't food on the table, but the welfare check could buy hooch the same as it could buy food. Poor BJ. He was just a little boy and he needed milk, butter and eggs. Instead, all he got was thin potato soup made with dry skim milk. Poor BJ. All eyes, scared eyes, that watched the doorway waiting for Papa to come home. Praying he wouldn't. And Mama, grim mouth, hunched shoulders, red hands from too much laundry and trying to keep the place clean.

Papa advanced on her, striking her in the thigh with his heavy boot. "How long have you been hiding that little bastard? You tell me or I'll give it to you. I'll finish you for good!"

The words were different, but they meant the same. Just like the night Papa had come home and heard BJ crying. BJ had never cried again. But Brenda—she had never stopped crying.

Elva, was back in the poverty-ridden shack in the Pennsylvania foothills. The smell was the same. Liquor, dirt, fear. And the smell of dry urine from where little BJ slept. But this was the second chance she had always prayed for. BJ would be all right; she'd seen to it by making him run away.

She could hear the low intake of her father's breath; it sounded like the growl of a beast. He moved toward her with sure, slow steps. She could sense his lust for the kill; she could almost taste it. An icy finger touched her shoulder, but she was too paralyzed to move, trapped in his gaze like a rabbit in the beam of a headlight. Somewhere in the back of her brain she heard her mother screaming: "Don't touch my baby!"

His hands were in her hair, yanking her to her feet. "No! Leave her alone!"

With all the force she could muster, she kicked, aiming between his legs. She felt him flinch and heard his sudden gasp. He flung her from him, sending her on to the floor. The pop-up rocked wildly on its moorings as the world tilted before her.

Pop-up? This wasn't Papa. Mama wasn't screaming, those were her own screams. BJ was dead, long dead. Cowering in a corner beside the refrigerator, Elva shielded her head with her arms. This was Cudge and he was just like Papa. Nasty, mean—a killer. Before the cast-iron frying pan came crashing down on her, Elva had an insight that she'd never been quite able to put together before. She didn't have to wonder any more why she stayed with Cudge—she knew. He was her punishment. She'd always known it would end like this. He was Papa all over again and, because he was, he gave her a certain security. Violence had been her birthright. And violence was Cudge. Through him, she would be able to pay for her sin of not saving BJ. She would die, just the way her little brother had died, and then her soul would be saved.

Her arms came away from her head. She allowed his weapon to fall, allowed herself to succumb to the blows. And always there was little BJ's face, eyes watching, waiting for her.

The round, plastic disc on the zipper of his jacket bounced against his neck as Davey ran through the woods, his breathing harsh and ragged. *Faster,* his mind screamed, *don't let him get you. You have to find Aunt Lorrie.* He was getting tired. And then he heard the words, and his Reeboks picked up speed.

"I'll get you, you little bastard," the man yelled. "You ain't getting away from me!"

The trees were thinning so it was easier to run between them. Perspiration streamed down Davey's forehead as he staggered ahead. It was so hard to breathe. Maybe he could hide somewhere and wait till he felt better, just a little while. *No,* he couldn't stop. If he did, the man would find him and kill him. If only Duffy were here. If only Aunt Lorrie were here. But they weren't—he was alone, and he had to find Duffy and Aunt Lorrie all by himself.

Saliva formed in the corners of his mouth as he heard curses coming from his left. His gasping breaths were making too much noise; his hand over his mouth to seal in the harsh sounds, Davey floundered ahead. He was slowing down now and tears of frustration gathered in his eyes. He stopped and listened to the early morning stillness. He was at the edge of the woods; ahead was a row of young trees then an open field. Davey looked ahead then back behind him. If he went across the field, he would be out in the open. If he stayed where he was, the man would catch him. *Hide*, he thought. He had to hide for a little while and rest. Davey looked around. There was no hiding place among the saplings.

Quickly he veered off his straight path, almost backtracking, but to the right. Hardly daring to breathe, he crouched down behind a wide tree and clamped one hand over his mouth to still his harsh gasps. His other hand fumbled with the zipper on his windbreaker. His eyes closed as he anticipated the sound the zipper would make as he pulled it down. It moved down but got stuck in the metal at the end. He needed two hands to make the jacket open. A second was all he needed, but he had to decide which was more important— keeping his hand over his mouth or getting rid of the red jacket. He crouched lower against the tree trunk. He crossed his fingers then yanked at the plastic disc and struggled out of the jacket, careful to make no sound. What should he do with the jacket? Mom would be mad if he left it behind. She always said you had to value your things and take care of them. He looked at his Reeboks. He might get away with the ruined sneakers, but not the jacket as well. He had to take it with him. If only it wasn't red. He looked at it with disgust and saw that the inside was brown. Dirt brown. He pulled the sleeves inside out and put the jacket back on. Now he blended in with the forest colors. The man would have to have real good eyes to find him. He felt confident as he started out again, but a sharp noise close ahead made him drop to the ground.

"I know you're here somewhere, you little twerp. I seen your jacket. You ain't gonna get away from me this time. I took care of Elva, and now I'm gonna take care of you."

Davey flinched. The voice was so close, almost at his head. The tone changed from threatening to cajoling. "You know I'm gonna catch you, so you might as well come out from wherever you're hiding. You come out now, and I'll take you to your folks. I'm gonna count to three, and you come out, okay?"

Davey remained still. The man was lying. He was trying to trick him, to make him come out, and then . . .

"One, two, three. Okay, you had your chance!"

Sounds of crashing and swearing fell on Davey's ears. How close the man must be. Davey was shaking with fear. He didn't dare lift his head or make any movement at all. It was a good thing he'd turned his jacket inside out. Gradually, the sounds grew quieter, as if the man were moving farther away, but his curses and threats could still be heard. Davey lifted his head and risked a look; there was no one staring back at him. A long sigh escaped him.

He struggled to his feet and looked at his watch. The little hand was on the seven and the big hand on the twelve. Seven o'clock, he told himself. Seven o'clock in the morning. If he were at home, Mom and Dad would be in the kitchen eating breakfast. He wished he'd had time to take one of the cupcakes out of the bag on the refrigerator before he left the pop-up. But he couldn't think about food now. He had to get out of the woods and find a road where there were cars.

Davey trudged back through the woods. The man had gone in the other direction, so he didn't feel he had to run. His legs ached furiously, and the knee that needed the brace kept bending when he put his weight on it. His hands were scratched and bleeding, and he could feel where the side of his face had scraped into a tree. Touching it lightly, he brought droplets of blood away on his fingertips. When had he had his last shot? Was it still working? Would the bleeding stop? His ankles and knees felt tender. Was it from running, or was it like before he started the shots?

Painfully tired and frightened, Davey hid in the brush under the trees. He would sit there and listen, watchful for the bad man. Lying on his belly, head cradled in his arms, he tried to stay awake.

Twelve

Sara Taylor stepped out of the bathroom after her morning shower, dry, powdered, cologned and naked. Slipping her toiletries into an Yves Saint Laurent cosmetic case, she placed it at the top of her suitcase. Andrew would bring both their suitcases home on his late afternoon flight. Sara hoped no unexpected problems would arise, and that Andrew's appearance in court would be completed by the afternoon. She could count on it, she thought, remembering how well she had drilled him on his testimony.

She must see about breakfast. For Andrew, hot cakes, sausages, one scrambled egg, and toast. For her, half a melon. A large pot of hot coffee for the two of them. She had to eat something to get her thoughts in order. She didn't want to think about what had happened in the shower ever again. She would put it out of her mind and never let it resurface.

Sara opened the door and handed the ever-present guard her breakfast menu. "Would you please tell room service that Mr. Taylor and I would appreciate our breakfast now. We have to be in court by nine." Without waiting for a reply, she closed the door, then walked over to the bed and gently shook Andrew awake.

"Time to get up, darling. All you have to do is shower. Everything is laid out for you. Breakfast will be up shortly. I don't want to rush you, Andrew, but sometimes you have a tendency to dawdle. Today you have to hurry—it's already seven o'clock." If Andrew noticed her annoyed tone, he didn't say anything. Instead, he dutifully got up, went into the bathroom and took his shower.

Sara stood outside the bathroom, listening to the sound of water splashing against the tiles. Her thoughts strayed back to DeLuca and her sexual fantasy. She shook her head to make them go away but they wouldn't. Maybe the television would distract her. The set came to life with a sexy, light-hearted comedy show. Sara frowned—everything had sexual connotations of one sort or another. She changed the channel to an early-morning talk show. An author was describing her latest book about men's sexual fantasies. Damn. Again, she pushed the button on the remote. Cartoons. That was certainly safe.

She heard the shower being turned off. Andrew would be in the sitting room in another minute, and she could question him again, give him a short run-through to be sure he hadn't forgotten his lines. What was she going to do on the plane for two and a half hours? She would have all that time to think, to fantasize . . . Davey—she would think about Davey, and Lorrie, and what she was going to say to her. How could Lorrie lose her son? How dare she allow him out of her sight? Yes, Davey and Lorrie would be safe ground.

Andrew was fixing his tie when a knock sounded at the door. A waiter carried in a breakfast tray laden with plates and silverware. After he'd left, Sara lifted the stainless-steel covers. She shook out Andrew's napkin and handed it to him.

"Looks good. Aren't you eating, darling?" he said.

"Just some melon. You know I don't like to eat before a plane trip. This is more than enough. That little round scoop of butter makes the hot cakes look so appealing, don't you think, Andrew?"

Andrew nodded as he chewed industriously. "This breakfast is a surprise—all my favorites!"

"You deserve only the best, Andrew, and that's what I want for you." Sara knew her voice lacked conviction, but Andrew was so busy eating he wasn't paying any attention.

"Are we taking the bags to the courtroom or do you think I should come back for them?" he asked minutes later, as he pushed his empty plate aside.

"You might want to freshen up before you leave for your plane. Leave them here or they'll just be a hindrance. The limo will be waiting, so there shouldn't be any problem. You might even want to shower. I heard just a short while ago that it's going to be eighty-nine degrees today."

"I'm glad we don't live here anymore, I can tell you that," Andrew volunteered as he pushed back his chair. "I like the change of seasons at home. What about you, Sara? Do you ever miss Florida?"

"No, darling, I don't. Perhaps though, we

should start thinking about moving out of New Jersey. It's so . . . so crime-ridden. Connecticut would be nice; let's consider it in the spring. I'm ready when you are."

"Then let's go and get this over with, so I can be home with you and Davey for dinner this evening."

"We don't know for certain that Davey has been found. As of last night he was still lost, but I'm sure they must have found him by now. He did miss his shot though, and that's what worries me."

"I feel just as you do—Davey will be waiting for both of us when we get back. Sara, instead of punishing him for wandering off, why don't you make a wonderful dinner with all his favorites? We'll make a party of it, and afterward have a serious talk with him. We don't want him to think we're angry with him, but he has got to realize what he's done. My father used to do that with me. The real punishment came from having to stand there with no defense for what I'd done, and my father understanding perfectly. My mother, too. They were never divided when it came to me. Whatever one said, the other agreed. Like we do with Davey."

"It sounds like a tremendous idea." That was something she could do on the plane ride. She could plan the menu and think about the talk she and Andrew would have with Davey.

"I, for one, won't be sorry to see the last of this hotel," Andrew said, closing the door behind him. "You'd better give me the key, Sara."

"Darling, I really don't want to go and leave you here. I'd much rather be here with you, but our son . . ."

"Sara," Andrew said, putting his arm around her shoulder, "I don't want to hear another word. We agreed and the matter is settled. I'll be fine. I'm just sorry that I made such a botch of things yesterday. Today I'll do much better. The State will have no problems. Mr. DeLuca will be more than satisfied."

"I rather doubt that," Sara said, sotto voce.

"What was that, darling?"

"Nothing. Just woolgathering. It wasn't important. We're fortunate that we left when we did. The traffic is building up. You're going to be the first witness, so it is imperative that you be on time."

Thirty-five minutes later the limousine pulled up at the curb outside the courthouse. Sara hated the pushing and shoving crowd of reporters shouting questions. As she walked beside Andrew up the stairs, she kept her gaze straight ahead, her step firm and sure. It wasn't till one of the security guards opened the door for Sara that she saw Roman DeLuca. She felt a flush creep up her neck.

"Good morning, Andrew, Mrs. Taylor," DeLuca said. Sara wondered why DeLuca called Andrew Andrew and her Mrs. Taylor. Andrew was whisked off by two court bailiffs, and Sara was left standing next to Roman DeLuca and one of the men from Sanders's unit, Michael Jonas. Stuart Sanders had introduced Jonas to Sara and Andrew, identifying him as an assistant supplied by the State of Florida. Sara wondered if he, too, was part of the syndicate.

"You don't strike me as the type to make foolish mistakes, Mrs. Taylor." DeLuca's eyes narrowed. "Why didn't you take my advice? You'll have no one to blame but yourself."

Sara felt herself grow rigid. "I don't make mistakes. I always take full responsibility for my actions. As for your advice . . ."

"Spare me, my dear. You had your chance last night and you ignored it. We don't play games." DeLuca turned to his associate. Sara felt mesmerized as she watched him. His lips barely moved. "Take care of the lady, Jonas."

"Yes, sir," came the clipped reply.

It happened so fast. One minute the three of them were standing alone, the next minute there was a swarm of reporters around them. Sara stepped aside, clearing the way for DeLuca to take center stage. Jonas moved at the same time, jostling against Sara. She knew, without seeing the gun, that the man was wearing a shoulder holster; she felt the hardness of the leather as she was thrown against him. The color drained from her face as she understood what DeLuca had meant by "take care of her." He must have thought she wasn't leaving. It was her own fault for allowing him to think she wasn't giving in to his threats. The fact that she was on the verge of telling him meant nothing. She couldn't tell him now, while he was holding court to the press. She would leave now while all the commotion was going on. DeLuca would find out sooner or later that she was on the flight. As she turned to go she felt a touch on her arm.

"We'll leave together. Don't say anything, just move casually."

"Take your hands off me," Sara hissed.

Jonas's grip became more secure. "Smile, pretty lady, so the reporters can snap your picture. I mean it."

He did, she could feel it. "You wouldn't dare do anything here in full view of all these people. You aren't an associate of Stuart Sanders. You're one of

DeLuca's thugs, not a government agent. I also know what you're wearing under that custom-tailored suit."

"Then you know I mean business. Keep smiling and walk slowly, straight out to the car."

"Why? Where are we going? That's assuming I go with you."

"For a little ride. You talk too much."

"I was just going to the airport." Sara didn't like the man's looks or the cold, controlled way he spoke, knowing that he had no intention of taking her to the airport. The shoulder holster said all there was to be said. She had to think quickly. Where was that seedy-looking reporter from the slick tabloid? He had offered five hundred dollars for her exclusive interview late yesterday afternoon. Her mind raced. What was his name? Peter? Percy. Percy Strang, that was it.

"Let's get on with it, Mrs. Taylor. You're wasting time. I'm not going to tell you again."

"I can see that," Sara smiled up at him. "One moment and then I'll be glad to join you for coffee." She made her voice purposely high and shrill, knowing one or more of the reporters would look her way. She gave them all a dazzling smile then asked for Percy Strang. The reporter from the *Miami Herald* looked disgusted. Sara could almost read his mind—the gossip tabloids always got the dirt because they paid for it. It always came down to the buck. An honest reporter had to hustle, and then he was lucky to get two inches of printable news.

"Yo! Here I am, Mrs. Taylor. Changed your mind, I see."

"Why not? I can spend five hundred dollars just as easily as the next person. Why don't we go for coffee?" Sara asked.

"You got it. I'll even buy."

"How generous of you." She felt panic rise in her chest as the clamor around Roman DeLuca stilled; everyone was listening to the exchange between the wife of the State's star witness and the reporter from the *Informer*. "When will you pay me?" Sara demanded as an afterthought.

"As soon as these nimble fingers get everything down in black and white."

"A lady could hardly ask for more." Sara felt all eyes on her as she shook Jonas's hand off her arm. "I'm so sorry, Mr. Jonas, to renege on our breakfast date. However, five hundred dollars is five hundred dollars. I'll see all of you later. Gentlemen." She nodded to the crowd and moved quickly to Percy Strang's side.

Sara linked her arm through Strang's, walking him down the corridor, out the door and down the steps to the street. The limousine was standing at the curb; the driver inside was reading the paper and smoking a cigarette. She dragged the reporter with her as she leaped into the backseat of the luxurious car. "Take me to the airport, driver, and please hurry. You don't mind, do you, Mr. Strang? I mean about going to the airport. If we have time, we can have coffee. I thought it would be best if we talked on the way. This way you won't feel I'm trying to put you off. I don't have much time, and we'll have to stop the interview when I board."

At the reporter's disappointed look she went on hastily. "Of course, you can always come to New

Jersey, or call me long-distance. My son disappeared yesterday, and that's why I'm going home now. No one knows yet. It's your exclusive, Mr. Strang. However, I don't want to talk about that just yet. We'll get to my son later. For now, why don't you and I get to know each other? You tell me what it is you want to know, and I'll answer to the best of my ability."

"Are you saying your son's been kidnapped? Jesus, Mrs. Taylor, I don't know what to say!"

"I knew you'd feel like that which is why I said we would talk about it later. I do have one rather small favor to ask of you though."

"For an exclusive like that, Mrs. Taylor, I would try to walk on water for you."

"Yes, well, that won't be necessary. I want you to stay next to me every minute till I board the plane. Don't leave my side. If you see . . . What I mean is, if you suspect . . . Just don't leave my side. Is it a deal, Mr. Strang?"

"Of course it's a deal. This is the kind of stuff reporters only dream about. How am I ever going to thank you?"

"By staying next to me and not letting me out of your sight."

"Is there a microphone in this limo? How do you give the driver instructions?"

Sara felt faint. "I don't know . . . I'm not sure."

Percy Strang fiddled with the small grille above the ashtray. "Is this a rented limo or did the District Attorney provide it for you and your husband?"

"The district attorney?" Oh, God. "Mr. Strang, look outside. Is this the way to the airport?"

"Beats me, Mrs. Taylor. I'm based out of Chicago—I was sent here to cover the trial. We could be going to Cuba for all I know."

"Press that gadget and ask the driver how much further it is. Do it now!" Her voice was shrill. Percy did as he was instructed.

"Another five minutes, ma'am," came the reply. "The turnoff is just ahead. You can see the sign from here."

"Thank God," Sara sighed.

"Mrs. Taylor, I don't know why you're nervous, but I do think there's something you should know. When we pulled away from the curb back at the courthouse, a car pulled out right behind us. It's been following us ever since. Being a reporter, I'm trained to notice such things," Strang said importantly, hoping the elegant woman would be impressed.

"Oh, God," Sara moaned. Whoever was in the car wasn't following her to the airport to see if she got on the plane. If she knew nothing else, she knew that for a fact. She was going to be killed. She could taste her own death; a bitter sourness in her mouth.

"Do you read the *Informer*, Mrs. Taylor?"

"All the time. My housekeeper buys it and leaves it in the kitchen," Sara said feverishly. She should have told Andrew. Left a message, or something. What lies would Roman DeLuca tell her husband? Poor Andrew, he expected to get home to a wife, a wonderful celebration dinner, and everyone living happily ever after. "Shit!" she said succinctly.

Percy Strang frowned. He pursed his narrow lips in disapproval. Mrs. Taylor had slipped a notch in his esteem. Back at the courthouse she had seemed so elegant, so regal, like a princess, and she would certainly look smashing on the front page, right next to his story about the woman who had grown another kidney—a genuine medical miracle.

The chauffeur leaned his head back and spoke. "Which airline, ma'am?"

"Airline?" Sara repeated.

"Yes, ma'am. Where do you want to be dropped off?"

Sara's mind raced. Eastern? Delta? Pan Am? She couldn't remember. They had come down on Eastern, but that was no reason to assume DeLuca had made her return reservation on Eastern. However, "Eastern," she said firmly. The check-ins couldn't be that far apart.

Sara's mind raced as the limousine pulled up at the curb. Perhaps the driver would deliver a message to Andrew, or should she have the reporter deliver it? She couldn't make up her mind. If she did write a note to Andrew, she might place him in danger, and Andrew didn't function well in a crisis. He needed her and she was failing him. Should she write the note or not? The decision was taken out of her hands the moment she stepped out of the car. Just as the porter asked if she had any luggage, DeLuca's man, Jonas, leaped from his car.

"Mrs. Taylor, Mrs. Taylor, wait for me," Jonas shouted, a smile on his face.

Sara could hear Percy Strang calling to her to stop as she ran for the Eastern check-in counter, but she ignored him. Where were the police? The security guards? Miami had a crime rate to warrant an officer every twenty feet, but she couldn't see anyone to help her. How could Jonas kill her in a public space?

It had been so long since she'd prayed that Sara felt the words catch in her throat. She couldn't remember the simple prayers she had learned as a child. She had never been one to rely on the Almighty to help her, preferring to handle her own affairs in her own way. If she didn't see a uniform soon, she would have to go to the check-in and tell the reservation clerk. *Tell him what?* her mind shrieked.

"Mrs. Taylor, where are you going? Why are you so upset?" Strang had caught up with her. "Didn't you hear me? There's a man running after us who wants to talk to you. Perhaps he's got news of your son."

Sara turned. "That man you are so concerned about, Mr. Strang, is trying to kill me. He may even kill you. That's why I'm trying to get away from him. Where is he?"

Intrigue, kidnapping, killing—all the ingredients for a first-class story. Some journalist in the sky must be looking out for him, Percy thought happily. He almost tripped over his own feet as he tried to keep up with Sara. "He's right behind us, and I think you should know he's gaining rapidly. Look, Mrs. Taylor, I'm no he-man type. Why don't you find a cop?"

Sara picked up speed. "I would if I could. Do you see one anywhere?" she shot back.

"You could shout for help," Strang said.

"And then what? The man following us is connected with the syndicate. He works for the District Attorney, who is also connected with the syndicate. Where do you think that leaves me, Mr. Strang?"

Sara wanted to scream with frustration. Where was she going anyway? Who was she fooling? If she did find a policeman, what was she going to say? Jonas would whip out his credentials and tell the officer that she was distraught. The officer would gladly hand her over to the District Attorney's right-hand man. She didn't stand a chance, and she knew it. She wasn't going to be allowed to get on any plane. Jonas could even say she was mentally unstable. Who was going to believe her against someone with his credentials? He had Madison Avenue, Ivy League, the military, and law enforcement on his side. And what did she have? She was just a highly strung, perspiring, middle-aged woman being trailed by the star reporter from the *Informer*. Once she was in Jonas's custody, that would be the end. The local police would probably give him an escort out of the terminal.

"Andrew, Andrew, I'm so sorry," she murmured. Frantically she looked around, trying to see some way of escaping the man trailing her. Maybe she would be better off outside; she could walk around the airport building endlessly and still not get away. She needed an exit. A diversion. It was getting difficult to breathe.

"I don't understand any of this," Strang bleated. "We really have to stop and catch our breath. Mrs. Taylor, are you listening to me? If you sit down calmly to talk and think, we might come up with a solution to this . . . this predicament. What I'm saying is, this is a busy, well-policed airport. The man behind us isn't going to . . . Besides, isn't he one of the men assigned to guard you and Mr. Taylor? Mrs. Taylor, you aren't listening to a word I'm saying. You're overwrought; you must be mistaken."

"You're right, Mr. Strang, I'm not listening, and that's because you don't know what you're talking about. Back in the courthouse I purposely singled you out to get me away from the man following us. He is wearing a gun in a shoulder holster. As long as you walk directly behind me, as you're doing now, he won't dare shoot me. I'm frightened, and I don't mind if you know. You should be frightened, too, Mr. Strang. These people are evil; they will stop at nothing. They've already kidnapped my son. Now do you see why I have to get away from that man? He has no intention of letting me board any plane. I did something foolish this morning, and I'm going to pay for it with my life. But I'm not giving up without a fight, I can tell you that." Her voice was barely a whisper, hoarse and frightened.

"Come now, Mrs. Taylor, you're upset about your son, and the fact that your husband is a key witness in a murder case. It's understandable that you're building mountains out of molehills. What do you say to a cup of coffee?"

Oh, God, she was going to die and he wanted a cup of coffee. She felt like throwing up. Then she saw the diversion she needed. A group of South American soccer players was advancing down the concourse with good-natured backslapping and hilarity. If she quickened her stride, she could reach the exit sign at about the same time the players did. And if Strang could manage to join the crowd of players, he could stall for time and allow her to get outside where she could run.

The words came in controlled gasps. "Mr. Strang, will you help me? If you do this, I promise you the story of your life. Ten minutes, that's all I need."

The story of his life! The big scoop! They were the words every journalist dreams of. The big by-line. He would do it—it would spread across pages one and two. The woman with three kidneys would have to wait for another issue. This was the big one, the one he had dreamed about ever since walking into the *Informer* office to apply for a job. They had asked him two questions only. Can you type? Can you spell? He had answered "yes" to both and they'd hired him on the spot. And now his big chance had come! Even if Sara Taylor was crazy, it was a great story.

Sara felt the color drain from her face as she closed the distance between the soccer players and herself. How lightheaded she felt. Maybe she could get out of this after all. The exit sign blurred. "Now," she whispered hoarsely.

She thought Strang hadn't heard her, but suddenly he threw up his arms and walked smack into one of the approaching players. "My God, you're a sight for sore eyes," he shouted as he wrapped his skinny arms around the player's neck. "I want you to endorse some new soccer balls for me. You and your friends move right over here." He pushed the players together into a huddle under the exit sign.

Sara gasped—she'd made it! She was through the door. The question was, what was on the other side? Where was she? Paying no heed to the signs which read "Authorized Personnel Only," she raced along the concrete corridor and down a short flight of stairs. Red letters on the door ahead shouted "No Admittance" but Sara was beyond stopping now. She pushed open the door; behind her she could hear the pounding of footsteps. Jonas knew what she had done, and he was following her again.

There wasn't much time left. Still, she had to try. She felt a rush of cold air on her face—she was outside. Her mind was racing, her thoughts incoherent. Maybe she should have taken her chances with the airport police. Maybe, maybe, maybe. But the end would have been the same, of that she was convinced. Only the location would have been different—a lonely road with a bullet through her head, or worse, a blow to her head and the car set on fire. She knew she had to die. She had disobeyed Roman DeLuca, tried to outsmart him, and now it was too late! He'd never let her get away with it, especially if Andrew helped the State's case on the witness stand. She should have obeyed DeLuca's rules.

Sara ran wildly, legs pumping furiously, breath labored and painful. She was heedless of her path, aware only of open space around her and concrete beneath her feet.

Dimly, in the distance, she heard a voice on the public address system. "Unauthorized persons on the runway! I repeat—unauthorized persons on the runway! Clear the runway! I repeat—clear the runway!" Over and over the message was repeated, and each time the volume increased. Sara realized they were referring to her, and to Jonas. She saw running figures converging on her path—help was on the way. She was within a hair's breadth of winning!

"Clear the runway! Will somebody clear the goddamn runway? A man and a woman are on runway six. Clear the runway! Aircraft approaching! Aircraft approaching!" the PA shrilled.

Sara kept running, knowing her life depended on it. She risked a glance behind her. Jonas was still there, grim and determined. Safety was only yards away. There was a roar near her head, loud and piercing. She mustn't stop, mustn't think! She was almost home, a winner again.

The aircraft appeared out of nowhere. Out of the corner of her eye she could see a monstrous moving object but she had to get across—she *would*.

The whining in her ears became louder. Then, a shadow pressed down on her. She was losing control of her movements in the turbulence. It felt as if the plane would flatten her onto the runway—but of course it wouldn't land flat—there were the wheels.

But it was the wheels that cut that thought short.

Seconds later, Michael Jonas skidded to a stop next to the motionless form crumpled on the runway. His chest heaved with exertion, and his eyes were wide with horror. But he'd seen worse. He had known exactly what he was doing when he chased her onto the runway. DeLuca might protest, but he would be pleased. If there was one way to climb to the top, it was by obeying orders. DeLuca had said to take care of her, and he had. Aside from being windblown and out of breath, he was none the worse for wear. It was over.

Sanders trudged into the campground just as dawn broke. He felt more certain than ever that Davey Taylor was close by. Feeley wasn't back yet and he wondered who was going to replace the blond policeman behind the desk. A quick catnap was what he needed now, so he could make a fresh start when Feeley returned. Sanders nodded curtly to the young officer, who was slipping a long-handled comb back into his shirt pocket.

Feeley shook him awake at eight forty-five and handed him a cup of coffee. "You know something, Stu, I can't drink coffee out of a cup anymore," he joked as Sanders roused himself. "If it doesn't come out of a Styrofoam container and have a lid, I can't get it down."

"Never mind the coffee. What did you find?"

"The same thing the cops did—traces of blood. That apartment was a hellhole—I wouldn't let a dog live there. I rousted the landlady and, let me tell you, she was a piece of work. She was nipping on a bottle of beer at five in the morning. Said it beat coffee for a pick-me-up. She'd heard sounds of a fight and a lot of banging around—same thing she told the cops. I did find a couple of mates to this," he said, holding out six mothballs. "I found them on the steps. I looked all over the apartment but couldn't find any more. There was an empty box in a paper bag by the sink. No other trash. I hung around till the workforce crawled out of the woodwork. If there wasn't someone to hold up the corners at seven A.M., Newark would fall apart. No one saw a thing," he said disgustedly.

At Sanders's bleak look, he added hastily: "I don't know if this is worth anything, but as I was getting into my car—thanking God it was still there—a little kid came up. He wanted a quarter, probably to play the numbers. The long and the short of it is, he was playing stickball outside the building when Balog and the girl came out carrying an ironing board which they loaded into the pop-up. The kid said Elva—that's her name—always carried the dirty clothes in a paper bag to the laundromat around the corner. He said he saw her do it lots of times. The kid was a regular little wise-ass, said you don't take ironing boards to the laundromat because you can't iron there. He also said the clothes looked heavy, and that Balog was sweating. I gave him a few bucks." Feeley could tell Sanders was pleased.

"Heavy, huh? This kid say anything about talking to the cops?"

"You gotta be putting me on. He's a street kid. Street kids don't talk to the cops unless it's to tell them to drop dead. Nah, he thought I was a relative."

Sanders put two Rolaids into his mouth. He'd give his right arm for a home-cooked meal of French toast, or pancakes, or scrambled eggs with lots of bacon on the side.

"They could have been carrying a body," Feeley said. "You have to admit it was a clever idea, if that's the way they got him out. This Balog is our man, I'm sure of it. The locals must know it too, only they think they've got the jump on us. And who are we, anyway? Just some tired men looking for a lost kid."

Sanders nodded. "It's adding up, that's for sure. The mothballs sort of frost it, if you know what I mean."

"Yeah," Feeley said, mangling the soggy end of his cigar. "While you were playing Rip van Winkle, I was watching the bird on the phone desk. He kept looking over at me while he was carrying on this conversation. Call came in a little after eight. I asked him point blank if it was something we should know, and he told me it was a personal call. You want to check it out?"

Sanders rubbed the stubble on his chin. "Do *you* think it was a personal call?"

Feeley shrugged his shoulders.

"Then let's check it out."

Sanders got right to the point. "Now, let's make sure we understand each other," he told the officer manning the phone. "This is a bureau office. Any calls that come in pertain to our case. My partner said you received a call a short while ago. Let me see the log sheet."

The officer's face drained of color. "It was a personal call. A pal of mine was going off duty and they put him through here to me."

"We can call your pal, but that would take time. Make it easy for all of us."

The pale face flushed. "Well, you see, what I mean . . . My buddy and me know this hooker. She's okay, if you know what I mean," he added hastily, watching Sanders's face. "Anyway, she got busted up during the night. Some dude from out of town fed her a line about making her a showgirl in Vegas, and she fell for it. Somebody found her and called the hospital in Point Pleasant. She's being operated on right now. My buddy went over after he finished his shift to see if he could get a line on how it happened."

"And?"

"All he came up with was some guy driving a pickup which he left parked behind the garage. Gus, the guy who runs the garage, said this dude came in late yesterday to have a tire fixed. He steered him to the saloon where Candy dances. That's it."

"Did the guy from the garage say anything about the truck, like what color it was?"

"No, but my buddy said it was one of those hip-
pie rigs, all painted up and—Oh, Jesus, that was
the guy, right? Jesus!"

"Which hospital?" Sanders barked.

"Point Pleasant General. She's being operated
on now for a busted spleen, fractured collarbone,
and two cracked ribs. My buddy says her face will
never be the same again."

Sanders's stomach turned sour. He chewed up
two more Rolaids and turned to Feeley. "Sack out
for an hour or so. I'll check the police report. No
point in hanging around the hospital—we'll get to
her doctor later on this morning."

"Go away, I'm asleep already." It was true, Sanders thought in amazement. Loud, gusty snores
rippled around the room. The cigar hadn't moved.

Outside the office, Sanders stopped to gather
his thoughts. Balog was still in the area—everything
pointed to it. The beaten-up woman, the flat tire,
the description of the pickup by the garage owner.
But where was Davey? He would have staked his
life on it that Davey was with Balog and his traveling companion. Sanders snapped his fingers. Right,
there were two of them. One could have stayed
with the boy while the other went into town. But it
didn't fit. A man on the run with a kid in tow just
didn't take the time to visit a hooker. It didn't fit.

Unless . . . unless Davey was already dead. He'd
seen too much; Balog knew it and had disposed of
him. Still, it didn't feel right. What about the
woman with Balog? Elva, Feeley had called her.
Would Balog have left her behind to guard the kid
while he took himself off for a little relaxation?
Nah, no woman would stand for that. Okay, so this
Elva didn't know Balog was paying a house call.

He'd left her alone somewhere with the camper and Davey—but still, where did Davey fit?

Perhaps he'd been right earlier. Perhaps Davey *had* seen Balog burying Lombardi. Davey had been spotted; he'd run. Balog couldn't have caught him, or he'd have killed the boy right there at the campsite and dumped the body into the grave with Lombardi. Sanders snapped his fingers—*that* was why the grave had been left open. Balog had chased off after Davey, and then panicked when he couldn't find the kid. He'd packed up camp and made a run for it. But where was Davey now? Sanders remembered Duffy's attempts to communicate with him. Perhaps Davey had hidden in the trailer, not realizing he was getting himself into worse trouble.

The thought that Davey had already spent a night with a probable killer, and was still nowhere to be found, made Sanders's blood run cold.

Tired and hungry, Davey made his way to what looked like a farm. The roof of a large barn caught his eye, along with the silver silo standing beside it. He almost laughed aloud at his discovery, but some inner voice warned him that he couldn't count on victory just yet. There was still the open field to cross, and then he had to find someone to call his aunt. Whoever lived near the barn might take him to the police, and they would let him wear a police cap and give him an ice cream. They always did that on television.

Cautiously, Davey walked to the edge of the forest and looked across the open field. He had to cross it to get to the barn. But what if the man saw him? Overhead, a squirrel scurried out onto a low-lying branch then dropped to one beneath it. Petrified by the sound, Davey dropped to his belly and dug his head into his folded arms. He waited, lying motionless, barely breathing, until the squirrel was a foot in front of him. Davey opened one eye and stared with relief into the shiny brown buttons that were the squirrel's eyes.

Crawling on his belly, he inched his way out into the field. He wriggled and squirmed across the muddy terrain. Mom sure was going to be mad when she got a look at his clothes. Aunt Lorrie would never be able to get them clean. Davey felt part of the earth now, and for a few brief seconds he reveled in the sensation of his fingers clawing through the muddy ground, pulling him closer and closer to the red barn. By the time he reached the barn he was exhausted but exhilarated. He had done it; he had gotten away from the man. Now, if only he could find someone to call Aunt Lorrie, everything would be all right.

Davey got to his knees and brushed his hands together to get them clean. Mud spattered every which way. He laughed delightedly. If Mom could see him now she would take a fit. Aunt Lorrie would just laugh and turn a hose on him. But he couldn't think about that now—he had to find someone to help him. He looked over his shoulder to see if the man was anywhere near but the open field was empty.

The hems of his new jeans flapped at his ankles as Davey trudged around the side of the barn. There were turkeys there, daintily picking at the corn that littered the barnyard. Everything smelled sweet and clean. He wished he had a drink; even toothpaste would taste good in his mouth now. As he walked toward the turkeys, they started to gobble and scatter. A white-haired woman came out of the barn, holding a pitchfork.

"Well, well, what have we here?" she said kindly.

"Lady, I need someone to help me call my aunt. Will you call her for me?"

The woman laid the pitchfork on the ground. "You're lost, is that it? Bet you wandered off from the amusement park. I thought it was closed for the winter."

"It is. I was camping there with my aunt, and I don't know how to get back."

"How old are you?" she asked.

"I'll be eight after Christmas," Davey said proudly. "I would 'preciate it if you called my aunt. I have to get a shot at noontime. Do you know what time it is now?"

The old woman looked up at the sun. "Pretty near one o'clock." She reached out and took his hand in hers. "You come along with me and I'll try to clean you up a little. You need hosing down in the trough, but it's a mite too chilly for that. Wait on the back porch while I make the call. Would you like some cookies and milk? I make the best ginger cookies in these parts."

"I'd like that," Davey said agreeably. They walked side by side toward the farmhouse.

"Do you know the campsite number?"

"It's close to the pond—I don't know the number. But we have an RV and it's the only one in the campground."

"How did you get so muddy?"

"I crawled on my belly across the field," Davey replied truthfully.

"You ask a dumb question and you get a dumb answer," the old woman laughed. "I'll be back in two shakes," she said, leaving him on the porch.

Davey sat down on the step. His leg was aching and he was tired. The cookies and milk were going to taste good.

The screen door banged shut as the old woman brought out his food. "Here you go. What's your name so I know who I'm talking about when I call the campground?"

"Davey Taylor, but my aunt's name is Lorrie Ryan."

All of a sudden the turkeys started gobbling again. "Mercy me, what's that ruckus? Looks like we have another visitor. Land sakes, weeks and months go by and nary a soul stops by, and today we have two visitors."

Davey laid the cookie he was about to eat back on the plate.

"There you are, you little rascal," Cudge Balog accused playfully as he climbed from the pickup. "Thought you would give me a scare running off like that, did you? Excuse me, ma'am, this is my son, and he ran off on me this morning. You see, he didn't want to do his chores around the campground. I have a rule that each child does his share but this rascal likes to play. I'm sorry if he gave you any trouble, ma'am."

Fear gave Davey the impetus to get to his feet. He moved over to the woman and clung onto her dress. "He's not my father. He's a mean, bad man and he's telling you a lie. Please, call my aunt and tell her to come and get me. He's not my father."

"Now, why are you upsetting this nice lady with your stories? Someday this boy's going to write books. I just know it," Cudge said airily. "He does have some imagination."

"You're a bad man! You killed that man and tried to bury him. And you kicked my dog!" Davey stared with imploring eyes at the old lady. She didn't believe him, he could tell.

"That's enough of that," Cudge said. "Come along now and give this nice woman some peace and quiet."

"Now, just a minute," Elsie Parsons said sharply. "This little boy don't look like no liar to me. What's it gonna hurt if I call the campground to see if his aunt is there? It's only going to take a few minutes."

"What's going to take a few minutes?" a nasally voice inquired from inside the house. "What's going on here?"

"Sid, this here boy is Davey Taylor. This man claims to be the boy's father but the boy says he ain't. I found him by the barn this morning looking like this. He wants me to call the campground for his aunt. I think we should call the police and let them straighten it all out."

"Now, Ma, you don't want to go sticking your nose in someone else's business and get yourself in trouble," Sid said warily. "If the man says he's the kid's father, he is. Who you gonna believe—the guy or the kid? Kids lie all the time. He probably done something wrong and lit out." There was no way Sid wanted police around the place. First thing they'd be tramping all over and find his patch in the cornfield. Smoking pot was one thing, but growing it was something else.

Cudge grinned and slapped the youth on the

shoulder. "You're absolutely right. Davey wasn't in the mood to clean up the campsite this morning and just took off. He's a mighty big source of worry to his mother, I can tell you." He turned to Davey. "Now you get your butt in that truck before I take a switch to you. Apologize to these nice people for the trouble you caused them, and we'll be on our way. Ma'am, I do want to thank you for taking care of my boy here." Cudge held out his hand to the old lady.

Elsie backed off one step and then another. What could she do? She'd seen the look in Sid's eyes at the mention of police. Good Lord, what had he done this time? Well, your own came first, and then you worried about someone else's kids. Davey seemed like a nice little boy, well-mannered and polite. The father—if he was the father—left something to be desired.

"You mean you aren't going to help me?" Davey asked incredulously.

"No she ain't gonna help you," Sid told him. "You go on with your old man and stop bothering people and telling lies, or you're going to wake up some morning with a nose a mile long."

Davey threw himself against the old woman's legs. "He's not my father! He's not! He kills people! He kicked my dog." He could feel the lady tense as he tried to hold on to her. Just as Cudge reached for him, Davey dropped to his knees, crawled quickly around him and down the steps of the back porch.

Sid raced after him, caught him by the collar of the windbreaker and literally lifted the little boy off the ground. "Where's your respect for your old man, kid? Now you get in that truck and act the way you're supposed to. I'll personally tan your hide if I hear another peep out of you."

Before Davey knew what was happening, he'd been thrown into the cab of the pickup. Sid's leering face staring at him through the passenger window made him want to cry, but only babies cried. He wiped at his eyes with his muddy sleeve, leaving streaks of dirt on his cheeks. He was never going to get away now. He was going to be dead. His eyes went to the CB unit on the dashboard and then to Cudge, who was stepping down from the front porch. Quickly Davey locked both doors. He had the CB speaker to his mouth before Cudge's feet had hit the ground. He switched to the emergency channel. "Breaker, do you read? This is Panda Bear. Breaker! Breaker!"

Cudge felt the heat of his anger the minute he saw Davey with the CB. It was all over if the kid knew what he was doing. His rage intensified as he raced to the pickup. Out of the corner of his eye, he saw Sid walk around the back of the house. The old woman had gone inside the moment Cudge had stepped off the porch. He was alone with Davey.

Davey looked around wildly. "Help, help me. This is Panda Bear. Breaker, Breaker, do you read? This is Panda Bear! Breaker, he's coming. Somebody answer me. Do you read?" Frustration gripped him when he saw Cudge dig in his pocket for the keys. He had to get out before Cudge got in. If he stayed in the truck, the man would kill him. Whatever he was going to do, he had to do it alone, just like before. There was no one to help him. He had to think; above all, he couldn't cry. If he cried, he

wouldn't be able to see. Swallowing hard, Davey
tossed the speaker onto the cracked leather of the
driver's seat and pulled at the lock on the cab door.
The moment Cudge opened the driver's door to
climb into the truck, Davey opened his side. He
jumped to the ground and took off down the road,
away from the farmhouse, back across the open
field toward the woods. He knew that if he had the
farm at his back, the amusement park would be
ahead of him. That meant Aunt Lorrie would be
close by. He had to run straight, and he couldn't
stop for anything. Run, run, run.

His tattered shoelaces slapped the wet ground
as his short legs pumped away. Danger was behind
him; he could feel it, smell it. On and on he ran,
his arms flailing the air as he fought for breath.
Once he fell sprawling in the muddy field. He
picked himself up and raced on, not looking behind him to see if Cudge was gaining on him. He
knew Cudge must be close, but he couldn't run
any faster. He made himself think about Aunt Lorrie
waiting for him, her arms outstretched to hug
him, mud and all. She would laugh and tell him a
story about making mudpies, and then he would
laugh too. He wanted to hear the story, he wanted
her to hug him. If Cudge caught him, he would
never see Aunt Lorrie again. His Reeboks picked
up speed. Behind him, curses sailed through the
air, but he ignored them. Careening wildly from
right to left, Davey headed into the welcome darkness of the forest. He didn't stop. *Faster. Run. Aunt
Lorrie.* A sob caught in his throat.

A thicket of low underbrush caught his eye as
he raced ahead. Without thinking, he dived down.
Brambles and stickers scratched at his face as he

burrowed deep into the undergrowth. Cudge was close; Davey could hear him now, feel the cold stream of danger getting closer and closer. He waited, his eyes squeezed shut. He didn't want to see. He had to be quiet and still.

At first he couldn't comprehend the sound. It was a roar, a deep, hard rumble that came from the belly; like when his dad threw back his head and had a good laugh. He wanted to lift his head to look around to see where the sound came from, to try to identify it. The man chasing him didn't make this kind of sound. This was something different. Davey tilted his head and listened as the rumbling was repeated. It was from the wildlife reserve. He must be close to the animals. That meant that on the other side was safety. His breathing eased; he wasn't afraid of the animals in their cages.

Cautiously Davey inched his way out of his nest. Everything looked so big as he lay on his stomach; even the scrubby bushes looked immense. He waited a moment, hoping the animals would roar again so he could tell in which direction he should go. If only he hadn't been so afraid he might be able to remember now. For the thousandth time he wished Duffy was with him.

He crawled backward on his belly from his hiding place and looked around again. Satisfied that the man wasn't anywhere around, he stood up. A wave of dizziness overcame him and he swayed, feeling sick to his stomach. Both hands grappled for the bushes; he needed all his willpower to steady himself. He couldn't get sick now. He shook his head several times; he was hungry and he really didn't feel well. How much farther did he have to go?

The old woman stood at the screen door, looking out at Cudge. Her son Sid watched him too, waiting to see if he was going to run after the boy, or jump into the truck and try to overtake him before he ran across the open field into the woods.

"Watcha lookin' at, old lady?" Cudge bellowed. "If you two had minded your own business, I would've had him!"

Elsie Parsons stared at him a moment longer, then retreated into the house, closing the door firmly.

Sid was belligerent. "Ma don't think that's really your kid."

Cudge turned on the teenager. "Oh, yeah? And what do you think, punk? You should've kept out of it, and I would've had him."

Sid gathered his courage. He really didn't want any trouble with this man, but he felt compelled to stand his ground. "I agree with Ma. I don't think that boy's your kid, either."

"I don't give a damn what either one of you think. That's my kid and I mean to get him and beat the tar out of him. What's on the other side of the woods?" Cudge demanded, stepping closer to Sid.

"Wild Adventure Park. Only it's closed now."

"Where's the campground from here?"

"Due north . . ."

"I didn't ask you that, did I?" Cudge bellowed in rage, reaching out and grasping Sid's shirt front. "I asked you *where*."

Sid pointed across the field to the right, in the opposite direction from that the boy had taken. Cudge grinned; he knew Sid was afraid and it made him feel powerful.

"Stay out of my way." He shoved Sid aside. "I eat punks like you for breakfast and spit them out before lunch. I knew a kid like you once. I took care of him, and I could do the same for you." He saw a defiance in Sid's eyes he didn't like. "Don't think about calling anybody. A man has a right to his own kid, don't he? Besides, you may not like it if I told anybody that you've got a patch of marijuana growing out behind the house."

Sid was amazed. "How do you know?"

"I always know, punk. You reek of it. Besides, you just told me all I need to know. Even if you weren't growing the stuff, you'd be real unhappy if the cops came beating at your door and found your little stash."

Cudge jumped into the truck and fired the ignition. It wasn't going to be easy to find that kid, but he'd do it, just the way he'd tracked him here to the farmhouse. He'd drive back to the park and leave the truck in the cover of the trees where it wouldn't be spotted. Then he'd grab the kid and shut his mouth for good.

Cudge took his time driving back to the campsite. He didn't need a broken axle now, not when the kid was within his reach. "It's either him or me. And it ain't gonna be me!"

The turns in the road took his full concentration. The weather was blowing up and storm clouds were gathering. For a fleeting moment he thought about Elva lying in his pop-up. He was glad she was dead, and he didn't have to listen to her squawk-

ing that he should leave the kid alone. Elva had
never been a survivor, not like him. If he could just
get his hands on that kid, his problems would be
over. "It's always the little things that trip a guy
up," he muttered aloud, "little boy, little dog. Elva
with her little bit of brains. Candy Striper for a little piece of ass. Lenny, for a little bit of money." He
groaned. How had this all happened? This wasn't
the way things were supposed to work out! When
he was a kid, he had believed he'd be able to overcome the poverty, the filth, his ignorance. And all
he'd done was carry it all with him.

As he drove he kept his eyes trained on the edge
of the woods, expecting a mud-smeared figure to
emerge at any moment. Christ, that kid was smart.
Still, when he got his hands on the brat's neck, he
was going to finish him for good.

The CB in the truck squawked. "Breaker, Breaker.
Do you read me, Panda Bear? Come in, Panda Bear!"

Panda Bear. Where had he heard that before?
Then he remembered. He'd been cruising around
in north Jersey, looking for a place to dump
Lenny, and Panda Bear had come on the CB channel and talked about the campground. *So that's
your name, eh, kid?* Cudge thought. *Panda Bear.*

"Breaker, Breaker, do you read? Come in, Panda
Bear."

Cudge reached over and flicked off the CB. The
sharp click made him think of how he would snap
Panda Bear's neck when he caught him.

Thirteen

Stuart Sanders checked in with his chief then set out in Feeley's motor-pool car. He couldn't explain why, but he knew Davey Taylor was close by, close enough to touch if he could just reach out in the right direction.

Up and down the dirt roads he drove, but with no success. He braked hard and sat for a while, pondering his next move. His instincts told him to head for the Wild Adventure Park, the same route he had followed on foot last night. There was something out there, something he'd missed.

It was well after one o'clock when he returned to the camp office to clean up and get on with the day.

Lorrie was sitting on the steps of the motor home. She looked as beat as he felt.

"Hi," he said, when he got within speaking distance.

"Hi, yourself. Anything new to report?"

Sanders shook his head. "Not yet, but not to worry. Everything is going to be okay."

Lorrie tilted her head sideways and gave him a questioning look. "How can you be so sure?"

"It's just a feeling." He shrugged.

"A feeling," she repeated.

He hunkered down in front of her, his hands braced on his thighs. "I've been in this business a long time, Lorrie, and after a while you start to rely on your gut instinct. And mine tells me Davey is alive and well."

Lorrie bowed her head. "I hope you're right."

He could see the tears welling in her eyes and, without thinking, reached out to touch her face. "When this is all over and Davey is safe and sound, you and I are going to get to know each other a little better."

Lorrie smiled at him through her tears. "There's nothing I'd like better but . . ."

"But what?" he asked, worry creeping into his voice.

"I may not be alive after my sister gets through with me."

"Your sister . . ." Sanders began, anger welling behind his words. "I still can't believe she refused to come with me. What kind of mother—" He broke off, realizing he had spoken out of turn.

Lorrie leaned forward and put her arms around his neck. "It's all right. I feel the same way you do."

The anger Sanders had been carrying around with him dissolved when he gazed into Lorrie Ryan's eyes. "Lorrie, I . . ." Whatever he'd been about to say was forgotten the moment Lorrie's mouth pressed against his. Slowly, he rose to his feet, drawing her up with him. Needs that he'd left too long unsatisfied rose to the surface. There were other feelings too—new feelings he couldn't put a name to. Together they created a terrible hunger.

Lorrie broke the kiss and stepped back, a look of surprise on her face. "What were you going to say?"

Sanders shook his head. "I have absolutely no idea."

"Oh."

"Yeah . . . oh."

Lorrie smiled sheepishly. "Well, I guess I'd better go inside and fix something to eat." She started to turn away.

"And I guess I'd better head for the showers," Sanders said, moving backwards. "I'll see you a little later."

Lorrie climbed the steps to the motor home and disappeared inside.

Sanders went to the camp showers, where he cleaned up quickly. Out of season the campgrounds offered cold water only, which seemed appropriate under the circumstances. A loud knock startled him. "Come in," he shouted as he put away his shaving gear.

"Yeah, what is it?" he demanded of the reflection that met his eyes in the mirror over the sink.

"Your man thought you would want to hear about this."

It was Officer Delaney. Sanders liked him on sight, from the top of his neat haircut to the tips of his polished shoes that were buffed to a high sheen.

"Feeley? I thought he was asleep. Something

come in that sounds important?" He noticed the alert look in the young officer's eyes.

"Yes, sir. He was asleep, but he sleeps like me, with an eye open. You have to do that when you're in law enforcement."

"Tell me about it," Sanders mumbled as they walked through the sodden leaves. "That was some storm we had last evening."

"Good thing it was over early. As it was, the power company was out all night working. We get storms like that around here this time of year. I hear there's another blowing up." Delaney's tone was easy but his respect for Sanders was evident. "There was a call from a shut-in who monitors police calls, Citizens Band, short-wave, you name it. He said he didn't know if it was important or not, but he heard a child calling for help on the emergency channel a little while ago. I have to be honest with you, this turkey calls in on a regular basis. He sees UFOs once a week, hears calls for help, and once he said he heard a gang rape going on in the back of an eighteen-wheeler."

"The kid have a handle?" Sanders waited, hardly daring to breathe, for Delaney's answer.

"Yes, sir. Panda Bear."

"Jesus Christ!" Sanders exploded as he broke into a run.

"Your man has the caller on hold," Delaney shouted. For a big man, Sanders moved fast as he raced ahead to the offices. Delaney looked after him, wondering if he would ever join the state police. That was the big-time. He'd get to wear a snappy uniform, a snap-brim hat and, of course, those polished sunglasses.

Delaney took his work seriously; he was even

willing to forgo marriage so he could devote his life to law enforcement. That was the supreme sacrifice. A talk with Sanders could be helpful. He hoped the caller had his marbles all in one bag this time around, and that the child on the emergency channel *was* the Taylor kid, and that he was okay. Dr. Ryan was a nice person, she deserved some good news. There was a chance that he would be the one to tell her. He would get pleasure out of that, seeing her eyes light up. Childishly, he crossed his fingers.

He nodded briefly to Feeley as he took his position again behind the desk. Sanders was just hanging up the phone. Delaney waited, not sure if he liked the look on Sanders's face. It was Sanders's case and the agent didn't have to confide in Delaney. Delaney crossed his fingers again.

"Feeley, you stick around and work the phone. Find out if anyone else heard the call. Let's see if we can't pinpoint it a little more accurately." Sanders looked at the scrawled note in his hand. "The guy's name is Rob Benton. He lives right here in Jackson. Delaney, find out how many turkey farms there are around here. This Benton is certain he heard turkeys in the background." Sanders grimaced. "He said he hates turkeys—actually what he said was, he's afraid of them." He looked directly at Delaney, defying him to say the caller was a crackpot.

Delaney's gaze was unblinking. "You ever have a bunch of turkeys gang up on you? It's hairy—I know what he's talking about. And yes, there are three or four turkey farms around here. As a matter of fact, there's one right next to the amusement park. The bottom end of the farm runs parallel with the wildlife reserve. An old lady owns the farm—her son is on every cop's list from here to Forked River."

"Check it out, Delaney. I'll see you in a little while." Sanders wished he had a lucky horseshoe, or a rabbit's foot.

As he steered the high-powered car down the dirt road, he tried to calculate how long Davey had gone without a shot, but he gave up. Waiting for the lights to change at the main road, he spotted some newspapers in a vending machine on the corner. Leaving the door open and the engine running, he picked up a paper—Davey's picture was on the front page. The traffic light changed and several horns beeped. He ran back to the car, tossing the paper on to the seat beside him.

"I know you're on the loose, kid," Sanders mumbled to himself. "You can find your way back, I know you can. I got a steak dinner going on your getting back okay. You just hang tight. I'm going to find you."

Ninety minutes later Stuart Sanders was back at the same light, waiting for it to change again. Rob Benton's story was unshakable. The guy had heard exactly what he'd repeated on the phone. He also reported that he'd monitored the channel from that moment on, and there had been no more calls. Sanders believed him.

Davey started off, looking back over his shoulder every few minutes. He still didn't feel well, but it wasn't as bad as it had been a few minutes ago. Something jingled in his pocket—the three quarters Mr. Sanders had given him. They clinked companionably together. The flashlight should be in the zipper pocket on the sleeve of his windbreaker. He felt for it—it was still there. If he could just keep away from that bad man, he would be okay.

He cocked his head and listened. The woods were silent, except for the rustling of the leaves overhead. From time to time a squirrel raced through the treetops. Davey grinned. The squirrels were getting ready for winter. Just like he was getting ready for whatever was going to happen to him next. So far he had missed two lunches, one dinner, and one breakfast. He ticked the meals off on his fingers. Four! He would tell Digger he had missed four meals and was still alive. When you didn't eat, you turned into skin and bones and died. Digger knew what he was talking about. He said it had almost happened to him on one of his trips to the hospital. They'd fed him with a tube because he was almost skin and bones. Davey's face puckered up as he tried to figure it all out.

Davey walked slowly on through the woods for another half hour. His leg ached and he wished he had someone to talk to. It would feel so good to have Duffy scampering around his feet, even if he was too tired to play with her. Duffy would be able to smell Cudge if he got too close. She would bark to warn him in time to find a hiding place. Davey would have to tell Digger how good he was at finding hiding places. Digger would appreciate his low-flying dives into the brambles. Poor Digger, he hoped the doctors fixed his legs right this time.

Davey stopped, every sense alert. It was quiet. There were no squirrels, no rabbits running through the brush. He was still safe. Then Davey noticed two things: a loud banging noise, and the way the

woods were thinning out. He strained to identify
the banging sound. He had heard it before back
home, or had it been Aunt Lorrie's house? He
grinned—how could he have forgotten? He himself had helped make the sounds. Last year, Aunt
Lorrie had let him bang in the nails for the tree
house they'd built in the backyard. Aunt Lorrie had
hurt her thumb and then quit to go make lemon-
ade.

He walked slowly to the very edge of the trees,
careful to shield himself by not stepping out into
the bright sunshine. He dropped to his knees and
then to his belly. It looked like the muddy field by
the old lady's house, but different. He propped his
elbows on the ground, letting his chin rest in the
hollow of his cupped hands. It took a moment to
make sense of what he was seeing—all kinds of
posts, gravel . . . It was a parking lot, he thought ju-
bilantly. He hadn't realized it at first because there
weren't any cars. Now he knew where he was—the
amusement park. If he was really smart, he might
be able to find his way back to Aunt Lorrie without
anyone's help.

In his mind, he had begun to think of Cudge as
a wild animal—a wild animal who was chasing him,
wanting to eat him. He remembered how Cudge
had sounded like an animal tearing through the
woods, pounding the ground. Davey had heard its
heavy panting and pictured a red-eyed beast with
sharp horns and hoofed feet. A hard knot in his
stomach seemed to squeeze out his breath, making him feel he was going to be sick.

He needed to find the man who was banging in
nails. He had been successful once by crawling on
his belly; he would do it again. If he stood up he

would be an easy target. The ground was muddy, and a shard of broken glass winked at him from the left. He would have to be careful. When he reached the other side, where would he be? Shielding his eyes from the sun, he peered across the parking lot. He could see the tip of a roof, some trees and bushes, and a very high fence, the kind that had little holes in it. Dad had told him it was called chain-link. Fences had gates, he knew, like at home where the gate was always closed so Duffy couldn't get out of the yard. Sometimes Dad locked the gate when they went on vacation.

Davey was fifty feet from the end of the parking lot when he heard the animal roar. "Hey, kid!"

Davey's heart pounded in his chest. He lifted his head to look around and saw Cudge at the far end of the parking lot, pointing at him. Davey shot to his feet and scrambled to the fence. Frantically, he looked for a gate. He couldn't let Cudge get him. He tripped and sprawled in the coarse gravel, and he saw a small hole under the fence. Using his hands, he dug at the wet earth. He dug faster, sending the loosened earth flying this way and that, the way he'd seen Duffy do it. He heard Cudge yelling at him and knew the beast was close. Lying flat, he pushed his head through the opening, then wriggled one shoulder under, then the other. He winced as the points of the fence dug into his jacket and his back. He worked his way loose and pulled himself through to the other side.

"Get back here, you little bastard! You ain't getting away this time," Cudge yelled. He grabbed for Davey's leg.

Davey shrieked in terror as Cudge pulled at

him. He jerked his leg and felt his Reebok slide off his foot. He was through! Safe! Cudge only had his sneaker. Davey struggled to his feet to see Cudge's rage-filled face staring at him through the fence. Slowly, Davey backed away, then turned and ran.

A roar ripped from Cudge's throat. "I'll get you yet! You ain't getting away from me this time, you stupid kid. This place is all closed up. You won't be able to get out, and there's no one in there to help you."

Davey knew he had to move fast to find the man with the hammer. Screaming for help, he ran toward the center of the park. Where was he? Why couldn't he hear the banging now? Maybe the man had finished his work and gone home. The thought was so terrible, he wanted to cry.

Cudge dropped the single Reebok as though it had burned his fingers. He'd been so close—he'd almost had him. It was becoming impossible to think; there was a roaring noise in his head, or was it the thunder? Panting with rage, blind with frustration, he was unable to think what his next move should be.

An eight-foot-tall fence separated him from the kid; by the time he climbed it, the kid would be long gone. He twisted the small black-and-white leather shoe in his hands. Panda Bear—it was a stupid CB handle if ever he'd heard one. Only the kid wasn't so stupid—Cudge would give him that.

Cudge had been smart, too, when he was a kid, but he wondered how smart he was now. Here he was, chasing a little boy, when he should have been planning his own escape.

* * *

Stuart Sanders tapped his fingers on the steering wheel while he waited for the light to change. He'd been riding around for what seemed like hours, thinking, reviewing, but always on the lookout for Davey.

A car full of teenagers passed him just as the amber light flicked to green. Surprised, he checked his watch; it was two-thirty already, and the high school was letting out. That was when he noticed a billboard with an arrow pointing to Wild Adventure Park. Maybe he could spot the turkey farm on the way. He allowed a van and a sports car to pass him before inching into the moving traffic.

Within minutes the main gates to the park were in sight, but it was the appearance of a secondary road, probably for employees, which caught his interest. After following a circuitous route for several miles, the road ended in a graveled parking area. The gates were chained shut.

Sanders turned off the engine and surveyed his surroundings, attempting to pinpoint his location. Last night he hadn't come this far through the woods. On the map, the distance between the park and the campground hadn't appeared so close. He knew he wouldn't have any difficulty gaining admittance to the park; all he had to do was flash his credentials. He could even climb the fence if he had a mind to.

Back at the car he retrieved the binoculars he'd borrowed from Feeley. Training the sights on the horizon, he scanned the treetops, spotting the tall girders of the Ferris wheel. Rides, thrills, and adventure, all waiting till spring, when flocks of children would swarm over them, laughing and shrieking. He wondered if Davey Taylor had ever ridden on a Ferris wheel or a carousel.

Lighting a cigarette, Sanders turned to his left, and walked along the fence. He took a drag on the cigarette as he retraced his steps past the gate, along the perimeter of the parking lot. He would have missed it if he hadn't dropped the cigarette to grind it out with the heel of his shoe. There was a hole under the fence. Dropping to his heels, Sanders saw the small mud-caked Reebok lying close by. He hadn't realized he had been holding his breath until it exploded from his lungs, making him lightheaded. Both hands reached for the bedraggled leather shoe. The hole under the fence was just about big enough for the kid to belly through, and it was freshly dug.

"Good boy. You're almost there. Just a little longer and I'll find you, Davey."

The pain that had been gnawing at his stomach stilled. Davey was free, not in Balog's hands. At least not for the moment. Sanders gripped the shoe hard, as though trying to squeeze information out of it. Looking at it, thinking about Davey, the chewing in his stomach began again. Davey wasn't the kind of kid who was careless with his things. He would never have left his shoe behind unless something had prevented him from retrieving it. Or someone. Balog.

Davey Taylor was on the run. His path took him across a park-like area littered with outbuildings that looked like the Quonset huts that came with his army and soldier set. All the buildings had wide doors like garages, and there were stacks and stacks of trash cans nestled inside one another. There was no safety to be found here, nowhere to hide. He ran on blindly, not stopping to take his bearings or note his surroundings. Past the utility buildings, alongside the storehouses and equipment garages he ran. His stockinged foot hurt from the pebbles on the ground and his sock was cold and wet from the puddles left by last night's rain.

Ahead of him was the visitors' area of the amusement park. The rides looked stark and alien against the vibrant golds and reds of the autumn leaves. To Davey's right was a tall, semicircular amphitheater with a blue dolphin pictured on the stark white concrete. Beyond this, the brick path widened into an expanse of cement where the desolate rides were located. Between two towers hung a huge pirate ship, painted bright red and suspended over a now-empty pool.

Glancing up at the sky, Davey saw the tall pylons which supported the guide wires for the Sky Ride. There were lots of buildings dotting the area between the trees. Once, for an instant, he drew up short, staring at a candyland structure with peppermint sticks for columns, supporting a sugar-frosting roof and ice-cream-cone facade. He was reminded of how long it had been since he'd eaten, and how good a cupcake would taste right now. The chocolate browns, vanilla whites and shiny reds of the building fascinated him.

Then he remembered his predicament and, with great effort, forced his weary legs on. The knee that usually had the support of the brace was sore and throbbing. Mustering his courage yet again, he ran onward, heading for a small building where he hoped he could hide.

The building had two doors. By stretching back, Davey could see the pictures on them: a lady and a man. He reached for the knob to the men's room then hastily withdrew his hand. The man would definitely look for him there. Without another second's hesitation, he opened the door to the women's bathroom. The heavy hinges stopped the door from closing immediately. Davey leaned against it to push it closed; now he felt almost safe. But then he noticed there was no lock on the doorknob. If he'd gotten in, the man could get in too. Frantically he looked around for something to block the door.

He could see sinks, toilets with doors, and a garbage can—everything looked clean and forgotten, as though no one was coming back. There was nothing here, not even a sliver of soap on the sink. He decided not to wash his hands and dirty the sink, but he had to go to the bathroom. Six of the doors had silver coin slots, and were locked shut, but one door at the end stood open. He had only Mr. Sanders's three quarters—he didn't want to spend them going to the bathroom. He looked in the open door as he unzipped his jeans. Carefully, he held up the seat while he urinated. He liked watching the steady stream as it hit the water. As he zipped up his pants a door slammed close by. Arrow swift, Davey had the door closed and locked behind him. He hopped up onto the seat and braced his hands against the door. He sucked in his breath.

He could tell Cudge was mad by the way the door banged against the tiled wall. Davey waited while footsteps sounded. Looking down from his perch, he could see heavy yellow boots, caked with mud, appear and disappear as the man stalked back and forth. With a growl, he moved toward the door. Davey waited for the sound of the door closing, but he didn't hear it. Did that mean the man hadn't pulled it closed, or did it mean he was still there, waiting to catch him? Davey wished he could hear the sound of the workman banging the nails. He was tired, and his arms ached, but he would wait a little longer. He couldn't get caught now, not when he was so close to Aunt Lorrie. He had to be more careful than ever.

Just when he thought he couldn't stand another second of waiting, Davey heard the snick of the closing door. There were no more footsteps, no muttered curses. The man was gone. Davey gingerly pulled back one arm and then the other. Dropping to the floor, he reached out a quivering arm to flush the toilet, but then quickly withdrew it. The frothy bubbles would have to stay—toilets made a lot of noise in places like this. It wasn't safe here; he had to leave. If the man came back, he would see the open door, and then he would know Davey had tricked him. The thought pleased Davey—he really had tricked him.

Now, when he walked out of the bathroom, he would go to his left, because if he went right he would end up back at the hole in the fence. He had to keep going in the opposite direction; he had to stay behind the man.

As Davey started out, he listened for sounds of hammering; his entire body was alert to any movement within his line of vision. He shivered, it was getting cold. Now that he was moving again, he realized he still didn't feel well. If only he could lie down and take a nap, but he couldn't. It was important to keep going, to find Aunt Lorrie. If he lay down and fell asleep, the man would find him.

Davey gradually slowed as he trudged around the park, bewildered by the shadows the giant rides created. He knew he had to be quick to hide at the first sound that fell on his ears. He wished he could read better so he would know what all the signs meant. Why couldn't he find the man with the hammer? Why hadn't he seen anyone to ask for help? Then he saw Cudge, just ahead, stalking the area in front of a hamburger restaurant. The little round tables and chairs were painted to look like polka-dotted mushrooms and toadstools, and Cudge was bending down, peering underneath them. Davey crouched low. Sometimes, like now, he was glad he was small. When you were little, there wasn't so much of you to see. He maneuvered his way behind a big red trash can and watched Cudge work his way around the perimeter of the restaurant. His heart hammered in his chest and he felt as though the ocean was slapping at his ears.

He was getting colder and he was so tired. He stifled a yawn, never taking his eyes from Cudge's slouched form. He drew back suddenly. Cudge was standing upright now and looking around, deciding which way to go. Davey risked another quick look and saw him head for a low, white building with a red and black sign. He watched as Cudge opened the door and looked inside. He didn't go inside, just looked. Then he closed the door and moved on. As soon as Cudge was out of sight,

Davey ran across the space and into the building. If Cudge had already looked in there, he probably wouldn't come back there again.

One wall was lined with lockers, the other with open-stall showers. To the left, in a room littered with cartons and boxes, Davey saw a desk with a push-button telephone sitting on it. Frantically, he dialed 911. He waited and waited but no one picked up the other end. He tried again but achieved the same result. Defeated, he sat down on the swivel chair, his face puckered with despair. Mom had told him to dial 911 if ever he had an emergency. But it didn't work. There wasn't anybody there.

Maybe this telephone was broken. Maybe if he could find another telephone it would work. Outside, in the locker room, he saw a pay phone on the wall. He knew it was a pay phone because he'd been with his mom once when she'd used one to call his dad. For almost a full minute Davey stared at the phone. He couldn't reach it. Maybe if he dragged the bench over and stood on it . . . He had to try.

Pulling and tugging, he managed to drag the heavy wooden bench directly underneath the telephone. He climbed onto it, lifted the receiver and listened to the dial tone. He wasn't sure if he was supposed to put the money in before or after he dialed.

Again, he dialed 911 but, as before, no one answered. He tried it again, putting the money in first. No answer. When he'd gotten out his money, he'd felt Mr. Sanders's card in his pocket. He would call Mr. Sanders! Mr. Sanders would help him. He would know what to do.

With shaking hands Davey dialed the numbers

on the card. A voice came on the line and told him to deposit fifty cents. He dropped two quarters into the slot and waited. Three, four, five rings.

"Hello, this is Stuart Sanders," a voice said. "I'm away from the phone right now but you can page me at—"

"Hey you," a gruff voice shouted outside. "What are you doing in here? The park is closed, mister. How did you get in?"

"I climbed the fence, that's how!" It was Cudge. "My kid got in here by digging under the fence out by the parking lot. I had to climb over, because the hole he dug wasn't big enough for me. Are you sure you ain't seen him? He's about this high, has blond hair? I gotta find him before his mother takes a fit!"

Davey put the receiver back on the hook. He wanted to run outside and ask the man Cudge was talking to for help, but he was afraid to because of what had happened at the farmhouse.

"Mister," the other man continued, "I haven't seen any kids around here. I've been working all day over by the roller coaster, dismantling the cars and getting them ready for next spring. There's no kid around here. You'd better be on your way before I call the police."

Suddenly the man's voice changed, as though something had choked off his words. "Now look, mister, if you want I'll go around and ask the shutdown crew if they've seen anything." He was speaking faster, higher pitched, as though he were scared. Davey knew that the man was afraid of Cudge too.

"I want to find my kid. I'm not leaving till I do!"

"I know, I know. I've got kids of my own. Come on with me, we'll go around and ask the other guys.

We'll be punching out for the day pretty soon. Maybe somebody's seen him."

Panic-stricken, Davey dropped the phone and jumped down from his perch atop the bench. He had to get away.

He looked around—there was no back door! Saliva dribbled down his chin; he was too frightened to swallow. Into the small storage area behind the locker room he ran, hoping there might be a door through there. He saw some double doors with a big red exit sign above them. Silently, he inched open one of the doors and peered out.

The sun was gone now and the sky looked dark. A strong breeze that smelled of rain was sending fallen leaves and paper spiraling along the ground. He could hear voices outside. His heart pounding, he inched the door back into place then ran. Faster and faster—up the incline, past the miniature golf course, around the bend to the haunted house, down the rise to the old-fashioned carousel. Sobbing, gasping for breath, he ran blindly, not caring where he went as long as he was putting distance between Cudge and himself.

Would Cudge go into the building? Would he notice that the bench had been pulled up to the phone? *He'll catch me!* Faster, always faster, Davey staggered onward. He had to keep running away. He had to make himself safe. Safe so Aunt Lorrie could find him.

Fourteen

The police station was located behind the city hall, and it was here that Stuart Sanders found a distracted Chief Allen. The ensuing confrontation added further fuel to the fire in Sanders's digestive tract.

"What's this bullshit you're giving me about not having any available men? You have a fifteen-man force here—or is that just for the taxpayers' benefit?"

"I do have fifteen men, but two are out with the flu, one's on vacation, and one has a death in the family. That leaves me eleven—count 'em, eleven!" Allen glowered at Sanders.

"Call in for help if you need it," Sanders suggested.

"Don't need it. This is our baby and we'll handle it. Eleven men, two murders."

Sanders remembered the beaten-up prostitute. "When did she die?"

"Who?"

"Who else—the hooker your boys are so fond of." He restrained his rising temper. Discipline, he told himself. Discipline.

"No, Candy is holding her own. We're not stupid here, Sanders. We found traces of rotting apples on the floor and bedcovers in Candy's cottage. All her shoes were clean, so we knew it had to have been tracked in by whoever beat her up. Turns out we were right. A few of these dirt roads leading out from the orchards are littered with dropped apples that bounce off the trucks."

"Another little tidbit that didn't appear in the police report. Just like the mothballs," Sanders slipped in. He was rewarded by the surprised look on Allen's face. "So, what did you find?"

"A pop-up camper. The same one that Balog was pulling, according to the plates. And a woman. Beaten the same way Candy was. Only it's too late for this one."

Sanders clenched his teeth. "Balog. That man is responsible for beating up two women and killing one, as well as the murder of the body you dug up in the campground. He's involved with the Taylor boy. Wherever Davey is, you'll find Balog close by. Now, are you going to make a move, or do I have to move you myself?"

"Forget it, Sanders. This doesn't involve you. Whatever you do about the kid is fine with me, but stay out of my business. We'll handle the murders." Allen reached for his hat.

"Where are you going now?"

"Out to the camper. The body hasn't been removed yet and I want to take a look for myself. Another thing—there's a storm brewing, due to hit here in the next hour or so. A good rain will obliterate any leads so we've got to work fast."

"I'm coming with you," Sanders said. "I'll follow in my own car."

Bouncing down the track behind Chief Allen, Sanders hit a pothole big enough to swallow the front end of the car. The pop-up was parked less than a mile from the main highway; Allen's men were already crawling all over it.

"He doesn't need a rainstorm to 'obliterate his leads,'" Sanders swore under his breath, "his men are doing it for him."

Hopping out of the car, Sanders moved quickly toward the trailer, elbowing through the uniformed men. The pop-up was rocking on its moorings with the extra weight of Allen's men. The interior was dark and filthy, littered with cartons, discarded cupcake wrappers and empty soft-drink cups. The clear vinyl windows were all in place, keeping the air within stale and close.

Sanders noticed an odor he couldn't immediately identify. Whatever it was, it was hours old, and smoking had weakened his sense of smell. He turned to one of the other men. "What's that smell?"

"Smell? Oh, yeah, it must be the mothballs. We found a few of them rolling around in here."

"No, it's something else. Ammonia?"

The young policeman shrugged his shoulders. "Urine maybe. Now that you mention it, it sort of reminds me of my kid brother's bedroom when he used to wet the bed."

That was it—dry urine. Poor Davey, trapped in the camper, no way to get out, not even to go to the bathroom. Sanders could imagine the little boy's discomfort.

"There she is, Mr. Sanders." Allen drew his attention to the form beneath the blanket. "Not a pretty sight, is she?"

"Seen worse," Sanders told him, meaning it.

The girl was small and scrawny; she could only be seventeen or eighteen. The coroner would know for sure. The side of her face was battered, and one arm was twisted at an unnatural angle. From the way she was lying curled on the floor she had probably been trying to defend herself from being kicked. Sanders's eyes followed the line of her body, coming back again to the girl's hand, relaxed now, and open. Her nails were bitten down to the quick.

The man who had done this was an animal. And every instinct told him that Davey was marked as his next victim. Sanders went back to the campground to call in for additional men.

Mac Feeley knew better than to utter a single word when he saw Sanders stride into the camp office. He had that look that said he was at the end of his rope.

Sanders grabbed the phone and punched out the section chief's number. "Buzz, there are some new developments here and I need help." Quickly, he reviewed the situation.

"Can do, Stu," his chief responded, "but they won't get there till around five this afternoon. It's the best I can do. Take it easy—we'll get him before it gets dark. If the kid's in the park and moving around under his own power, we're okay. Sounds like your theory was right. I want to meet that kid when this is all over."

"You and a lot of other people. Talk to you later."

Sanders turned to Feeley. "A second body's turned up. Have Delaney . . . Forget it, he's being recalled. Where is he?"

"He left just before you arrived. The body you're talking about was found on the other side of the highway in a pop-up camping trailer. According to Delaney, there was no positive identification, but it seems likely that the woman was traveling with Balog. I don't understand where this guy is, or what happened to his pickup. Beats the hell out of me why we haven't come up with something on that rig. From the description I've heard, it should be easy to spot."

"I need someone to stay here by the phone." Sanders chewed his lip. "Hey, wait a minute—I'm forgetting Dr. Ryan. Go get her, Feeley, and bring her back here. She can handle the phones. You camp out in Allen's office in case something comes in and he's not generous about passing it on. I'll go to the park myself. It's the best we can do till five, when Buzz's troops arrive. Doesn't this remind you of the time we were in Birmingham and only had three men, working around the clock for four days?"

Feeley's eyes were dreamy. "There was this waitress that made the best damn goulash I ever ate. She had other talents too, but the goulash was her specialty." He shook himself back to the present. "I'll call and see if I can get the park opened up.

And if it comes down to Allen being the only one with authority, I suggest you storm the gates. Let Buzz take the heat."

Lorrie burst through the door, out of breath from running. Sanders quickly filled her in, ending by showing her the Reebok he'd found. Lorrie collapsed on to a chair and let her tears flow as she held the muddy shoe. "Is it a positive or a negative sign?" she asked eventually.

"I think it's safe to say it's positive. I'm going back out there now—I'm convinced Davey's somewhere inside the amusement park. I'm taking Duffy with me. I've called in for more men but it'll be awhile before they get here. If you could handle the phones—"

Lorrie stood up. "No! I'm going with you." Sanders shook his head but Lorrie went on. "I mean it, I'm going with you. You forget, I'm a doctor and Davey is a very sick little boy. The sooner I get to him, the better chance he'll have of coming through this."

Sanders knew she was right, but it was against everything he believed in to take her with him. If Balog was still in the park too, things could get dangerous.

"All right, but there are conditions," he said finally. "You have to do as I say. No going off on your own. We stay together—you hear me?"

Lorrie smiled. "I hear you." She started for the door. "Let's go!"

* * *

Davey was tired of running. He leaned back against the rough bark of a tree in a sheltered grove overlooking the entrance to a giant flume ride. He knew he wasn't safe here, that he should keep going, but his knee hurt and he needed to rest a little while.

He was so tired. He wanted to just curl up somewhere and fall asleep. And he was hungry—hungrier than he'd ever been before. Spaghetti would taste good now. He would suck the long strands through his teeth and not care if little drops of the sauce splattered all over his cheeks and shirt. Mom was always showing him how to roll it on the fork. His mouth started to water. Suddenly, a sound behind him made his heart leap in his chest. He relaxed again when he saw it was only a fat, gray squirrel searching through the trash cans.

He couldn't go much farther. He needed to find a place to hide so he could take a nap, but everything was locked up or out in the open. He needed somewhere enclosed. The sky was getting blacker by the second. A streak of lightning tore across the sky, making Davey's heart pound in his chest. A rumble of thunder echoed around him, frightening him still more.

It was almost dark when he thought of hiding beneath the carousel's platform. He dropped to his belly and crawled underneath the circular structure; there was more room than he'd expected. Torrents of rain beat against the colorful carousel, and the heavy thunder and lightning made a Fourth of July display.

Davey curled into a ball. Embraced by the darkness, he was shielded from the warring elements overhead.

The storm was building as Lorrie and Sanders pulled up in the parking lot just outside the gates of Wild Adventure. Duffy sat between them, her nose keen for Davey's scent.

Leaving the car, Lorrie matched Sanders's athletic stride. Both glanced at the ominous gathering of thunderheads, each dreading the rain that would delay their search for Davey.

"We don't have time to wait for someone to open the gates, Lorrie, so the best thing we can do is climb the fence. I'll give you a hand up and you go over first. Find a garbage can and toss it over the fence, and I'll follow you."

"Okay." Lorrie placed her foot into Sanders's cupped hands and grasped the fine links of fencing. They cut into her fingers. She was going to feel this tomorrow, she thought, as she dropped to the ground. The first roll of thunder sounded. She tried to ignore it—to acknowledge it was to accept that Davey might be caught in the storm, unsheltered and afraid. Quickly she found a trash can and ran back to the fence with it.

"This storm is worse than I thought. I think you'd better come back to this side for now," Sanders said. "We can sit in the car until it blows over."

Seconds after Lorrie got back over the fence a river of rain came down out of the sky. They made a mad dash for the car.

"I guess you know we're stuck here. I can't even see to drive in this. Jesus, I haven't seen rain like this since I left the farm thirty years ago, and then only once. Later on the weather guys said it had been a hurricane."

Lorrie reluctantly resigned herself to waiting. "You know something, Stuart, I'd give everything I own, everything I hope to own for the rest of my life, if I could see Davey safe and sound right now. I love that little boy more than you can possibly imagine."

"I'm sort of nuts about him myself," Sanders admitted. "There's just something about him that makes you want to hold him and love him, and it doesn't have a damn thing to do with his medical problem. It's Davey. He's a very special kid."

"Do you get this involved in all your cases?" Lorrie asked.

Sanders chuckled. "No way."

A brilliant flash of light ricocheted off the windshield. Sanders swallowed hard as he caught the look on Lorrie's face. "Stuart, tell me that Duffy is in the backseat."

He would deserve the whiplash he got from the quick swivel he did. "Oh, Jesus. She went under the hole in the fence where I found the sneaker. She must have picked up Davey's scent. When you got the trash can, did you see her?"

"No, but I wasn't looking. I thought she'd stayed with you."

"If I were a crying man, I would bawl my head off about now," Sanders said.

"There must be something we can do. We can't just sit here. That dog weighs all of six pounds— the wind will kill her if she doesn't find a safe spot to take shelter. She's not an outside dog, Stuart, she's a house dog. She won't even go outside to pee when it rains. The cook spreads a paper by the back door for her. She's frightened to death of thunder and lightning."

Sanders hated negatives of any kind. "I know. I also know that you are an intelligent woman. No one with reasonable intelligence would even think about opening this car door. Believe me when I tell you I know what you're going through."

Lorrie's head fell back against the headrest. "We wait, is that it?"

"At least until it starts to let up. Come here," he said, putting his arm around her shoulders and pulling her toward him.

It was shortly after eight when a call came in over the radio from the campground manager, asking Sanders to return to the camp offices. Though it was still raining cats and dogs, Sanders was able to inch the car out of the parking lot and onto the road that led to the campground.

"I have good news, excellent news as a matter of fact," the manager said importantly. "Your man Feeley called in just a few minutes after you left. He said that an elderly woman stopped by the police station shortly after he arrived; she was carrying a copy of the *Asbury Park Press.* She said Davey had been at her turkey ranch around noon."

"Oh, Stuart, he's all right!" Lorrie threw her arms around Stuart's neck and hugged him.

"What did I tell you?" He hugged her back. One of these days he wouldn't have to let her go.

The manager went on. "Mr. Feeley says all the roads are flooded, especially the causeway, so your men might be delayed even longer, Mr. Sanders.

They closed off the parkway an hour ago. He's been most kind, calling in every twenty minutes or so to keep me alerted. Lordy, I almost forgot. The woman from the turkey ranch said that a man who claimed to be Davey's father came after him."

"Balog?"

The manager shrugged. "Feeley didn't say. The woman told him she didn't think the man was the boy's father because he was too mean."

"Anything else?" Sanders inquired. It would be easier to get blood out of a turnip than the full story out of the campground manager.

"Feeley said . . . I'm not sure, but I think he said that the woman's son put the boy into the man's truck." He shook his head. "Well, anyway, the woman said the boy started talking on the CB. Then, when the man got into the truck, the kid jumped out and ran across the field toward the amusement park."

"That clinches the shut-in call," Sanders mumbled. He hated to ask but he had to, for his own peace of mind. "Did Feeley say anything about how the boy looked?"

"I asked that and apparently the woman said the boy was hungry but looked right as rain to her. Oh—and he looked like he had been wallowing in the pig trough." The manager laughed, but sobered at once.

"Then he *is* in the amusement park. I knew it."

"What about Balog?" Lorrie asked. "Did he follow Davey?"

The manager shrugged. "I don't know. Feeley didn't say."

"If he'd followed him to the turkey ranch, he'd probably follow him to the amusement park," she surmised. "How long can Davey elude him?"

"I don't know, but so far Davey's given him a run for his money," Sanders said.

"If Balog does find Davey, do you think he'll kill him?" Lorrie's voice was unsteady.

Sanders couldn't answer any other way. "Yes."

Lorrie sucked in her breath. "Are we going back out there now?"

"As soon as I can find us some raincoats or slickers." Sanders's gaze shifted back to the manager. "It's still coming down in torrents. When our back-up men arrive, you'll have to direct them to the park. You can do that, can't you?"

"Of course I can. I'll stay right here by the phone and write everything down."

"Here we go—best I could do." Sanders handed Lorrie a pair of knee-high green boots and a bright orange hooded slicker. "I think I should warn you, if we fall into a pond or a lake we'll both go straight to the bottom. This stuff must weigh eighteen pounds."

Lorrie leaned over to kiss Sanders on the cheek then wrinkled her nose. He smelled like mildew and detergent. "Come on, let's go find Davey," she said.

Sanders drove carefully through the heavy rain. No matter how bad the storm got, there was no way he was going back to the camp offices now. He knew Davey Taylor was in the amusement park and he was going to find him—tonight.

"We aren't going over that fence again, are we?" Lorrie asked.

"Hell, no. We're going to do it the way they do

in the movies. We're going to shoot off the locks and walk right in."

"Good. I was wondering how we would make it over the fence in these Armani originals."

"That's what I like about you, Lorrie—your keen wit and utter logic," Sanders laughed. He felt more confident now, sure they would find Davey soon. He wouldn't think about the cold rain and the dark. "I should be back at the offices waiting for the others right now. And having you along with me is a no-no, right off the bat. We never involve civilians in anything that might be dangerous. I'm not going by the book is what I'm saying."

"To hell with the book," Lorrie said briskly.

"That's what I say. Okay, we're here. Let's hope the thunder muffles the shots."

Lorrie stood back, holding the flashlight while Sanders aimed the gun. Two shots and the lock was still intact. "Just how the hell rusty can it be?" he asked, not considering for a minute that he might have missed. He fired again and the lock fell off.

"Okay, here we go!" Sanders swung open the wide gate.

Lorrie held the flashlight in front of her as she waded through six-inch-deep puddles. When was this rain going to let up? She shouted for Davey and Duffy till she was hoarse. The wind and rain just carried her cries back to her. It was eerie—she didn't like it. Over and over she shouted, though she knew it was probably useless. Even if Duffy heard her calling, and barked in response, would she be able to hear the dog?

"I know you're out there, kid," Sanders mumbled. "Give us a break, Davey. Do something—anything would be a help at this point. Help me to help you." The rain was running down his arm, and he switched his flashlight from one hand to the other to shake the water from out of his sleeve. It was cold; the boy must be freezing.

The agent stopped to check their surroundings. To their immediate left was the roller coaster and the thrill rides; to their right was the Lehigh Valley Express train for little kids. Beyond the tracks, a small section of the park was devoted to the children's rides. None of the areas offered shelter of any kind. All he could see were the steel skeletons of framework. Should he go to the left or the right?

An hour later they were almost ready to give up. Just then the rain slackened, then stopped. In the dim, yellow-white glow of the flashlight, Sanders could at least see where he was going now. Just ahead were the carousel and the end of the children's area—they had almost reached the wildlife preserve. He doubted Davey would go in there, not if he knew about the wild animals. Something teased at him, some comment his nephew had made last spring. One of the animals—Delilah, the lioness—had given birth to six cubs. That was it. Her mate, Samson, was extremely protective of Delilah and the cubs. God help anyone who strayed into the lions' den.

Everywhere Sanders looked there were fallen branches and uprooted trees; anything that hadn't been nailed down had been scattered by the storm. Swinging the flashlight wide to get a better view, he was startled to see a monstrous oak lying across the Lehigh Valley Railroad. It would take a team of ten men to move it.

He didn't like the destruction he saw all around. "Where are you, Davey?" Maybe he was crazy; maybe Davey had never come back to the amusement park at all.

Fifteen

Upon awakening, the little boy's movements were slow, sluggish. At first he was unaware of the softness nestled close to his chest. But when he came fully awake, he wanted to howl with glee at the comforting feel of his little dog.

"Duffy!" he cried. "How did you find me? Where did you come from? Where's Aunt Lorrie? Good girl, you can lick my face all you want," Davey laughed happily. "I'm so glad to see you!"

He put his arms around his dog and hugged her, then suddenly remembered why he was hiding under the carousel. "We have to be quiet, Duff. You can't bark and don't run away this time. It's good you're here, Duff. I don't know my way back to camp and you can show me the way. Boy, is everybody going to be surprised when we come back together. Just you and me, Duff. We're a team, just like Mom and Dad. I only wish Mr. Sanders was with you—he'd know what to do. But he's in Florida with Mom and Dad."

It was good talking to Duffy. Davey felt reassured that soon he would be safe at home. "You're all wet," he noticed suddenly, "and so am I." But Duffy's companionship relieved some of his hunger and weariness—as long as Duffy was with him, he could talk to her and it would make the hike back to camp easier.

Brows puckered, he decided it must be very late. "We'll just have to wake Aunt Lorrie up, right, Duff?" He smiled to himself in the darkness, visualizing the expression on his aunt's face when he opened the door of the RV. Duffy whined low in her throat and continued with her furious licking.

"You're tickling me, Duff! We've got to get out of here. Do you think you can find your way in the dark?" Davey grunted the question from the effort of inching out from under the carousel. He shivered in his wet clothes. Now that he was exposed to the wind, he could feel the cold all the way down to his stockinged foot.

"Be quiet, Duff, real quiet. I don't know where that man is now but I know he's here somewhere, waiting to catch me. I'm going to be right behind you. If he catches us this time, he's going to kill us both. I don't want to be dead, and I don't want you to be dead, so don't bark," he cautioned in a firm voice. Duffy trotted off with Davey following close behind.

The rain was coming down steadily and Davey was cold. Duffy must be cold too. The pavement dipped—Duffy growled but it was too late. Davey's foot slipped and he found himself in water up to his chin. He thrashed about wildly as he struggled to reach higher ground. The rain continued to beat down in steady driving torrents. Carefully, not allowing himself to panic, he trod water till he was at the edge of the little pond. He groped for a handhold, only to find himself slipping back into the water. Duffy stood sentinel, barking loudly to offer encouragement. Her stubby tail swished furiously against her haunches as she crept up to the edge then backed off.

"It's no use, Duff," Davey called out. "I can't get out of here—there's nothing to hold on to. I need someone to pull me out. Quiet Duff, stop barking and go get Aunt Lorrie. Go on, girl, go get her. I'm not going to drown. I know how to float on my back. Go on, girl. Go!" Purposely, with all his might, he forced his voice to be like his mother's when she gave an order. "It's the best thing for me, Duff. Go get Aunt Lorrie."

Davey watched Duffy run away and hoped she'd understood him. He rolled over in the water. It was better lying on his back than playing dead-man's float. He never wanted to play that game again, not now that he knew what being dead meant. Blackness engulfed him, closing off the world. He could feel fear closing in too, choking off his air. He stiffened, feeling himself going under, the weight of his clothing dragging him down. Tentatively, he straightened his legs, the one shoeless little foot stabbing out a speculative toe to touch bottom. There it was, not very far down, but it felt slick and slimy, unpleasant. Yet, by standing on tiptoe, his head and face were out of the water.

He could feel the tears pricking at his eyelids, but then he imagined what Mom would say at a time like this. "David, crying solves nothing. You must use your brain and think. Tears are a sign of immaturity. You must reserve your tears for impor-

tant things, such as grieving and weddings." He
wasn't exactly sure what grieving was, and he only
had a vague idea about weddings, but what he did
know was that Mom wouldn't consider that the position he was in called for tears. He swallowed hard
and wished for a light so he could see how big the
pond was and find a way out. He had a light! Mr.
Sanders had given him the penlight and it was still
in the zippered pocket of his sleeve. He would
have to unzip his jacket and take it off, or at least
get his arm free of the clingy, nylon windbreaker.

Experimentally, he shifted his arm, trying to
take it out of the sleeve, working at the zipper and
sleeve under water. He had to balance himself on
his toes so he didn't go under. He yanked at the
zipper and managed to get it down halfway, and
then it stuck. His toes gave out and he slipped beneath the water. Gagging and spluttering, he rose
to the surface and flailed out with his arms. His
teeth began to chatter and he had to control them,
because the more noise his teeth made the colder
he felt. Flopping over on his back, the way he'd
been taught, he let the rain drizzle down on him.
It reminded him of a waterfall he had seen in one
of his picture books. He wasn't afraid of the rain
or the water. He just had to think of a safe way to
get out of the pond.

He was concentrating on testing the bottom with
his foot to find a shallow place to get a foothold,
when he heard a muffled curse. A dim circle of light
played near him. Cudge! If he went under the
water, he could only stay under until he counted to
four. He would make noise coming to the top and
then he would have to take deep breaths. Cudge
would be sure to hear him.

When the light reached the edge of the little pond, Davey could make out the big man's work boots and wet trouser legs.

"You're really a pain in the ass, kid. You made me tramp this goddamn place in the rain for hours. I thought you might have gotten away while I went back to the truck to get the flashlight. Guess I was wrong. Get over here and I'll pull you out. C'mon, over to the edge. Move it!"

Davey hesitated. To put himself into the hands of the man was unthinkable.

"Better do what I say, kid. I got your dog. I'll hold her under the water and finish her off real fast. Move it!"

He'd got Duffy?

"You hear me, kid? Get your ass over here so's I can grab you. You want to see your dog drown?"

He *had* got Duffy! Davey obeyed unwillingly. Maybe it was better to be out of the water. Maybe he could get away from him again. As long as he didn't hurt Duffy. *Please don't let him hurt Duffy!*

The little dog snapped and snarled as Cudge reached down to lift Davey out of the pond. He hauled him out effortlessly. "I thought I heard this mutt of yours. Even the rain couldn't muffle her barking." He set Duffy down on the ground and immediately she attacked his leg. "Call her off, kid, or I'll kick her from here to kingdom come."

"Duffy! Duffy—down girl. Down!" The dog sat back on her haunches and tilted her head, deep growls rolling in her throat.

"Pick her up!" the man ordered. "Pick her up and carry her. I got someone I want you to meet. As a matter of fact, he's dying to meet the both of you."

"My aunt is going to find me," Davey said, feeling his lower lip quiver. "She's going to come and get me and take me away from you. And Duffy, too!"

"Well, ain't your aunt gonna be surprised when she gets here and you're not. C'mon, walk! My friend is waiting."

Davey knew he didn't want to meet anyone this man knew. Still, he couldn't resist asking "Who?" in the hope that it might be Brenda. Maybe he was wrong and Brenda was okay; maybe the man hadn't hurt her.

"The sign says his name is Samson. A real live lion, like in the jungle. The kind that eats kids like you and doesn't even burp. Now shut up and walk!"

Lorrie and Sanders came to a standstill in front of the Space Port. When the park was open it would be packed with kids plunking their quarters into video games like Space Invaders and Indy 500. Now it was deathly silent.

"He's here," Sanders said bitterly, "I know it!"

"What now?" Lorrie asked, despair in her voice.

"I'm going to call in to see where our backups are. And I want my section chief to get in touch with somebody to organize turning on all the goddamned lights in this park. Even if Davey's not in the park, but somewhere nearby, the lights should attract him."

"Good idea. But wouldn't the storm have knocked the power out?"

Sanders's face fell. "Well, it's worth a try. Anyway, it's time to call in." He walked over to the closest building and sheltered under its eaves.

Lorrie waited nearby, her nerves shattered. As soon as Sanders had finished the call, she was at his side. "Well?"

"They're on their way."

"And the lights?"

"I don't know. They're going to try, maybe use the generator."

"Let's go back down the main concourse," Lorrie suggested. Even though she was exhausted she just couldn't give up.

"Right," Sanders said grimly. It was worth another try.

They walked side by side, their flashlights fanning the ground, searching for clues that might lead them to Davey. Each kept their thoughts to themselves. It was beginning to look as though they were on the wrong track. Every lead was cold.

"Hey, watch out," Sanders cautioned. "What's that?" His light sought out the shiny object that had reflected the beam back at him. "There!"

Lorrie's eyes followed the beam of light. The disc was silver, shining and new. A quarter. She picked it up, holding it for Sanders to see, her manner almost reverent.

"Hot damn!" Sanders slapped his thigh. "That's one of the quarters I gave Davey. I know it is because of the nail polish on the edge!"

Suddenly their steps were lighter and their gloom lifted. "Davey!" Lorrie called, loud and clear, the rain drizzling into her mouth unnoticed. "Davey!"

Strong fingers reached out and yanked at his collar, pulling him backward so violently that he almost lost his hold on Duffy. Davey hadn't realized how heavy the little dog was until he'd had to carry her for so long. They had left the main amusement park behind now and were circling the far side of the parking lot, heading for the trees again. The rain had almost stopped and the wind had died down. The air was cold and Davey was colder. His one shoe squished with each step he took, and he could feel a blister growing on the bottom of his foot.

They came to a cyclone fence like the one at the parking lot, only this one was higher and had spiked wire strung along the top. Davey could hardly see the top, even when Cudge held the flashlight high. Duffy was nosing into his neck and sometimes he could feel her shiver. She was cold too. He wrapped his arms protectively around her, warming her, trying to keep her from Cudge's notice. Somehow the responsibility of looking after Duffy gave Davey the courage to go on.

Cudge was searching for something. He kept lifting the flashlight, scanning the fence, then looking off into the distance. Eventually, Cudge prodded Davey on again, leading him across the field toward the next stand of trees. The grass was short and the ground was soft and muddy. Several times, Davey almost fell, his knee refusing to support him. But he thought of Duffy and what Cudge might do to her, and he kept pushing forward.

After what seemed to Davey like forever but was only a short while later, Cudge reached out and yanked on his shoulder. "This is as far as we go. We're gonna sit down over here, right where you can see the lion and he can see you. Bet you thought lions slept at night, didn't you? Well, they don't, especially not this one. He's got his old lady in there and some cubs. He stays up all night to watch over them and protect. He don't want no wiseass kid coming near that fence to upset things. Know what I mean?" Cudge snorted. "You ain't even gonna make a good bite for that big guy. He's gonna chew you to pieces in one gulp."

"Are you going to kill me?" Davey asked fearfully.

"Yeah. Well, no. It's gonna be my fault but that there lion is the one what's gonna do the actual killing. All day long I been thinking about wringing your neck, but then I came across Samson here and decided he'd have the pleasure instead. Besides, why should I hang for killing you? You ain't nothin' but a little brat. I don't like brats, and you especially. I wouldn't be out here if it wasn't for you. Elva would still be alive, and we'd be on our way to Florida. You spoiled everything. Wringing your neck is too good for you."

Davey was frightened. He sat on the cold, wet ground and watched Cudge pace back and forth. Duffy curled into his lap, making herself into a little ball to keep warm. When Cudge's pacing brought him too close to Davey, she lifted her head, bared teeth and growled.

"Shut that bitch up," Cudge warned.

Stopping to think for a minute, he lifted up his army-colored jacket and pulled off his belt. He leaned down to reach for Duffy and was rewarded with the threat of snapping jaws. "Here," he threw the belt at Davey. "Make a leash out of this and hook it to the fence there. Now!"

Davey's fingers fumbled with the belt. He wasn't

sure how to put it on Duffy. It was wide and made of thick leather, like his good Sunday shoes. It wouldn't fit around Duffy's neck without choking her. The next best thing was to put it around her middle; he slid the strap through the buckle then threaded the strap end through a hole in the fence.

The man seemed satisfied. Now he could stay just beyond the reach of the belt and Duffy couldn't get to him. "You know what kind of fence that is, kid? It's called horse fencing. I noticed this afternoon that they use it to section one kind of animal off from another. It keeps them from eating each other." The man seemed to find that funny, because he threw back his head and laughed. Davey didn't like the way he laughed. It wasn't nice, not at all like his dad's laugh.

Davey could make out the curving stretch of the horse fencing. The highest wire had been pulled down by a giant tree which had fallen against it in the storm.

"Don't like the look of that, hey kid? Neither did I when I come across it earlier today. Old Samson there gave me a scare when he charged the wire. Only he don't seem too interested in getting over. Guess it's because his wife and kiddies are in there."

Davey was silent, looking through the darkness to where Cudge was pointing. Duffy was restless, straining to the full length of the belt, trying to get close to her master.

"You don't believe me, I can tell. You're just as stupid as Elva ever was. Look, kid—I'm gonna show you something that's gonna make you wet your pants."

How did the man know he'd wet his pants? It had happened so long ago, when Davey was locked in the camper.

Cudge picked up the flashlight and stepped closer to the fence. There was a fallen branch lying on the ground and he picked that up too. Immediately, Davey's eyes flew to Duffy. "Worried about your little doggy? I'll tell you when it's time to worry. Look! Look over here!"

Davey did as he was told. Cudge ran the end of the branch against the fence; it made a harsh grating noise which was loud in the still night air. Immediately a yellow streak charged out of the darkness and threw itself against the wire. The earth seemed to shake with the impact! Davey felt it in his belly, like he'd once felt the big bass drum that came marching behind the parade. Boom! Boom! Samson's roar was the loudest noise Davey had ever heard, like all the thunder in the world put together in one big sound that made your ears pop and your backbone melt like ice-cream on a hot day.

Duffy yelped with fright and tried to crawl away from the fence, but the short length of leather held her back.

Davey clapped his hands over his ears and squeezed his eyes shut. He wanted the noise to go away. He had been scared before, but now he was terrified. Again Samson roared, a rumbling which began deep in his chest and exploded through his fanged, cavernous mouth. Yellow eyes reflected the light of the flashlight, watching, daring, defying.

"How do you like him, kid? Pretty big, huh?" Cudge laughed but the sound was smothered by another of Samson's warnings. "I'm gonna toss you right over that fence. That old lion only has to lift his leg and *bam!*" He smacked one fist into the other hand. "Just like that! Only I'm gonna rile him up a little first, sorta whet his appetite, if you know what I mean. Then he'll be in fine form when you hit the ground."

"You'd better watch out 'cause Mr. Sanders is looking for me," Davey lied, hoping to frighten the man. "And when he finds you, he's going to lock you up."

"Mr. Sanders, huh? Who's he?"

"He's the FBI agent that stays at our house. He gave me money to call him when I needed him and I called him from the pay phone by the Ferris wheel and told him where to find me."

"FBI agent? Who're you kiddin'?"

"Okay, don't believe me, but it's true."

Cudge lashed out and cuffed Davey on the side of the head. Dizzily, Davey shook his head to try to clear it. He should have kept quiet. Tears brimmed in his eyes; no one had ever hit him before. He didn't like it one bit. He was helpless and scared. He focused on the fence, watching the lion pace back and forth, the animal's feline eyes reflecting the light from the flashlight and adding a light of their own.

"If that Sanders fella does show, kid, I'll throw him over to the lion right after you. Then that damn dog. What do you think of that?" Cudge bellowed. When he saw the dread on the little boy's face, he smirked.

Suddenly all the wind seemed to go out of Cudge, and he wanted to sit down someplace dry and warm. He was exhausted, physically and mentally. Thoughts of Elva kept popping into his head and he had to push them away. It couldn't be that he missed that stupid, scrawny broad. Why had he ever gotten mixed up with her anyway? He sat down heavily opposite Davey, leaning back against a tree. A match flared as he lit a cigarette.

Davey saw Samson walking away from the fence. *He's going back to his family*, Davey thought. *I wish I could go back to mine.*

"I used to have a dog," Cudge said quietly. "Well, she wasn't exactly mine. She belonged to my grandmother."

Davey glanced at Cudge then back toward the fence again.

"Don't believe me, do you, kid? It's true. I wasn't any different from you when I was a kid. Matter of fact, I was just like you. Trouble, always trouble. Leastways that's what my mother used to say. 'Edmund Balog,' she'd say, 'I don't know what's come over you. You used to be such a good little boy. What made you change?' I used to pretend I didn't know what she was talking about. Only I did know, and I knew when I changed too. I wasn't any older than you when I found out what lives inside me. Only I never told anybody. Couldn't. And when I look at you, kid, I know the same devil that lives inside me is inside you too. Think about what you did to mess me up with the law, with Elva, with everybody. Yes, I know it's there inside you too."

His voice droned on but Davey was only half listening. The man wasn't his biggest fear right now. His biggest fear was right there, behind the fence, with its tearing jaws and thunderous voice. Samson.

"There were times when I didn't know why I'd ever been born. I ain't never had a friend. You know that, kid? Never, except for Elva. And she wasn't a friend as it turned out. *You* made her turn against me! She was all right till you came along. So what if I did think she was stupid? And maybe I did think about getting rid of her, but I never would've done it. Never! But then you had to mess everything up.

"Don't get me wrong. Maybe you couldn't help yourself. I never could when I was a kid. This thing inside my head would always mess me up. What's yours like?" Cudge lowered his voice, whispering conspiratorially. "Mine is like a bull, black and tough. It's got hooves that cut into my brain, and long sharp horns that fill up the inside of my head till I can't think! And it's heavy, real heavy. It pounds around in there till I can't stand it. And then it takes over, makes me do things I'd never do on my own. It was the bull that made me kill Lenny. And Elva too. And the other night I beat up this girl for no reason, except maybe she was breathing. It ain't my fault," he whined.

Cudge's voice had a strangely soothing effect on the little boy. Although his eyes never left the fence, he found that by reaching out with his fingers, he could touch the fur on Duffy's neck. It was reassuring. Suddenly, there was a movement on the other side of the fence. The man's voice must have disturbed the lion again. But no, it was too small for Samson. It was one of the babies, a cub, bigger than Duffy but a baby nevertheless. Davey felt sorry for the cub as it sat lopsided on its haunches, looking out at him. It must be terrible to live with a fence around you all the time. Beyond the circle of light, he could discern a larger form, or were there two shapes? The mother and father lion, he decided. A smile touched his lips. There were more cubs nursing from the mother. The thought delighted him; the mother must be sleeping, and the father was watching out so nothing happened to his family.

It wasn't like that in his family. If Aunt Lorrie had kids, she would be like Samson—watching and protective. But his family was different. Mom was the one who watched and took care of them, the one who said what was good to eat and where it was nice to play and work, and how things should be done. Mom liked things to be perfect, Davey thought. And she wanted him to be perfect too, but he wasn't. Maybe if he didn't need to get a shot every day, or wear a brace sometimes, he *could* be perfect. "Picture perfect" was what Mom liked to say.

A loud, belly-rumbling roar startled him. Cudge was still talking but Davey stopped listening. Samson had come back to the fence; he was standing over his cub, anxious and uneasy about the intruders. He picked up the cub by the scruff of its neck and marched back to the lioness, dropping his bundle between her front paws.

That's what fathers are supposed to do, Davey thought, comparing Samson to his own dad. They're not supposed to let the mothers do all the important things.

Cudge was off in a world of his own, rambling through his memories, revealing things he'd never spoken about before. And as he talked, the differences between the little boy and himself became less clear. He felt like a child again, as if he was Davey's age, scared of the night-walking monsters that haunted him, and recognizing the monster that inhabited his own body, compelling him to destroy and to kill. In the dim flickering light, Cudge came to believe that Davey was the young Edmund Balog, capable of all things evil, and the future stretched out before him. Every moment of pain and suffering, every weakness, was inevitable. There was only one way to stop it from ever happening again and Cudge was going to do it, before it was too late. The child might look innocent but the evil had already taken hold. The young Edmund Balog was as much to blame for Elva and Candy as the adult was. And now, because of that little boy, Cudge was going to have to kill again.

Samson's roar, when it came, made Davey clap his hands over his ears. Cudge stopped his ramblings. "I thought I told you to sit there and not move. I ain't ready to dump you over that fence yet. The only reason that lion is bellowing like that is because he *wants* me to toss you over there. He probably ain't had anything to eat for a week. You're gonna be real sweet meat to him, kid."

Davey drew his knees up to his chest. He was so cold he couldn't feel anything anymore. "I didn't do anything to that lion," he whispered to himself over and over. Again, he saw a movement by the fence. A smile tugged at his lips. The little cub was back, looking at him through the wire.

Lightning swift, Cudge was on his feet. He clambered up the slippery tree trunk that straddled the fence, ignoring the soggy leaves and branches that were sticking out in every direction. Mesmerized, Davey watched as Cudge broke off a branch and proceeded to pound at the top of the wire fence. Horrified, he couldn't bear the thought that Cudge might hurt the lion cub.

Samson's roars ripped through the night as Cudge pounded again and again at the wire. Duffy joined in the noise, barking and growling, straining to escape the belt.

Cudge turned, almost losing his footing on the slippery trunk. "Don't even think about moving, kid."

Davey was stunned. Why hadn't he run off the minute Cudge started up the tree trunk? He could be away by now, looking for a hiding place. He was angry with himself, and angry that the little lion cub was occupying his thoughts, that the father lion wasn't taking it back to its mother. He could still run now if he wanted to—Cudge was halfway up the tree. He would have a small head start if he got up now; but the cub held him rooted to the spot. The cub wasn't afraid of the pounding noise, and it wasn't afraid of its father's anger.

Samson backed off then advanced again. With one monstrous paw, he gently moved the cub to one side, then pushed with both front paws against the tree where it was leaning against the fence. A storm of sound erupted from the lion's cavernous mouth; Davey shuddered but was pleased to see that Cudge was afraid and had started to back off down the tree trunk. The cub was safely back with its mother. Davey sighed with relief.

"That was just for starters," Cudge said, wiping his hands on his sodden jeans. "I wanted to show you that that lion means business, and so do I. You getting the message, kid?"

Davey nodded.

Cudge returned to his spot against the tree trunk. He started talking again. Davey knew that was good—he didn't seem so mean when he talked. He kept saying the same things over and over and Davey wished he knew why. He didn't really want to think about Cudge, or why he did anything, but he needed to think about what to do if Cudge dragged him up the tree trunk and tossed him into the lion's mouth.

The lion continued its pacing close to the fence.

Cudge's voice was making him sleepy, but Davey couldn't give in now. He had to stay awake and plan how to escape.

"Come here," Cudge said hoarsely, crooking his finger for Davey to get up and go to him. "Making me come and get you ain't gonna help now."

Davey didn't waste a minute. The second he was on his feet, he bolted off into the trees, away from danger, away from the man. Cudge crashed through the trees after him, grunting and panting, but Davey was running fast now, down the hill, towards the level ground. The earth was muddy and soft, making it difficult to run, but he wasn't going to stop until he was safe.

Suddenly he heard a bark from behind him. The sound pierced him. *Duffy!* He had run away and left Duffy!

"Hey, kid! Guess what I got that's yours!" The bellowing laugh was followed by an angry yipping and a whimper of pain. There was nothing else to do. He had to go back. He couldn't let Cudge hurt his dog.

Heedless of the branches scratching his face and neck, Davey stumbled back up the incline, gasping as he fell over tree roots and slipped on the wet leaves. At first, he thought Cudge had gone and taken Duffy with him. He could hear Samson snarling, but couldn't see him.

Then Davey heard that hated voice. "Up here, kid. I thought you'd come back. Look what I've got—but I won't have it for long!"

Davey looked up at the fallen tree straddling the fence. Cudge was lying on his belly along it, his arm hanging down over the wire. He was laughing. Duffy swung from the belt looped around her middle, just feet away from Samson's reaching claws, her short legs twitching, her head arched back in terror The lion snarled, its jaws snapping, saliva stringing from its mouth.

Davey felt as if his heart would burst. "No! No!" His feet found a hold on the tree trunk; it was slippery and wet, and he had to dig into the bark with his fingers to hold on. It was so high, higher than he'd ever been before.

Duffy swung out again, lower this time. At the last second, Cudge yanked on the belt, pulling her out of Samson's reach.

The lion stood on its hind legs, clawing at the furry object swinging overhead. Growling, it attacked again, just falling short of its prey.

Davey climbed higher, faster, reaching out for his dog. The trunk was too wide for him to hold on to, and he slipped, falling into its lower branches, nearly going over the fence himself, right down into Samson's mouth.

Cudge didn't seem to notice that Davey was just underneath him. He swung Duffy out again and the belt came to within inches of Davey's grasp. It hung there for a breathless moment before Cudge hauled Duffy out of Samson's reach.

"Hey, kid, come and see. Where are you? Don't you want to feed the lion?" Cudge shouted out, laughing nastily. "You'd better answer before your dog turns into this cat's breakfast!"

Davey stretched out, feeling the branch bend under his weight. He held his breath. He had to be ready; his hands had to be strong to grab Duffy away from Cudge.

The next time Cudge swung Duffy out over the lion's head, Davey reached out as far as he could. He caught the dog but she was too heavy to hold. He felt himself losing his balance. Grasping the end of the belt, Davey swung the dog toward the fence. He prayed it wasn't too high, that Duffy would survive the fall. At the last second, he released the belt, and waited for what seemed an eternity to see that Duffy had cleared the fence and dropped to safety on the other side.

"Hey! What the—?" Cudge looked around wildly, then spotted Davey below. He reached down through the branches to grab him but Davey ducked, avoiding Cudge's hand by a narrow margin. Again, Cudge groped for him. Cowering backward, Davey was afraid to move for fear he would fall into Samson's mouth. Curses sounded above him. He couldn't see Cudge, but he knew where he was by the arm searching through the branches.

Samson roared again, his yellow eyes staring at a point above Davey's head. The strength flowed back into Davey's limbs. His brain started to send signals to his body. *Wait*, he told himself, *wait*.

He heard the shift of Cudge's body above him, and saw the man's change of position in the lion's yellow eyes. As Cudge's arm came reaching out again, Davey gripped it with his knees, locking his ankles together. He heard Cudge grunt and saw

the lion ready itself to spring. Swiftly, with all the
strength he possessed, Davey pulled hard at the
trapped limb.

The sudden action caught Cudge off guard and
he lost his balance. He began to fall through the
branches and reached out for something to stop
his fall. But there was nothing. Only the yawning
jaws of fate waiting for him.

Davey closed his eyes and forced himself to shut
out the terrible sounds from inside the lion's cage.
He was safe at last. Safe.

He slid down the tree limb, feeling a sense of his
own power. But the minute his cold, numb feet
touched the wet ground, his legs gave out on him.
He needed to rest a minute. Rest. Just for a minute.

There was a soft sound close by. Duffy. He wanted
to see her, to check if she was all right. But it was
still too dark. He needed the flashlight. A sigh escaped him as he forced his fingers to work. Off
came the jacket and down came the pocket zipper.
His fingers worked at the switch but nothing happened. He banged it against his knee; it was too
wet. Again, he flicked the tiny switch and this time
was rewarded with a feeble light. Quickly, before it
faded, Davey shone it on Duffy. His fingers felt all
over her dark fur, searching for bloody gashes and
wounds. Only once did the little dog yelp with
pain—when Davey was removing the leather belt
from around her middle.

"You're gonna be fine, girl. Your tummy's just
sore. Let's see you walk, Duff. Can you walk?" The
optimistic tone of her master's voice revitalized
Duffy. She could be her old self again if Davey
could.

"Come on, Duff," Davey said. "We're going to find Aunt Lorrie."

Davey wasn't sure which way to go to find the hole in the fence. He started toward the Ferris wheel then heard someone call his name.

"Aunt Lorrie?" he called back. "I'm here! Aunt Lorrie, I'm here." He tried to run but his legs and feet were too painful.

Lorrie stopped. "It's Davey. Oh, my God. It's Davey." She began to move again, listening carefully to work out where Davey's voice was coming from. A moment later, Duffy came tearing toward her. Behind her, Lorrie could see Davey limping.

She held out her arms and Davey fell into them, hugging her with all his might. "Oh, honey, are you all right? I've been so worried about you, so afraid for you."

"I'm okay," he said against her neck. "I'm better now."

"Hey, Davey," Stuart Sanders said.

Davey leaned back. "Hi, Mr. Sanders. I did what you said and called you, but all I got was an answering machine. I couldn't leave a message because that man was chasing me."

"What's his name, Davey?"

"Cudge."

"Where is he now?"

Davey looked back the way he'd come. "He fell out of the tree and . . . and Samson got him."

"Samson?"

"The daddy lion," Davey explained.

The color drained from Lorrie's face. She pulled

Davey closer and pressed his head against her shoulder. "Don't think about it, Davey. Don't think about anything but going home."

"I'm hungry, Aunt Lorrie."

Lorrie swallowed hard. "I bet you are."

"I lost one of my shoes."

Lorrie grinned. "Who cares about that?"

"And I ruined my new jacket."

"No big deal." She was still grinning.

"Where's Mom and Dad?"

Lorrie looked to Sanders for help with that one. The agent ruffled Davey's hair. "They're still in Florida, son. But you'll see them soon."

Davey's features closed up. "Did you call Mom and Dad and tell them I was lost?"

"You bet. Right away."

Davey nodded. "I'm kind of tired, Aunt Lorrie."

Concern filled Lorrie's face. "Then let's get out of here and get you back to the motor home and into bed." Tenderly, she held Davey against her and began to walk toward the exit.

"Are you coming, Stuart?" she asked, when he didn't immediately follow.

"Yep, sure am. I'll take care of this mess later. Right now Davey's the most important thing."

Lorrie sat next to Stuart on the motor home sofa, waiting for Davey to wake up. A little over an hour ago, Feeley had called and given them the news about Sara. Lorrie hadn't been able to believe it at first. Sara dead—it just didn't seem possible. She had always believed Sara to be indestructible.

"Poor Davey," she said, squeezing Stuart's hand.

"Don't say anything to him right now. He needs to recuperate from this trauma first."

Stuart had expected Lorrie to go into shock, but she hadn't. He supposed it was because she was a doctor and dealt with death on a daily basis.

The moment Davey stirred, Sanders got up and tiptoed over to the bunk. Davey lay with his eyes wide open, staring at the roof of the RV. Duffy, freshly bathed, was snuggled against him.

"How's it going, kid?" Sanders asked as he sat down on the edge of the bunk.

"Okay, Mr. Sanders."

"I'm real proud of you, Davey. I think you're the bravest little boy I've ever known. You can join my team any time."

"You aren't leaving, are you?" Davey asked.

"Not on your life. I made a date with Duffy to buy her the biggest steak in town. I have a date with you too, and your aunt."

He could feel that lump in his throat again.

Roman DeLuca was being escorted down the studio corridor by an assistant director. The jury had reached its verdict during the early morning hours, and now DeLuca was going to be interviewed on a television news program.

The accused had been found guilty, which made DeLuca a winner in the public's eye. It would probably help to put him in the governor's seat. He was ready to smile for the cameras, and tell the world that justice had been served, but inside he was seething. It hadn't been meant to turn out this way, and all because he had miscalculated the determination of one person—Sara Taylor. He had achieved his goal—Jason Forbes's killer hadn't been linked to the syndicate, and probably wouldn't be now—but it would all have gone a lot more smoothly if Sara Taylor had been more cooperative.

The moment DeLuca stepped into the studio, the reporters began shouting out their questions. They liked Roman DeLuca, they knew he was climbing the ladder to success. He even looked the part with his bronzed face, his immaculate white shirts and custom-made suits.

Flashing his brilliant smile, DeLuca listened attentively to the first question. He sobered at once as he replied: "I'm shocked. There are simply no words at a time like this. My sympathy goes out to Mr. Taylor who made such a brave and admirable contribution to justice."

"Mr. DeLuca, do you know of any reason why Mrs. Taylor would ignore the warning shouts to get off the runway? Is there something the press isn't being told?"

DeLuca put on what he called his sincere, humble smile. "Haven't I always been open with the press?" Not waiting for a reply, he continued somberly: "I understand there was some personal problem at home concerning the Taylors' son. Mrs. Taylor was distraught so Federal Agent Jonas was assigned to take care of her. The whole incident was very unfortunate and I'm truly sorry. Mrs. Taylor was a remarkable woman in many ways."

"What kind of personal problem, Mr. DeLuca?"

"Now, if I told you that it wouldn't be personal any longer, would it?"

"The Taylors have a hemophiliac child, don't they?" A chunky man in a sweat-stained blue shirt shouted to be heard over the chattering throng.

"Yes, they do. Now, if that's all, gentlemen, I have a hard day ahead of me and I'm expected at WKBA's television studio."

"Mr. DeLuca, do you still have 'no comment' on your plans to run for governor?"

DeLuca grinned: he was on solid ground now. "I think, ladies and gentlemen, that . . ."

Agent Jonas listened to the suave, controlled voice. That bastard. He hadn't lied, he hadn't fabricated a thing. Up front all the way with the media. What right did the attorney have to use him like that? Implying that he, Jonas, had overplayed his hand and used a thug's tactics. DeLuca was the one who'd said "take care of her." How could he have known that the prosecutor just wanted her kept out of the courtroom. Christ, even Sara Taylor had misunderstood!

Davey's mind wandered as he sat quietly in the small chapel. He wished he could be outside with Duffy, running through the leaves, or talking to Digger on the CB. He didn't understand the meaning of the words the minister was saying, and he didn't like the way people kept looking at him. Most of all, he didn't like the words Memorial Service. He began to fidget.

Lorrie watched Davey out of the corner of her eye. The little boy didn't understand what was going on; he shouldn't have to be here. Instantly, she was contrite. What an awful thought. Of course he should be here! After all, the service was for his mother.

How sad, she thought as she let her gaze circle the small chapel. Aside from her and Andrew and a few of Andrew's business associates, the only other person present was Stuart Sanders. Private memorial services were very lonely, but Andrew had wanted it that way. How sad that only she and Andrew were grieving; but, as long as she was being honest, she was also relieved in a way.

The short service was soon over. Outside, in the brisk, autumn air, Andrew didn't seem to comprehend where he was. His luggage was in the car parked at the curb; he was going away. He knew he should be saying something to Lorrie, but he couldn't think of the words. If the service had been for him, Sara would have known the right thing to say. Now that he was on his own and had to think for himself, he felt lost. Davey. He had to say something to Davey before he left. God, what could he say? Where were the words? Where?

Davey stood awkwardly between Stuart Sanders and Lorrie. His round gaze was speculative. "Dad?"

"Yes, son."

"Will you be gone a long time?"

"I don't know, Davey, I just don't know. But you'll be fine with Aunt Lorrie. She'll take good care of you."

"I know. Aunt Lorrie is going to get all my things and my CB and take them over to her house this afternoon."

Something pricked at Andrew's eyes. "I know that, Davey."

Manfully, Davey extended his hand to his father.

Andrew felt his eyes begin to smart. He took his son's hand in his own. "I'll call you when I get settled." For an instant Andrew felt as though Sara were with him, arranging the last-minute details, offering her approval.

"Okay, Dad. Drive carefully and don't forget to stop for gas."

"I won't, Davey. You take care now."

Davey nodded.

Stuart Sanders's penetrating gaze rested on the small boy in the gray suit. His lips narrowed to a grim, white line and he nudged Lorrie. "Is it my imagination or did Davey get taller in the past several days?"

Davey watched his father climb into the blue sedan. His eyes didn't leave the road until the car was long out of sight. Then he turned to face his aunt and Stuart Sanders. His eyes glistened momentarily in the chill October light. "Can we go now?"

"You bet," Lorrie said, smiling down at him. "Get in the car, we're going home."

Davey ran for the car and climbed into the front seat. He concentrated on fastening his seat belt. When he'd finished, he looked out the window and saw Aunt Lorrie and Mr. Sanders standing by the driver's door, kissing. They had been doing a lot of that in the last few days—kissing and giving each other mushy looks. And they'd been hugging and kissing him a lot, too. He had pretended not to like it, but he did. He liked it a lot.

Aunt Lorrie had said that he'd suffered no ill effects—whatever that meant—from not getting his shots and that he was going to be just fine.

Mr. Sanders opened the car door and Duffy jumped in. She climbed onto Davey's lap and licked his face. Mom would have scolded Duffy and made her get down but Aunt Lorrie just laughed.

Be sure not to miss the next novel in
Fern Michaels's thrilling new "Sisterhood" series.
Turn the page for a special preview of
PAYBACK,
now available from Zebra Books.

Prologue

Myra Rutledge, heiress to a Fortune 500 candy company looked around her state of the art kitchen at the pots bubbling on the stove and at the table set for two. Even though it was late afternoon, the sun danced through the stained-glass ornaments hanging on the kitchen window, creating rainbows on the white walls all around her. The girls—that's how she thought of Barbara and Nikki—had made the colorful ornaments for her as gifts one year at summer camp.

She'd adopted Nikki at a young age, but she and Barbara couldn't have been more alike than if they'd come out of her womb at the same time. Barbara was gone now, killed by a hit-and-run driver in the District—a man with diplomatic immunity.

Myra tried her best not to let maudlin thoughts overcome her, but sometimes, like now at the end of the day, she thought about her two girls and the dangerous path she'd embarked on. She needed to fortify herself against such thoughts because she knew they weren't going to go away on their own. A snifter of brandy helped a little. She poured generously, eyes watering at the first massive gulp. She always gulped brandy even though she knew it should be sipped. She took another mighty gulp as she looked at the clock. The girls of the Sisterhood would be arriving before nightfall to prepare for their second mission. The thought warmed her more than the brandy did. They were like daughters now, and she loved them all.

She was worried a little about Alexis, though. She'd mentioned her worry to her live-in companion, Charles, the way she mentioned everything that bothered her, and he'd agreed that perhaps Alexis *wasn't quite* ready for her mission. If not, they'd open the shoe box, fall back and regroup. It wouldn't be a problem. With Charles at the helm, it would all go smoothly.

There was another problem, though, outside of the Sisterhood. Assistant District Attorney Jack Emery, Nikki's fiancé. Ex-fiancé to be more precise.

Myra set the glass down on the table and massaged her temples.

"You're at it again, eh, Mom?"

Myra's head jerked upright as she looked around. One of the stained glass ornaments, a red tulip hanging in the window was jiggling on its little hook. "Barbara?"

Dear Sweet Girl, I was sitting here thinking about you and Nikki when you were little. I miss you so.

I know, Mom, but I'm always close by. I'm looking at you right now. Don't worry so much. Things will work out. Trust Nikki.

But Jack . . . Jack could ruin everything.

Nikki won't allow it, Mom. I think what you're doing is super. That first mission of Kathryn's was really kick-ass. Thanks, Mom. I know you're doing it for me, and I can't wait till it's your turn. I'll be with you every step of the way.

Myra looked down into her brandy glass. Was she really talking to her dead daughter? Was her dead daughter actually communicating with her? Or was it the brandy? She finished it off, not wanting to let go of her daughter's voice.

Easy on the sauce, Mom. I'd hate to take away a vision of my Mom dancing on the table. I know how rowdy you can get. I'm teasing, Mom.

I know, dear. I'm feeling a little light-headed right now just talking to you. I wish . . . oh, Barbara, I wish so many things.

Don't, Mom. You can't unring the bell. I just want you to know how proud I am of what you and the girls are doing. Sometimes . . . sometimes you simply have to take charge and make things come out right. Kathryn is a new person these days. You're right about, Alexis, too. She isn't ready, but, Mom, let her be the one to tell you she isn't ready. Don't make the decision for her. And, Mom, just keep doing what you're doing."

Oh, I will, dear, I will. I just thank God I have the money to fund this venture. And to think I don't even like candy.

I hear Charles coming. I'm going upstairs to spend some time with Willie. I love you, Mom.

Myra smiled at the mention of Barbara's tattered teddy bear.

When Nikki moved back here to the farm she started to sleep with Willie so he wouldn't miss you so much.

I know, Mom. Trust Nikki. And, don't worry about Jack. Nik has it under control. Love you, Mom.

Myra was up and off the chair in the blink of an eye. She ran over to the kitchen window to touch the stained-glass ornament that was now still. Her hand flew to her mouth to stifle a sob.

She felt Charles's hand on her shoulder. She turned around to bury her head in his broad chest. "She was here, Charles. We talked."

Charles Martin, ex-M16 operative who had devoted most of his life to Her Majesty, eyed the brandy bottle and the empty glass. "I'm glad, Myra. I'll finish up here. Why don't you check the bedrooms to be sure everything is ready for the girls. Did you buy something special for Kathryn's dog, Murphy?"

"Yes, Charles, I did, a chew toy and a box of jumbo biscuits. He's a wonderful animal, isn't he?"

"Yes, Myra, he is."

"I love you, Charles. I wish . . . I wish . . . never mind. Barbara said . . . it's all right, Charles. I'm not dotty. Isn't that a term you Brits use?"

"I'm an American now, dear. I say nutsey cuckoo like the rest of you. You are my dear, sweet Myra and I love you with all my heart. Scoot!"

Myra smiled. She adored flirting with the love of her life. "I'm going. I might have overcooked that mess on the stove, Charles."

"I'm throwing it all out, Myra, and starting over. It's all right, dear. You have other wonderful talents." He twirled the dishtowel and then playfully swatted her backside.

Myra laughed all the way down the hall and was still laughing as she climbed the steps to the second floor.

One

Alexis Thorn frowned as she looked around her small apartment. There was nothing about the tiny place to suggest permanency of any kind. There were no knickknacks, no green plants, no family pictures. It was a place to sleep, a place to come home to at the end of the day, nothing more. How could it be anything else when her name wasn't even Alexis Thorn? Alexis Thorn was an alias. She'd taken a new name with the help of her lawyer, Nicole Quinn, when she got out of prison for a crime she didn't commit. She didn't want to think about why she was living in this run-down apartment but she had to think about it, like it or not.

Without Nicole Quinn she didn't know where she'd be. Nikki had gotten her a job as a personal shopper to some of Virginia's older, wealthy residents. It was a far cry from being a high powered securities broker in her other life, that was for sure.

Today, in just minutes, she had to climb into her little Mini Cooper and head out to McLean, Virginia.

There at Nicole's adopted mother's palatial estate, she would join the other members of the Sisterhood. She'd joined a year ago, again, with Nicole Quinn's help. The Sisterhood wasn't just any organization. Myra Rutledge had formed the organization after her daughter was run down and had been killed by a diplomat's son. With the aid of Nikki's legal expertise, Myra formed the Sisterhood to help women get the justice and the revenge they deserved even if it meant going outside the law to do so.

The Sisterhood consisted of six women, seven if you counted Myra, all recruited by Nikki. They'd gone on one mission so far and it had been successful. At the end of that successful mission, they'd drawn names to see whose case would be next. Alexis's name—not her real name of course—had been drawn from the cardboard shoe box.

But she wasn't ready yet to seek the justice she deserved. She needed more time to wallow in her misery and to build up her strength and resilience. She didn't know why that was, it just was. She would have to tell the sisters they needed to choose someone else for the second mission. She knew in her gut she was still too fragile, too broken with her thirteen month stint in the federal pen. She tugged at her lavender dress, straightening it over her slim hips. The dress was one she'd chosen from her pitiful wardrobe and a knockoff to boot. It went well with her brown skin and dark hair. She'd chosen the dress because she thought she looked best in pastels. The days were long gone when she didn't think twice about buying high-end designer clothes. Everything from her past was gone. Every damn thing she cared about. Even her dog.

Alexis started to shake when she tried to imagine what the other sisters would say when she told them she wasn't ready for her mission. Kathryn, the most verbal and the toughest of them all, in her opinion, would narrow her eyes and tell her to grow up and get with the program. Isabelle, who saw things other people didn't see, meaning of course that she was psychic, would shrug and close her eyes maybe in the hope of conjuring up the reason for Alexis's pass on the mission. Julia, a retired plastic surgeon, who had contacted AIDS from her philandering senator husband, would stare at her as if she were a speck under a microscope. She'd say, "You need to make those bastards pay for what they did to you and get on with your life because you *have* a life to get on with." Yoko would nod and say she understood, whether she did or not. Nikki would use logic to try to convince her to take the bull by the horns, and Myra, sweet, gentle woman that she was, would smile wanly and say, "Honey, if you aren't ready then you aren't ready and we'll choose one of the other sisters." At which point she'd feel like a fool and probably start to cry. The others would look at her with disgust and she'd cry harder. They might even become so disgusted with her they'd try to drum her out of the Sisterhood.

She'd done so well with Kathryn's mission. It couldn't have succeeded without her expertise. She could take nothing and transform it into something wonderful and exciting. She was a master with a makeup brush and she knew it. Costume design was something she loved doing. Nikki said she was a master at that, too. She'd been so proud when Nikki had said that. All the sisters had complimented her. So, what the hell was her problem?

Alexis eyed her suitcase by the front door, and

then let her gaze go to what the sisters called her
Red Bag of Tricks complete with everything she
needed to alter a person's being. Makeup, spirit gum,
latex, costumes, wigs, glasses. She had the talent to
take an ordinary person and transform them into a
movie star. Where she'd come by this particular talent, she had no idea. Everything in the Red Bag
had been updated or replenished by Myra.

Alexis looked at her watch. Time to get on the
road. The Sisterhood's hosts, Myra Rutledge and
Charles Martin didn't like to be kept waiting. She
smiled when she thought of Charles, Myra's right-
hand man, and the one who planned each mission. Charles was an ex-British M16 operative who
had once worked for the Queen on the other side
of the pond until he'd been compromised. In the
spook world, according to Charles, the bad guys had
found out who he was and steps had to be taken to
keep him safe. Now he worked for and lived with
Myra. Charles always said being a superspy for Her
Majesty had equipped him to head up the Sisterhood. On top of all his other accomplishments,
Charles was a gourmet cook. Alexis felt her mouth
start to water at some of the wonderful meals he'd
cooked for all of them. Today, she hoped, would
be something just as wonderful.

Suitcase in one hand, the Red Bag of Tricks in
the other, Alexis still somehow managed to lock
the flimsy door of her apartment. She didn't look
back because there was nothing to see except a
bunch of shabby, secondhand furniture. She hadn't
felt the need to buy new furniture, preferring to
bank all her money until she was sure where she
was going with her life.

Alexis tossed her suitcase into the back of the

Mini Cooper, then climbed behind the wheel. Before she turned the key in the ignition, Alexis looked around the ratty looking neighborhood and the building she lived in. They should just demolish the entire three blocks. Once she'd lived in a pretty little house with window boxes and flowers on her front porch. She had furniture that she'd saved for, beautiful linens, fine dishes and crystal. And she'd had a dog she'd loved dearly. It was all gone now, sold to pay her legal fees. She'd been told that one of the security officers who arrested her had taken her dog.

If anyone should be ready for revenge, it was she. She knew in her heart of hearts, deep in her gut, that the two partners who framed her for their own crime did it because she was a black securities broker. She'd been careful not to play the race card in her defense. Now, she wished she had. Maybe her problem was that she couldn't come up with a suitable revenge that would make her whole again. Nothing she could come up with was bad enough, horrible enough, ugly enough to make her whole. Death was the only thing she could come up with but that wasn't an option. She had no desire to go to prison again.

Ever.

The engine of the Mini Cooper turned over and Alexis drove down the road to the highway. Another glance at her watch told her she had just enough time to make it to McLean. A smile tugged at the corners of her mouth. It would be good to see the sisters again.

As she drove away, Alexis noticed for the first time that spring had really arrived. The trees were dressed in their fledgling greenery, and here and there she could see flowers buds. Spring. A new beginning. She crossed her fingers the way she had when she was a child. Maybe this spring would be a new beginning for her.

As the miles ticked by, Alexis settled herself more comfortably in the driver's seat. She felt better already.

Myra Rutledge, Charles at her side, stood under the portico and watched the cars inch their way through the open gates. Her smile rivaled the sun. "They're here, Charles! Every single one of them. I was so afraid they might have second thoughts. They look wonderful, don't they? I love the way they poke one another and make each other laugh. I am so relieved that they all get along just like real flesh and blood sisters."

Charles beamed! "Luv, they are beyond wonderful. Julia looks particularly good, don't you think?"

"For now, she's in remission, but yes, she looks wonderful, just awfully thin. Look how they're all smiling, Charles. That means they're glad to be here. Turn off the power to the gate. We don't want any intruders today." Myra's voice dropped to a whisper when she said, "Nikki didn't say anything about . . ."

"No, Nikki didn't mention Assistant District Attorney Jack Emery at all. I didn't want to open any old wounds by asking. They broke off their personal relationship and as such, Nikki is touchy on the subject of Jack Emery."

"A District Attorney prowling around here with binoculars makes me worry, Charles. I know Nikki is still in love with him. I also know Jack Emery is not going to give up. He suspects that we were responsible for Marie Lewellen's disappearance. He told Nikki so. That's why the two of them are estranged. They were on opposite sides of that case. He's trying to . . . to . . . get the goods on us, Charles."

Charles patted Myra's hand. "Not to worry, my dear. That will never happen. I want you to trust me."

Myra stared into Charles's bright blue eyes. God, how she loved this man, her daughter's father. "I do, Charles. I do. Now, let's welcome our new little family.

"Girls! Girls! Welcome back to Pinewood! Charles prepared lunch for all of us and we'll have it on the patio. Oh, how I've missed you," she said, opening her arms wide to gather all the young women close.

Murphy, Kathryn's dog, barked sharply for attention. Myra laughed. "You, too, Murphy. Charles fixed you a special treat." The big shepherd literally purred at her words.